About the Author

Michael Jenkins MBE served for twenty-eight years in the British Army, rising through the ranks to complete his service as a major. He served across the globe on numerous military operations as an intelligence officer within Defence Intelligence, and as an explosive ordnance disposal officer and military surveyor within the Corps of Royal Engineers.

His experiences within the services involved extensive travel and adventure whilst on operations, as well as many major mountaineering and exploration expeditions that he led or was involved in. He was awarded the Geographic Medal by the Royal Geographical Society for mountain exploration and served on the screening committee of the Mount Everest Foundation charity. He was awarded the MBE on leaving the armed forces in 2007 for his services to counterterrorism.

The Failsafe Query is Michael's first novel, and this is the second edition. The second novel in his spy thriller series is *The Kompromat Kill*, and *The Moscow Whisper* completes the trilogy.

THE FAILSAFE QUERY

THE FAILSAFE QUERY

MICHAEL JENKINS

Failsafe · Thrillers

ASIN (eBook): B088LKFB3L

ISBN (Paperback): 9798643498377

Cover Design by Mecob

Cover images:

© iStockphoto.com © Shutterstock.com

To my wife, Rebecca,
and my children Matthew, Holly and Ramina

And in dedication to the close family of British army
bomb disposal teams and high-risk searchers of the Corps of
Royal Engineers and bomb disposal teams of the Royal Logistic
Corps

'We take the long, lonely walk together, watched over by our brave friends in a special Valhalla'

(The term 'The Long Walk' or 'The Lonely Walk', is used by bomb disposal operators to reflect on how a short distance can seem a very long way when you're walking alone towards a suspect explosive device.)

FAILSAFE

Something that is designed or made in such a way that nothing dangerous can happen if a part of it goes wrong.

Prologue

Moscow 2005

The team commander sat in his parked car, watching intently for any unexpected movement along the road. After all this time, he didn't want anything to blow the operation apart. His nervousness was palpable, his mission almost complete, and his team were going through the final stages of a thoroughly rehearsed plan.

He sat and waited, fidgeting occasionally with his lighter, but poised to spring into action when needed. He was quietly confident that his team, who were a short distance ahead of him, would see this mission through to success. To be caught now would be a travesty. But who might be watching this final act, he wondered?

He stepped out of the car and walked slowly towards the shadows of the figures ahead. The moon was absent. It was hidden behind the tall skyscrapers, providing ample darkness over the banks of the river in which his team could operate. It was chilly, a slight breeze in the air, and the ambient illumination of the street lights was enough to allow the team to see what they were doing, yet remain disguised from any peering eyes on a midsummer's night.

The ripples of the river could be heard below as the water broke and swirled around the shallow, dilapidated pier, crashing past the bridge stanchions and providing enough noise to quietly subsume the splash into the river from above.

He walked past his team, looking around again to make sure no one was walking along the embankment late at night, and casually handed over a rusty container to another man stepping out of a car that had slowly approached and turned off its headlights.

A second man remained in the passenger seat, looking on. No words were exchanged, but a mutual nod concluded their roles. The list of moles was safe.

Meanwhile, the other members of the team opened the rear doors of their small van and carried a number of dark sacks, with some difficulty, over the six or seven paces to the walls of the river.

Anyone looking across the road from the adjacent park would have seen the glistening river as it bent towards the city, with a foreground of the dark shadows of the four men under the trees, before watching them ease the sacks gently over the walls of the river. The splash of the drop was masked by the rustling wind in the trees and the calming sounds of the river in full swell.

With the lights of the city in the background, the men turned and slowly got into the van before driving off into the night.

Their mission complete, a civil servant signed a red-coloured file in London some days later.

He tied a grey ribbon around the three-inch file, and placed a large white sticker onto the cover that stated, '*Placed in suspended animation.*'

PART ONE

LEGACY

Chapter 1

Central Asia 2001

Sean Richardson had a sense of impending fear as he stood in the shadows of a tattered, poverty-stricken housing estate. Sometimes he knew danger was lurking. The unfamiliar environment gave him a strange feeling of isolation as he smoked a cigarette in the dimly lit open courtyard that accessed each block of solid-grey apartments. He noticed the knee-length wooden fences and the sporadic but quite colourful blooms amongst the tufts of sun-seared grass.

The realisation of what he was embarking on dawned on him and the consequences of being caught there gave him a deep, stomach-churning feeling. The fear crept back...

A mixture of old people, young kids and streetwise teenagers meandered past in the ghostly darkness. Only the pale images of pruned apple trees, curiously marked with white paint at their bases, broke up the dour landscape.

'*Dobryi vecher*,' uttered a fierce-looking, middle-aged man who squeezed past Sean with a grim look endemic to those trying desperately to survive the hardships of making a living in a city full of poverty.

'*Harosheva vechera*,' Sean replied, observing the man's movements carefully. The man raised a hand, limped on, then turned as if to process Sean's dubious pronunciation and curious Western manner. He looked him up and down in a slightly hunched but muscular fashion, and projected a barrage of strong, guttural Russian. He indicated for Sean to offer him a cigarette.

Sean winced at the waft of rancid vodka – a consequence of the man's evening foray with a few other like-minded Russian pals. A gruff retort swirled in the air as Sean offered him the packet, which was eagerly snatched before the man shuffled away into a urine-spattered block of flats. Sean watched with curiosity the way of life of these people in a land that was completely unfamiliar to him.

It was late 2001 and he was stranded in the middle of Central Asia, a region of the globe both mysterious and harsh in equal measure, and he told himself on many occasions that it would take him more time to become accustomed to it. But he knew that he was well up to it.

Sean imagined looking at himself with the eyes of others who were around him that night and wondered what they might see and think. He did not speak the language too well, and his body language, gait and aura differed hugely from those of the people he was surrounded by. He knew he had to work harder to remain inconspicuous. He also knew the Russian Mafia ruled the roost, that corruption was rife, serious and petty crime were endemic and the people led horrific, impoverished lives. Yet this was a place of great mystery that intrigued him.

Despite the year, he felt and imagined it to be the early or mid-1970s deep in the communist Soviet Union. Nothing had really changed here. It was exactly how he imagined it would have been when he had been fighting the cold war as one of Her Majesty's intelligence officers. The huge Russian symbols of communist life were here right in front of his eyes. Sprawling cold facades of government buildings, the pitiful Lada cars with their frost-damaged, shattered windows, the wide, straight boulevards with cavalcades of government black cars with blue lights spinning, sirens on, whizzing past the oppressed people.

The greyness of the light and the wafts of smoky air and putrid industrial smells made everything seem bleak and barren. He could see the Kazakhs were a very proud people, most of whom were descended from the Genghis Khan hordes of earlier centuries, and it was a nation of immense strategic importance to the West. And of course, there was oil. Lots of it...

As he mulled his presence, Sean sensed trouble when he stepped out of the shadows. The hairs on the back of his neck gave him an overwhelming sensation, strong enough to taste, that danger was present – a sensation he had honed after years of living right on the edge. His sixth sense kicked in as he glanced over his shoulder and saw the shadows grow closer to him. It took a split second for him to realise the danger to his life. And to the person he had secured in the flat.

'Shit,' he muttered under his breath, turning to confront the approaching men. His eyes were drawn to the pistol in the hand of the smaller man, low down close to his thigh, and shadowed from the incandescent light behind.

He heard the sirens of police cars in the distance, tossed his cigarette away and shrugged his shoulders. In that split second, the sounds around him waned, his breathing calmed and a vacuum of air exploded as he instantaneously made a half turn and crouch, drew the Glock from the back of his jeans and fired a double tap of nine-millimetre rounds straight into the chest of his immediate adversary.

Sean hit the ground. His eyes focused on the second man, whose muscles and body appeared freeze-framed. He fired another two rounds that pierced the man's neck. The cordite lingered in the air, a pleasurable smell for Sean. He rolled over, sprang to his feet and fired another double tap of rounds into the twitching body. Glancing behind him, he set his eyes on the half-glazed double doors that provided quick passage to the safe house where the General was hidden.

He ran with detonating speed to the doorway, knowing the chasing men would be on them both quickly. Death was coming – he felt his leather bomber jacket ride up his back as the air swelled around his frame, eyes firmly fixed on that door handle – every second was vital as he ran, and ran. He heard the crack, thump and sharp piercing whistle in the air as the first shot went straight through his jacket collar, before ricocheting off the wall. A second round crashed through the window. Sean hit the ground, slammed the door shut, bolted it at mid-level and crawled rapidly to the ground-floor flat located immediately behind the far staircase.

His heart was pumping now, moving quickly to the entrance door and imagining his next moves – exactly as he had rehearsed many times before to ensure he was fully prepared in the event of compromise. He placed the key firmly in the lock, twisted it, opened the door and shouted to the General at the top of his voice.

'*Poydem, Poydem.* Get out, Get out!'

Unhesitatingly, and acting on the prompt, the General burst into the kitchen and out onto the veranda, initiating the well-rehearsed escape plan.

Sean pulled the green dual-core wire that held a small stainless-steel pin. It detached from the white box fixed to the wall in the entrance hall, the green light flashed and Sean felt a sense of relief as the victim-operated improvised explosive device armed its electrical circuit. The peroxide-based explosives he had mixed were placed in a three-inch projectile that would shower the torso of anyone initiating the pressure mat with searing blades of copper fragments.

Sean sprinted to the kitchen, through the external door to the veranda and jumped straight into the manhole, before lowering himself to the concrete floor of the large power duct below. A quick grapple with the manhole cover saw it click sweetly into place as he simultaneously grabbed the head torch hanging on a hook next to his shoulder. He slipped the torch over his head and, in a crouched position, reached up to grab the kernmantle rope, pulled it down to below his feet and clipped it to a silver ring on top of the small box of explosives that was rigged with a high-explosive detonator. He had primed the booby trap to make sure anyone opening the manhole cover would be showered with ball bearings from the explosion, which would simultaneously collapse the walls of the tunnel.

He made a final adjustment to the rope, ensured it was fully tense, turned and followed the General's route down the narrow tunnel of the power duct on his hands and knees. He was now a third of the way down the tunnel, swatting the odd rat out of his way as he made progress, and sweating profusely. He then heard the thunderous explosion behind him.

Sean pictured the person who had probably stepped on the large doormat when entering the flat, which concealed the pressure plate below it. He expected that they were either dead or writhing in agony from the burning copper and blast wave they had initiated as they entered the flat.

Grimacing, Sean made his way to the end of the tunnel and climbed out of the exit into the moonlit park located some distance across the road from the decrepit complex of flats.

He pulled out a transmitter from his sleeve pocket, pressed the small embossed button and looked into the dim and dark distance at the flashing blue lights next to the apartment they had escaped from. A wry smile spread across his rugged face as he saw the flash, then heard the boom of the explosion before he watched the fire take hold of the apartment he had left. The incendiary devices had worked a treat.

Sean checked that the General was safe and in one piece. He was a senior Uzbekistan Army General and a prime intelligence source that Sean was recruiting. A man of vital significance to his mission.

The General stood up, brushed himself down and patted Sean on the back.

Chapter 2

Almaty, Kazakhstan 2001

Cold dark shadows. Moonlight sparkling on the mountain ice. Almaty's glacial backdrop of the Tien Shan range cast a mysterious aurora above the city that night. Sean glanced at the snow-clad peaks high above the canopy of the grey suburban streets, pulled the door shut and turned the iron key twice. He checked its resistance.

Mist in the lane. Bitter cold in the air. Sean waited in the shadows, having showered and changed into a casual suit, ready for an appointment he would rather not have to fulfil. He wondered who had targeted him that day, who his next adversary would be and reflected on how a change of job had led him to this curious part of the world on a very odd mission with General Yuri. He knew it had been a close call that afternoon and that someone had probably leaked information about his mission with the General, but who?

Satisfied he had secured the General after their narrow escape, Sean waved to the taxi as it appeared through the early evening fog and made his way to the British Embassy residence on the outskirts of the city. Despite his clandestine mission to nurture his intelligence source, he had been invited by the Embassy staff to the house of the Defence Attaché. An awkward invite he could really do without. But maybe he'd glean some useful information for his future travels.

Sean had travelled the world extensively in his role as a British intelligence officer. He was athletic, slightly tanned, adorned with slightly greying wavy brown hair, now in its long mode in a ponytail, and had the rugged features of an outdoor man. He was a tough, no-nonsense operator with a blend of charm and guile to suit his quiet but determined persona. Highly skilled, adept, harnessing a fierce loyalty and with talented spy tradecraft, he was quick-witted and comfortable amongst different people, cultures, languages and customs, and with the hidden perils his service brought.

This was different though – he was distinctly uncomfortable and wary of his new surroundings behind what was once the Iron Curtain. What made it precarious was that he was conducting a deniable operation, leaving him to the mercy of the secret police if he was caught. There would be no British Embassy sponsorship or diplomatic saving grace here.

Sean was introduced to Graham Morris, the Defence Attaché, a large man with short grey flecks of hair, who wore a Cavalry Officer tie.

'It's a pleasure to meet you Sean,' the attaché announced as he walked across the spacious living room to greet Sean. 'I'm glad my staff invited you here this evening. It will be good to get your views on what London is thinking.'

'Good to meet you too,' Sean said, grasping the hand in front of him.

'It's a strained time for us all at the moment,' the attaché continued. 'Especially with the relative unknown of what our American friends will do next. I have a funny feeling it could get rather busy over here.'

'I think you're quite right,' Sean said assuredly. 'This is probably the beginning of an awkward time for us all over the next year or so and it could get very busy for you and your staff.'

'And all the rumours suggest Afghanistan will become the focus for us now.' Graham smiled, having posed his rhetorical suggestion looking for insider information.

Sean paused and took a sip of his Georgian red wine. 'Well, it all looks pretty ominous now that the US Secretary of State has said he wants regime change in Afghanistan and the Middle East.' Sean avoided any detail but gave the attaché a nuanced appraisal of the geopolitical and military activity happening in Washington and London after the 9/11 attacks in America.

'So, what brings you all the way over to Kazakhstan then?' the attaché asked, probing further.

Sean, dressed in a tailor-fitted light grey suit and white shirt with a navy blue tie, had prepared his responses before this moment, knowing it would come. He took a caviar blini from the Kazakh waitress stood at his side and answered, enjoying the company of senior Embassy staff.

'I'm passing through Almaty and onwards to Tashkent, so I thought I'd grab the chance to visit the Embassy staff and get a few briefings here before I meet up with your opposite number in Uzbekistan.'

'Sounds very sensible Sean.'

'I need to know the ground and the situation over here better. Get more streetwise, so to speak,' Sean added. 'Jon Bellingham in Moscow suggested I ought to make a quick visit to catch up with you guys on local and regional matters.'

Sean could see in the attaché's eyes that he wanted to ask more about his mission – knowing full well that Colonel Morris understood military protocol by not asking too deeply about another officer's mission and intent. It was unwritten military etiquette not to probe too intently with those who might be working on sensitive matters.

'We always called him Jonny 'Two Vests' Bellingham,' the attaché said, chuckling. 'He had an affinity for wearing two vests under his shirts in the cold Embassy offices in Moscow.' They both laughed.

'The nickname must have stuck then – he did the same at the staff college where we served together all those years ago,' Sean said with a grin. 'We always called him J2V for short.'

'Shrivenham?' the attaché inquired.

'No, we both went to staff college in Quetta.'

'Pakistan? Wonderful place. Seems you've had a few exotic postings in your career.'

'Occasionally. And quite a few tedious ones too.'

'Indeed. Just as it is tedious for me to be hauled away now to make small talk with the masses. This is quite an enjoyable discussion.' The Defence Attaché was escorted by his staff to meet some of the other dignitaries and guests for the evening.

Sean enjoyed the social break and felt at home in such convivial settings. In his work, he had become immersed in fast-paced covert operations across the globe, and lived off the adrenalin of clandestine service. It was an honourable and satisfying job, despite the enemies he had made and left in his trail. There was always danger, and for the rest of his life he'd always be looking over his shoulder.

He turned and walked a few steps to admire some of the Central Asian paintings on the long corridor wall and pondered momentarily. He reflected on the complex journey that had lulled him into this dubious deniable operation following the terrorist event of the century on 11 September 2001. It occurred to him that he was caught up in a new game of fast-moving intelligence and he had little idea of how his world might change as he began his unprotected mission across Central Asia.

Exactly two weeks earlier, Sean had been sitting in a high-level intelligence community meeting at the MI6 headquarters at Vauxhall Cross in London. His mind drifted back to that day.

He had raced down Whitehall, clutching a small black briefcase under his arm, grimacing as the wind-lashed rain worked against him. He knew he would be late for the daily meeting of those involved in providing human intelligence updates to the Prime Minister and the government's COBRA committee.

He arrived at the meeting, made his apologies for being late and sat next to his boss, an experienced hand of fifty-two years, who was addressing the agent running representatives of MI5, MI6 and Defence Intelligence.

Sean normally didn't take much notice of the GCHQ representative, who was oddly not present. But in his place at the end of the table sat an attractive female, who he assumed was in her mid-twenties, and to whom he nodded as a gesture of welcome. Sean briefly glanced at her name card in front of her. Samantha Braund. He memorised her name, then smiled wryly at the remaining souls who knew him well and passed his boss a note. The senior MI6 officer paused, scanned the note and continued to chair the meeting.

'I'll ask Sean to explain this note in a moment. In the meantime, I can't stress enough how our particular niche specialisms are now vital to shape the Prime Minister's next steps.' The team were the leading officers involved in Operation Cloud-Hawk who, somewhat unusually, provided direct human intelligence to the chief of MI6 and, subsequently, the PM.

Sean laid his briefing notes out on the table and took a sip of water as the Chair continued. 'These are high-end stakes for us all following the 9/11 attacks and I needn't remind you all how the Americans are spoiling for war, not just in Afghanistan but on several fronts now.'

Sean glanced at his notes and zoomed into an area he had marked with a yellow highlighter. As well as the US plan to invade Afghanistan, the recent cross-Atlantic missive suggested that Iraq was now high on the agenda for regime change. He continued to listen to his boss, knowing full well he'd be on a plane the next day as part of a high-tempo intelligence operation needed to satisfy the strategic imperatives of the PM and the US President.

'Washington and London are very concerned about weapons of mass destruction ending up in the hands of Al-Qaeda terrorists,' the Chair continued. 'Especially given their previous threats to use them. Radiological and nuclear terrorism is now seen as a very prospective and catastrophic threat. I need all the teams to gather intelligence quickly on how far Al-Qaeda has gone in realising this aspiration – above and beyond what we already have. We need to be talking to every agent regularly on this and I'm expected to get something new to 10 Downing Street very soon.'

He paused. Then he moved his chair back slightly and turned to his left. 'So, Sean, what do you have for us?'

'Well sir, the Americans are moving quickly after 9/11 and want us to collect intelligence on quite a mix of threats.'

'Related to weapons of mass destruction I assume?'

'Indeed sir. They've been very specific. And I'll start some of this work when I arrive in Moscow tomorrow, before I move into Central Asia. They have substantially changed our objectives. They want us to find direct evidence that Iraq is buying special nuclear materials on the black market.'

Sean grimaced at the change of mission and brought his mind straight back to the reality of the cocktail party at the Defence Attaché's residence – and the paintings right in front of him.

He had learnt much from General Yuri in the two weeks since that meeting in London, and the intelligence didn't fit with what the Americans wanted. He walked along the corridor, admiring the art. He mulled over the words of his boss and the complete change of direction sanctioned by Washington and the PM.

Why were the Americans so disorganised in their thinking? Why the speed rather than precision? Was this about conjuring up intelligence? As he pondered these questions, he became engrossed in one particular picture on the wall. He marvelled at a portrait of Sir Alexander 'Sikunder' Burnes, who was one of the most accomplished spies Britain had ever produced. Burnes was dispatched by the British Government when the Russian and British empires collided in Afghanistan and they needed intelligence urgently. They sent Burnes to get it. Burnes' desert missions resonated with Sean.

'Dark seduction, dark intelligence,' Sean mused. He smiled at the irony. Would his own mission harvest some of the modern-day intelligence that was now vital to London and Washington? And what would come next from the Americans? He knew this was likely to be a long, protracted and disparate intelligence effort to put such a jigsaw together. More pressing for the Americans though was to close down the jihadi efforts in Afghanistan first, before taking the fight anywhere else. He felt sure this new Central Asian great game would keep him trapped for a long time.

'Sean, come with me – I'd like to introduce you to someone,' the attaché said. He turned and beckoned Sean to follow him across the room, past a low, square coffee table and across to the large French windows with a large balcony.

'This is Dominic Atwood,' the attaché said with an oddly quiet voice. Sean shook hands with a tall, lean man in a dark grey suit. 'Dominic, this is Sean. He's passing through and works in the old War Office building in the same field as you. I'm sure you both have similar business over here, so I'll leave you chaps to have a chat. I need to welcome the British Ambassador to Russia, who is arriving shortly with my ambassador.'

Although they didn't talk about the sensitive and classified work they were conducting separately in Central Asia for post-9/11 intelligence, both men were working on the same broad, but highly complex, intelligence question. Sean, a defence intelligence officer and seconded to MI6, was operating illicitly. His mission was to establish key contacts and sources that could provide information on the radiological and special nuclear material racketeering that was happening across Turkey, the Caucasus and Central Asia. Concerns remained that such material could end up in the hands of terrorists from the former Soviet states who still retained cold war nuclear weapons on their land, and had numerous unsecured sites holding radiological material. His new objective from Washington was to find evidence that such materials were being surreptitiously harvested by Iraq.

Sean would remember this moment forever. His first meeting with Dominic Atwood. The man with the flimsy toupee. Sean's instincts kicked in when he met Dominic. His gut told him that Dominic was likely to be a career MI6 intelligence officer, probably operating under the more formal Embassy diplomatic cover to gain intelligence on the goings-on in Central Asia. Sean had met enough MI6 operational officers to know their peculiar traits, and Dominic exuded all of them. Particularly the pompous ones. Something wasn't quite right about this man, but he couldn't put his finger on it. There was an odd stand-off between the pair he thought, neither giving an inch of information to reveal their clandestine activities.

The cold air snapped at his lungs. The security gate gnawed on its icy cogs as it slowly drew open for the approaching car. Almaty was dark and bitter that night as Sean left the Defence Attaché's house, content with his brief encounter with government staff and feeling that his lengthy chat with this curious fellow called Dominic Atwood had gone reasonably well.

He headed back into the city to plan the next stages of his mission with the General – and a journey to Tashkent, the capital of Uzbekistan.

Chapter 3

Uzbekistan 2002

Sean watched General Yuri Yakubova arrive at Tashkent train station just before eleven o'clock on the busiest day of the week. The station was awash with loud and vibrant trading activity at the stalls outside – reams of noisy traffic slowly bustled their way through the massed crowds.

The dense smoke of breakfast stalls and barbecues lingered in the air as Sean greeted Yuri with a strong handshake and a pat on the back. Sean was unshaven, dressed in a black T-shirt, beige mountain trousers and sand brown desert boots and a large, black North Face rucksack. He looked to the entire world totally out of place as a Westerner amongst the large crowds of native Central Asians, all of whom were actively trading and bartering around the station. Sean was immersed in the quirky atmosphere, but his senses were sharp. Sharp to the risk they could be being watched or followed if anyone had latched onto the fact that Yuri was his agent, and effectively an Uzbek traitor.

Yuri looked around incessantly as he shepherded Sean towards the station entrance, his eyes glancing across the array of faces in the crowds. Yuri was smaller than Sean and slightly overweight, with a balding head that contrasted with his thick black rimmed spectacles. He was a calm and intelligent Uzbek, brought up in the universities of Moscow and well-travelled throughout the former Soviet Union. He did, however, have a penchant for the good life, but for all his worldly goods, he simply wanted to escape to the West. He felt this was his only opportunity to leave Uzbekistan for good.

Sean had finally recruited this charismatic Uzbek some months ago. It hadn't been easy, and Sean had spent many a day verifying the secret data he had provided, his credentials and the veracity of his motivation. He had probed Yuri deeply in the safe house in Almaty and, in the end, it came down to Sean's gut feeling to offer him a provisional deal. The trust between them was cemented during the escape from the safe house. That trust relied on cash for General Yuri and a surreptitious escape from Uzbekistan for him and his family. But only if he provided evidence of the intelligence Sean needed on the smuggling of nuclear materials.

What the General had requested from Sean resonated deeply with him and he was empathetic to Yuri's desire to make a new life in Europe or the USA. Sean found it incredible that he was now dealing with Yuri on intelligence related to terrorist improvised explosives devices. Not just normal IEDs, but highly sophisticated chemical, biological and, chillingly, radiological or nuclear devices. The extraordinary speed of events after 9/11 had propelled him quickly into this dangerous new era of covert activity to support the strategic aims of the US and UK. Sean's world was intelligence. His life was counterterrorism. He had given fifteen years of service to HM Government, and they had bared his soul on more than a few occasions.

Sean and General Yuri boarded the cranky old train bound for Bokhara via the great city of Samarkand. They were destined to spend twenty-four hours together in a small double-bunk compartment situated in the second-class carriages towards the front of the train.

Sean entered the compartment, placed his rucksack on the top bunk and sat at the small table next to the window. The carriage windows had an ancient set of curtains pulled back on an old wire that hung by its threads, and the musty smell of the compartment lingered deep in the nose. The table held two small Uzbek bowls for drinking green chai, and a blue-mosaic-patterned teapot.

It wasn't long before the train had rolled out of Tashkent on its way to the historic Islamic cities of Samarkand and Bokhara. The wide landscape of the Karakum desert provided the mysterious backdrop for Sean to quiz Yuri on the criminal underworld activity of radiological smuggling that was happening across Central Asia.

Yuri didn't stop talking.

'There's an extensive network of cross-border smuggling going on, radiological sources moving across the region, and I've been monitoring exactly how it works.'

'Exactly what we wanted. You've developed this operation well, and we're pleased with your work Yuri.'

'I'm glad it's to your satisfaction,' Yuri replied, in his slightly strained, but very understandable English.

'We pay people here Sean. They are poor, and in this country, we trade in whatever we can. It might be furs, sausages, illegal drugs, vodka or even special nuclear material. It's our way of life and bargaining markets occur all across the deserts where buyers and sellers will come together. The illicit trade in caesium and uranium is managed by the Russian Mafia.'

Sean was fascinated at the extent of knowledge Yuri had acquired. The information he had been relaying back to London over the last few months was chilling and he was eager to learn more. He leant back into the sofa opposite the bunk beds, whilst Yuri sat cross-legged on a cushion near the table. Yuri continued.

'The Mafia use normal traders, low-level workers and simple men to try and sell the stuff. You know, hustlers. Middlemen. If they sell, they give the largest cut back to the Mafia. They are shit-scared of them and know they will be hurt if they try to renege on any deal and run off with the items.'

'So, who's buying, Yuri? Where is it moving to? And who are the end users and where are they from?' Sean asked the questions, remembering the classified intelligence he had read of 220 specific cases of smuggling of special nuclear material across Georgia, Turkey, the Caucasus, Kazakhstan, Ukraine and Uzbekistan.

'We only have a handful of deals that we've managed to uncover here, but it moves across our territory into the Caucasus and Turkey and onwards to wherever the end buyer is. The stuff comes from our old refineries and metallurgy processing plants: some here, some in Kazakhstan. Everyone is corrupt and it's easy for the Mafia to buy the stuff from security, the workers or even the police. Money speaks here. They then use the hustlers to move it across the deserts into Turkmenistan and then across to Georgia and Ossetia.'

Sean knew the hunting ground for the buyers was in the broken Russian states of Ossetia and Abkhazia and often in the black market bazaars of Turkey. It was in these countries where you could buy anything from dried fish to gold, drugs and even weapons-grade uranium.

'Ossetia is lawless and it's the biggest duty-free market in the world,' Yuri explained, gesturing with his hands. 'The market bazaars are full of people who come from all over the region to buy everything from gasoline to pasta with no taxes that you'd pay in mainland Georgia.'

Yuri placed some Uzbek documents on the table and explained the case of Tamaz Davitadze. Yuri pointed to his picture on the table next to his Kent cigarettes, and placed another picture showing four vials of green, powdered, highly enriched uranium.

'He brought this through Bokhara three months ago,' Yuri explained. 'We intercepted him to see what was happening in the wider network. We then allowed him to continue where Davitadze headed out of Bokhara towards the Uzbek–Turkmen border in an old Niva four-wheel drive with Vazha Lortkipadze. He's a corrupt, middle-ranking Uzbek Interior Ministry official. They met with two Iranian agents just over the Turkmenistan border in Türkmenabat.'

Sean listened, aghast at the extent of duplicity and corrupt, state-sponsored activity. Yuri had managed a clever intelligence operation and had recruited Davitadze, who was now on his payroll. He watched Yuri light a Kent cigarette and opened the window. The desert wind whipped in. Yuri then explained how Davitadze had carried over four kilogrammes of the greyish-green powder. Not quite enough for a nuclear bomb, but for a buyer with the right equipment and experience, a damn good start.

Yuri added some detail to the plots. 'There was the problem of the Uzbek–Turkmen customs post, just a few miles from Türkmenabat. Lortkipadze smoothed the way with payments, probably on a regular basis, to the commandant of the flat desert outpost.'

'They're all on the take then?' Sean asked. 'Uzbek military officers and government officials? All easily bought off I assume?'

'Exactly. This means the Iranians can, and do, operate at will – masterminding their own nuclear smuggling racket. I'll introduce you to two of my agents from the criminal underworld in the Ferghana valley. They'll be able to show you the evidence you need.'

The door creaked open. Sean glanced round. Was it a threat? No. Just Hazim the porter bringing them bowls of the local beef delicacy, Bishbarmak. Hazim worked in a small kitchen towards the front of the carriage and it was his job to bring each compartment their chai, lunch and dinner and to provide them with any service that might be required on the long desert journey. Hazim was a portly and smiling gentleman from Azerbaijan, who began to set the table, allowing Sean to take a moment to revel in the spectacular views of the large desert. He marvelled at the huge desert vista brimming with heat waves seen low across the sands, giving him a sense of myopia as the horizon blurred. He felt privileged to witness the evocative and charming nature of the land as they travelled gently across the huge expanse of Uzbekistan towards the western frontiers.

Yuri pushed his finished plate aside. With a glance, Sean saw him pull out a hefty dossier. Yuri indicated to Sean that he should read the dossier he had compiled on the frightening magnitude of the illicit trading.

What Sean read, all fully translated, was alarming. He knew he would need to verify the intelligence but also knew there was enough to mount major operations using US and UK strategic assets to precisely track and trace the threats. Yuri had provided him with a dossier full of illicit trading in special nuclear material – and everything pointed to Iran, not Iraq.

Two incidents stood out as he read. One was a report where Yuri's intelligence officers had searched vehicles in the dead of night just outside Bokhara. Their equipment and searches had revealed a cargo of fifteen kilogrammes of zinc oxide destined for Iran with traces of caesium-127 emitting 240 microroentgens per hour. Border checks showed the transporter did not have the appropriate permits and was using falsified documentation to move from Uzbekistan and onwards through Turkmenistan completing the short distance to Iran. In the other incident, a cargo of molybdenum, a silvery metal used in metallurgy processes, was searched again at night en route to Iran via Turkmenistan: it contained within its load, radium-226, uranium-234 and uranium-238.

The third incident that he read about made him shiver. Yuri's officers had searched a car, based on a tip-off from Davitadze, where they had found a container with an estimated two kilogrammes of caesium-137, alongside the special device for opening the lead container as well as a number of explosive detonators. According to Davitadze, his fellow hustler had received the container of caesium-137 from a member of the Uzbek Counterintelligence Department at the Tashkent district police headquarters. He was instructed to transfer the caesium-137 to an unidentified person in Bokhara, later identified by Yuri's team as an Iranian agent. Sean could see immediately that the caesium-137 isotope could be used as a radiological dispersal device, a dirty bomb, and that this fitted with Iran's capability of possessing a high-grade, state-sponsored terrorism threat.

'Yuri, who else knows of this operation you're running?' Sean asked, sipping his hot Uzbek tea from a blue mosaic bowl.

'No one other than my team at the moment,' Yuri replied. 'I thought it might be useful to you. I can't trust anyone in government, but if they learn of what I'm doing, and I'm linked to you, I'm a dead man.'

Sean was astonished by Yuri's courage and the outrageous risks he was taking, all driven by his motivation to leave the country and live in the UK. Yuri was despondent at the tyrannous nature of his country's regime, who were quite obviously operating illicitly with the Iranians. This crossed Sean's mind a lot as he continued to debrief Yuri. 'Have you got any evidence that any of this stuff is going to Iraq and not Iran?' Sean inquired. 'Any evidence of contacts or criminal activity linked to Iraq?'

'None at all. Most of the linkages we've found are direct to Iran, except the criminal and Mafia movements of some stuff going into Georgia and Turkey.' Sean knew this was now a critical source of intelligence for linking duplicitous Central Asian activity to the wider concerns of the West – and he started to think how he could exploit these leads further. London were desperately looking for an Iraqi connection to support the US-led war that was centred on Saddam Hussein having weapons of mass destruction, but everything here pointed to Iran.

The train lurched heavily as it jogged slowly over some points, shaking the crockery on the table. 'Yuri, here's what we do,' Sean said. 'We develop this operation you're working on over the coming months, and you keep reporting the leads and intelligence direct to me. We can't get you out of the country just yet because I need you here to craft these leads. When the time is right, I'll see what people think about defection but, to be perfectly honest, we don't have enough yet.'

Sean wanted more from this journey to Bokhara. He was confident the intelligence would lead to critical results very soon. And he had a gut feeling that none of it would relate to Iraq at all. It would be some years on, and a few more intelligence roles, before he would uncover the truth.

God he was tired. Sean needed a break to think things through and to stretch his legs. He tugged the compartment door open and stepped into the narrow corridor connecting each of the individual compartments. A waft of Hazim's cooking hit him as he walked to the front of the carriage and pulled the window down on the door. He needed some fresh air.

He had been reflecting on how the US had wanted a war for some months. And how they seemed determined to invade Iraq next. But first they needed the burden of proof that weapons of mass destruction existed in Iraq – even if their spymasters and mandarins had to manipulate, or invent, a trigger.

He fiddled with his lighter momentarily and recalled his last private chat with Jonny 'Two Vests' Bellingham in a secure three metre-square room in Moscow. The room had been built within another room and was the only place in the Embassy where officers could speak on sensitive matters without fear of a bugged environment. Within those secure walls, Jonny briefed Sean that there were others, like Sean, on similar missions. Other carefully disguised intelligence officers clandestinely employed across Turkey and Central Asia to watch, listen and try to interdict the illicit trade in nuclear material.

'Read this file first Sean,' Jonny said. 'And then these others in order. There are lots more you need to digest before your next steps south.'

'Who knows all this Jonny?'

'It's compartmented intelligence so I'm guessing only a few back at the centre will know the aggregation of all the material. Add all this to your briefings in London and you have far more than I.'

'OK, so just your immediate staff know of this then?'

'Yes, but remember some of this is already widely known anyway. Kazakhstan and most of the other former Soviet Central Asian states still have access to stockpiles of nuclear resources. Most of it is still in a state of decay and poorly secured. Worse still, Central Asia is the classic black market for this kind of stuff.'

'Russian Mafia hands all over it?'

'Precisely. You'll see that racketeering and corruption is their way of life and sets the conditions for lots of unscrupulous trading in radiological sources.'

'Not looking good at all then,' Sean said, scratching his temple slowly.

'Well, you know as much as me on that score. We know Al-Qaeda has tried many ways of getting the right radiological sources over many years from these markets.'

'And our worry back home is they could easily get the right material to improvise a nuclear device. We don't know how close they are to that.'

'Put it this way, Sean. We know the trade is there and the Russian Mafia have no qualms at all about making a large buck from selling material to them. The question is whether the right material is for sale of course.'

Sean leant back and glanced around the sparse room, which had an odd feel created by the ghostly flickering of the fluorescent lights. 'The speed at which the Americans are moving is staggering,' Sean said. 'And political expediency has seen some very odd decisions being made in the dark halls of Whitehall.'

'Pressure no doubt. Incessant pressure being put on Whitehall mandarins and then onto us.'

'Yep, and it looks like the pressure is on to get the UN atomic and chemical weapons' inspectors into Iraq as soon as possible,' Sean said. 'The start of the search to find smoking-gun evidence.'

'Well I know they've just appointed Professor Margaret Wilshaw to start looking at that. A quiet, unassuming woman by all accounts. I read about her this morning. Woman in her mid-sixties from Gloucester and a nuclear expert.'

'Interesting,' Sean said followed by a pause. 'Meanwhile, it looks like there are a few of us lined up, from different agencies, to try and uncover this type of evidence.'

'Plenty of dodgy nuclear trading going on,' Jonny said. 'Question is, can we find evidence of it getting into Iraq or to AQ terrorists?'

Jonny explained that there were likely to be other officers in the region with the inherent mission of finding intelligence to show that Uzbekistan was supplying 'yellowcake' uranium to Iraq, which could then be enriched and used as weapons-grade material for nuclear devices.

Had Sean read the ultra-secret MI6 dossier on this critical intelligence objective, which he wasn't privy to, he'd have known Dominic Atwood was on a similar mission to his own. Neither knew of each other's objectives but the intelligence they were providing was being graded at the highest compartmented level within the intelligence services – and shared with the Americans.

The Great Game of the modern era had arrived in Central Asia with similar duplicitous, clandestine and murky activity to the last. This time it was configured to propel the US onto a platform for war across the region. The fallout from this road map would eventually be cataclysmic for politicians and spymasters alike in the UK and US over the coming decade.

Sean closed the train window and walked slowly back to the compartment, eager to learn more from Yuri. He was impressed with the detailed and diligent documenting of Yuri's intelligence operation, and wanted to help him reap high-grade intelligence to enhance the bird's-eye view of illicit radiological trading in the region.

Yuri had arranged with Davitadze to let Sean see for himself the routes and tactics being used for smuggling from Bokhara. The stage was set for Sean to look at the front-line activity and get amongst the live intelligence collection operations on the ground.

The long desert journey came to an end and was made all the more worthwhile when Sean finally stepped out of the carriage and into the searing heat of Bokhara train station. He sensed the magnificence of the place, spying the high minarets in the distance. There was no platform – he jumped out of the carriage onto the red sand and noticed a few small huts acting as the station entrance. He stood and watched for a few moments. Uzbeks were sat alongside the rails, proffering their wares from trestle tables, and smoke wafted from the station charcoals on which shashlik was cooking. The vendors escaped the direct sunlight by sitting under large parasols, chatting and drinking chai. Bokhara was an oasis in the sands and was to become a place of great curiosity for Sean, who was immediately captivated by its mystique.

They walked the short distance to the centre of the city, which had often been dubbed the most interesting in the world because of its murky and mysterious history. Named after the Sanskrit word for monastery, *vikhara*, the city could not have been more inappropriately labelled given its image of iniquity, which had reached a nadir with the reign of the deranged despot Nasrullah in the nineteenth century.

Sean saw little evidence of such historic cruelty and death, but he recalled the history of the Great Game which he had read at length, knowing that it was here that two British officers had been executed by the emir in 1842. It was chilling for Sean to walk amongst this evocative place that was wrapped in British military history, and he was mesmerised by its impressive gems and by the breath-taking blue and white brickwork of its mosques, minarets and mausoleums. Wearing a light rucksack, sunglasses and black cap, he walked alongside Yuri, feeling every bit a tourist on a very special tour.

They stopped for a while in the huge central square, sat in the shade and gazed at the impressive Kalon minaret. Sean started sketching on a small pad. The square was surrounded by a colonnaded arcade of columns and arches and was a peaceful sanctuary for Sean to enjoy a reflective moment in the late-afternoon sun. He treasured such moments. He paused to wonder about his own life, grappling with his vision of one day following the duty trail into Civvy Street, holding down a steady job and wage, and having a family. He heard himself entertaining those domesticated thoughts as he took in the magnificence. But could he see himself ever being fully extracted from this life of chaos? He wondered if he'd forever be looking over his shoulder at the trail of nemeses left in his wake. He had a yearning deep inside him, at the very core of his being. Some indefinable sense that one day he could cleanse his soul of the killing and death he had been embroiled in. And that one day, maybe, he could find peace with himself. And with another.

Yuri's voice made him flinch as he was brought back to reality. 'Tonight, you will see your radioactive sources Sean. We'll take you to a fleet of trucks parked in the desert, and to one in particular which has been waiting to be called forward by the Iranians.'

Sean lifted his sunglasses to look Yuri in the eye.

'How do you know the material is on board? How long has it been there?'

'Two days,' Yuri said. 'My team have been watching the smugglers for weeks and Dimitri has confirmed the vehicle has the material on board. He's arranged the transit across the border for tomorrow afternoon. We've also got some equipment for you to confirm the radiological source.'

Sean wanted to make sure that Yuri's intelligence and operation were legitimate and not a set-up, but he grappled with how he could do this other than by trusting that Yuri was being totally up front, and not staging the whole event just to get a free defection pass to the UK.

Nevertheless, Sean would now see first-hand the smugglers methods and verify that real fissile material was in play. He knew it would be risky getting himself on board the vehicle at night and unnoticed, but he had no option other than to trust his gut feeling and the competence of his Uzbek intelligence hosts.

As they walked to their small hotel, Sean kept an eye out for any recurring faces in the crowds.

Chapter 4

Bokhara, Uzbekistan 2002

Uzbekistan was remote. It was like virtually stepping back in time. The deserts surrounding Bokhara gave Sean a sense of history, as he considered how British officers had first traversed this great land in the nineteenth century. He felt privileged to operate in this mysterious region as he travelled covertly across the sands, just as his forbears had done over 150 years ago.

Sean was driven that evening to the outskirts of Bokhara and onwards to the edge of the Karakum desert. They travelled in an old Gaz van with sliding passenger doors. Sean sat on an old sofa in the rear compartment, where he used a hand-held GPS receiver to track his route and position. Sat between him and Yuri on the corrugated metal floor was a small black Pelco case containing a high-tech radiation detector, a small endoscope and a range of small hand drills.

Dimitri sat in the front of the Gaz navigating the driver along the M37 to a conurbation about fifteen kilometres to the west of the city. Sean sat quietly in the back, contemplating the hours ahead, dressed in a black fleece, gloves and beanie to ward off the plummeting desert temperature.

The journey took less than thirty minutes before Dimitri turned to let Sean know they were now on the approach. He would lead Sean and Yuri to the target vehicle and then prepare the lookouts, allowing Sean to climb on board and search the vehicle. Dimitri assured Sean that there was a radiological cargo on board, but he didn't know what type. It was destined for Turkmenistan and the money transfer with the Iranians would happen tomorrow afternoon, just before the border guards were bribed to let the vehicle through.

They arrived in total darkness at a sprawling warehouse complex with an outdoor market, some bonded warehouses and a large overnight lorry park situated next to a rickety accommodation block. Sean quickly walked the few paces to a small shack, where he was greeted by two bearded men sitting on canvas chairs around a small trestle table. They both rose to shake his hand.

'We have plenty of time Sean,' Yuri said. 'Let's have a coffee and my good friend Akram will tell you about the vehicle. I'll translate for you.'

'Good, can he show me the exact location?' Sean replied. 'I'll be running this task from now on and these guys need to know that.'

They sat down, and Yuri slid the hand-drawn plan of the car park across the table so that it faced Sean. Akram pointed to the location of the target vehicle next to the lorry park accommodation block. Sean was annoyed to see how close the vehicle was to the external ablutions. He could easily be disturbed. 'I'll need to get into the cab as well as the trailer. Can your guys do that for me?'

'Akram is an expert in this,' Yuri said, pointing towards his tool box. 'It's the kind of thing we would do as a kid. Nothing more than a simple wire coat hanger and some plastic banding is needed. He'll make it happen for you.'

Akram led the way to the lorry, taking a convoluted route behind the warehouses, with Yuri and Sean following. Sean made sure their night vision was suitably adjusted by making all four of them sit outside in the cold damp air, gently regulating their eyes to the reduced light conditions. No specialist equipment was being carried, no night-vision goggles and no radios. Just the basic tools needed to get into the truck and the radiation detection equipment Sean had decanted into his small rucksack.

Sean observed the dark areas across to the lorry park, paying attention to the low-level illumination which gave a gentle fuzziness of misty light across the park. It seemed quiet, with little human activity. He sat and watched for a full twenty minutes, studying the comings and goings from the main accommodation block about sixty metres to their left, and the lights of the restaurant slightly further on. Sean could just make out the faint noises of dinner plates being washed through the open windows and the gentle hum of a generator behind the kitchen block.

Somewhere in front of him lay the target vehicle, still unseen behind a row of other articulated lorries, each neatly parked across the huge expanse of tarmac. Sean reckoned there were around eighty-five vehicles in all, probably destined for travel down the busy M37 into Turkmenistan.

They moved in pairs and emerged just behind the target vehicle: a large, Czech-made, four-tonne Tatra lorry. Sean signalled for them to go to ground then made his way around the truck, looking for the best access point into the cab and superstructure. The truck had standard canvas belts securing the canopy, which provided easy access for him to the rear of the truck.

He looked at his watch. 1.20am. 'Perfect,' he thought, happy that the darkness would allow him to operate with some degree of autonomy and safety. He switched on his beta and gamma detector which gave him an immediate reading of 145 millisieverts. He sucked in hard at the shock of such a high reading. This was a live source. This was a real situation. The intelligence was spot on. He wanted to know whether it was beta or gamma radiation being emitted, and needed to enter the lorry to confirm what the source was. He was taking a huge risk putting himself in front of live radiation: he knew if it emitted more than four hundred millisieverts per hour he would be permanently damaged. If it reached six hundred, he would be dead within a day or two. This was the risk these smugglers were taking all the time. He grimaced and hoped the smugglers had shielded the source with some sort of lead container.

He pulled out his red filter torch and began to undo four large buckle straps at the side of the trailer next to the cab. This gave him enough of a gap to push his rucksack inside before levering his body in behind it. He struggled at first to get a foothold on the underside of the superstructure, but eventually managed to get himself inside the canopy. It was ungainly wriggling that finally got him in and he groaned and tutted at his lack of grace. He crouched inside the truck with his back against the freezing-cold metal tailgate while he tried to get a grip on his breathing. Then, once he was composed, he switched on his green torch and looked around. It was empty except for two large crates strapped to the bulkhead near the cab. He looked at the detector screen. The reading from half a metre away was now 280 millisieverts per hour.

'Madness,' he muttered, with a degree of trepidation. This wasn't just some sort of radioactive dust: this was likely to be a fully-fledged strontium or caesium device. But he needed to measure both the beta and gamma emissions to be able to identify the type of source they were smuggling. He knew it was vital to identify the radiation source to confirm what the Iranians might secretly be using it for. His mind raced as he pulled out his hand drill. He made a hole in the underside of the crate with a five-millimetre bit, gently pushing the probes into the crate.

Just as he had finished pushing the probe inside, he heard footsteps outside. He froze. Another scrunching noise. 'What the fuck was that?' he whispered as the sound stopped. Then it began again. He waited, then quietly moved into a sitting position and remained still. The footsteps appeared to have gone. Was it Akram walking around? Was it someone moving to their vehicle? He could only hear the distant howl of wild dogs scavenging the conurbation for food.

He waited for the silence to engulf him. A soak time to judge the threat. He continued checking the readings, and felt the gooseflesh tingling on the back of his neck. He was exposed. Had a trap been set? A whiff of kerosene caught his throat. Liquid to keep the radioactive source stable perhaps.

He prised open a small wooden slat, creating a hole large enough to see what kind of shielding was in place. He struggled with the pungent smell of kerosene and was now convinced the source was strontium, with all the dangers that brought. He swabbed the metal casing with a chemical trace kit and took a few more readings, deciding it was safer to analyse them back at the hotel. He knew any extended length of time spent in front of this material would kill him.

Sean clambered through the canopy and dropped to the floor.

Bang! Something hit him hard on the back of the skull. He reeled, felt a searing pain and turned to see two men attacking him with brutal force. His sight began to blur as he crumpled to the ground, sensing death. The next blow came in the form of a hefty boot to his kidney.

With reflexes, and fierce instinct, Sean used all his power and kickboxing skills to roll away from the danger zone, lashing out instinctively with his right leg in an arcing motion, catching the first man straight on the shins. He fell to the floor yelping as Sean lashed out again – striking from a coiled position and blitzing the man's head with a brutal kick. With lightning speed and ruthless force, Sean moved out of the second man's grasp and jab-kicked his hamstring behind his left knee. The man buckled. Sean launched two scything jabs to the nose, followed by a straight kick to the man's shins that made him collapse to the ground at his feet, screaming in pain.

Crack. The air vacuumed. The first gunshot whistled through the truck canopy, before a second shot zinged past Sean's face directly into an adjacent lorry. He was under fire from another gang member. Yuri had sensed the attack and sprang into action, firing rapidly down the alley and killing the first attacker from eight metres away. Sean grabbed the second attacker and ripped his eye sockets with two fingers. He held him in a headlock and reached for the Makarov pistol in his waistband. He pumped two shots into the man's neck before releasing his grip, allowing the body to fall to the floor like a crumpled mannequin. Just as he did so, a bullet ripped through the air directly into Yuri's torso, propelling him backwards into the dirt.

Yuri screamed in agony. Akram ran to him, desperately trying to stem the massive blood loss as he lay on the ground. Crack. Sean heard the thump as the second bullet ripped into his left shoulder, feeling a searing pain as the bone was crushed. Blood oozed garishly. A third attacker continued to spray rounds down the alley before Yuri lurched over to fire three shots, each of them penetrating the attacker squarely in the head.

Sean sat back against the lorry wheel, clutching his shoulder, agonising at the disastrous end of the operation.

He looked to his left and moved nimbly on his knees towards Yuri, who was now in a state of deathly, slow breathing, calm. Sean held Yuri's head in his hands as he watched his life drain away. He grimaced, as a man's dream of a better life lay shattered in his hands.

Sean was gutted. He wondered who the hell the attackers had been and at the enduring damage they had caused. This was the second compromise of this mission and, this time round, a fatal one. Who was it that was behind all this? Who the hell had the inside track on him and General Yuri? Who was leaking information? And to whom? This was a catastrophic security breach, and he was incensed that it had cost Yuri's life.

His pain fused quickly with fierce anger. Anger that he had been compromised and that someone, somewhere had leaked secret information that had led to the death of a good man.

Chapter 5

Two Years Later

Central London, October 2004

The metal detector alarmed as Sean walked through the security archway into the Metropolitan Police Service HQ in Victoria. Already late for a critical meeting, he cursed as the security officer decided to conduct a full body search.

He found New Scotland Yard tedious to navigate with its cramped spaces, and being late for his third counterterrorism meeting of the day meant that things were not looking good. These were frenzied days for Sean in his new role. He made his way calmly to the lift lobby, which was crammed with people waiting for the elevators to arrive. He checked his phone as he waited, noticing another text from his boss.

'Can you call me tonight around 9pm – something urgent has come in.'

'Not another one,' he thought, as the lift doors opened. He knew that his new role would be frantic but wondered when the high-paced tempo might drop off just a bit. He was flying around the world going from job to job with little respite in the heady days of the country being on high alert for terrorism at home and overseas.

Sean knocked on the meeting room door and entered. He scanned the large room quickly. Five faces he didn't recognise looked directly at him. He closed the door, smiled and made his way to an empty seat he spied at the end of the oblong table. 'Sorry I'm late,' he began. 'I hope you got my message and I've not held you up too much.'

'Absolutely fine Sean,' the Chief Superintendent at the head of the table said. 'We held off on the specifics of the debriefing until you arrived. Let me introduce you to everyone.'

Sean was introduced to five individuals, each representing different police, forensic and counterterrorism departments who wanted to hear the intelligence from his latest mission in Iraq.

Two years after the death of Yuri, when he was permanently based in London, Sean had been promoted and assigned to MI5, where he led teams gathering intelligence on terrorist and bomb-making cells in the Middle East. His work brought him into a tight fold of people hunting for terrorist caches and he spent many long hours briefing senior police and forensics officers on the capabilities of the most dangerous Al-Qaeda bomber cells across the globe.

'So, Sean, can you let us know what you found with your hunter team?' the Chief Superintendent asked. 'We're keen to hear how you managed to find the body and the links to the AQ death squads. The deceased was a British citizen, so we want to investigate his death thoroughly.'

Sean glanced at the pictures on the wall of the burial site and the target compounds he had searched in Iraq. Grim business. A brutal murder. He chose to stand to brief the team. 'Well, the mission was to find the body of the British Foreign Office diplomat who was kidnapped when he was visiting Baghdad. We searched a number of residences which eventually led us to where he had been buried.'

Sean pointed to the first house on the wall, a large high-walled compound with multiple annexes. 'This is where we found the evidence that led us to his murderers.'

'These three men you mean?' the chief superintendent asked, pointing to the faces on the wall.

'Yes. You'll receive a full report tomorrow, but the death is very much linked to the Tawhid Islamic extremist group, led by Abu Musab al-Zarqawi. We used a mixture of intelligence, dogs and air-imagery to eventually find the body which was buried in a shallow grave.'

Sean knew that this would be a long meeting, and he glanced occasionally at the photos of the terrorists shown below the target houses on the wall. The leader reminded him very much of General Yuri. He felt a cold shiver as he recalled his missions in Uzbekistan. Despite several years having passed, he continually wondered who the mole was who had leaked intelligence about his clandestine operations. How many other agents were compromised too? The ruminations never went away. Especially at night. MI6 had decided to extract him from all Central Asian operations and had assured him that a team were investigating the intelligence leaks. He had never heard anything in the intervening years, and the loss of Yuri continued to play heavily on his mind, especially as he had saved his life.

The years had been kind to him though. Sean had met and married an MI6 lawyer with whom he had worked during his secondment. They lived in a large military house on the river Thames just to the west of Central London.

He returned home late that evening, glad he had put the grim murder to bed. He chatted with Katy in the kitchen for a while before he sat at his painting easel. Three paint brushes. Titanium white oil. Linseed oil. A battered palette. Katy peered over his shoulder as he continued with his latest oil painting, skilfully adding the white crests of the waves below the fighting bow of Captain Cook's ship, *The Endeavour*. The setting sun, glancing below the ship's ensign, gave the painting a crimson vitality across the rampant waves, gently echoing the ocean twilight he loved.

'Have you thought any more about adoption?' Katy said, massaging his shoulders.

'Lots, why?'

'Well, you know, after nineteen months of trying I think we really need to start the process.'

'I know my love. We do have more time though. Don't give up hope just yet.'

Katy kissed him on the cheek. 'Let's get the process started anyway. Promise?'

As he painted, he spoke quietly with Katy of his hopes for a family and a safe City job with a steady day-to-day life one day. But he silently knew he was hooked into his world of adrenalin too.

It was 9pm. He leant back to check his work, then reached over to pick up his phone. He punched in his boss's Quick Dial and dabbed at the palette.

'Sean. Thanks for calling. I have an urgent job for you.' The Colonel didn't pause to allow Sean to interject but forged straight on, announcing that Sean needed to be in London by 8am the next morning.

'That's fine,' Sean said. 'What's it all about?'

'I haven't been given any detail at all but the FCO want to discuss a very sensitive matter concerning your next overseas job. They explained that it's close-hold and that only the minimum number of people are to know the details of the task. This one takes priority.'

'OK, sounds curious. But yes, I'll get down there tomorrow and find out more. Who's the contact?'

The Colonel gave Sean the details of who to meet and explained that he would not be told about the task until Sean briefed him, and that no one else in the team was to be informed. 'They've classified it as Top Secret Strap three. You'll need to come and see me tomorrow evening at my home once you've got the initial brief from London.'

Sean smirked a little. His heart raced for a moment, and he grinned at the intrigue of it all. He put his brush down as his boss continued. 'The only steer I've been given is that it's a delicate overseas job with your track and trace specialism needed, and they want you to scope the task. Seems you've built up a reputation for searching for bodies now. I've told them you'll look at it but don't commit anything until I understand the whole show.'

It was a short and simple conversation. Sean was to scope the job and report back to his boss. But he had no idea where in the world this would take place. It was the strangest of phone calls, Sean thought, and he was anxious to learn more the next day.

'Anything interesting?' Katy said, handing Sean a cup of tea before sitting next to him on the sofa.

'Just another early start tomorrow,' he said. 'My next job by the sounds of it and doubtless I'll be late again as normal.'

'Oh well, it's about time you became more punctual and sorted your admin out,' Katy teased. 'I still can't believe you missed your flight back from Iraq last week. You live in total mayhem.'

'Wasn't my fault,' Sean retorted. 'Damned FCO buggered that one up for me.'

Sean took a sip of his tea and they relaxed together quietly. The late nights in West London gave him the chance to explore his dreams, share his fears and rationalise his future with Katy. He relished the time when he was at home with her. She listened well, and he often shared with her his dreams, his guilt and his thoughts of who may have been behind the killer leaks in Uzbekistan.

Chapter 6

Central London, October 2004

Sean woke early the following morning. He turned, strained his eyes and reached over to the bedside table to silence the alarm. Katy was fast asleep. He kissed her on the forehead. It was pitch-black and the aesthetic sound of gentle rain brought him to his senses as he sat half hunched on the bed. He stood, scrambled for his slippers, felt his way around the bed and silently crept downstairs before flicking the hall light on. It was 5.20am and he had to be in London by 7.45am.

His mind started racing. He flicked the kettle switch, grappled for a mug and found himself immersed in a train of thoughts that confused the actions of making a cup of tea. Slowly he came to his senses, drank his tea and struggled out of the door and into the silver Vauxhall Omega, cowering as he ran to avoid the rain.

The windscreen wipers were operating at full speed as he drove down Whitehall with the screech of the blades annoying him. It was a dark and chilly morning as Sean glanced at the MOD building to his left whilst the traffic moved slowly down Whitehall. He thought about the curious nature of the call from the FCO, what risks might be involved and any diplomatic issues that might crop up. He turned into King Charles Street and parked in the FCO compound.

He was late again. Living the dream, he mused, as he entered the FCO. He wasn't to know that this bizarre mission would lead to his life changing direction.

Sean was given a visitor's badge by a flamboyant cockney woman and instructed to take a seat in the foyer. He didn't have to wait long. The gentleman who greeted him was a diminutive, slightly overweight man in his late fifties dressed in a crisp white shirt and an immaculately knotted blue tie. His glasses were a little askew, with a spectacle chain protecting them, and his hair was slightly balding at the front. He was Sean's only point of contact for this mission.

They introduced themselves. Sean was immediately struck by the man's demeanour. He was a middle-ranking career civil servant and had a defined and stringent routine. He fidgeted a little, seemed a bit nervous and appeared not to be comfortable with making small talk. Nonetheless, he appeared to be a nice fellow and Sean was sure that he must live somewhere in the home counties, got to work early, left late and was immensely conscientious about his work. Sean had no doubt he was meticulous in all he did.

Edward escorted Sean downstairs into a large open-plan office with no signs on any of the doors. He was then taken through to a small room with a round table and four seats with a few foreign pictures on the wall, including one of the newly built British Embassy in Moscow. Edward then left to make some coffee.

When he returned, he had an old, tattered red A4 folder with the relevant government marking 'Top Secret' on the front cover. The file was bursting with documents and Edward placed it in front of Sean, thanking him for coming to see him. The coffee followed, and Sean asked him how long he had worked for the FCO.

'Oh, a good number of years and probably about three years on this desk,' he said, fiddling with the folder. 'I was on the Middle East desk before this one for many, many years. Now, if I may, I'd like to start by explaining that my contact has asked for some detailed assistance from you and he'd be pleased if you can oblige.'

Sean knew there would be very little small talk before Edward launched straight into the business of the day. He decided he'd grill Edward a little later, at the end of the business. He always found it worthwhile finding out about people, simply to develop a friendly rapport just in case they could be of some use in the future. Sean was a confident, gregarious operator, always able to sense how he could elicit information from new people he met. He was competent at spotting personality flaws and people's underlying insecurities, and had studied psychological and attachment theories, as well as elements of neuro-linguistic programming. A classic intelligence officer's education.

Sean sipped his coffee as Edward continued.

'We made our first contact with your superiors earlier this week and we will issue them with a formal request for your services if you think the job is viable. I'd like to give you the background to the case.'

He gently nudged the red file marked 'Top Secret' towards Sean before telling the story.

After he had finished, Sean sat and read every single detail of the file alone. He was not allowed to copy any of the material or take any notes. It was a fascinating story about the evacuation of a British Embassy in 1980 and gossip about a supposed list of Russian moles in the British establishment. It was all captured in handwritten memos, typewritten letters and numerous internal notes. It was a thick file and told the story chronologically. Sean came across a memo that explained the details of previous attempts to close the file, each having failed. No one had ever found the secretive list.

Edward returned thirty minutes later with more coffee.

'Well, the job is certainly doable,' Sean explained. 'I will need to~visit the place first and I want my best operators on this one. I'm presuming you'll deal with the relevant clearances I need through your channels?'

Edward nodded and gently adjusted his tie. 'We'll get you out there on a visit as soon as you're available. Our people are expecting that. We'll arrange everything: travel documents, hotels, support and contacts. We've already thought about your cover story.'

Sean sat back, checking Edward's expression. He was deadly serious and showed no emotion. 'I'll need a team of four operators, all under diplomatic cover.'

'That may not be entirely possible,' Edward said, looking at his watch. 'My people are very nervous about the whole affair and the risks attached to it, so they want this kept totally under the radar. This could be one of the biggest secrets ever to come out of the cold war. If it exists.'

With little emotion, Edward asked Sean if he'd like a look around the FCO before locking away the file in the high-security cabinet in the corner of the room.

Sean lit a cigarette in the neatly manicured grounds, chatted with Edward about his past, his hobbies and his family and finally asked him who he could disclose the information to.

'No one Sean, not even your boss. Leave that issue with us.'

Sean suddenly became very conscious that he could end up in a prison cell if he got this mission wrong.

It was while Sean was overseas conducting this mission some three months later, that he was called into the British Embassy Defence Attaché's office in Moscow.

He only ever remembered the first sentence.

'I'm very sorry to have to tell you that your wife was taken ill, and she has sadly died Sean…'

A sudden seizure had left Katy with an abrupt and devastating brain haemorrhage that no one could save her from.

Sean's face narrowed before he dropped to his knees.

PART TWO

CONSPIRACY

Chapter 7

Eleven Years Later

Canary Wharf, London

Braking harshly, the Tube train lurched into Bond Street station. Nestled amongst the crowded morning commuters, Melissa Morgan stood her ground as those around her jolted awkwardly before settling again as the train came to a halt.

Inclining her head, and holding onto her space, she became irritated as two youths entered the carriage and bumped into her with their small work rucksacks. 'Idiots,' she thought momentarily, thinking twice about telling them to take their rucksacks off and put them on the floor. She shuffled into pole position again, composed herself and remained annoyed that she had another seven stops to go, most likely standing.

Those thoughts led to her looking at her shoes. Dark blue high heels, which were beginning to cripple her toes. She lamented that she had put them on that morning, with pretty much no thought for her comfort, in a weary state after a long weekend back home in Cardiff. She'd bought them in John Lewis on a shopping trip with her mother.

'I know it's difficult finding someone these days,' her mother had begun during lunch, 'but have you thought about maybe looking back here at home?'

'Mum, really!' Whilst she loved Cardiff, she never ever saw herself moving away from London, away from her job and its travel. 'It's a tough city to find anyone decent. Mainly lunatic boys and we never seem to find any real men,' alluding to her forays with her best friend.

'And your work, my love? How's that all going?'

'Oh, you know most of it Mum. A pedantic weakling boss, with no real balls, and me seemingly bashing out all the hard graft for no real value in return. But don't worry, it's fun and I'm gonna show the idiot how good I really am.'

Standing there on the crowded train, it suddenly dawned on her that she would be late for the meeting with a secret source of information who could dramatically change her life if she got the break she needed. After five years of working for the Global Bureau of Investigative Journalism, she damn well knew her time was ripe for recognition. She instinctively felt it, and at thirty-five, she was revelling in the challenges of deep-delve investigations, having learnt her craft well.

She really had to nail this. She had nurtured her source, Alfie Chapman, extremely well over the last six months. Alfie was a military intelligence officer who had decided to use the Bureau as an outlet for leaking a variety of stories exposing government and establishment figures for their indiscretions. She recalled how fate, and a short dysfunctional relationship with Alfie, had brought this opportunity to her. His revelations on the Iraq war were particularly appealing.

Melissa was confident, but slightly apprehensive, as she emerged from the giant Canary Wharf escalators into the Jubilee Gardens of East London. Her standard fare was researching and reporting on human rights abuses and Middle Eastern terrorism, but this was a complete shift from her status quo. Alfie had inadvertently provided her with gold dust.

She knew the pain Alfie held, and of his inner turmoil, but also about his determined desire to go through with a plan he had shared with her some weeks ago. She felt self-assured and vindicated in agreeing to help him with his escape plan and to look at the detail of how Alfie could release his secrets to the world. Melissa had no direct feelings for Alfie anymore and she had moved on to a number of other short-term relationships since she had broken up with him. Nevertheless, she felt a real friendship and true bond with Alfie, qualities that none of her other erstwhile boyfriends had ever presented her with.

She knew of his emotional insecurities and had begun to recognise his disordered mind and fickle emotional state. But she marvelled at how Alfie, with his starkly handsome features and authoritative figure, could wear his mask and remain outwardly confident, yet vulnerable beneath it. She knew he was emotionally dysfunctional, but she knew she had a duty to help this kind soul. It was just a shame the spark was not there for her with Alfie and she winced as she reflected on her own poor judgement in men, and her despair at never finding anyone suitable in a city of millions of young professionals.

She walked across the gardens, straining in the cold air, and studied the clocks neatly placed around the square showing the time in different global cities. The share price ticker tape scrolled around the building as she cast her eyes at the people whizzing by. She felt uplifted by the greenery and the deep blue spring sky as she tied her brunette hair in a bun before walking the few minutes to Canada Square Park to meet Alfie.

Melissa walked into the restaurant, immediately sensing other men's eyes gravitate towards her. These were City men sitting on leather bench-style seating in the canteen restaurant, with its large ceiling voids and high glazing that provided great views into the banking world of Canada Square.

She wore a navy skirt just above the knee, black high-heeled shoes, a white blouse and a sleeveless tangerine top that accentuated her breasts. Her favourite blue handbag was slung over her left arm, with a white jacket draped over the other.

She spotted Alfie sitting in the far corner of the restaurant and immediately noticed how exhausted he looked. 'Hi Alfie, crazy journey. Sorry I'm late. A right bunch of idiots on the tube,' Melissa said, as she kissed him on both cheeks and gave him a hug. 'You look tired, are you OK?'

'I'm fine Melissa, come and take a seat. I'll get some drinks. Erm, you look great by the way.'

'Thanks, I love early morning breakfast meetings on such gorgeous days.'

'Wonderful,' Alfie said. 'I'm really pleased how you've helped me so far. You know you're the only one I can trust with this and, to be frank, I don't think I could do it without your help.'

Melissa sat and leant forward, her arms on the table as they sat opposite each other. Alfie had ordered some grapefruit juice and water before they ate. He looked thin in the face but cheery, she thought. 'You look gaunt Alfie. Are you sure you'll be OK with all this?'

'Yes, don't worry too much about me. How have you been getting on with the work?'

'Well, I'm due to meet my editor in person tomorrow,' Melissa indicated. 'And I have his guarantee of no disclosure and a prepared plan to get you somewhere safe when the time comes.'

Melissa crossed her legs and drank some of the juice, looking around to ensure the area Alfie had chosen was quiet, with no prying ears. Exceptionally bright, Melissa had planned in detail the way that Alfie would expose his story and how she could help with his escape. Wise enough to know she had to be cautious with her own career, she had mulled over the political ramifications of her own role within the Bureau as an investigative journalist.

'The editor doesn't know who you are Alfie, but he's agreed to fund the logistics and a couple of high-grade private facilitators for you. He knows you're an anonymous source right now, and the initial documents you gave us have convinced him that the Bureau can act to protect you.'

'That's great Melissa, bloody good work.'

'But remember Alfie, there's a long way to go yet. You can go through with it right?'

'Go through with it? I'm nearly there,' Alfie replied tersely. 'And yes of course I can, it's just very stressful right now.'

'OK, let's get down to business then, lots to sort out now.'

Melissa leant back and placed her handbag to the side as she watched Alfie remove a black book containing an immaculately written plan. He passed it to Melissa and started to describe his exit plan in detail, including the precise locations and timings. Alfie had been impeccable in crafting the minute-by-minute stages of his exit plan from the country.

Melissa had read many of the exposés that Alfie had researched and had remembered falling back on her sofa in utter astonishment at the shameless facts Alfie had unearthed when she first read them.

As an investigative reporter, she felt her stomach churn as she read the revelations he was about to release to the world. Feisty, and with an edge, Melissa was a straight-talking and respected journalist following a short career as a financial forensic investigator. She loved investigative work and had become fascinated after reading the documents Alfie had given to her some weeks ago. She went through a whole bottle of white wine on the first night she read them, intrigued by the carefully crafted résumés and the historical facts of what she could see were dark forces in operation. She awoke with a hangover and a new drive to help Alfie, who had clearly mulled over his plan on how to expose all the secrets he had uncovered. Her love of risk had surfaced again. And she saw her opportunity to rise to the top.

'I have to expose all of this, no matter what it takes,' Alfie quietly mentioned, looking her straight in the eye. She sensed his anxiety but remained quiet.

'I can't wait to go through with it,' Alfie continued, putting his hand to his mouth to cough. 'Erm, but we must keep this very tight Melissa, I can't have anyone knowing my identity at all until the exact hour. It's too risky with the security service connections in the press world. Make sure you erase your tracks and keep your digital footprint tight for God's sake. It only takes a small sniff from anyone on the inside and I'm toast.'

'You know very well that I know what I'm doing,' Melissa said sharply. 'You have nothing to worry about from me on that score.'

'I know, but it plays on my mind a lot. I really don't want to end up in some stinking jail to rot.'

'Alfie. You won't. Get a grip now.'

Melissa watched Alfie sit up straight, as if affronted by her hardness. 'Snowden fucked up his escape plan because he didn't think through the detail Alfie. You have.'

'Thanks.'

'That's why he ended up floating around the world as a fugitive before the Russians agreed to let him hole up there. Look at how some of his data was lost by the arrest of the reporter at Heathrow. Sheer amateur fuck ups. This is different. We've planned this tightly.'

Melissa watched Alfie's face tighten. 'I know how I want to store and hide the data in case anything happens to me and the failsafe plan to expose it is in good shape too if I'm arrested or, God help me, if I'm kidnapped by the intelligence agencies.'

'This is all very obvious Alfie, but you need to keep calm, it's all OK. I'll make sure my side goes perfectly but you need to let me know what some of these failsafes are. You have to bloody well trust me you know.'

Melissa began to write down the dates she could meet with Alfie to finalise the exact detail. She had an edge for risk-taking and didn't take any nonsense – even from a military officer.

'Now have a look at these dates Alfie, and don't worry. This is very, very, complex and worrying but I won't let you down and the Bureau are right behind you. It's the right thing to do and our planning is meticulous.' Alfie looked calmer, she thought.

'I know,' Alfie said solemnly. 'Thank you. You will be fine. It's the others who will get me, and just one slip, one tiny slip of our tongues or amongst our online activity, and the net will close in. I have 68,000 files and five huge revelations about government secrecy and cover-ups. I can't release it all to you until the time is right. And the trail we leave must be watertight.'

Melissa noticed the beads of sweat on his forehead and she wondered if he'd been taking drugs to keep his traumas at bay. She was alive to the risks she was taking and savvy on how to operate clandestinely, knowing full well the gravitas of the secret world she was dancing with. She kept her irritations with Alfie at bay for now, noticing how he wanted to keep talking.

'There is something else I want to tell you,' Alfie said. 'This is very sensitive and could mean someone losing their livelihood, and their life, if it gets out. But before I leave for good, only you will know the full extent of what I've been doing, and how.'

Melissa perked up. 'Sounds intriguing – go on.'

'I've been getting information from another whistle-blower. He has been one for many years and has been a thorn in the government's side ever since he left Russia.' Alfie explained how he had met his main source of classified information and what they had achieved together over the last twelve months across the dark net, a hidden place of internet encryption that allowed them to exchange secrets, and where no one else was likely to monitor or trap them.

'His name is Jonathan Hirst,' Alfie explained.

'OK. So, who is he?' Melissa asked. 'What does he do?'

'Hirst is a renegade. At least to the Foreign and Commonwealth Office. He was the British Ambassador to Russia during the early 2000s. He was very popular in the British Embassy in Moscow and across the regions in Uzbekistan and Kazakhstan.'

'Bloody hell,' Melissa chipped in. 'An ambassador who's gone rogue then?'

'Exactly that.'

'But what happened to him then – why did he go off-piste?'

Alfie described how Hirst was an unconventional ambassador, youthful and exuberant, yet shrewd and pragmatic. He loved a drink. He loved a party. He enjoyed the company of good-looking women and had a reputation amongst the staff for being a bit of a lad.

'The trouble was that Hirst was not toeing the party line,' Alfie explained, coughing again. 'The FCO expect their ambassadors not to cause any turmoil or rock the boat and, in those dark heady days, anyone who missed a beat on the government's stance would be fair game for political assassination. Hirst was politically slayed for not remaining on message and was sacked by the FCO. They had saddled up their first ambassador whistle-blower, with ramifications lasting for years. He's leaked a lot of information to me.'

Melissa was hugely excited about this new revelation. 'Absolute dynamite,' she thought, wondering how she could profit from this.

'Hirst had first-hand knowledge and detailed reports on yellowcake uranium that was supposedly being sold to Iraq by Uzbekistan in 2003.'

Alfie touched his forehead, as if comforting a headache. 'Hirst exposed this as being thoroughly false and showed evidence that these sales were never destined for Iraq, but in actual fact were being negotiated with Iran. Exposing this scam got him the sack and the government hushed it all up.'

'Bloody hell Alfie,' Melissa said. 'This is stunning stuff. When can I show this to the editor? How will we get this out there?'

'All in good time Melissa.' Alfie continued to describe the extent of the subterfuge perpetrated by the UK's Secret Intelligence Service and someone known as Dominic Atwood, an MI6 field officer. 'It was Dominic Atwood's intelligence that had been spun and weaved to provide false evidence to support the aim of invading Iraq.'

Melissa, fascinated by this turn of events, took a sip of her coffee and sat back, feeling an adrenalin surge, as Alfie went further into the detail.

'So, what else has Hirst exposed then?' Melissa asked.

'Well, the other case he has helped me on is that of Professor Margaret Wilshaw. She is said to have taken her life in 2003 as a result of exposing dubious intelligence that emanated from a very secretive clique in MI6 called Operation Cloud-Hawk.' Alfie looked down and paused.

Melissa sensed his tears.

'I'm still working on the case,' Alfie said. 'But effectively it looks like she was probably murdered.' Alfie was clearly shaken by this tragic death and Melissa put her hand on his shoulder.

'That's a horrible thing to find out. I remember the case well. She was hounded by the MOD and all because of the despicable warping of intelligence by the government to justify war. Makes me sick,' Melissa said.

They sat in silence for a short period before Melissa asked what else the Ambassador had revealed. Still slightly stunned, Melissa watched as Alfie collected himself before answering. 'He's been pretty active actually, with newer stuff. He's started to feed me some puzzling information about the UK Brexit referendum and the US presidential elections coming along later this year.'

'You mean Britain exiting the European Union?' Melissa queried.

'Yep – well, the vote to remain or leave at least. Looks like there has been some underhand Russian meddling there too, as well as the Russians trying to destabilise the US elections in

November. Hirst has good connections with the Russians you know.'

Melissa took a spell to breathe and think a little. She looked around the restaurant nervously. 'Wow. Be careful Alfie. If the Russians are all part of this puzzle, there'll be lots of nasty vultures hovering about.'

'I know. But with all these revelations, the public really deserve to know. People will be culled or neutered for all this Melissa. It's just a matter of time. What's more, my biggest investigative case is going to bring even more eruptions to the very heart of Westminster. I can't tell you all about that one yet. It's very powerful stuff and involves a list of Russian moles in the country all captured from a legacy operation in Moscow about eleven years ago in 2005.'

'Wow.'

Melissa's thoughts were finely tuned to the success she could achieve with Alfie's astonishing secrets. She knew he had turned – forever. And for her, there was no going back.

Canary Wharf life passed them by as they went into the details of the carefully written plan that Alfie had crafted. Melissa was excited by the full extent of what she had heard that morning. Excited about how this could propel her journalistic career into the big time.

An hour later they left, and agreed to meet next time at the Tate Modern to avoid being seen together at their homes.

Neither of them noticed the suited businessman sitting on a bench in the park reading his Kindle as they left.

Chapter 8

Kabul, Afghanistan

Warren Blackburn, known as Swartz to his friends, watched the ground crew take their positions from the shade of the terrace located in the discreet terminal compound for VIPs and dignitaries.

Swartz had not aged well. Life at the very edge of living had taken its toll, emotionally and physically, and he wore a face that would not welcome chance or opportunistic conversations with strangers. His pockmarked face, short grey hair and steely gaze projected a man who had seen and tasted life to its fullest, whether it was hard partying or gritty and deathly combat.

Swartz watched the Gulfstream G550 long-distance jet struggle with the fierce Kabul crosswinds as it lurched and swayed before landing with a heavy thump at Afghanistan International Airport. A recent sandstorm had left an orange fog swirling in the air and it was hard for him to make out the small craft as it taxied to the decrepit terminal building and its VIP parking zone.

He smiled assuredly to the petite VIP stewardess, who followed him with her eyes, he was sure, as he walked through the sliding terminal doors onto the secure area of the tarmac. Had she looked closer, she'd have seen his left hand only had one finger and a thumb.

Swartz was dressed in a black T-shirt, tan fatigues and desert boots. He was wearing a thigh holster with a Sig Sauer P226 pistol and had body armour slung over his shoulder. A seasoned hand with twenty-six years of army experience, hugely respected within the Special Air Service, and deadly at executing interdiction missions on terrorist targets. He had been on major operations across the globe virtually non-stop over the last ten years, and had dozens of house assaults to his name, each one resulting in terrorist kills.

He slipped on his wraparound sunglasses, walked a few metres to the security barrier and stood awaiting the arrival of his charges. His mind wandered back to the encrypted signal he had received the day before. Swartz pondered why he was being tasked to collect his old SAS commanding officer, JJ Jones and a civil servant from the UK. 'What the fuck is going on?' he muttered curiously, especially as he knew that JJ had left the SAS some years ago.

Swartz watched the small jet taxi close to the old building before being directed to turn right by the ground marshal, who was waving his table-tennis bats with metronomic precision. 'I feel a bloody big ruse coming on,' Swartz muttered again, as he watched the two men walk across the tarmac. He recognised JJ Jones immediately as the taller of the two. JJ gave a short wave, accompanied by a big beaming smile, and walked towards the security barrier to greet him. 'Here we fucking go,' Swartz murmured. 'Another day living the dream.'

JJ Jones was a former commanding officer of the SAS who had masterminded the British special forces' black ops across Iraq and Afghanistan, taking out terrorists on an industrial scale. Swartz and JJ had been part of an enduring US-led strategy of black ops across Central Asia and the Middle East that had been hugely successful in carrying out precision strikes on the leaders of major terrorist cells. Shrouded in public and diplomatic secrecy, the American strategy had been the master plan of General Stanley Beeton, before his ultimate demise after being caught libelling the US Vice-President in a press article. The British SAS had played a major role in striking at the heart of these terrorist groups and, for years, they were propelled into the toughest of killing assignments in Baghdad and beyond. Beeton had an almost empirical love of the SAS and had become good friends with JJ.

JJ was fondly revered by his men, who always referred to him as 'Jackdaw' Jones, or JJ for short after Beeton's nickname had stuck. JJ had seen the effect that a few score troopers had in Baghdad during the darkest days of the Iraq wars.

Swartz knew JJ well from the regiment and had operated as his second in command in 2005 when the SAS undertook house raids to chase down the 21 July London bombers. He smirked as he remembered how JJ had introduced himself as JJ to the guys – and as Richard to all the political monsters he came into contact with. But why is JJ here now, he thought.

Swartz's team ran human intelligence agents across the Afghan region, and he had previously been visited by government officials who would undertake audits of cash that was being dished out on behalf of the British government. All in return for high-grade human intelligence. Ministers wanted to be assured of value for money. He wondered if this was the same kind of snap inspection. He remained sceptical on that idea. He was no fool and had seen his fair share of political shenanigans and SAS soldiers being used by MI6 in irregular ways. His gut feeling was that this visit was something irregular.

'Great to see you again Swartz,' JJ said, holding his hand out. He was dressed in a dapper beige suit and white shirt. 'It's been too long eh?'

Swartz smiled, his fingers held just inside his sleeveless body armour by his armpits, legs astride. 'It is mate. I certainly didn't expect to see you again,' he joshed. 'For fuck's sake, you've become a respectable businessman, haven't you? Or have you been caught out and sacked already?'

They laughed, then patted each other on the back. Swartz knew more than most about JJ's gung-ho, cavalier and renegade reputation. He was a fighting man through and through, yet had the charm and swagger of the best of senior officers.

Swartz turned towards the civil servant. 'I'm Warren but most people call me Swartz,' he said. 'Long way to come for an inspection if that's why you're here?'

'I'm Jack. Pleased to meet you Swartz,' the suited official said. 'I'm afraid it's a bit more than just an inspection but something I'm sure you'll enjoy.'

Jack was small, probably five foot eight, slightly scraggy with a weathered face, but also had boyish looks with the classic short-back-and-sides. Nothing special Swartz thought, noticing how the man was quiet of voice. Yet Swartz sensed he probably wasn't the normal diplomat that he was used to seeing come out on inspections.

'Follow me chaps and we'll saddle up and get ourselves through suicide alley.'

Swartz ushered them towards his white, armour-plated Landcruiser. His driver opened the doors and Swartz threw his body armour into the front before moving to the rear compartment to switch on the radio-frequency jammer. A vital piece of equipment to provide a secure electronic bubble around the vehicle which would protect them from radio-controlled improvised explosive devices as they travelled. He jumped back into the front seat, made a quick radio call to his operations room and they set off to Bagram airport on a route they alternated from day to day to avoid the threats of suicide-vehicle bombers.

Swartz switched on his dash-mounted phone and sent a quick text before his driver steered them down suicide alley, all the time skilfully avoiding the larger trucks to remain on heightened alert as he drove past any potential threats. It was forty-two degrees and the height of summer as they breezed past the rickety roadside stalls, manoeuvring the Toyota Landcruiser with skill amongst the Kabul traffic mayhem, which was now in full flow.

No one talked during the initial part of the journey, but as they neared Bagram airport, Swartz turned to the rear. 'Well, I'm looking forward to hearing what you have up your sleeve this time JJ,' he said. 'If we can possibly avoid a diplomatic incident before you fuck off home that would be good.'

JJ and Jack both smiled. 'Not on your nelly,' JJ said. 'This is all very kosher you know Swartz.'

'That's as maybe mate, you always used to say that. Remember Kosovo?' Swartz asked. 'You nearly got me and half the squadron sacked for that little escapade you conjured up.'

'Yes, you did rather save my ass back then,' JJ said, chuckling, before addressing Jack. 'You ought to know Jack that you're in highly qualified hands here with Swartz.'

'Great to hear,' Jack said.

'Swartz is first-rate at this sort of stuff. When it comes to the crunch, he'll deliver.'

'Spare me the shit JJ,' Swartz agitated. 'Besides, our best ever excitement came with you leading the charge across open ground on an Iraqi compound you nutter.'

'If you liked that, I think you'll find this job will be far more exciting,' JJ uttered as the vehicle approached the entrance to their ultra-secure Bagram airport base.

Swartz shook his head, smiled ruefully and said 'Fuck' as he opened the door. He knew the ruse was coming.

They got straight down to business when they walked into the special operations compound.

'Only bunk beds and Brillo Pad army-issue blankets I'm afraid,' Swartz said. 'Rooms are through there guys, and we can talk safely in the interview room just by here.'

JJ mentioned that Jack would not be staying there. Swartz shrugged his shoulders. The compound was a tiny piece of Britain on a US airbase. Not only that, it was one of the most secure yards on the base, set behind reams of five-metre-high corrugated steel frames so that no one could see in or out. No other British HQ contingents were allowed behind the steel walls, largely because the compound was used to debrief Afghan agents who would covertly arrive at night through two air-locked gates in trashed-out cars with full blackout windows.

This was a dark-ops world: cocooned amongst the safety of the American base, but a UK eyes-only facility. The compound consisted of an MI6 officer, two GCHQ operators, a handful of intelligence officers running interrogation ops and a small team of specialised, task-specific SAS troopers. This was exactly what Jack wanted.

Swartz set the mugs out in the centre of the interview room table and ushered his radio operator into the room, he brought in a tray of biscuits, water, coffee and toast. Swartz had checked the vetting clearances of JJ and Jack to ensure they had the right level of credentials to allow access into the highly vetted compound. Each had impeccable clearances at STRAP and DV level. This immediately struck Swartz as odd given that JJ had left the army years ago. What was he up to now he wondered?

Swartz was now a major in the SAS having risen through the ranks since joining at seventeen as an ammunition technician at the Army Apprentice College in Chepstow. His trade as a bomb disposal officer saw him undertake six tours of Ireland and eleven short tours of Iraq and Afghanistan. He became embedded in the regiment in the '90s as their black ops bomb disposal officer before completing selection training and becoming a fully badged soldier in B Squadron. Swartz was short but stocky, with cropped fair hair. He was a taekwondo enthusiast, and a calm, experienced operator.

Swartz took off his radio headset, adjusted his thigh holster and then sat down opposite Jack, with JJ to his right.

'Swartz, the official story is that we have come to interrogate one of your sources and look for intelligence linkages into the Maghreb,' JJ said. 'But we won't discuss that again: you can explain that away as a STRAP 3 Level, UK eyes-only piece of info. Jack is from box, MI5, and will explain the help we need.'

Swartz listened intently to JJ before switching his gaze back to Jack.

'We need your help Swartz: some firepower and trusted men to carry out a slick, short job for us in Kabul.'

Swartz perked up, shuffled in his chair and held his palms together to lean forward over the small table. He had a sense of excitement, but was cautious about what was coming his way.

'The UK needs a very important intelligence officer brought back to the UK. He went missing, and we need him for some other business back home,' Jack said. 'I've managed to track down where he's being held in Afghanistan.'

Swartz stayed quiet as Jack sat back and shifted his eyes to look at JJ.

JJ took up the story. 'Jack has asked me to make this op happen, and to get this guy back to the UK,' he said. 'As you've gathered already, and I know you get it, it's a deniable operation. You and I will carry out the job and Jack will cover our diplomatic trail and step in politically if we fuck it up.'

Swartz breathed in hard.

'Why can't you use the guys attached to the intelligence services? Or bring in a team? Seems odd to me to use my guys if it's all kosher?'

Swartz knew JJ would have anticipated this question and he watched as JJ stood up and looked at the aerial imagery of Kabul on the walls. The images showed blue insertion and red extraction routes, used to covertly bring Afghan agents back to the compound for debriefing and paying off.

'I can't blag you Swartz – it's a *side op* not known about by the agencies back home. But it's sanctioned very high up in the centre. And actually, it's not too tricky a job.'

Swartz leant forward again and rolled his eyes in disbelief. 'For fuck's sake JJ' he said angrily. 'That means no fucker in the regiment knows and my ass is on the line after all these years of approaching an honest pension. I'll be hung out to dry, denied by the UK and probably chucked in a cell. I like a bit of fun, but shit mate…'

Swartz leant back, opened his posture and gestured with his palms up in the air.

'I know,' JJ replied calmly. 'But I have something here which I hope will convince you.'

JJ slid a passport-sized picture of a man across the table for Swartz to look at. Swartz was shocked at who the man in the picture was. A man he knew well. A close friend. He looked up and noticed Jack smile.

It occurred to Swartz that this had all been set up by JJ and he imagined him and Jack plotting this ruse in some grubby East End London hotel, which was where plenty of side ops had been hatched. He wondered who the main boss was. What was the aim here? And what was the risk to him as he approached his latter days of service before retiring? The fact that he was in command in Kabul, at exactly the same time that a good friend of his needed rescuing, was probably a total fluke. Swartz began thinking through the detail of the mission. It had a bloody good chance of success, and he relished the deviation beyond the norm.

He was relieved knowing that it was JJ on this mission: that was a level of trust he could accept. But he was concerned about the risk of the whole side op remaining unknown to government agencies, and the deep shit he would be in if they found out. But given who it was he had to rescue and needed his help, he knew he had no choice. It was a close friend. Honour amongst military friends and never leaving a man behind was the SAS ethos. 'This is full on fucking daring,' he muttered, 'and how many times have I heard the words *This is very tight hold, only a few people know.* Bullshit by the truck load I reckon.'

Swartz was seasoned enough to know that such statements were never true and that invariably there were hidden people who knew what else was going on. Such was the standard fare of the deceptive world of intelligence operations: no one ever knew who was pulling the strings or who else had a hand in the outcomes.

Swartz wondered who else knew about the task he had to complete, and who exactly was Jack's boss? He made a note to find out.

He had a thought or two about Jack and his poker face, along with his amenable and smiley engagement. A career spook he thought, nothing special, but as with all spooks Swartz had met, he knew they were all utterly treacherous.

Jack had clearly arranged things well. Swartz noted how he had disappeared to the British Embassy in Kabul, no doubt keen to maintain the guise of an official visit, another deception Swartz felt Jack was very skilled at.

Swartz arranged the satellite imagery of the target site so he and JJ could come up with a plan to see if it was feasible to rescue the officer. He passed two files to JJ showing old HUMINT reports that gave detailed information on the target building from those who had worked on the inside.

'This could all be out of date,' Swartz said. 'Let's get on the ground to have a look and I'll get the boys to put together some close target analysis packs with high-resolution imagery. We need to get this guy out and back to Britain with as little fuss as possible.'

'Agreed mate. I think we need to rehearse the insertion too.'

'Definitely. I'll get the boys to rig something up.'

'Good, let's recce the place.'

Swartz and JJ spent the next couple of days looking at the precise layouts of the buildings, the corridors, the key people inside and any weakness or vulnerability they could expose to pull it off. Swartz's team carried out helicopter reconnaissance, and JJ drove around the target building where the Brit was being held. The drive-bys and aerial reconnaissance were backed up by Swartz's intelligence from interrogating two Afghan men who knew the place well. Swartz arranged for collection of each of the men over two nights, extracted them safely from their separate communities in Kabul, smuggled them blindfolded into a battered old French Renault van and brought them back to the compound for questioning.

Each man was duly paid with official UK Government funds, enough for four months' earnings, and returned home unscathed and unseen by their local neighbours, who were none the wiser regarding their collaboration with coalition forces. Swartz chuckled at the irony of it all.

Swartz considered a blagging-type scam: approaching the entrances and reception area of the building with an air of high authority whilst dressed as diplomats in suits and ties and escorted by some big burly protection. The lax security, and lack of will to stop authoritative figures striding in purposefully, had certainly worked in the past. But, after discussion with JJ, he felt a simple, no-nonsense, direct approach with surprise as their main weapon was a better strategy. And they would deal with whatever came at them as it emerged.

They needed to extract the man and get him back to the compound to allow Jack to surreptitiously whisk him back to the UK.

Chapter 9

Outskirts of Kabul

Swartz checked his watch. It was 2.40am on the darkest night of the week. He was chuffed there were no CCTV cameras or high-tech electronic security measures to be defeated. Just a number of poorly trained, lightly armed, Afghan Police guards in one-piece grey coveralls who were patrolling listlessly. He watched their sluggish manner through his night-vision goggles.

Swartz had rehearsed his team well. He glanced to check they were poised and ready to go in their four black Landcruisers, tactically positioned for the pre-prepared assault. Each was armed with two nine-millimetre pistols, holstered on their thigh and waistband, and each carried a shorter barrelled version of the MP5 automatic machine gun used on house raids. It was a nimble weapon that could be easily trained on the target using the red laser-targeting sight.

Swartz pulled his goggles over his eyes and checked the activity around the target. It was a large, sprawling colonial fort with whitewashed mud walls at the base of the sheer ramparts and red-brick watchtowers. Entry over the walls was a non-starter, but Swartz knew exactly where the guarding weakness was: right at the heart of the entry into the site through its giant iron-framed gates.

Swartz spoke quietly into his hands-free radio, ordering two of the SAS operators, Dell and Bob, to move into position to make a final approach to the small wooden hut where the external bearded guards wandered lazily.

Swartz was revelling in a slightly different job from the norm. A jailbreak.

The moonless night and cloud-laden sky were ideal for concealing their approach. The guards could be heard chattering around the corner, smoking and kicking their heels, doing little to look like professional guards. Swartz had observed their amateur behaviour on each night of their detailed reconnaissance. 'Should be a breeze,' he murmured, as he hogged the darkness, moving to his assault position. Swartz checked the safety catch was released on his weapon, felt the adrenalin rise and sensed his heart beating at an elevated rate now. He was charged and ready. He patted Dell on the shoulder, spotting the glint of light from the blade in his right hand.

Emerging from the shadows, like a cheetah striking a gazelle, Swartz charged at the closest guard. He grabbed the guard from behind, one hand on his forehead, the other around his neck, and then hurled the man to the floor in a rolling motion. Within seconds he was disarmed, face in the mud, with Swartz's knife positioned to slit his throat.

Swartz glanced to his side to see Bob attack the second guard by punching him straight in the face – he was immediately knocked out. The silence remained. He watched Dell and Bob handcuff the guards as he moved silently around the right-hand side of the recess, just behind the huts, to the main gate.

He waited. It was perfectly quiet and still as he ordered his team into their next assault positions. It was time to tease the other guards out from behind the walls.

Six minutes later the gate opened. A dark figure walked cautiously through the small gap. Swartz grabbed the unsuspecting guard and threw him to the ground with a brutal judo throw that knocked the wind right out of him. He signalled for Dell and Bob to rush through the gate to storm the control room, where three other guards sat behind their desks – another guard stood up just inside the door and made a ranging movement with his hand and weapon.

Right on his shoulder, Swartz watched Dell pop two nine-millimetre rounds right into the guard's thigh and saw the man crumple to the floor with a loud moan.

'Get your fucking hands on the desk now,' Bob shouted. Swartz sprinted through the middle of the front desks to put his hand in the guard commander's face, pushing him back violently. The guard commander toppled over his chair and Swartz rolled him over before forcing his right arm up his back, just to the point where a click took place. This was followed by a loud cry of pain. With clinical speed, all four guards were bundled into the corner with plastic tie strips on their hands and makeshift gags around their mouths.

Swartz spoke in Pashto to the guard commander, who had been dragged to the other side of the room and showed him a four-inch-thick wad of cash. 'You won't be killed if you cooperate with me and you'll have enough money for the rest of the year,' Swartz whispered, making sure that the other guards did not hear him or see the cash. 'Take me to the white man,' he said.

Sheer speed and total brutality had allowed Swartz to get right into the very heart of the prison, with the now very compliant guards restrained and neutralised. He looked the guard commander in the eye, tugged him by his shoulder and headed for the exit.

'Watch the courtyard Dell,' Swartz whispered. 'Move quickly boys, the police station is next door and I don't want to be their next fucking guest.' He led his team into the courtyard, along the edge of the square, and veered right into a long corridor lined with men sleeping, coughing and spluttering.

The mud walls were cracked, the floors rutted and the entire building reeked of decay and poor sanitation. The corridor stretching before them was flooded with inmates in striped uniforms, their faces full of despair.

Swartz nudged round the corridor, sweating hard now, his weapon at the ready in his right hand. He put his other hand across his nose to lessen the filthy stench, urging the Afghan to move quicker. It would be fatal to be caught now after their act of surprise. The guard commander stood to the side and ushered Swartz into an eight square metre cell where a dozen or so Afghans lived, ate and slept. 'Jeez, this is fucking desperate,' he said, scanning the room, where rusting bunk beds hid the walls. The floor, on which a few men slept in total squalor, was strewn with rubbish and covered in dirty blankets.

Through a thick shroud of smoke from a dying charcoal grill, a light flickered, revealing occasional smears of excrement and mucus on the walls. A radio blasted out Afghan music.

'*Salaam Alaikum,*' Swartz said to the occupants, some of whom were now standing with obvious fear. Two Afghans with long beards and grey turbans began praying on their knees. Swartz looked into the far corner, where a bald, gaunt Westerner had just sat up on his bunk bed to see what the hell was going on. He approached the bed and shone a small torch straight into the Westerner's face.

'Sean, you wanker. Get bloody dressed. We have a rugby match to go and watch.'

Chapter 10

The Compound, Bagram Airbase

Sean got the shock of his life when he saw his old pal Swartz standing over him after months of being incarcerated in Kabul's most fearsome prison. It was a hell of a welcome surprise and a curious reunion as they chatted over a beer back at the compound that night. They laughed loudly at the audacity of breaking him out of one of Afghanistan's most terrifying prisons. It was a great celebration.

Sitting holding a bottle of beer, Sean experienced a sense of utter disbelief that he was finally free. Hurting emotionally, wounded physically, dejected at his demise, mentally on a knife edge but pleased that Swartz, an old mate, had enabled his freedom.

Sean looked at Swartz, who was not holding back. His eyes were intense, his posture taut and he wanted to hear every single detail of his internment. Sean smelt like a decaying rat, but Swartz didn't seem to give a shit. All Sean felt was a sense of euphoria, helped by the beer, as he listened to Swartz's questioning on how he had ended up in a hellhole.

He struggled hard to focus his mind which was now relishing the effect of alcohol. Wearily, he began recounting with brutal honesty, how he had fucked up a mission that had eventually led to the lowest point in his career: being arrested and incarcerated in prison for having a stash of heroin blocks and illegal weapons in his hotel room in Kabul. He was looking at fifteen years inside. No remission. Probably death.

It was a relief for Sean to finally convey his pain to someone who knew him so well. He felt the physical pain subsiding. The sores didn't feel as harsh and his cracked lips felt less damaged, but he felt deep shame.

'It all went downhill on a stupid civilian job in Central Asia a couple of years back and after I had left the service,' Sean began. 'That's why I eventually ended up in that fucking hellhole. A place of the living dead.'

'Go on,' Swartz urged. 'It must have been bad for you to have been pensioned off by the service, or sacked, as I think we say.'

'They forced my hand really – I had no choice but to leave and find contract work,' Sean recounted. 'I lost my vetting, so I was of no use to them. They could just toss me aside.'

'Blimey. How the hell did you lose the vetting?'

'Long story my friend. They offered me a desk job and a demotion, there was no loyalty from the bastards at all. We're just pieces of meat to the service mate, they are ruthless in all they do.'

'And the short story?'

'Mmmm, a rather foolish relationship with an Iranian agent. Vetting lost. Untrustworthy. Unemployable to them at that point.'

'Shit.'

'Yep – top class eh? No halfway house for me after Katy died. I just fucking plummeted.'

'Went out with a bloody good bang then!'

They laughed. For a long while. Swartz took the piss out of the indiscretions that had fouled Sean's entire life and career.

They both relaxed, drank a few more bottled beers and Sean continued to recount his colourful journey over the last few years of his service before his entry into the private sector. He explained how he had then fallen foul to a crime lord who was running drug-smuggling gangs with the Taliban in Helmand.

'I always loved excitement mate, it was great fun,' Sean said, merrily. 'I suppose my life had had an all-too-normal trajectory. Home counties schooling, middle-of-the-road university, military officer career and then into city life, working nine to five so as to settle down a bit. Get married and have kids, you know – all that good civilian career and family stuff. I didn't figure on intelligence work, let alone being suckered into it for twenty odd years. Katy's death led me onto a different path altogether and it was all too much after that. Many things went wrong, leading me to finally cock it all up by working with Frazer, a bent ex-copper, and his gang. It was definitely the lowest point of what should have been a normal life.'

For Sean, the death of Katy was a wound that would never heal, and a catalyst for the dark days and nightmares that continued to haunt him most nights.

'How did you end up working with these nutters then?' Swartz asked, cracking the top off another bottle.

'Contract work mate. It was a couple of years back when I left the service. Intelligence collection stuff, a bit of close protection for him and his cronies, liaising with the Taliban over routes through to Iran and how to conceal stuff. And some booby trap work he wanted me to do on guards at border posts who didn't play ball. His companies were all very dodgy and a front for his brutal drug-running work. Fuck knows how but he won UK Government contracts for Helmand region.'

'You mean he had legitimate businesses then?'

'Yep – and he had other big-money UN contracts across Iraq and Afghanistan. Probably from his corrupt contacts.'

'So, they were running the heroin routes through Iran and Turkey then?'

'Exactly – and he didn't like it when I queried his operations and when I probed too much into their backgrounds. They were pretty crap on the ground too and didn't care so long as they had the money coming in.'

'Got it. So you pissed him off and he decided to nail you?'

'Spot on mate. He had everyone in his pocket, from UK Government officials to border guards and Albanian gangs running his drugs ops in London. He spends six months of the year in Asia and the other six months at home. Wealthy as fuck but a nasty bastard who had people killed just for looking at him oddly.'

'How did he have the smuggling routes tied up then?'

'Big money. Nasty people. The real bosses of the heroin trade, those who make the most profit along the supply chain, were Turkish Mafia living throughout Europe. He had deals with most of them and much of his wealth from heroin is now invested in legit legal businesses, like casinos and even law firms. He recruited Albanian crime syndicates who have taken over a lot of the heroin business as it moves its way along various smuggling routes into Western Europe, through Greece, Albania, Kosovo and Serbia. Even Hungary. These twats are hard-core nutcases and have changed the face of London crime.'

Sean grabbed another bottle of beer, cracked it open with the edge of his lighter and smiled at the incongruity of it all.

'Big Bang Frazer he's known as. I'll get him one day – in fact we can plan it together mate. I can't believe I got suckered into it all, but it was good money and a good adventure when I had bugger all to live for. Then it dawned on me I needed to put things right and get the fuck out of the haze I was in.'

'Sounds like you were in it too deep mate. How the fuck did you find all this out?'

'I went too far. I started delving deep into his operations. I'm surprised he didn't have me slotted in the end. The bit that got me the most was when I learnt part of his legit business was to supply ex-coppers and bent lawyers to the Iraqi Historical Allegations Team.'

Swartz winced. 'Those bastards are the scourge of the earth. Hounding the fuck out of us for years with no justification at all.'

'Exactly. I worked with some of the investigators when they were transferred to my Afghan ops. Two of them gave me chapter and verse on how they were firmly instructed by their bosses to string the investigations out. Dragging it out, with no thought for the soldiers being investigated, meant more money. To the tune of millions. It was nothing short of racketeering and I let them know my views on that.'

'So, he felt threatened then? Enough to do you over?'

'I resigned and walked away. Then he found out I'd been meddling. Had me tailed and stitched up like a kipper. He was worried I'd whistle-blow, so he set me up. I was bang to rights when they tipped me off to the Afghan police, who arrested me on the spot. Frazer got me. Knowing full well I'd be incarcerated for fifteen years plus.'

'Maybe you'll have the chance to get at him one day Sean. Hopefully with me in tow to sort the twat out. I retire soon, thank fuck.'

'This could be the break I need Swartz and I'll get him and his cronies one way or the other, make no mistake about that.'

Sean marvelled at the irony of both their situations. Their black humour and no-nonsense lifestyles provided no measure of deep emotion. It was simply hard core get on with it, live it and fix it. 'Hog the pain,' as Sean would often say when the going got tough. Chuckling, they toasted each other's futures and clinked their beer bottles.

'Why the fuck did they ask us to break you out then Sean?'

'Haven't got a clue. But one thing's for sure, it's not because they felt sorry for me. Looks like something pretty dodgy to me.'

'Another fucking ruse,' Swartz muttered.

Chapter 11

Bagram Airport

Sean awoke the next morning to the sound of Bagram airport coming alive. The noise of a huge Galaxy C-5 air transporter taking off was a welcome relief from the screams of agony and the pitiful distress of those incarcerated in the Kabul jail.

It had been a disturbed sleep, as it always was. His mind breaking in and out of the flashing scenes of his dank cell, and the stinking bodies of a dozen filthy men. He took a few moments to let the pleasant smell of the fresh white linen sink in, feeling the comfort of the duvet and plump pillow devour his senses. He felt fresh but sore. He lay there, not planning on getting up for a while, but quietly thinking of the events that had led to his arrest and incarceration.

He had been watching TV in his hotel room in Kabul when he had heard the commotion outside. Seconds later the door smashed open. Two of Frazer's steroid-laden thugs jumped on him and he felt the sensation of cold steel pressed hard against his forehead. He was handcuffed and bundled into a van, where he was beaten by the thugs.

People cope with the shock of capture in different ways. For Sean, it was always his gut that wrenched first. Then total despair. He remembered that he had regained consciousness with a curious view. A tiny concrete room. One high window with bars and a deluge of dust gently cascading downwards, forming a mirage from the sun's rays.

The door creaked, and Big Bang Frazer stood above him. Ginger-haired. A huge nose. Sniffling from too much cocaine.

'Well Sean, you really thought you'd get one over on me, didn't you?'

Sean tried to sit up but failed. 'What do you mean?' he said, blood spurting from his mouth, as he bent his head to get some shade from the sun's rays.

'Talking. You talk too fucking much, and don't pay attention to how that might affect my manor. You're a little fucking squealer aren't you?'

'Bullshit. I've been doing my job. Fuck all else.'

'You've been squealing to the locals and digging into my business. Had a change of moral compass, have you?'

Sean stayed quiet, quickly thinking about how he could escape.

'I'm going to teach you a lesson, sunshine. One you never learnt in your cosy little spy training. A lesson you'll keep learning because you'll wake up to it every fucking day thinking of me.'

'Listen Frazer, I don't need any teaching. Just a fucking job. This is all bollocks.'

'You really don't know anything about me, do you? I know everything. You've been tracing my money and delving into my fucking personal business. Looking to stich me up.'

'Rubbish. I was trying to uncover a leak.'

Frazer laughed hard. 'Always trying to grasp onto your training, eh? Doesn't work, sunshine. There's nothing that makes me more pissed off than people going behind my back. It makes me itch hard. It makes me want to see you suffer.'

Frazer lifted his leg and drove it down into Sean's knee. He felt the patella twist and crack.

'You're a scumbag Sean. Enjoy your vacation. You may survive, who knows?'

With that, Frazer was gone, and four uniformed Afghan policemen arrived an hour later to arrest Sean.

The sun burst into his small bedroom. Sean took a moment to remember where he was. The gutsy sound of a Chinook helicopter reminded him he was now free, and he took in his surroundings again. An old, steel-framed army bed. A bedside locker and a jug of water. A military sign on the door, giving instructions in the event of a mortar attack. He hated his flashbacks, shook himself to relieve the emotion, and slowly exited the bed to make his way across the small room to the clothes Swartz had appropriated for him.

'Good man,' he thought, as he spied the brand-new, sand-coloured desert shoes under the armchair. His favourite. Swartz had left him a light blue short-sleeved shirt and a pair of tan jeans, as well as a black gilet for the cold. On the table were a pair of sunglasses, a bottle of water, a packet of Rothmans cigarettes, with a Zippo lighter on top, and a small note saying, '*Best of luck mate, see you at the next match.*' Sean opened the bottle, took two tablets to ease his pain, showered and got dressed. The peace of having time to himself was invigorating, and his thoughts switched between what was coming next, how to keep his freedom and the bastards who had stitched him up. He wondered what the 'ruse', as Swartz had described it, might be.

The brown leather squeaked as Sean nestled into his seat on the Gulfstream jet. He sat next to Jack and opposite JJ who was already immersed in his paperback: Fitzroy Maclean's *Eastern Approaches*. The jet had four small pods consisting of four seats, each with a small table in between. Sean thought about how such jets had been used by MI6 to move terrorists around the globe as part of the CIA-led extraordinary rendition scheme. Doubtless this plane, its cargo and manifest would not show up on any official records.

Jack began. 'You'll meet my boss tomorrow, but we have a critical job for you Sean, and you're probably the only man we have who can do it. A hunter job. Exactly why we got you out.'

Jack was not just a loyal Crown servant, but a spy who operated best in the deserts of the Middle East, the mountains of Central Asia or with the dark gangs of the Balkans, where he knew his craft well. This time, he was on a national security mission for his new boss, Dominic Atwood.

'OK, what's it all about then?' Sean said, leaning back into his plush seat and glancing over at Jack. 'I'm expecting there is some sort of deal to be had here.'

Jack smiled. 'Indeed. That's the gist of it. In essence, we have an intelligence officer who has gone rogue. And he's gone missing. Possibly kidnapped. He's a high-grade officer who was working at the National Forces Intelligence Agency based in the high-security bunkers of the Bedfordshire countryside.'

'What's he done then?' Sean inquired, wondering what Jack's role was in this, and about the motivation of the rogue intelligence officer.

'We're not entirely sure,' Jack replied. 'We only have a single source of intelligence on him at the moment. And that's where you come in Sean.'

'Who's the source then?'

'Well, I obviously can't divulge that, but the picture seems to be that the officer has stolen a huge quantity of highly classified digital documents.' Sean remained quiet whilst he watched Jack place his black leather briefcase on his lap. Jack continued as he opened the briefcase.

'It seems he was brute-force hacking deep into our intelligence network systems. He's highly vetted, and has direct access to a range of American and British intelligence and data-mined files stored on servers across both countries. His prized cyber-intelligence feeds included TS, SI and TK intelligence.'

'Top secret, special intelligence and talent keyhole then. That's big stuff,' Sean replied, stunned at the extent of access to secret intelligence the officer had. 'I'm assuming he had access to special compartmented information too?'

'He did, and our concern is this could be more damaging than the leaks of Edward Snowden, the NSA contractor who leaked US secret communications to the world. It seems that we could have the next high-grade, cyber-security whistle-blower – and the first ever British Intelligence officer.'

'Pretty serious – so you want me to find him? And his cache of stuff?'

'Yes, of course. Our source has revealed that the rogue officer had a series of secret files he was going to expose,' Jack said. 'From the little we know, he had information files that he had titled '*Russian Moles*', '*Police corruption*' and '*Iraq Intelligence*'. It looks to us that he's committed to becoming Britain's biggest ever wholesale whistle-blower. We need to find him fast.'

Sean smiled at the sheer gall of the man – recalling the British Government's wobbles in 2013 when they had declared that the Snowden leaks amounted to the 'most catastrophic loss to British intelligence ever.'

'This is bloody big then,' Sean said, as he opened the red-covered dossier that Jack had handed to him. 'I assume everything you know is in here?' he asked, looking Jack squarely in the eyes. He knew he would not get an affirmative answer.

The dossier reminded him of Edward, the civil servant, who had tasked him for that fateful mission he had been on in 2005, when Katy died.

Chapter 12

West End Hotel, London

Sean wore a small black beanie hat and smiled coyly at the receptionist when he arrived at the West End hotel. He was embarrassed at his demise. Head now shaven, he was a skeleton of his former self with numerous scars on his face from living rough in one of the most dangerous prisons in the world and a personality that had been battered over the years.

He was pissed off he was now forced to wear headwear. He was self-conscious about his looks and his scorched past. He was damaged goods having plummeted into a dark downward spiral, followed by jail and finally the absurd notion he was still on top of his game.

He wanted to return quickly to his physically fit and gregarious self. 'What a bloody fool,' he murmured, willing himself to become a winner in life again. His addiction was adrenalin, and the rushes it gave him as it pulsed through his veins as a result of living life right on the edge. He wanted his life back again. Sean dealt with grief in his own way. He took it to a private place, a small set of drawers in his mind, kept it all to himself and took each drawer out occasionally. The loss of Katy had a devastating effect on him, and he had grieved alone for many years, immersing himself in his work. He often awoke from harsh nightmares and dreams of the family he had craved, a family with three kids and a wonderful wife, of which he had been robbed by tragedy.

Sean had always dressed immaculately, yet here he was now in a London hotel in trainers, T-shirt and jeans, looking like some sort of football hooligan. He was bemused about why he had been summoned to a Mayfair hotel in the early evening with Jack chaperoning his every move – exactly as he had done to get Sean safely back into the UK with no questions asked.

Sean walked into the large suite on the seventh floor and was instantly shocked when he was greeted by a quite tall, but very lean, man in his early sixties.

Sean recognised Dominic Atwood immediately from his time in Kazakhstan back in 2001, but it was clear Dominic did not recall that chance meeting with him all those years ago. Sean was, after all, a few stone lighter, emaciated and bald. As was Dominic – his toupee had gone.

Dominic was one of the country's greatest spooks. A spy with MI6 for over thirty years, he had a fearsome reputation for getting things done. He was one of the establishment's most commanding, contentious and enigmatic mandarins – and now he was the Home Office's top security man, someone who had only recently emerged from the shadows of MI6. He had come a long way since his murky days in Central Asia.

Sean looked at his surroundings as he walked through the lavish suite, as if he was looking for bugs and other listening devices. The suite was large with a double bedroom and spacious dining and living rooms, each overlooking Hyde Park. He was ushered by Dominic to take a seat amongst the beige leather chairs around an oval-shaped glass coffee table littered with fashion and tourist magazines. He watched Jack remove a large vase of flowers, so they could sit and talk unimpeded. Sean sat down opposite Dominic and Jack poured each of them a glass of Saint-Émilion to establish a congenial atmosphere.

'I understand you had some success finding a kidnapped and murdered diplomat who was buried some years ago in Iraq?' Dominic inquired. 'Frightfully bad episode.'

Sean nodded. 'And a few more since then too.'

'Good,' Dominic said, pausing with the unhurried confidence of someone not expecting any interruption. 'I have a pretty serious job I'd like you to lead on Sean. An intelligence officer has gone missing and we fear he may be dead already. It's vital to the interests of this country that we find out what has happened to him and find the files he was about to leak.'

Sean swilled his wine around the glass a few times, releasing the fruity aroma, and glanced across the table to gauge Dominic's disposition. He seemed edgy, but spoke simply, without a public schoolboy's accent. Sean tasted the 2009 vintage. 'I wondered why the goodwill repatriating me to the land of comfort,' he said. 'Delighted to help if the terms are favourable of course. Favourable to me.'

'Splendid Sean. It's all rather complicated but it needs a loyal Crown servant like you who is, erm, not a Crown servant, if you get my meaning?' Sean gave a knowing smile as Dominic continued. 'It's far too close-hold to do this in a traditional way. As you know, Chinese whispers float across our world. I can't afford for this to be cocked up, so this will have to be a complete side operation, well away from officially sanctioned work, one that needs a good cover story and a few good men.'

Sean listened to his tone, observing his style and demeanour. Dominic, it seemed, was not arrogant about his accounting. Rather, he seemed impassioned that this was the right thing to do for the country. He was speaking with clear, sometimes pitiless, but calm, honesty and straight from the soul. Sean wondered why this task was so vital to Dominic. 'Perhaps the leaks of information might also implicate him?' he wondered. Sean was clear in his mind though that Dominic was a ruthless operator. Behind the facade was a man with serious ambitions and clear views on life that matched the research he had undertaken during the day. '*Woe betide those who failed him,*' Sean had noted from the words of his contact. '*His charming but unhandsome looks belie his fearsome and brutal manner – a reputation that ricocheted through the corridors of the Home Office when he began his new role.*'

Sean looked Dominic directly in the eye with his response. 'That means I become a fall guy if it all goes wrong?' Sean said. 'A deniable operation?'

'You could say that is the case,' Dominic replied irreverently.

'Look Dominic, if I decide to find this man and his files then it needs to be full details and facts on the table,' Sean replied tersely. 'I don't want anything hidden. These are never easy jobs and it could take months. Just like it did to find the diplomat in

2004. And besides, to undertake an operation like this I will need my old team to assist, and they'll need to be motivated to remain quiet. I'd prefer not to have any surprises and an up-front conversation about how you will remunerate us all. You probably already know my motivation?'

Dominic turned to Jack. 'Jack will explain the details on how to go forward on this and I'm sure he's briefed you on nearly everything we have. I need your word that this will not get out to anyone.'

'That's all well and dandy, but where are my guarantees?'

'I can guarantee you won't end up back in Kabul,' Dominic said. 'But you'll need to make a damn good job of this to avoid any other large holes. You'll get everything you need, and all the costs you need will be met. However, if you so much as utter a word to anyone about the detail of this problem, I'll ensure your world is crushed again.'

The implication, as Sean always knew, was clear. Another large hole loomed if he didn't play ball. 'Fuck it,' Sean said. 'I'll play, but I want out in full if I succeed.'

'Very well,' Dominic replied. 'A real pleasure to have you back in the game Sean.'

Sean knew this was an opportunity but that it was probably a game to Dominic. He began to calculate all the avenues in his mind that could be used to surreptitiously keep his game plan shrouded from Dominic. Sean also found out from his contact in the Home Office that Dominic was currently a very angry man. He did not suffer fools. By all accounts, he had been passed over by some nut-chewing pompous fool who had beaten him to be 'C', the chief of MI6. He apparently held a deeply buried grudge against the people who had failed him in his life's ambition to become C.

Sean probed a bit more. 'So, this might well be a side op, but who else is in the game exactly? Who knows what?'

'We're unsure who the opposition is,' Dominic said, pausing briefly. 'But someone got to him before we did. Someone knew about his plans, and someone probably knew the extent of the nuclear fallout such a story would provoke if it was allowed to happen. I need to make sure that the information he was going to release is safe and, if it isn't, whose hands is it in? In there somewhere is a virulent list of moles. I need it kept from other prying eyes.'

'Who is this intelligence officer then?' Sean said, looking at both of them before taking a sip of his wine.

Jack chipped in. 'His name is Alfie Chapman. His name is Alfie Chapman. We thought he was a good man, if a little odd and slightly insecure. It seems now that he's wrongfooted us. We only recently found out he had disappeared, just before he was about to release to the world thousands of secret files that would seriously hinder our US relationship and expose some of our historical cock-ups we would rather didn't get out into the public domain.'

'So, you actually know for sure he was on the verge of releasing all of these files then?'

'Yes, he was. So, it's a bloody dangerous situation for the country.'

'Anyone else involved with him?'

'We found out he had been planning this for years,' Jack said. 'And he had been meticulous in his preparation. He had a female aide, who was helping him to access investigative journalists in a similar fashion to Edward Snowden. But Snowden was an amateur. Alfie was a careful, wise spook. The information he plans to leak could monumentally fuck things up for us all.'

Sean knew that he would need to grill Jack in far more detail and was prepared for a long night of finding answers to his questions. He was already formulating a plan for tackling the thorny issue of finding Alfie. Dead or alive.

'So, why can't you get the Met Police search and missing persons experts, oh, and box, to tackle this?' Sean said. 'It's their bag in MI5.'

'No one knows about this and he's just a missing person right now. This is too high-grade and too toxic to allow it to reach the ears of the agencies,' Dominic said garrulously. 'I don't know who else is out there looking for him, or indeed the full extent of the information he was going to whistle-blow on. So far as I am aware, and I believe this, only we know what he wanted to expose. I don't believe the intelligence agencies knew of this. We just got lucky with a trusted source of information who gave us the heads up on what he was about to do, and we need this to be totally under the radar. Sadly, ministers get involved with all sorts of governing and prying fingers in intelligence ops these days. I simply can't afford to have anyone else know. Keep me informed about what you discover.'

Dominic stood to leave. 'And watch your back a little. We don't know who else is watching and moving in this nasty cloud. Somebody got to him and I'm pretty pissed off at that.'

Sean stood up and politely bade him farewell. He decided to keep his own counsel on this case. He trusted no one. Something was not right. Not right at all. But on the other hand, he knew Dominic could easily have him arrested and banged up again on some false pretence of absconding from international justice. At least this offered a way out, even if he didn't quite know how. He also knew the chances of dark forces operating would mean he had to make sure he left no trails and adequately countered any surveillance on him. Time to stiffen the sinews he thought.

'So, Jack. What do you think? Was it MI5, MI6, the Yanks or the Russians who lifted Alfie? Who is linked to all this? Who could have got the tip-off and how?'

Jack had now rolled his shirt sleeves halfway up his forearms, slackened his tie and was slouched in his chair.

'We simply don't know,' Jack said. 'Not 5, I can guarantee that, and the exact link on who would be implicated in the exposés, other than Her Majesty's Government, isn't fully known.'

Sean warmed to Jack and his calm, agreeable character. He had managed to find out that Jack had two daughters, was a keen family man and lived in Marlow. His youngest daughter was three and severely ill with MS.

'We do know Alfie had researched old intelligence operations,' Jack continued. 'You know, things like the Iraq dossier, the death of Professor Wilshaw, Moscow spy cock-ups and bits and bobs on the mole hunters in MI6. We know there's a list of Russian moles in there too. One piece of high-grade intelligence on these suspected moles could implicate former and current ministers. Government could tumble too. A few things are certain. First, he was meticulous in his planning and would have had a contingency plan if he was got at. He knew that could happen. Secondly, he knew high-profile people would have been destroyed both in Moscow and on our side.'

Jack was in full flow now. Sean kept quiet and listened.

'We only had a single source who gave us the clue he was about to release these secrets. He's a very credible source but didn't know the full extent of what Alfie held. We need to find the files Alfie was going to release, and we need to get them first before anyone else does. Alfie was careful about what he exposed to tease the journalists into siding with him.'

Jack sipped more wine as Sean continued his probing. 'He had a good escape plan too? New personality, new life?'

Jack nodded. 'What's worrying for us is we don't know what he's put in place as a contingency to release this information in the event of him going missing. We need you to trace him Sean. And do a deep-delve into everything he came into contact with. I've done some work on this. I managed to get his friend to a safe house very quickly. Her name is Melissa. And I've got his flat sealed off too. It's been searched by the police as part of a simple missing person case, nothing more. They didn't find anything. We were about to lift him when he disappeared.'

'OK. I'll have a look at it,' Sean said. 'Can you get into some intelligence systems for me? Line up some funding to bring some people in, and sort me out a new identity? I'm going to need to meet his friend too. She could hold the key to this.'

'No problems with any of that,' Jack said. 'I've already squared away a new passport for you, some credit cards, club memberships and loyalty cards. Melissa is in our safe house in Suffolk being looked after by Jane, one of our best operators.'

'I need a couple of secure phones and a secure encrypted laptop too Jack.'

'Done. Who will you be calling in?'

'I'll probably bring the old team of experts together if we find out he's been killed. Chances of him being alive are slim as there is no value in extortion for him. He may have left some clues as to where he has hidden his files, but I'll probably need a number of your intelligence capabilities to investigate this properly.'

'That's all easily arranged through my team. You may want to reconnect with Samantha Braund in GCHQ as well Sean. Or TABASCO, as you fondly refer to her.'

'How do you know about her?' Sean asked quizzically.

'Come on Sean. You know the score. I've done my homework on you for every aspect of your life, as you'd expect me to.'

Sean grinned. 'Yes, I know. But Samantha? Blimey. I kept that very quiet for years.' He took a swig of his wine and shrugged his shoulders a little. He visualised his last meeting with Samantha and the times they had shared on an undercover job in Ireland where she first gave herself the codename TABASCO. They had been in touch on and off over the years since they had first met at that crowded meeting for Operation Cloud-Hawk in London way back in 2001. But Sean found her too heavy and forthright for anything more than the occasional dalliance. Might be good to see her again though, he thought whimsically.

He nudged his mind back to the mission in hand, juggling with his thoughts, before teeing up his most immediate needs. 'I'll need to bring the old team back together for this. Starting with Mike and Billy Phish, who are in Barbados these days. They'll both be vital if we're to have any chance of successfully getting this over the line. Can you fly them over? I'll also need John 'Jugsy' Stokes ready to move too – if only to have a beer with the old scrote.'

They both laughed. Each of them was familiar with the legend of Jugsy in the intelligence world. They got through two bottles of Saint-Émilion's finest Bordeaux that evening as they planned the next stages of the operation and the team Sean would need.

Chapter 13

Baker Street, London

Sean arrived at the Baker Street complex alone. He pressed the bell next to the intercom. Alfie was now an official 'Missing Person' case with the Metropolitan Police and access to his flat was strictly controlled following a forensic search. Jack had arranged access to the flat, which was on a mezzanine floor in a set of Mansions close to the Tube station in Marylebone.

The porter opened the door to Bedford Mansions and greeted Sean with a very polite nod, a smile and the words 'Welcome sir'.

'I'm here to see Ron,' Sean explained. 'I'm the agent for number twenty-four.'

He was politely asked to enter and invited to sign the visitors book. Ron was sitting in his small office situated just to the left of the large reception area, which was decorated with large black and white pictures of the enormous mansions located near to the Tube station, all of them from the '30s. It was useful to have an ex-army manager he thought – someone with whom he could build a rapport to see who had been visiting or entering Alfie's small dwelling.

He agreed with Ron that he needed a couple of hours inside the flat to make an inventory and take photos for the owner.

'Did he have many visitors over the months?' Sean asked.

'Hardly any that I was ever aware of,' Ron replied, taking his glasses off. 'We can have a look at the visitor book and I'm happy to help in whatever way you need whilst you're here. Did you know him?'

'Not very well,' Sean said. 'Just the odd occasion when he popped into the office. I noticed your military pictures in your office by the way, and the marching music. Who did you serve with?'

'Twenty-two years in the Royal Green Jackets, man and boy,' Ron said. 'Retired a few years ago and landed this job as the facilities manager. Love it.'

Ron escorted Sean upstairs, explaining his career history as they went. 'Best thing I ever did, retiring,' he said. 'This company looks after me well and I get a tidy little flat plus they give me time off for my regimental association work too.'

'Sounds like a really good deal,' Sean said. 'Nice to see you landed on your feet and they value your service.'

'Love it when a plan comes together,' Ron said with a beaming smile as they arrived at number twenty-four. 'Feel free to do whatever you need, and pop in if you need me for anything.' Sean shook Ron's hand, turned the key to enter the flat and made a mental note to check the CCTV later.

He wondered if there were any hidden cameras as he stretched his neck looking around the apartment. He couldn't be sure of anything being safe now. Especially after Alfie had been so easily lifted and nabbed by the opposition before Jack could get to him. From this point onwards, he knew he could be followed and wondered exactly who the opposition were.

'Shit,' he muttered, scanning the small flat. 'Too many places to hide things, old-style decor and wooden floorboards everywhere.' He suspected Alfie would have been ingenious if he had hidden anything in the flat relating to his escape plan – and he also knew that the police search teams could easily have missed anything Alfie had cleverly concealed.

He tried to put his mind into Alfie's. He sat on the leather seat in the small lounge that overlooked Baker Street and thought. How would Alfie have done it? Where would he hide something important? He sat there for a good fifteen minutes, the sounds of traffic on Baker Street occasionally interrupting his thoughts, and then set about his task. If it was him doing this, what would he do to leave a clue in the event of being kidnapped? What kind of trail would he leave? Where would he hide such a clue?

He felt sure Alfie would want to leave a clue, a trail, a jigsaw puzzle to lead to the files as a contingency if he was lifted or killed. A kind of failsafe plan. He figured that Alfie would want to have done just that, to show he was committed in what he was doing. He believed in exposing the truth and would leave his own unique, indelible mark on the world once he was gone. His own legacy, but how? What did Sean need to look for? He knew any IT devices would have been forensically searched by the police and wondered if *box* or MI6 were at all involved at this stage and, if so, what did they know? Did they know anything at all of Alfie's plan to whistle-blow? Was Dominic right that only he and Jack knew? And the other agencies didn't? He cast his mind into the track and trace world of an old master spook of the past. What would Wynthrop have done he thought?

He began in the bathroom and looked carefully for any subtle changes to pipework, decor or panels that would, to a very observant eye, show the absence of the normal or the presence of the abnormal. It was his eyes that did the searching, nothing else. He knew Alfie wouldn't have concealed items in obvious places as the police would have found them. Sean knew it would be a devious, cleverly thought through concealment. Next, he moved to the hall and looked for small cavities, openings and recesses that might conceal small credit cards or notes. He looked at the balustrades for any sign of tampering, and he looked at the fixtures and fittings for any signs of small voids, chip marks or paint missing from screws. He noticed some paint scratches on a low-level plug fitting, but the sealant looked OK and was undisturbed. He knew Alfie wouldn't have concealed anything in items that could be removed, such as TVs, radios or bedside lamps.

It took him over fifty minutes to search using only his eyes. And then he sat down for a rethink. He closed his eyes and tried to put himself inside Alfie's mind again. He wouldn't have used the floorboards, clothes or removable items and he discounted difficult to get at areas such as the ceiling.

'I know you've done it Alfie, but where, you devious bastard?' he mouthed out load.

It wasn't until he looked inside the tiny broom cupboard in the hall, just as he was about to leave, that something appeared odd. He noticed a light fitting but couldn't see the light switch. That was, until he peered round the inside of the door frame, with some discomfort, and saw that there was indeed an ancient, dysfunctional switch. He hadn't seen that before when he had first looked inside with a small torch. He flicked the switch. Nothing. He then manoeuvred himself by bending his back and reversing into the cupboard to look more directly into the darkness at the switch cover. No good. He couldn't see a thing. He tutted. Then he squeezed out of the space to stretch into a more upright position.

'That's bloody hard to get at,' he said. He went to the kitchen to grab a larger torch from a toolbox he had looked at earlier and then squeezed himself back into position. His heart began racing at the prospect of finding a possible clue. He shone the torch, noticing that the switch cover was not firmly fitted to the wall, and that the seal on the paint around it had been broken. He could immediately tell that the cover had been removed after painting had taken place and that a gap had been left in the seal. He used the tiniest of Phillips screwdrivers to remove two screws with some ease. It was the smallest of voids, but enough for a plastic-wrapped package. Sweat dripped from his brow and he started breathing faster, knowing he had found something important.

He extracted the wraps in the light from the corridor. Inside were two credit cards, a passport and a number of pieces of paper with codes on them. Some seemed like bank PIN numbers: others he didn't recognise at all. On another piece of paper were numerous email addresses. And on another, writing that seemed to be the username and codes for a web portal. He looked at this one more closely. There were only three pieces of extremely small, but very immaculate, handwriting:

Erg58@gmail.com – DF452Hdc – PB

'Bingo,' Sean said out loud. 'Nailed it.' He popped the packages into his right jacket pocket, turned the door handle to exit the flat and left.

He left Baker Street, heading south towards Oxford Circus. The sun blinded him as he strode purposefully, but at a slow pace. A distant siren, merged with the heavy traffic, accompanied the persistent noises in his mind. His heartbeat rose. His thoughts became intense as he reminded himself of the trauma that people had inflicted on him.

He had one more thing to tend to before he left London. And it involved a kill.

He turned right onto Crawford Street, then back on himself, and made numerous turns down the quiet Marylebone back streets. He headed back towards Edgware Road and made a deliberate U-turn, browsing occasionally at some of the antiques in shop windows. Finally, he turned left onto Enford Street and walked quietly into the Thornbury Castle pub.

He made his way to the bar and ordered a pint of Rebellion beer. He paused, turned his back to the bar and cast his eye around the few local punters before making his way to the far corner of the pub, which provided an excellent view of the entrance.

Exactly twelve minutes later, 'One-Eyed' Damon walked through the entrance. A beast of a man, just shy of six foot seven inches of sheer bulk, he made his way to the bar with a white stick. No words were exchanged as the bearded barman slipped a pint of pale ale across the bar and indicated with a glance that Sean was sat on the higher deck in the corner.

One-Eyed Damon was a Northern Ireland and Iraq war veteran. A surveillance and weapons expert who, even with only one eye left, was still at the top of his game and who had contacts in the city who could do anything that was needed. Pick a lock, Damon was the man. Provide a weapon or plant some bugs, Damon was the man. He shuffled up the small steps and crouched over his pint next to Sean.

'Long time mate,' Sean said.

'You're looking old and angry,' One-Eyed Damon replied, smirking widely as his false eye glistened and twinkled in the low light. He was wearing a union flag lens.

'Fuck off mate, you know I'm never angry. Just badly mad,' Sean retorted. 'And you can wipe that smile off your face, at least until you've paid me back for keeping your arse out of jail all those years ago.' Sean had provided a glowing reference at Damon's court martial in Colchester after Damon had 'accidentally' beaten up an RAF officer for touching up a woman in a Southend bar.

One-Eyed Damon broke into laughter. 'Great days those mate – he deserved it and you did indeed save my arse. But I hear it's you who's been in jail getting your arse pounded this time.'

'Very fucking funny,' Sean said. 'Anyway, what's the SP?'

'No one is on your tail,' Damon said, lifting his head from his beer and looking cautiously around the bar. 'I followed you from that swanky hotel, all the way to Baker Street and then on your very obvious counter-surveillance route around Marylebone. You really need to sharpen up on your skills you know mate.'

'My mojo is coming back – don't you worry about that.'

'What's next then Sean?'

'A kill,' Sean said. 'A slow one, but a purposeful one that I need you to look at. I'm going to be busy for a while with a job. Are you happy to do some stuff for me?'

'Yep. Normal fees please though.'

'Not a problem.' Sean pulled out a small business card. 'I need you to find this man. Find out everything about him, where he's living, his pattern of life, who he's shagging, what he loves, the lot.' One-Eyed Damon turned the card over. The name on the card was Frazer, with a telephone number and a company address.

'I assume this is the guy that got you shafted then?'

'You could say that. Be careful though. He's running Albanian gangs in the city as well as major drug-running operations across the continent. He takes pleasure in hurting his friends too.'

'Fine. A real bastard then who needs sorting out. I'll find out everything about his movements and people. I look forward to hearing your plan on the kill.'

Sean stayed silent, smiled and stood up ready to leave.

'Go via Samantha,' he said. 'She's the conduit for this job. And feel free to leave a marker for him – just so he knows.'

Chapter 14

Enfield, London

S ean walked briskly to Baker Street tube station heading straight for the Jubilee Line, making a mental note of the faces he saw in the street and those around him.

He began a series of counter-surveillance moves on the escalators and concourses of London's underground until he was sure no one could have tailed him. He emerged in Enfield north London and made his way to an internet café on the high street.

Sean had firmly set his plans out in his mind. He had found the secret codes that might lead to the whistle-blowing files that held the list of spy moles Dominic so eagerly wanted, or at least one of the clues to the case he thought. He was due to leave from Liverpool Street on the 1910 to Ipswich that evening to meet Melissa at the safe house that Jack had arranged on the Suffolk Coast. He wanted to check the web account first, but was wary of anyone following him to an internet café and then interrogating his online activity after he had left. He had to continue to make sure he was not being followed.

He found a snug corner in the internet café and logged on to the internet. What he found in the account Alfie had opened was incredibly curious. PB stood for Photobucket: a cloud-based photo and imagery portal. He opened the cloud account, punched in the passwords, and looked inside. Alfie had produced his own obituary and uploaded it as a jpg photo file. 'Steganography to conceal secrets?' Sean wondered. He also found a series of documents with passwords related to the credit card bank accounts, other email addresses, and passwords to get into his iPad, iPhone - and two laptops he held.

The obituary was curious, the remainder being standard email accounts with yahoo, google and BT. Sean then spotted a series of photos, but one stood out – it was of a cottage. He spent some time analysing this photo of a low roofed single-story cottage with large hedges surrounding it. Nothing large, in fact, just a small cottage with two windows, a back garden gate, a chimney, a pastel painted blue front door, and some potted plants outside. Sean knew this was key to his next moves and pondered if this was where Alfie would have used as a *bolthole* before exposing his secrets and starting his new life somewhere else in the world.

Sean magnified the image of the cottage in stages then finally at eight hundred percent saw a series of text too small to view at lesser scales. In the bottom right hand corner were the numbers 66190. He didn't quite know what to make of it. It certainly didn't represent a postal address. Could it be a UTM Grid reference he wondered? Or a postcode of some sort? Sean got to work trying to decipher where this cottage was. It wasn't as easy as he thought it would be until he began to think that Alfie would need to get away from the UK and have an escape plan overseas. Eventually, after wrestling with his foolishness for not thinking of it earlier, he cross referenced all European postcodes with that number. His search revealed a small fishing village in south-east France – Collioure.

Sean checked in with Jack to see if Mike and Billy Phish were on their way from Barbados. They were. He then made his way to a café, sat down in a quiet corner, and ruminated for a while fiddling with his lighter. Finally, he worked up the courage to call Samantha.

'I knew you'd call sometime,' She said cheerily. 'You just can't help yourself can you Sean.'

'Of course I can't, but I need your help on a job this time Sam.'

'Oh, do you now? You must have missed me lots. Where the hell have you been?'

'Away, overseas.'

'Hope you stayed away from any tarts,' she joshed, flirting as ever with him.

'Oh, I did, believe me. Not a sniff where I was living.'

'Good. I'm your lady as you well know. When are you coming to see me? We have lots to catch up on you know.'

Samantha was always insistent that Sean would become her man on a full-time basis – one day. Whenever he was ready. She had the charisma and intelligence to nurture her quarry with a style that any other man would have succumbed to by now.

'Won't be for a while I'm afraid. I'm caught up in something big.'

'You bastard. Not happy with that.'

'Do you know a bloke called Jack H from MI5?'

'Yes. He mentioned you'd call – said you were a tit.' Sean laughed.

'Good. We both need your help on this case Samantha.'

'I'm all yours as you well know, for whenever you get your ass in gear for my needs.' Sean smiled, then coaxed her into the more pertinent necessities he had. Asking her to be a little more patient.

'I'll send you some details of some target phones I need to be tracked and traced. I need some geo-location data Sam. As stuff emerges, I'll send it over to you.'

'Right you are. I'm here to help – send it over and give me call whenever you want me to come into the field. It will certainly be worth your while.'

Sean was only too aware that Samantha always enjoyed being on the ground as an operator rather than being cooped up doing analytical work as a signals intelligence liaison officer in MI6.

'Great. Oh, and by the way. One-Eyed Damon will be in touch at some point too. Just relay his thoughts. Catch up soon Sam. Take care.'

Sean signed off with a wry smile, happy he had called her. A close friend for many years since he first met her back in 2001, he had borne her persistence for a long time - wishing it wasn't always so.

Sean changed his mind and decided to play safe by hiring a car in his new name and drive to Suffolk under his own steam and timings. He would trust only himself from this point onwards. He collected his hire car in Enfield and made his way to Suffolk.

As he drove, he considered the options to track where Alfie may have gone from his seaside cottage in Languedoc-Roussillon. He also thought about the logistics of getting a small team there to operate undercover on French territory. But for now, he needed to find out how much Melissa had been involved in Alfie's plan.

He wondered why Melissa was still alive when Alfie had been taken. Especially when whoever had taken him would be keen to make sure no residual threat of information lay, even subconsciously, with Melissa. She was damned lucky that Jack had gotten to her first, whisked her to the safe house, and got her off the radar.

Chapter 15

Safe House, Suffolk

S outhwold was draped in a dense drizzly fog as Sean drove into the town, struggling to read its street signs through the dirty haze. Sean liked Southwold: a quiet Victorian town with a large white lighthouse on a hill that dominated the town, and some of the most picturesque beach views in England. A quirky seaside town with the air of old Britain, an ageing population and a range of boutique shops whose quaintness drew many American tourists.

Sean spotted the street where the safe house was located. It was halfway down a narrow lane with a slight incline and tucked in around a small bend. He made sure to park well away from the house and started his instinctive walk around the area, checking for escape routes and the security of the building if they were compromised. He looked for any telltale signs of people observing the street and the best avenues of approach to the cottage, including the back garden. He made a mental note of what he perceived would be good escape options, then walked up to the front door. Melissa was being protected by an ex-intelligence officer called Jane. It was just after 10pm.

Jane greeted him and took him through a small narrow hallway, down some steps and into a long narrow kitchen. Melissa, dressed in a blue dressing gown, sat at the far end of the small kitchen table with her iPad propped up in front of her next to a jug of sunflowers.

'Melissa? Hi, I'm Sean.' He smiled, indicating with a hand that Melissa need not rise. Melissa stood up anyway, shook his hand and moved to the other end of the table. Sean watched her pull out a chair and turn off her iPad.

'I hope you've brought me some good news,' she said. 'Take a seat.'

Jane put the kettle on and Sean sat down.

'Not great news I'm afraid and I expect this has been quite traumatic for you for the last few days. I assume Jane has briefed you?'

'Jane has been terrific,' Melissa said, leaning forward. 'And I feel very safe. But no one has told me what the hell is happening other than apparently, I'm in some danger now that Alfie's gone missing. I'd like to get back home soon and can't stay here forever. What exactly is going on?'

Sean saw Melissa's eyes waver. She looked fearful despite Jane's protection. 'Well, I'll be frank with you. You won't be going home anytime soon. There are people out there who are probably trying to find you and I think you know that already. They're not friendly people and they will do anything they can to get information out of you to get to Alfie's files. They will probably kill you. After they've interrogated you first.' Sean paused as Melissa crossed her arms and pushed her chair back, as if to find a safe space. 'I'm sorry to say there's also a high chance Alfie has been killed by now.'

Melissa's eyes welled up and Sean watched as she tried to hold it together, the seriousness of the situation suddenly dawning on her. Jane placed a teapot and cups on the table, smiled at them both and retreated to the lounge.

'My job is to find him and then figure out what we do from there,' Sean continued. 'I need to talk with you to see if there are any clues that might help me to find him. I'm very sorry how this has come about but that's how it is right now. I need to be quite straight with you.'

Melissa looked run-down and exasperated by it all.

'Thanks. I know he planned everything to perfection, so I don't understand how this has happened. He only revealed to me what he absolutely needed to during our discussions and was clinical about not giving me too much. Just enough to give me credence with my editorial contact. I'm bloody pissed off it's come to this.' Sean nodded, sensing her anger.

'What about you Melissa? How did you get involved in all of this?'

'We'd been working on this for months. Alfie was an old boyfriend who stayed in touch a lot as our careers and lives sent us different ways. I think he was stuck and came to me looking for help and advice on how to get all these secrets out. He's unearthed a lot of bad stuff you know.'

'Do you know how he got hold of all these files at all?'

'Not fully, no. Although I knew he was hacking into people's computers I never let on. Nor did I ever ask where he got the stuff. I knew it was probably the only way he could get this information. He was furious about some of the things he found, and he shared many of the corruption stories with me, knowing full well I'd be furious too.'

'OK. But how were you going to do this. Through your contact? The editor?'

'Yes, that's right. Although he was dismissive at first, thinking I was after a quick buck or bonus. He didn't really get that this was one of the biggest whistle-blowers ever, and a huge investigative scoop for the Bureau.'

'What changed that then? What did you feed him?'

Melissa looked Sean in the eye for the first time. 'The veracity of the files eventually shocked him. He woke up to it all. Up until then, he had treated me like some dumb bird, thinking I was not serious, and was being a real chauvinist. Listen, I love my job, my friends and I have a comfortable life, but I'm not just some bimbo without brains. And I certainly don't like people taking the piss like he did. I agreed to help Alfie and that's what I'll do – even if he is dead. After all we went through, it's the least I can do.'

Sean watched her stand and walk to the kitchen bench, becoming more animated about the story. She turned, arms folded.

'Alfie gave me a particular file on the Gulf War that could be verified by a certain contact we had in the Bureau's global network and that's when the editor finally took me seriously. In fact, the more files I showed him the more active interest he took, pretty much ordering me never to talk to anyone at all about it, except him. He told me how this had to be manoeuvred through the right people and drip-fed into the public domain once Alfie had escaped and was safe.'

Sean sat back and listened, keen not to interject. She was talking and that's what he wanted. Melissa sat down again, leaning over the table.

'This was a great opportunity for me. A chance to take a serious investigation right the way through to the end. From cradling the contact, nurturing him, setting it up and profiling it in the right order, right through to publishing it across the global investigative network.' She sat back, collecting her thoughts, and then waved her hand in the air. 'In fact, that opportunity still exists, and I'll bloody well make sure Alfie gets his day.'

'I think we'll need to take one step at a time first,' Sean said. 'Your life is in danger, don't forget, and there are a heap of complexities now that we can't just go off-piste with.'

'I really don't give a shit. The more I think about this, the more I realise what Alfie was doing was right and people need to see the corruption that exists in our world.'

Sean listened intently. He was intrigued to see her strong emotions and to hear her gutsy, if somewhat misguided, view that she could carry all this off on behalf of Alfie. It was telling to see her true persona leaking out. But he was guarded about how much of this was the truth, and what she was holding back.

'How much did he confide in you? Did he tell you what he wanted done if he went missing?'

Melissa calmed herself, pushed her fingers through her hair and took a few sips of tea. She paused. 'Never. He was very precise about what he told me or shared with me, and he was always saying he didn't want me implicated if it all went wrong. He only ever gave me small bits of information or fragmented versions of the full stories. Enough for my editor to check on, but with plenty left out to tease the bastard into wanting more. The editor's eyes were agog when I watched him reading some of the more damning evidence Alfie had provided. He supposedly had a list of Russian moles too, he was always anxious that someone might be onto him and he gave me a hell of a telling off if I made a mistake. To which I reminded him who was the spy and who wasn't.'

'Did you see this list?'

'No.'

'And did Alfie ever explain the dangers to you? And the measures to be taken to protect yourself? I expect you never ever thought it would come to this?'

'Really? That's a stupid question,' Melissa said angrily. 'No, I didn't think it would come to this. But don't treat me like an imbecile. I've lived in the Middle East reporting on terrorism for fuck's sake.'

Sean let her vent.

'Of course we discussed the risks. He explained all that operational security stuff a dozen times. It was quite obvious what he was uncovering would be catastrophic if he was found out, but I never ever thought about him being killed. Nor me being a target for that matter. It only bloody well dawns on you when the shit hits the fan.'

Melissa stood up and made her way across the room before pouring a glass of water. Sean felt her angst. 'I feel exhausted by all this so if you don't mind, I think I'll turn in.'

Sean nodded, noticing the tears in her eyes. He suspected she might be holding back on the full story and, in truth, he thought Alfie's lack of security measures was lazy, but now wasn't the time for candour. He watched Melissa grab her iPad and walk upstairs, weeping as she went.

Sean wondered how Jack had got to Melissa so quickly and what had triggered the alert to get to her. What was he missing here? He discussed this with Jane for a while as well as asking her about the operational security she had put in place. Jane was a redhead in her early thirties with a sharp-witted mind, and totally capable of protecting her charge. Quiet when the necessity arose, she was an accomplished kickboxing instructor and a committed rower. Sean liked her style and professionalism and she was a good fit for Melissa due to her age and similar personality.

'So, what have you set up here Jane? Are we looking good?'

'Not bad,' she said. 'Come and have a look at the monitoring screens.'

Sean followed her into the lounge, noticing an array of laptops and seventeen-inch monitors. She'd set up a full command and control set-up for intruder detection and alerts. 'Cameras and movement detectors?' he asked.

'Exactly. I've got covert cameras covering all the approaches to the house and each of them has got passive infrared motion detection too. They'll alarm on the screens and on my mobile phone. I've also set up a few active infrared beams along the fence and the doors will withstand brute-force attacks for a few vital minutes.'

'Good. What's the plan if you're compromised?'

'Well, this will obviously come in handy for a start if I need it,' Jane said, showing her nine-millimetre Beretta pistol. 'But we also have a grade-three cellar designed to withstand a direct attack, plus all the normal panic alarms back to the control room.'

'Response time?'

'Assured at less than fifteen minutes for armed response. And enough steel to survive an onslaught.'

'Great,' Sean said, impressed with Jane's meticulous approach. 'Sounds like we have a good plan then. We need to stay sharp on this one. I have no idea what we're up against.'

Sean didn't sleep much that night. He thought about the entire case and how he could conclude it. He knew he didn't want to press Melissa too early, but she was the only human lead he had which required him to develop a rapport with her to gain her full trust. He could see she was sharp, intelligent, had a good deal of guts, was very articulate but quite animated when angry.

He got a few hours blackout interspersed with his normal traumatic dreams and awoke wondering where the hell he was. He could have fought his way back to sleep at 5am but, instead, chose to clear his head with a morning run.

The early morning sea air was invigorating as he jogged down the hill past the huge white lighthouse that overlooked the idyllic sands of Southwold. Only the circling gulls gave him company as he watched the sea mist rise to provide a glimpse of the long Victorian pier in the distance. He had lots of thinking to do and running was the best way for him to find time when he was alone and refreshed to do so.

He glided down the hill and did a U- turn at the end of the road, increasing his speed vigorously before hitting the sandy beach to continue past the pastel-coloured beach huts. Once he was on the beach, he pushed himself hard to get his heart rate up and started some speed training along the sands. In between he rested and breathed deeply as he looked out to the sea, which was like a millpond. The tide lapped at his feet.

It was a glorious place to recuperate after the hellhole of the Kabul prison, and he reflected on his thoughts about what might come next after this bizarre episode in his life. The only way out for Melissa was for him to find Alfie. He had carefully quizzed her the night before, probing deep into her psyche and listening to her closely.

He had studied her eye movement and body language. She didn't seem to be lying, or indeed to harbour any traits of deception. He felt she was secure, didn't like being mucked about and was very ambitious. She seemed responsible and loyal, but he had to probe further to see what else she might be hiding. Purposefully, or not. He considered hypnotism, as well as deep interrogation techniques that might reveal any hidden clues she didn't know were hidden in her memory.

Jogging slowly, Sean wondered what the hell had happened to Alfie and tried again to put himself in his mind, thinking through what kind of plan he would have hatched if he had suddenly been taken. How would he have ensured his secrets were still exposed? How would he have used Melissa for his plans? What type of trail would he have left?

A lot went on in his head during the morning run. He wanted to ensure his own trail was covered and reminded himself to ask Jane what she had done to make sure Melissa had left no electronic footprint by communicating from the safe house on social media or the internet. He also decided he needed to get more information from Melissa and had a plan to explore deep inside her memory. He needed to sharpen up on the techniques he had been taught a couple of years ago on agent interrogation using neuro-linguistic programming.

The run back up the hill and through the narrow streets was a killer, and the chilled air hurt his lungs. Sean pushed himself hard, as he always did at the end of his run. He arrived back at the gate to the cottage totally exhausted.

Jane was up and on the computer in the lounge when he walked back in at 7am. It was a couple of hours later before Melissa surfaced, by which time Sean had conjured up his plan for the day and how he would tackle the French part of the job. He decided that he would take Melissa and Jane to France the following day and begin the investigation to determine what the hell had happened to Alfie. He wanted it that way.

Melissa sat in the kitchen at her iPad having made herself some tea and toast. She had had a restless night ruminating. She was incensed at having had her life tipped upside down and that Alfie was likely to have been killed, with no worthwhile ending for him. She hoped deep down he was still alive. An element of determination gripped her when she looked on Twitter and other internet sites and saw no mention whatsoever of Alfie's disappearance, knowing immediately how government machinery was making sure nothing existed of this sad episode. It compelled her to act.

How did she know she was safe, she began thinking? Who is this Sean bloke anyway? Who can help me now, she wondered? She checked her Twitter account for activity before deciding to craft a message to her most trusted contact in the police. She had first met the policewoman as a paid source of information when she had investigated how a lorry load of files had gone missing from Scotland Yard – all linked to paedophile rings in London going back to the '80s. Melissa had been adept at gaining her trust and nurturing her source to reveal the extent of the cover-up from within. She sat and smiled before checking that Sean and Jane were still in the living room.

Melissa then wrote a short message to her contact. She was keen to see what help she could provide to help expose the Alfie case and wanted to ask her advice.

Sean spent the rest of the morning contacting a number of his old team, asking them to be ready to move to support his urgent task. While he felt the task would not need too many people at this stage, he needed to line them all up just in case. He was aware that the Met Police would also be searching for Alfie, but judged they probably had very few leads, and he wondered if anyone else had beat him to any other crucial clues beyond the cottage near Collioure in south-east France.

Melissa returned to the kitchen wearing a turquoise dress cut just above the knee. Sean couldn't help noticing for the first time how attractive she was and that she had put make-up on. He was immediately drawn to her tanned legs as she glided across the kitchen to sit down in the same place she had sat the evening before. Her long dark hair was flowing, and Sean felt her allure.

They sat and chatted. She explained who the editor was and how they had a plan for releasing Alfie's files. Only he knew the full detail, according to Melissa, but Sean doubted that to be the reality. She was too trusting of the editor and had little concept of the politics involved when a paper deemed it fair game to release such files. He would have had to have consulted with lawyers, chairmen and key owners to make sure they had a watertight plan, just as they did when Snowden came to their lair. This was one avenue for a leak that could have led to Alfie's kidnap.

Sean then questioned Melissa about how she knew Alfie had gone missing. 'He texted me the day before we planned to meet in Paris. I got the train from London and waited at the Hilton hotel. I had booked a room and waited there all day. He didn't arrive, and I immediately knew something was wrong. That's when I let my editor know. The next thing I knew, Jane arrived at the hotel and took me straight here. I knew something had happened to Alfie straight away and he hasn't texted me since.'

Sean surmised that Alfie would have been careful with his texting activity, and that he would have ensured at that late stage of his operation that he had driven far away from his bolthole in Collioure to text Melissa and not give away his safe location. Alfie would have known the capability of state agencies to triangulate his position from any texts that may have been hacked from Melissa's phone. Sean was also sure that people had monitored Melissa's movements and her phone activity. It looked to him like state agencies were involved, but which ones?

'Did he ever text or email you explaining which route he was taking to meet you in Paris?'

'No. He never told me where he was, and I never asked. He knew that I wouldn't ask so he never told me how he was getting to any of our meeting places. He simply gave me a time, date and venue.'

'And did you ever know what date he was going to start leaking all these secrets and what his escape plan was?'

'Listen, Sean. That part of the plan was all his and his alone. He told me that I'd know the point at which I would never see him again, probably at the point the first of my articles would be released. But again, the editor didn't tell me when he would break the story. I wrote the leaders and Alfie told me he would be in touch to drip-feed the next stories through the editor and I'd be asked to create the stories with another journalist. That was the deal.'

Sean knew that it had probably been state actors using electronic surveillance on Melissa that had eventually led them to tracking Alfie's movements, and that they had clearly picked their time to close in on him and take him out of the game. Was it the Russians after the list of moles? He sensed Melissa was getting agitated and decided to change tack.

'I told you that you wouldn't get your life back for a while and the problem is I don't know how long that while will be. You're certainly in danger and we need to move quickly, so we'll be moving out of here tomorrow to a place where we can begin to piece Alfie's last movements together.'

'Good. Because if you're going to search for Alfie, I'm damned well coming with you, whether you like it or not,' she snapped.

Sean watched her scrunch her face. 'The time will come when we will get you back home Melissa, and I'll determine that time. These are brutal people and we don't quite know who else may be involved in trying to find him.'

'But you still haven't told me who the hell you are. I'm not just going to disappear, and don't forget I've got some bloody good contacts in my world who might be able to help me.'

'You mean us?'

'I do, but only if you agree it's us, and not just you. I'm going be part of this whether you like it or not Sean.'

Melissa had an edge to her and was letting Sean know it. 'So, are you any good at this stuff?' she said. 'I don't know if I should trust you or get the hell out of here. Have you ever killed to protect, or made crap situations like this go away?'

Sean knew Melissa was agitating. He remained quiet, turned slightly and briefly thought of the adversaries he had blown away at point-blank range in cold blood.

'Yes, I've made things like this get better and, sure enough, you've been plunged deep into something people like me exist to make right. It's not a good business at all.'

He left the temptation to push back at Melissa's stubbornness any further – yet.

Chapter 16

Collioure, France

Sean arrived at the cottage in a rusted Peugeot van and parked next to a small blue gate giving access to the garden. He stepped out of the van and caught a gust of the stiff ocean breeze that forced him to grab his cap quickly. Sean was dressed in paint-spattered white overalls and was anxious to get on with the job in hand: breaking into Alfie's bolthole.

The rear of the van was full of painting and decorating gear which he began to ferry through the gate and onto the expansive garden, with the ladders leading the way. It was suitably enclosed with high cypress hedges, allowing him perfect cover from view against any prying neighbours in the small French commune.

The views across the lawn towards the small fishing village of Collioure were stunning. He gazed for a moment down the hill at the architecture of the quaint seaside town, which was located just north of the Spanish border on the Vermeille coast. It was a picturesque area that attracted the artistic community, with the castle and church creating an impressive backdrop and the beach and harbour being amongst the most scenic in southern France.

Sean liked the place. He could see why this was the perfect retreat for Alfie. It was invigorating, quiet and very discreet, with no prying neighbours. The garden was strewn with the remnants of Alfie's outdoor life. Two seagoing canoes could be seen in the far corner, next to a pink rhododendron bush, and he spotted two mountain bikes under the veranda. The centre of the garden had a sundial and a couple of deckchairs, with a bin and a table between them. Strange, he thought. Two bikes, two deckchairs. Why hadn't these been locked away in the large shed? It looked exactly as if someone was at home having just returned from a bike ride or a foray to the sea. Sean knew that wasn't the case and was eager to get on with searching the house.

He began to break into the cottage. Using a couple of screwdrivers, he began to shake the locking arm on a high-level kitchen window, which took him less than five minutes to crack. They were old frames allowing easy access. He climbed onto the short window ledge, stood on his toes, and reached through the window with his left arm. He then juggled the latch to open the larger window below. Crouching now, he steadied himself before jumping through the aperture to the tiled kitchen floor below.

The room smelt musty from damp. He studied a small noticeboard in the kitchen with a couple of blue notes on it, just shopping lists and a small map of the village. On another board were a few photos. Two of them showed Alfie with his canoe in the garden, and the third was an aerial photo of the cottage.

Sean walked around the cottage to familiarise himself with the building's layout. There were two smallish bedrooms that were built into the attic space of the small cottage and a tiny square living room below. The main living space seemed to be a quaint dining and breakfast room adjoining the kitchen and hall.

The cottage had a maritime feel to it: pictures and paintings of the local harbour and coastline adorned the whitewashed walls, and Sean imagined how Alfie had probably adored the solitude and peace of his small, neat little bolthole.

He could see how Alfie would have enjoyed planning his operation here, probably in between cycling, walking and sea canoeing to keep him fresh and invigorated. There were no signs of any struggle or break-in. No signs of anyone having disturbed furniture or ornaments while searching the place. Sean ran his finger over an oak dresser in the hall. No dust. The place was immaculately clean, and he smelt the faint whiff of chlorine. Had there been a clean-up operation?

He sat in the leather armchair in the corner of the dining room next to a bookshelf which was built into the wall, and a small round table by its side. He imagined what Alfie would have done here. No doubt he would have relaxed in his chair, mulled over his options and created his plan to succeed on his mission. Sean reasoned that Alfie would have planned to escape the country from here. He also felt that no one had beaten him to find this location, other than whoever had lifted, and possibly killed, Alfie. How and where had they done that, he wondered?

He sat awaiting the arrival of Mike and Billy Phish to conduct the next stages of the search. Sean had arranged to meet them at the cottage a few hours after he had made sure that Jane and Melissa were safely ensconced in the hotel at Port-Vendres, a few kilometres to the south of the village. It was the right decision to take Melissa and Jane to France and he had ensured Jack had made all the necessary arrangements for them all.

He had a thought. He stood up and started to look around for the electricity master switch and the water stopcock. He found it odd that the taps weren't working, and that there was no power to the cottage. He put his forensic gloves on, looked in the outhouse and switched the power and water on. He then looked for any sign of a washing basket in the small utility room bolted onto the kitchen. There were no clothes in the tumble dryer, but a full load of unwashed T-shirts and underwear was in the washing machine. He carefully put a white T-shirt and pair of socks from the washing basket into a large forensic plastic bag and then placed that into a second larger plastic bag, before sealing it. He placed that on the kitchen bench for later.

He spent the next two hours searching the cottage and found nothing that gave him any suspicions or suggestions as to where Alfie may have secreted his files or any other information he may have hidden. Sean reckoned that whoever had got to Alfie had done so without any need to break in and that he may even have simply opened the front door to his attackers. He needed some kind of forensic evidence to provide clues as to where Alfie had been taken or disposed of, and he still didn't know whether Alfie was alive or dead.

Sean heard a vehicle screech to a halt outside the cottage. He walked into the garden and stood at the gate to see Billy Phish getting out of a black pickup truck. He watched Billy Phish tug his jeans up, throw a cigarette to the floor, then stamp it out before looking up to Sean. 'Watcha,' he said. 'Fucking long way to come for a cup of tea mate. None of that French shit either, I'm parched and need a big bowl of English please.'

'Kettle's on old man,' Sean said, smirking. He watched Billy Phish give him the finger before opening the tailgate. Mike, his nine-year-old cocker spaniel, leapt out first – closely followed by a much younger spaniel called Foz. Sean watched both dogs go crazy with excitement. It had been many years since he had seen them all, Billy Phish included, and he had a soft spot for Mike in particular. In his spare time, Billy Phish was a forensic cyber-detective, hence his nickname 'Phish'. But his real talent was training dogs – forensic dogs.

'Great to see you Billy, you're all as mad as you ever were,' Sean said, patting him on the back as the dogs scuttled around frantically in circles before jumping up at Sean. He stroked the dogs, watching Billy Phish place a big bowl of water on the ground before the spaniels darted off to slurp away in contentment, relishing their new-found setting.

'Well, this is a right turn up for the books mate,' Billy Phish said, giving Sean a big handshake and a rare smile. 'I'm guessing it's going to be fun, whatever it is.'

'It'll be better than the rest, I can assure you of that.'

Billy Phish laughed, pulled a face and continued in his strong Yorkshire accent.

'Well, whatever happens it will beat the hell out of sitting on my arse in Langley trying to be a CIA cyber intellect,' he joked.

Billy Phish was a gregarious, full-blooded ex-soldier turned canine specialist, and now a part-time cyber trader and cyber-forensics sleuth. His gruff manner and 'say it as you see it' philosophy shrouded a more intellectual and broad-thinking mind.

Sean led the way to the garden chairs, explaining the story to Billy Phish. The dogs started to relax on the grass, basking in the early morning sun. 'I'm really interested to see what we find in the cottage with the dogs,' Sean said. 'I'll bring the rest of the team in if we get any forensic clues here. You brought the vapour-trail dogs too, right?'

'In the back of the pickup mate. I'm not getting them out too – they'll all go nuts together and it'll be a fight fest.'

'Great, I'll get the tea on. Cup and saucer squire?'

Billy Phish flicked a V-sign, rammed a breakfast-cereal bar into his mouth and then started patting little Foz, who had scuttled over to his side to get some attention. Mike remained chilled out, lying on the grass scratching his head with his paw and gnawing on a plastic bone.

Mike was the world's leading crime scene cadaver dog trained to find dead bodies. He had over two hundred cases to his name and had never failed in any murder or missing person case. Mike never gave false alerts and had only ever indicated where a dead body lay – with an incredible success rate. Billy Phish, on the other hand, was probably the best forensic dog trainer in the world, despite his part-time cyber-sleuth work in America.

Sean led Billy Phish into the cottage to a mammoth-sized mug of tea with four sugars, and then showed him around the place. He wanted Billy Phish to see the layout before getting the dogs in. Mike would be first up and Sean stood to one side, quietly watching Billy Phish go through his routine with the unleashed but excitable spaniel.

Sean loved watching the double act at work. Bloody impressive sight he thought, as Mike set to work in his usual frenzied manner. He scooted around the kitchen with his head held low, sniffing for the scent that would give him the reward from his 'dad', as Billy Phish was known to him. Sean watched him move rapidly from corner to corner, under shelves and tables and nosing up to cupboards around the kitchen. If he didn't pick up a scent, Billy Phish would channel Mike to other areas of the room with a wave of his hand and a short, sharp call of 'Move on boy'.

Mike was Billy Phish's pride and joy and the sole love of his life. He was irreplaceable. Sean recalled how he had worked with Billy Phish on countless covert cases to search for buried bodies of kidnapped diplomats in the Middle East and beyond. Sean had become a lifelong friend of Billy Phish. They had bonded, he remembered, after he had saved Mike's life when he saw him suddenly drowning in a swollen hillside river in Wales many years ago. Sean had dived in and pulled Mike out of the river by the scruff of his neck before landing him on the bank next to a distraught Billy Phish. Mike had nearly died that day on the riverbank during an incessant day of rain on the hills and Billy Phish cuddled him for nearly an hour under a poncho in the driving rain before Mike recovered. Billy Phish remained indebted to Sean for having saved Mike's life. Mike was his lifeblood.

Sean followed them both around the cottage and it wasn't long before Mike was in the hall leading to the stairs. He got an early waft of vapour and headed straight to the far corner, close to some golf clubs by the staircase recess.

Mike went wild.

He stood rigid, barking incessantly, arching and turning his neck to look for his 'dad'. His tail wagged like a flag whipping in the wind. He had found his reward and had smelt the scent of death. Billy Phish had a chest-mounted video camera to capture all of Mike's moves, indications and postures. Sean had seen Mike react this way many times before – it was an unequivocal hit.

Sean felt a chill run up his spine, followed by goose bumps. He grasped its significance: a dead body had lain there. He watched Billy Phish move Mike around a bit just to try and fix the exact spot. Mike was indicating that it was on the carpeted floor next to the stairs and by the alcove. Sean knew that this was proof that a dead body was either under the floor or had lain in that position at some time. He also knew that the body decomposition compounds that had seeped out of the dead body would have done so within less than an hour and that Mike was trained to hit on that scent. Mike had been fully trained on dead bodies in America and he could track and trace where in a building the body had lain, or had subsequently been moved to. The putrescine and cadaverine would leave a scent trace for many months.

Sean followed Billy Phish as he took Mike round the rest of the house just to check for any other cadaver signs or evidence of potential movement of a body from one part of the cottage to another.

'I'm not so sure there's a body under there Billy,' Sean said. 'It's rock-solid and no one would have gone to the trouble of excavating a hole through concrete to stick a body in it.'

'You're right mate. Very unlikely,' Billy Phish replied in a throaty voice. 'Now don't be touching fuck all. I'll bring Foz in.'

Foz was smaller and was trained to locate any tiny spots of blood. He was moving more slowly, and although it was frantic searching, he scurried around in what appeared to be a more precise way. He was trying to find the scent of blood and moved his nose around quickly, but much lower to the ground than Mike had. His nose was virtually stuck to the carpet. He didn't indicate in the kitchen or dining room, so Billy Phish moved him into the hall.

Foz made his way to the staircase alcove but, before he got there, midway across the hall from the kitchen to the stairs, he hit.

Foz stood utterly rigid, totally still – like a statue.

His nose was stuck to the ground millimetres above the carpet, and his head fully inclined. He didn't flinch or bat an eyelid. Only his tail was moving rapidly. He had smelt blood. Unlike Mike, he remained there in that position, totally still, until Billy Phish gave him a reward. On this occasion it was a few pieces of dog pellet.

Foz was one of the best blood detection dogs in the world. Sean knew from his previous jobs that he could detect the vapour of the most minuscule traces of blood, well beyond the capability of the human eye. Foz was ready to go again after his first hit in the hall and it wasn't long before he hit again. Billy Phish gave him another reward and he gobbled up the lot in one go.

Sean looked at the carpet where the first hit was and couldn't see anything at all. No distinguishing bloodstains or anything untoward. The carpet was not wet from cleaning and no obvious stains were present. Foz indicated the precise places where blood remained in five separate spots all around the alcove. There was not a sign from the human eye that there was blood anywhere.

It was almost certain now that Alfie was dead but where was the body?

Sean brought all the clothes from the tumble dryer and washing machine into the kitchen, laid them out alongside the shoes and let Billy Phish lead Foz to the next stage. Foz didn't hit on any of the clothing. There were no bloodstains on any items of Alfie's clothes.

The dogs had done their work and Sean had inspected below the carpet where Mike had hit. Not a sign of any disturbance in the concrete and Alfie's body was not in the house. He was convinced of that.

'A bit of a mystery here then, mate,' Billy Phish uttered as they both stood in the kitchen with the kettle on. 'It's a proper job I reckon, proper clean-up and quite a clinical hit I would have thought. They definitely killed him here,' he added before pausing. 'But let me do some tests with Luminol spray to find all the blood and I'll get some results on my mobile forensics kit courtesy of the CIA dollar.'

'I need this kept quiet Billy,' Sean said. 'I can't reveal what we've found to Jack or Dominic until we've probed a bit further.' Sean was thoughtful as he answered, his mind actively deciding the next steps to take, now he knew Alfie was dead.

'Liz arrives this evening. I need her to complete the forensic analysis for us and she's a trusted hand who keeps her own counsel.'

Sean remembered how Liz had been approached previously in her West Scotland cottage to identify some forensics from a case that MI5 were investigating. These people were from the FBI and she had spun them a tale of how it couldn't be done, despite the fact she had already solved it for MI5 some days previously. She knew where her loyalties lay and was clever with it. She was an expert freelance and independent forensic expert who specialised in soils, fibres, hair and pollens.

'I reckon she'll love taking this one on, Sean. None of this has to be to court-level standards, but it will give us the clues we want from any mud, blood and hairs mate. Don't be touching anything.'

Billy Phish scratched his greying stubble, turned to make the tea and lit his thinking pipe.

Sean sat down on the kitchen stool – he knew he couldn't let Dominic know of the finds at this stage and he began to think about how he would spin the case out and keep them in the dark until he was better placed to know what the hell had happened, and where they had taken Alfie's body. He started thinking about what Alfie's attackers would have done next in order to get rid of his body, and where and how they would have done it. This was like finding a contact lens in a snowdrift, which is why he needed Liz to help narrow down the huge search area he now had on his hands. The other person who could help him narrow down the search area was Jugsy.

'I've left a message with Jack to get Jugsy here as soon as we can,' Sean mentioned, taking a sip of tea. He checked for a reaction.

Billy Phish coughed, spluttered and spilt some tea down himself. He tried to regain his composure but was too shocked to say anything other than 'You're fucking joking me man! He's a bloody disaster and a nightmare to manage.'

Once Billy Phish had recovered, and Jugsy's character had been debated amongst considerable banter, they continued a long discussion over several brews in the kitchen to decide what else needed to be done.

'I'll get the vapour dogs primed,' Billy Phish said, his pipe still in his mouth. 'We should then be able to get an indication of where they took the body after they killed him.' Billy Phish pointed towards the plastic forensics bag on the side of the kitchen which held Alfie's old clothing. Sean nodded knowingly as he handed the bags to him.

'Liz will do her stuff with the forensics while we crack on mate,' Billy Phish explained. Sean agreed, knowing that forensics would be the key to finding Alfie. Billy Phish, Mike and Foz had done their job for now and it was up to the rest of the team to keep the trail hot. They had a target to find.

Sean sat alone that afternoon in Alfie's chair. He had partly anticipated this scenario and mulled the options open to him if Alfie was dead. And whilst he was mindful of other odd and wild scenarios, he was convinced Alfie had been murdered by someone who didn't want him to release his secret files to the world. These were high-level stakes, he thought.

It occurred to him that the killers might be from a national agency, either a foreign one or one from home soil. At this stage, he hadn't discounted there being an organised crime link to the case.

He looked around at the paintings and decor of Alfie's secret home. 'I wonder what drove Alfie to undertake these acts?' he thought. Sean also wondered how One-Eyed Damon was getting on with the task he had given him.

After a lot of thinking, he decided that he would not alert Jack and Dominic to any of the finds, clues or progress he had made. He would spin a few changes to the story just to give himself the space and time he needed, knowing that deception might just keep him alive in the landscape of irregular operations.

He needed to lose Jane on this one too at some point – just to keep his story tight and away from prying eyes and ears.

Chapter 17

Côte Vermeille

Sean took off his white overalls, threw them into the passenger seat of the van and grabbed a map of the Languedoc region from the glove compartment. He placed the map on the bonnet and put two small paint pots on each end to stop it blowing away in the gusting wind. He was exhausted but had an intense yearning to find out where the body had been taken. 'Where do we go from here?' he muttered, drinking his coffee from an aluminium mug and glancing up to see two large kestrels hovering above the cottage, doubtless looking for a kill he thought. It prompted him to call Jack.

'Jane will fly back tomorrow from Perpignan airport,' Sean said. 'I don't need her here any longer, but she can return to escort Melissa back when I'm finished with her.'

'That's fine,' Jack replied. 'Do what you need to. What about Billy and his dogs, has that worked out OK?'

'Yes, we did some good stuff this morning, not a bad start to be fair.'

'Go on, what happened?'

'Well, I've managed to trace Alfie's whereabouts. I think he may have gone up into the Pyrenees and secreted some stuff up there. I also think Melissa knows more than she is letting on so I need to keep probing her over the next few days. She could have some critical information that might help me nail this.'

'You can have whatever you need,' Jack said. 'Dominic just wants to know that the information Alfie had is safe and has not been exposed. Do whatever you must to make that happen. What else do you need?'

'I want Jugsy brought in ASAP. With all his kit too. I'll get him a hotel room here and we can reinstate Melissa in the safe house once I'm done with her.'

'Jugsy is ready to go. I'll come back in the next few hours to confirm timings.'

'Jack, I need you to do something else for me too. It's a big ask. Can you get someone to do some terrain analysis over Languedoc-Roussillon? It will need national assets, if you know what I mean?'

Sean hinted at using American capabilities to support his search to find whatever Alfie had deposited on the Pyrenean moors and he needed high-end technology to help him track and trace where Alfie had been on the hills.

Jack paused. Sean held his breath, hoping. 'I can inject a task into the imagery-intelligence centre, under some guise of a new operation Sean. It could be troublesome, but I'll see what I can do. Are you talking about using satellites?'

Sean breathed deeply, knowing that this needed special permission from the Americans to justify its use. 'Yes, that's exactly what I'll need. And hyperspectral imagery too please. It will help identify any areas that have been dug from the air. I haven't got a clue which sites yet, nor the date span I need for the terrain-change analysis, but this will help me narrow the search. Anyway, I'm working hard with Billy Phish to find where the hell Alfie went. He could well be alive and incarcerated – hard to tell right now.'

Sean was conscious he was calling on high-end intelligence capability that he needed to complement the world-leading geo-forensic expertise of Billy Phish, Jugsy and Liz. Only the full depth of forensic-intelligence layers would lead Sean to his goal. Whoever killed Alfie would have dumped his body in the sea or somewhere on the Pyrenean moors.

'I also need someone to check the CCTV footage in Collioure, just to verify Alfie was here and his last-known movements.'

'I'll get Samantha onto it,' Jack said. 'Send me a grid reference of the house and we'll do a search from there.'

Chapter 18

London

Natalie Merritt walked briskly through the crowds on the cramped streets of Ludgate Hill, striding forcefully through those who were dawdling and in her way. She wore a beige Karen Millen trench coat, which accentuated her brown shoulder-length hair, and she grappled fiercely to keep her handbag on her shoulder whilst gesturing vividly during her phone call.

She cursed the London weather as it began to rain, struggled to find her lightweight umbrella in the depths of her bag and gave up the instant she saw her destination. The rain promptly became torrential. She swore in haughty English, then broke into a gentle trot, cowering from the downpour for the last few metres. She was mightily unimpressed but hoped for a very quick reversal of fortune with her awaiting subordinates.

Natalie had worked as a political advisor to MPs at the Palace of Westminster for over five years. Five years during which she felt lucky that, until this point, no one had investigated and uncovered her affiliation to Russia's foreign intelligence service, the SVR. As an illegal sleeper, she was directed by her masters in the mysterious Directorate 'S' of the SVR. She used her elegance and charisma to good effect in the male-dominated world of Westminster. Calm, alluring and cautious, with impeccable tradecraft in spy methodology, she was the perfect hidden mole within the UK Parliament.

She was a new breed of spy: young, university-educated, intelligent, full of youthful female ambition and hugely attractive. Now in her mid-thirties, she had been groomed from a young age by her father about her dutiful allegiance to Moscow, and had spent long periods of time being held back from clandestine intelligence activity until Moscow felt she had developed her career well enough through her British private sector roles. Finally, she had been channelled into a key government role, and then made use of.

Natalie arrived at the modern office block halfway along Fleet Street and took a moment in the airy reception foyer to smarten herself up. She took her coat off, grabbed a brush for her hair and checked her make-up in a small vanity mirror. Mascara seeped down the sides of her eyes, which she quickly cleaned off. She was fuming because of the deluge and felt her irritation continue to rise. She stepped into one of the four lifts and made her way to the undercover operations room.

Natalie swiped her proximity ID card and passed through the high-security transparent revolving door. The air of a branded corporate-style organisation lingered as she strode purposefully towards the operations room. A set of secure grey doors sat prominently below the CCTV camera and a biometric eye scanner gave her access into the secure area of operations. She paused, drew breath, looked behind to watch the corridor lighting automatically dim and finally let a machine scan her iris before punching in a six-digit key code. She stepped into an airlock where the same procedure was required except that the last door required a different proximity card which she had collected at reception.

The door opened and she scanned the dimly lit open plan office. Desk lights were shining brightly on documents and maps that were being pored over by the evening shift.

The offices of the small company provided cover for a Russian eavesdropping and electronic cyber unit capable of hacking deep into complex IT systems, and conducting electronic surveillance to gather information on a range of British targets.

Her senses were electric as she strode into the room, excited that she was about to get her first big break towards finding Melissa and ultimately Alfie. Natalie had been informed by Moscow about Alfie and his confidante via a source they had in Westminster. Moscow was keen to protect its agents in the UK who were at risk from Alfie's investigations – word had reached them from London. Moscow had done its homework, had put

Natalie in charge of finding Melissa and had given her access to all the state intelligence apparatus at their disposal, including their clandestine cyber-operations centre located right in the heart of the City of London.

'Who wants to start?' Natalie asked firmly, as she walked to the control console. 'Are we ready to go?'

'Come and have a look at this,' Boris, the cyber commander, said. 'There's been a lot of activity all day, but the last three hours have been special. I think you'll be pleased with what's about to go down.'

Natalie was ushered to a cyber-operator's console where a detailed metadata analysis was being conducted on numerous human targets across the UK to try and confirm the leads for her. The Russian operators had been working for twenty-four hours using high-grade signals intelligence in an effort to get a head start on the operation. They were listening into a vast amount of telecommunications traffic, targeting known intelligence outlets.

The operation was a welcome break from their regular duties of feeding disinformation to the British media outlets and brute-force hacking into the computers of central government, universities and armed forces to surreptitiously collect secret data for different strategic aims. Much of this data was used for psychological operations to try to gently subvert a raft of British and European political efforts.

'You've boosted the surveillance team numbers I assume?' Natalie asked.

'Yes, exactly as you ordered. It took us a while to track the precise location of the safe house MI5 are using in Southwold. That's where this woman Melissa sent her message from. The metadata we've mined gave us the location of where she sent her tweet. We've been on the ground for three days now watching the house. The team have walked the grounds and have identified a number of electronic defences that someone has installed. We can defeat them whenever you give the order.'

Natalie knew the house would be the vital lead she needed to eventually get to Alfie's files. She had strict instructions from her handlers in Moscow to locate Alfie, whatever the cost.

'I think you'll see a bit of action in the coming minutes,' Boris said with no hint of a Russian accent. 'Come and have a look at the CCTV screens.'

Natalie looked at the large bank of screens, excited at the prospect of a breakthrough at last. Patience was not her finest trait.

'The female arrived a few hours ago,' Boris continued. 'She arrived at the house in a Mini Cooper, parked up and entered the house carrying a single red rucksack. This is her picture.'

'Do we know who it is? This isn't Melissa.'

'We used an IMSI grabber that locked into her phones and contacts. No second name, but her first name seems to be Jane. Probably the safe house custodian. The team are linking back to Moscow to get a full analysis on the contacts. Does it matter?'

'I don't know until we get in there and interrogate her and look at the forensics from the digital devices she has. No point waiting too long to find out either. I need results now.'

'Do you want us to tease her out? A direct assault will fail. We need to use some guile, and this is the best time to go ahead and do it if you want that.'

'Do it,' Natalie ordered, turning to sit down.

Natalie was firm and committed. She sat at the rear of the CCTV console and began tapping her fingers on the table. She was eager to watch. Within seconds the CCTV operator had patched through the live feeds from the ground operators onto the large screens. Natalie watched the live images from the body-worn camera of the commander as he triggered the first active infrared beam in the garden by putting his hand through it. Natalie instinctively knew this would alert the female occupant by way of some sort of intruder alarm in the house. An audible alarm, she thought.

She also knew that the occupant would expect false alarms, but that too many of them might eventually coax her out of the house to investigate. Natalie tensed her body, thrilled at what might materialise if this did indeed happen.

The commander triggered the same beam every six minutes. Then there was some movement from the house.

Natalie jumped out of her chair as she caught sight of the red-haired British agent on the TV screen. Jane had made the fatal mistake of opening the highly secure back door.

Natalie kept her eyes on the screens, watching with glee as the Russian leader grabbed Jane by the throat at the rear entrance and slammed her up against the wall before launching a fierce punch into the solar plexus. The internal lights of the safe house gave plenty of illumination to provide clear images of Jane being brutalised. Natalie revelled in the ruthlessness she was seeing at close quarters and felt her body shake through stimulation. It seemed perverted, but she needed this. As an illegal Russian wunderkind, she thrived on being involved in wet affairs, the SVR euphemism for killing, brutality and torture.

The body-worn cameras provided shaky pictures, but they gave a good enough view of what was happening right in the heart of the action. The live imagery captured the second Russian vividly ripping Jane's nine-millimetre handgun from her right hand, before throwing her to the ground. The loud thud as her head violently hit the floor reverberated across the operations room from the surround-sound speakers. Natalie watched with delight as Jane was kicked in the ribs before being punched square in the face. Brilliant, she mused with a sadistic edge, smiling at what she enjoyed seeing most: violence.

The Russians trick of teasing Jane out had worked. 'I want them to hurt her and find out where this woman Melissa is,' Natalie shouted. 'Make it happen.'

Boris nodded and gave the order over his microphone to the ground commander. The CCTV operator had hacked into the internal house cameras, providing images in each room of the house.

Natalie's interrogators began their brutal interrogation of Jane in the kitchen, all of it vividly captured on the CCTV screens and audio system. Jane was forced to stand in a stress position with her hands on the wall and standing on tip toes. Every time she began to crumple from the strain of the position, she was beaten with a baton across her back and shoulders. Natalie heard a horrible crack as the team leader's baton smashed into Jane's left shoulder with agonising force. Bright red blood was dripping from her eye sockets: two large fissures had been prised open by the interrogator, who had grabbed her from behind to rip her eyes apart and gouge the sockets. Natalie breathed deeply as Jane eventually passed out in unbearable agony, which was heard, seen and felt by everyone in the control room.

It was obvious to Natalie that Jane had been highly trained to resist interrogation and she decided early on to order her men not to bother with the soft stuff. Wet affairs, '*mokrie dela*' to her Russian friends, and brutality were the only way forward in Natalie's mind, and she really didn't have any patience for messing around. But Jane hadn't yet given any information away.

It was only a single tweet that Melissa had sent to her police friend from the safe house in Southwold. Even with the location services in the 'off' position on her iPhone, this was enough for her location to be traced using the hidden metadata which had been analysed using supercomputers by the Russian cyber team in Fleet Street. This had led Natalie directly to Jane and the safe house.

Natalie saw Jane's slumped body on the kitchen floor, jumped up and marched across to the microphone. 'Wake her up and give her the SP17 now,' she demanded. I need results quickly for fuck's sake.'

The CCTV operator zoomed in on the syringe the team doctor was holding. He placed the needle directly into Jane's spine and depressed the plunger, releasing the drug straight into Jane's nervous system.

'Now she'll talk like a banshee,' Natalie said with delight, pacing up and down the ops room. She had ordered the doctor to insert a small amount of scopolamine, known colloquially in Colombia as 'The Devil's breath', and made from the borrachero tree. The truth serum worked within an hour on ninety-five percent of recipients.

Two hours later, Natalie watched as the doctor injected a second dose. The convulsions began in seconds.

For Jane, life was over all too quickly.

Chapter 19

Côte Vermeille

Sean chose an old-fashioned hotel to conduct his operation in Port-Vendres, a curious seaside town that was a deepwater commercial port but also had a fishing and yachting harbour. He purposefully avoided any large hotels with nosy hotel managers, CCTV and distinctive security measures. He had arranged for Billy Phish and the dogs to stay at a small gîte in the hills to the west, which would allow the dogs plenty of space to roam.

Sean took Melissa for a walk along the bay at Port-Vendres and started to explain the next phases of his mission. She seemed a little more at ease with Sean now and walked close to him along the coastal promenade. It was a brilliant summer's day with the sun glinting off the dark green ocean as the haze on the horizon weakened. Sean breathed the air deeply, reaching for his thoughts. He wanted to elicit everything possible from Melissa's mind. He was competent enough at gaining the trust of people and remained convinced of his power to reveal the starkest of intelligence. He just needed time to develop a rapport with Melissa and to nurture her trust during periods of time alone together.

Melissa was dressed in a full-length, floral maxi dress as they strode slowly along the bay. To others looking on, they could easily have been lovers. Whilst he found Melissa to be feisty and irksome, there was also a deep intelligence to her, and a grounded personality that he liked. He revealed some of his thoughts to her. 'It's difficult to say what has happened to Alfie right now,' he said quietly. 'In fact, it will take me some time to get a real lead, but I'm bringing in a few experts to help.'

'Who?' Melissa asked.

'My old team. But I need you close so I can quiz you on Alfie, and in particular, about anything you haven't yet remembered that might be vital.'

'My memory is bloody good you know. I haven't missed anything, if that's what you mean.'

She turned towards the ocean and stood silently clenching the handrail overlooking the beach. A few youths were scrambling on the rocks and an elderly man took some photos of the bay. She turned abruptly and looked Sean right in the eye. She paused, then spoke unexpectedly. 'Why do you keep looking at me in that way Sean?'

Sean was shocked by the question and froze for a moment. 'What way?'

'The way you have since the first time we met. Do you fancy me?'

'Why on earth are you asking me that?'

'So we can get the decks cleared straight away and so there is no ambiguity. Looks to me as if we'll be here a while and I don't want any confusion going on.'

She was straight-faced, and Sean sensed her wanting to take control of the situation – again. She was hard-nosed and testing.

'This really isn't the time to discuss such matters, and anyway, I'm here to do my job – nothing else right now.'

'You haven't answered.'

'For crying out loud – no.'

'Good,' Melissa said. 'Just so we're clear on all this.'

'Excellent. We now know where we stand Melissa. I'll do my job, and I'd be bloody grateful if you can help me with that.' Sean was riled, and he knew she had struck a nerve. He turned to compose himself, intrigued by her abruptness.

'I'm still angry, and ready to fight these bastards, but I feel much better being here and being involved. Even if you are a pain,' she said, easing the tension she had created. 'I want to be a full part of this and I'll get stuck in too. I'm a bloody good investigator you know.'

'An investigator of sorts,' Sean said sarcastically, pushing back at her. He was encouraged by the honesty and trust that she had unknowingly begun to cement. 'Anyway, are you sure Alfie didn't say anything to you? Anything that seemed tenuous? I just think he would have given some sort of clue to you. Can you try to rack your brains over this and go through all your conversations and journey with Alfie step by step?'

Melissa nodded, as if to concede. She ran a hand through her hair as the sea breeze strengthened and turned her back to the sea. 'Do you really think I haven't been doing that already? Of course I have, and I'll keep doing so. Who are you working for Sean? I don't understand who is who anymore.'

'I work for the government Melissa, and for people who I believe will do the right thing for us and the country at large.'

'But is that MI5 or MI6?' Melissa asked.

'It's not as obvious as that: there are many blurred lines in these kinds of ops.' He felt that he had better not tell her the full deal and closed that part of the conversation down quickly.

He remembered the occasion when Jack had briefed him on Melissa in detail. She was indeed a shrewd investigator, but hadn't always been so corporate and precise. Her days at university had seen her asked to leave quietly as the Vice-President of the Student Union for surreptitiously obtaining university financial documents. Days that had also seen her wear a skinhead haircut and undertake endless days of campaigning against university fees. By all accounts, she had become a wild child away from the sobering mind of her conservative mother and her father, a Captain in the Merchant Navy. The university didn't know it at the time, but she had broken into the Vice-Chancellor's office late at night and found the password to his computer in an open drawer. She wanted to have the inside track on accommodation fees and to hold the university to account with the information her stealthy investigation had yielded. She had also found evidence on the VC's computer of salacious relationships with two academics, and she let him know it. By all accounts, the final negotiations went her way and accommodation fees were reduced for the first year and frozen for a further two.

Sean was astonished at her gall and stealth. It was her father, who had teased her away from university, perhaps, Sean thought, with an enticement by the VC. It was only then that she entered the corporate world of investigations. He had managed to get her to change her dress and hairstyle, and got her a break by landing her a junior research role in a publishing house in London, courtesy of his best man. It worked. She grew into life and gradually, through her immense dedication to work, moved on to journalism in Canada, the United Arab Emirates, Kuwait and a year-long stint in Lebanon, where she helped unearth a serious terrorist plot being hatched in the Maghreb. That was the case that had landed her the job with the prestigious Global Bureau of Investigative Journalism based in London. Sean knew she had guts and that she would be a hard nut to crack in order to obtain the information he needed. He liked how authentic she was.

His thoughts were again brought to a sudden halt by Melissa. 'How do you think you will find Alfie then?' Melissa asked nonchalantly. 'What's the plan?'

Sean decided to answer this one. 'Well, I work best when I put myself in the mind of the person of interest – to try and unlock the way their mind works. You know, where he would hide his secrets, how he would do the deed, that kind of stuff. You can do a lot by trying to act as the poacher despite being the gamekeeper. My work is about solving puzzles and mysterious problems, and to gather intelligence in many different ways. Then I can solve the bigger puzzle.'

For some reason Sean couldn't fathom, Melissa took Sean's arm. He didn't resist.

'This doesn't mean anything by the way,' she said. 'I used to do it with Alfie too. Just friends in a very mad world.'

Sean began to understand her. She put on a good act of defiance, but also had moments that showed her sensitive side too. The small touches and vocal resistance revealed a lot as he continued to build and nurture her trust. He felt himself being drawn in, but was guarded against her prominent appeal.

As they walked along the promenade, Sean smirked when he thought about Melissa's past but then found himself being drawn back to the question of Dominic Atwood. Who exactly was he protecting? Why on earth was he so obsessed with these files? Sean didn't know. Which is why he decided not to trust anyone or to reveal his full hand to anyone quite yet. But he did feel he owed Melissa more explanation about Alfie, deciding he had no option but to tell her the truth now.

'Melissa, this will be quite a shock. But I feel you need to know now.'

'Know what?'

'It looks like Alfie has been murdered. Killed in the cottage.'

He steadied himself, concerned about her response. He watched her retreat with a pang of sorrow as she turned towards the choppy bay. Sean saw her eyes well up. She took some deep breaths before placing her arms on the promenade wall where she broke down.

Chapter 20

Côte Vermeille

'It helps you think, I know,' Billy Phish said pouring two glasses of red wine at the table kitchen in the gîte. 'Big one or little one?'

'Quite a tonic for quite a day, big one of course.' Sean tossed a wad of cash across the table to Billy Phish, an early reward for a successful search at the cottage.

'Where's Melissa?' Billy Phish inquired.

'Back at the hotel, too much detail for us to talk about this evening Billy. She'll be OK for now.'

'Bit dodgy mate. Is she savvy enough?'

'Oh, she's very savvy, and very precocious,' Sean said. 'I told her she's to remain in the hotel and stay in her room for a couple of hours until I return.'

'You have a bit of a soft spot for her, don't you?'

Sean scrunched his face. No words were needed.

Billy Phish nodded, wisely not pushing his thoughts further. He lit his pipe. 'What else has been happening then? Any news?'

'Liz arrives tonight with her forensics kit and she'll start at the cottage first thing in the morning.'

'Fair play to her, she's never let us down eh?'

'Indeed. Hopefully her forensics will help us zoom into the sites we'll need to search, instead of it just being the whole of the Pyrenees, as it is right now.'

Sean laid out a huge map of Languedoc on the table, together with an A3 piece of paper showing a flowchart in pencil of the steps he wanted to pursue.

'My hunch is that they got rid of him somewhere in the hills of Languedoc or even high up in the Pyrenees,' Sean said, pointing to the map. 'My gut tells me they wouldn't want to get rid of the body altogether, and they might want to keep a record of exactly where they left him. More than likely he was buried.'

'I think you're bang on, I'd say the moors too,' Billy Phish chipped in. 'Easy digging.'

'Exactly. But I need to make sure they haven't just tipped him over the cliffs or taken him out of the region entirely.'

'Well, the vapour dogs will show us where he went, of his own volition or not.'

Sean needed a clue. He needed to find which area to concentrate on. Was it the cliffs and the sea? Or was it the vast expanse of the Pyrenees? Or had they killed him and taken him miles away out of the region?

'I think it would have been too risky for the killers to travel on major roads with a dead body in the car. So they wouldn't have moved him too far out of the area.'

'You're right mate. And I'm guessing they wouldn't just get rid of the body over the cliffs, just in case they needed to return to it at any point in the future.'

'What makes you think that?' Sean asked.

'Well, if I was them, I'd just want to hide the body carefully and not disrobe him. That would be bloody hard work too if they were burying him.'

'Maybe, who knows? We don't really know who the hell it was who had been tipped off about what he was going to do.'

'I reckon it was the Yanks myself, always involved somewhere and always cocking it up,' Billy Phish joshed.

'Could be Russians though,' Sean replied.

'No, they're always last past the post and last to wake up mate.'

'We'll see. Doubtless someone was going to be totally shafted once Alfie released his files. But I wonder who, and what was so important that they had to kill him to stop all this?'

'Just wait until Jugsy turns up with those big ears,' Billy Phish grumbled. 'He'll have us caught and jailed unless we keep him off the booze and away from any women within ten miles of here.'

'He'll give us a grin, I grant you that. But hopefully he'll also give us some clues to work on,' Sean said.

'It'll be great to have him back here on a job mate. I bet his nose is redder than ever with all that red wine he drinks. Remember that time in the Yorkshire hills? Jugsy had the whole bar singing, drank the hotel dry and stood on a wet patch shouting that he had solved the entire case from his imagery analysis. Bloody great fun mate.'

They chatted for a while and drank more wine, interspersed with the occasional pensive silence.

'I'm thinking of bringing in Larry too if it gets to the stage where we can't find Alfie.'

'Bloody great. Not just Jugsy but the nutty Italian geologist too. Jeez, this will turn this job into a laugh a minute with that pair mate.'

'Well, he's the best we have on geology and chemical analysis and you know he's helped solve a lot of cases. So, he's in. If I need him.'

'True, very true, my friend. But why are all these global experts all bloody nutters?'

'Have a look at yourself Billy. You're one of them,' Sean responded. They laughed.

Sean explained how he would use Jugsy to analyse key areas using his air-imagery analysis skills – based on how far the murderers might be able to carry a heavy body from a vehicle they had used to undertake a body deposition. It was a vast area that they had to narrow down which would then allow Mike to do his cadaver-detection work. If it was the cliffs, they could use Mike in a boat to try and detect the deposition area and then use tidal flows to analyse where the body might lie. Billy Phish suggested that the map analysis they were about to do would help them to identify hot spots across a wide area of the peat and forested Pyrenean hills where the potential deposition sites might be.

They would look to identify the key areas where vehicles could access and park, that in turn would then provide walkable access to remote areas suitable enough to carry the body. Then dig with some cover from being viewed. Billy Phish explained how these areas would generally be well away from well-defined tracks that would attract unwelcome footfall and may lead to someone spotting the body or the disturbance of turf.

'You know what Billy, I think we can do this. I just need to get in their minds to know how they would have planned this.'

'The Yanks you mean?' Billy Phish chuckled. Sean discussed the ease of digging in the peat and high forested hills, and also the ease with which ground disturbance would disappear quickly as the soggy tufts began to knit together again after having been replaced.

Sean began to draw vehicle routes on the map. He drew circles around the junctions and placed arrows next to potential parking spots on the hill and along the cliffs. He continued analysing the routes, knowing the killers would have needed to recce the area first.

Sean closed his eyes and mimicked their journey in his mind. He figured they would have had to retrace their route back to the body deposition site after they had killed him, both by car and on foot. And he based his assumptions on two men. Possibly a third to carry the body more easily. He worked on the basis they couldn't carry a body too far from the vehicle drop-off point.

This gave him some parameters to work with for the search and would allow Billy Phish to cover shorter distances with Mike sniffing for the dead body. He was anxious to start the search the very next morning, starting with Billy Phish's vapour-trail dogs.

Sean had a hunch he needed to find the body and that it would hold the clues he was looking for.

Chapter 21

Côte Vermeille

Sean and Billy Phish arrived at the cottage at 5.30am with the air-scenting dogs in the back of the van. It was a cold morning with glistening dew on the grass and a morning moon in the sky taking pride of place beyond the bay. Sean watched Billy Phish draw on the map having made his important first brew of the day. He lit his pipe and then drank tea from the world's largest Thermos mug.

Billy Phish started marking up each road junction for their next search. Using the dogs, they would try to find where the body had been moved to. Jack's GCHQ team had been working flat out for the last twenty-four hours searching the CCTV footage of Collioure and had confirmed early that morning that Alfie had been seen in the town. He had been into the town on three consecutive days around the time his disappearance had become known to Jack. It was time to see what had happened to him next.

Sean watched Billy Phish take Alfie's old T-shirt out of the forensics bag and hold it to the noses of the two English Coonhounds. The vapour-trailing dogs now had the scent article to begin trailing where Alfie had been moved to from the cottage. Sean knew these kinds of dogs were rare and he was mightily glad to have them kick-off the search. Very few had been trained to this level of track and trace in vapour-wake hunting.

It was a cold morning with fog over the village and the smell of recent rain hung in the air. The first dog, Winston, was released by Billy Phish to trail the lingering air at mid-height rather than having his nose on the ground, where the scent wouldn't remain. Sean watched Winston strain for a waft of Alfie's scent as he meandered along the road, nose high in the air, with Billy Phish following a few metres to the rear. Sean followed in the pickup truck a good thirty metres behind both of them, and watched Winston cover the sixty-metre stretch to the first T-junction with some ease and little delay. Winston then stood still at the T-junction. Sean watched him sniff around in circles for a while, before he headed left.

He had the scent of Alfie. Alfie had travelled in this direction for sure. The dogs were trailing the body scent right from the cottage gate and had followed his trail to the left of the first junction. Dynamite, Sean thought as he drove back to the gate to start the process again with the second dog. He watched Chester do exactly the same at the T-junction, but a little slower than Winston to gain the scent. Billy Phish always used a second dog to verify the actions of the first and they used this routine throughout the morning.

It was now a two-kilometre drive to the next junction that Sean had circled on the map. He had discounted the other roads off this quiet road because they led nowhere except to private, stand-alone cottages. He was proved right as he watched Winston continue straight past them.

Sean opened the tailgate to allow Billy Phish to quickly tuck both dogs in the back of the pickup, and they drove swiftly to the next junction to see in which direction the vapour trail would lead them. When they arrived, they repeated the process, and the dogs were more excitable trying to find the scent again. They knew a reward would come if they kept on going.

The scent of Alfie could remain in the air for weeks and would escape from any vehicle he was transported in. The crossroads at the next location was where Sean hazarded a guess that it would be straight on. Winston proved him right as he picked up the scent after about twenty seconds of sniffing around the junction. Sean was delighted. He had a trail, but for how long?

They continued for another two junctions, all the time heading inland towards the hills. At the next major junction Winston came unstuck. Billy Phish gave him a smell of the other clothes this time. But still nothing. The dog wandered around the junction slowly while Sean slowed traffic down, but it was no good. The trail had gone. Chester fared no better. Sean watched from the pickup window as Billy Phish approached looking dejected. 'Sorry mate, it's gone dead. I think we're now in an area where the scent isn't trapping and holding. Probably due to wind on high ground.'

'Yeah, real blow after such a great start.'

'Let's go further down the road to check the next junction out, just in case the scent comes back.'

'I want to have a look at the map and see what's what first,' Sean said, feeling gutted. He needed more of a clue here. The dogs, although the best-trained in the world, didn't quite get him the result he needed.

Sean jumped out of the wagon, pulled on a black gilet and placed the large map on the bonnet of the vehicle. He pointed out another seven possible junctions with his pen.

'We need to check the lot,' Sean said.

'That's a lot of ruddy scent trailing,' Billy Phish said reticently. 'Time's getting on and the roads are in full flow mate.'

'Well, no pain no gain,' Sean said, slapping him on the back. 'Let's get it done my friend. We'll check every damn permutation.'

They checked each and every one of the junctions that could have been taken by the killers to see if the canines picked up the scent again. They didn't.

Sean was burned. He was disappointed that they hadn't made it into the Pyrenean hills where his instinct told him that Alfie was probably buried in the secluded peat hills. He needed a closer launch pad than this to narrow the search down. He felt sure the body might hold a clue.

Then, at the very last junction, it happened. Chester, not Winston, picked up the scent, which Winston had missed only minutes earlier. They had found the trail again.

'Fucking amazing,' Billy Phish said to Sean as he smoked a cigarette leaning on the car window. 'I feel a bloody good day coming on,' he said in his gritty Yorkshire voice. He threw his cigarette on the ground and walked over to pat the dog on the head.

Sean was elated. He was allowed to throw a reward to Chester. His favourite type of lamb bone.

Chapter 22

Côte Vermeille

Sean threw his clothes on the marbled floor, slid the shower door open and stepped into the steaming shower he had been running for five minutes. He felt the windburn on his face ease as he lathered himself with the moisturising soap, scrubbing vigorously to bring his tired body back to life.

He thought through what he had uncovered. So far, he knew Alfie was dead and his body had been moved towards the Pyrenean hills – he also knew Alfie had been got at before Jack could lift him to safety. Who, he wondered, had got to him first? And had they extracted information from Alfie about where he had concealed the files? Had he been interrogated or tortured? Why had the search of the cottage not revealed any clues where he had hidden the files?

No clues, no computers, not a jot. He was intrigued by the fact that Alfie needed a fallback plan to expose the files and wondered who would have initiated that plan if he had been killed? His own inquiries had given him no tangible leads other than Melissa, and hopefully the location of Alfie's body. He had no choice but to pursue both leads, knowing full well no one else would have both of them.

He stepped out of the shower feeling rejuvenated from his ten-minute soak. The day's work had been productive, and he was relieved that Winston and Chester had given him a great head start. It wasn't faultless though. The trail had gone cold at a key junction high in the hills, despite both dogs trying to chase the scent down at further road junctions. What was clear though was that Alfie had been moved in a car in a specific direction that led only to the Pyrenees. The next stages needed to take them further into the target zone. But for now, at 7pm, it was a good day's work.

What would he have done in Alfie's shoes, he thought? He decided it was time to probe Melissa for any clues that had not yet surfaced in her story.

Sean had arranged to meet Melissa in her room at 7.30pm and he took the short walk down the corridor before knocking on her door. Melissa took a while to answer.

'Come on in. It's been a long boring day for me. I don't like being locked away. I need more action.'

Sean smiled, ignored the glint in her eye and stepped into the room, taking a seat on the bed. Melissa followed him and stood, arms crossed, by the TV.

'It's been a good day, and you need to stay patient. This is a serious game of life and death as you well know. I can ramp up the tempo a bit now, and I've got a few people flying in to help me on the case. It's going to get pretty busy from this point, and I need you to stay patient.'

'If you say so. I just need to get out of this place, it's horrendous deep cabin fever being cooped up all day.'

'How do you feel?'

'Still annoyed that you won't let me help and use some of my contacts, if you really want to know,' she said sardonically. 'You do know I'm getting fed up that you're not letting me get involved, don't you?'

'Of course I do,' Sean replied. He stood to face her. 'You're as eager and as capable as I am but, if you don't mind, we need to take everything a step at a time right now.'

'And what's the next step then?'

'Interrogation, I'm afraid.'

'Oh really? Sounds like a bit of fun. I might be up for that,' she said, chuckling at the notion.

'You've suddenly changed your tune.'

'As is my prerogative, and as well you know.'

Sean sensed the push and pull of their engagements. He had never imagined it would be this way. Like an elastic band, the pulling was now changing to her side, but he had a job to do.

'Listen, I know it seems somewhat amusing, but at this moment in time my leads on this case are limited to you, a few pictures in a cloud account which I've studied time and time again, and Alfie. I need to find the next lead, otherwise the trail goes cold and we're all in a whole heap of shit then.'

'I was just teasing you. Lighten up a bit, for goodness sake.' Melissa walked towards the balcony window and turned on her heels. 'I know this is serious, but how does all this interrogation work?'

Sean softened his tone. 'It's a chance to talk. Just us.'

'Well, if you really need to know, I actually enjoy talking with you. So, this might be quite nice.'

'Absolutely, good teamwork and me getting to know you better,' Sean said calmly.

'I see. An opportunity to see what's hidden in my mind and behind my mask then eh? Very sly,' Melissa said, looking Sean in the eye with hands on hips.

Sean smiled back, trying not to laugh. He could see Melissa warming a little bit. She seemed more relaxed and open now. He asked Melissa to take a seat and placed a notepad on the small round table.

'You know what Sean, I like how you're going about solving this puzzle. And don't think for one moment I haven't been scared about all this. I bloody well am. Petrified at times. But my way is to just get on with it, you can see that, right?'

'Yes, I do. You're a tough cookie on the outside but a little softer inside I think. That's absolutely fine.'

'That's exactly what my father always says. You're so much like him you know.'

Sean sat, and inclined his seat to face Melissa at an angle. Not too close to Melissa, and with enough space to provide a level of comfort and trust for the question and answer session. 'I'm not sure I can say much to that. But let me tell you, what we're involved in right now can be quite overwhelming, I know that. But don't worry, you'll be fine. You're with some very good people here you know.'

'Thanks, I can see that and I'm sorry I've been such a pain, but I do feel more settled now. So, what about your puzzle we need to solve?'

'Well, I'll use some techniques that were designed to debrief people who had been involved in traumatic incidents, such as being taken hostage or witnessing horrific events. The idea is that, together, we can uncover memory that has been lost or is deeply hidden. A bit like small bytes of memory in a computer that have been erased – but with skill they can be recovered.'

Sean felt he had developed a trust and rapport now, enough to be able to probe further into her mind about recent and past events and to explain the techniques they would jointly use.

'Wow. This sounds fascinating, but like I told you, my memory is fantastic. Isn't this all a bit silly though?'

'Well, we'll see. I have no choice, so just relax and work with me on this please.'

The techniques he had been taught were high-grade and efficient. He had previously used the skills to interrogate captured terrorists for snippets of intelligence that could lead to solving complex intelligence puzzles.

Neuro-linguistic programming required Sean to increase his rapport with Melissa and to use the techniques to improve the recall of Melissa's memory. Sean remembered Zara, who had instructed him in these techniques. She was a British intelligence officer who had studied psychological debriefing methodology all her life. He remembered Zara's famous line: *To put it bluntly, some people just don't know what they actually do know.*

Melissa sat forward and poured some water. 'OK, I'm happy to give this a go, on one condition though. That you start to involve me more in this case and let me get my hands dirty.'

'That's a deal. The beginning of becoming a close team I think we can say.'

'Absolutely,' Melissa replied, sitting back in the high-backed chair. 'Now let's get on with it and see what we can find out.'

Sean knew a major experience for Melissa would have had a specific set of meta-programmes attached to it. Processing that experience would be very different from the ones that Melissa might normally prefer to use. This was how a hostage or witness separated out events into space in time which seemed to have happened somewhere else, or to someone else, or become distorted in time. He had learnt conversational technique and natural psychological phenomena to assist memory recall.

'Nothing to worry about,' Sean explained. 'It will take a few hours and we'll go right back to the very first point in time when you met with Alfie.'

'Great, this is quite exciting actually. Who knows what I know eh?'

'OK, I suppose we can begin then. Now, I want you to take me, step by step, through the journey you took the last time you met Alfie,' Sean said. 'We'll stop at each stage. You'll look around you. You'll try and recall the faces that you passed and looked at on that day. Then I'll get you to look at small insignificant items. Items left on tables, what Alfie had with him, what he wore, what words he used to describe things. Treat it as a journey in your dreams...'

Melissa began to relax, closed her eyes and started a commentated journey in her subconscious mind and memory.

'Tell me what Alfie was wearing the last time you met. What was he carrying? What did he always carry with him? What did he fiddle with?'

'The last time we met was at Tate Modern and I think he wore jeans, a white shirt and a blue cardigan. He always wore a ring on his right finger and I know he had a recent tattoo on his forearm, which I saw when he rolled his sleeves up. He seemed quite calm, but oddly he crossed his arms an awful lot...'

'Tell me about the ring and the tattoo? Did he fiddle with anything at all?'

Sean spent just over three hours interrogating Melissa that evening, carefully noting her every response and mental carriage, adjusting questions to send her memory back in time to recall pictures and scenes of events.

Chapter 23

Whitehall, London

Jack arranged to meet Dominic Atwood at the RAC Club in Pall Mall and spent an hour refreshing himself in the Turkish baths before walking upstairs for lunch. Feeling confident about his plans, he waited for Dominic Atwood in the ornate central court, which had a 1966 Austin Healey 3000 as its centrepiece.

The magnificent surroundings provided synergy with Jack's persona of precision and immaculate design in all he did. He felt content with the progress so far and had prepared well for his meeting with Dominic, feeling very much at ease in the salubrious but egalitarian surroundings of the club.

Dominic arrived a few minutes late, and they were ushered to a discreet table in the main dining hall fully adorned with the accoutrements of a formal dinner setting.

'I have a meeting this afternoon with the Home Secretary Jack, and I'd very much like to provide some assurances for her,' Dominic began.

'I'm very happy to give you a full briefing sir and I think we've made some good progress so far,' Jack began. 'Though it will take some time to solve I'm afraid.'

The waiters left them alone in the corner for their early lunch and Dominic nodded with approval at Jack's remark before continuing. 'What about the police investigation? Do we have that tied up?'

'Well, I would say we do.'

'Good. Let me know the details. I want to make sure no one starts to trawl for suspicious motives.'

'Of course, sir.'

'Is the Intelligence Committee the same Jack?'

'Indeed. I think you can safely let the Home Secretary know that there are no dubious reasons for the intelligence officer's disappearance and that the police are not treating it as anything more than a missing person at this stage. They follow fairly standard procedures for people who disappear, as you know, and invariably they won't be deflected from their very standard operating protocols.'

'That's very good Jack. How much time does it give us? I really don't want any of the agencies smelling a rat you know.'

'We have some time,' Jack said. 'It's a joint inquiry with the military, who are helping the police with their investigation. But, sadly, nothing will come from those discussions and they'll simply continue to check different lines of inquiry. Sean seems quite happy no one has followed the trail he has uncovered – yet.'

'Good. I'd like to keep it that way, if you don't mind. We really don't want the Home Office flapping around because of all this. What about the press?'

'All under control. No need for D notices either. I've taken care of all that.'

'Splendid. Shall I report that all is well and that there is nothing of huge concern then?'

'I would say so, yes. So far, we have no murmurs of concern from the Joint Intelligence Committee, the police inquiry could last for some time, and there are no tangible leads to latch onto. Alfie Chapman was a pained man, and they may put this down to his mental state of mind. Our man is unearthing things relatively quickly in terms of his last movements and the safe house he was using to operate. So, all in all, we are in a reasonable place right now and we have a fair chance of uncovering the full puzzle.'

Jack was pleased that Dominic seemed comforted by all that he had prepared, which had included setting the deck of cards so that order was maintained and there was no reason for Dominic to intervene further. He knew Dominic liked it immensely when his people made things happen.

Jack poured some water into Dominic's glass as he looked musingly out of the large window into the neatly manicured gardens. Dominic continued after a short pause.

'The Home Secretary will not want any fallout over this Jack. She is acutely aware of previous cock-ups with our service and wants to know she is protected. That's my job of course – as well as keeping this well under wraps until I can judge the fallout and the way we handle it after that. There are some very anxious people right now.'

Jack knew that Dominic, for his part, would have been smoothing the ministerial lines, making sure no one was taking the matter to a high level or asking awkward questions. Except of course for the key men he was protecting. Men whose downfall relied on Sean finding the files first.

The first course arrived, and the pair moved onto more convivial conversation regarding the merits of the current economic outlook for the country and the issue of the forthcoming referendum on the UK pulling out of Europe. It was a well-rehearsed ploy to change conversation around the very nosy waiters in the London club zone. Jack adjusted his napkin and paused before providing Dominic with information on the current operation on the ground.

'He's definitely the right man for the job and he's made good progress so far. But I think you perhaps ought to let your people know that this will take time. It won't be days, it will be weeks I'm afraid. Sean has found Alfie's last movements but now it's a hunt to find where he has stored the files.'

'Very good,' Dominic replied as he began to eat, pausing after each mouthful, and looking back at Jack, awaiting more.

'We have searched his place in France,' Jack said. 'None of his friends and family knew of its existence and he covered his trail quite well, up to a point. I can only surmise that he made a serious error in covering his communication trail and that's when someone got to him before we did.'

'Where are the files though? That's what we need, nothing else. The mole files.'

'That's what will take the time I'm afraid. We think he may have left clues for their release in the event of him being killed or taken out of the game, but we haven't yet found those clues. The woman he confided in may hold those or they may be hidden somewhere in the surrounding area. It's a matter of tracking and tracing his movements from the cottage.'

'Push him on then Jack. He needs to know the urgency here. And back up the resources and effort as you need to. The clock is ticking if the other side get to them first, and then we're both done for my friend.'

'Already done, sir. He has everything at his disposal and we'll find where young Alfie is – dead or alive – and then we'll find the files before anyone else does. Unless he's already talked. But we'd know that immediately I assume?'

'Possibly Jack. Very possibly. But we don't know which side we're batting against yet. I'm working on that. Now tell me about this fellow Richardson. You told me he was the best we had before I gave the order to get him out of Kabul. But is he really? He seems a strong operator from what I saw but why is he the man for this?'

'He's one of our very best, sir. If not the best. He's the son of a military engineer and was told by his father that he'd have a great military career, if he listened to him and did as he asked. His father worked as a hod carrier before joining the Army. He was successful when he left, rising to CEO of his old construction company. He made his son do exactly the same. Sean spent three years hod carrying on London building sites, spent time in the toughest of pubs and rumbled with the best of them in the East End.'

'A curious route into our world though Jack, fascinating.'

'It's quite a story actually sir. He is also a talented artist, he spent his weekends and evenings selling his pictures in Covent Garden before going to Sandhurst, where he excelled. Tough, hardy and ultra-resilient it would seem. Learnt his craft in Northern Ireland on undercover operations as well as leading searches for dead soldiers and hidden IRA weapons caches. He became an expert in his field of covert operations and spent long periods on loan to MI5 and SO13 in the Metropolitan Police. By all accounts, his missions in the Middle East and Central Asia have left a fair trail of bodies too.'

'What went wrong then Jack. Why did we lose such a top operator?'

'The death of his wife apparently led to his own downfall. He spent a number of years on counterterrorism operations, back and forth into Iraq and Afghanistan, before losing his vetting and being asked to retire. Shame really. When he was on loan to MI6, the Fort Monkton staff had never before seen anyone with such a broad skill set. An accomplished explosives expert, very handy with weapons, forensics-trained and an uncanny knack of getting his sources to have total trust and faith in him. A magnetic personality to the death, many had said.'

Jack relaxed back into his chair noting Dominic was about to change tack.

'Listen Jack, you've done a great job on this so far. Sean seems just the chap we need here, and I have faith in his ability. But I do need it cleaned up quickly. I've got a few other issues going on with the damned Russians playing their active measures cards again, and with them hacking more intensively into different government departments. It seems they are playing with the US presidential election too, pushing out disinformation campaigns to influence the electorate and leaking party political secrets to the public. It will get very messy, you know. I've also got a whole heap of Brexit issues to deal with and a few dissident actors playing up on this. Let's get this whistle-blowing mess put to bed and put to bed quickly. Then we can focus on the real threats of the day – and keep our careers, if this is solved.'

Chapter 24

Côte Vermeille

Natalie arrived in Port-Vendre on the Tuesday evening and headed straight to the hotel's small reception desk. Comfortable, but not very classy, she thought. She was drawn to the pretty eyes of the blonde receptionist, and for a moment, found herself gazing idyllically at the young Norwegian woman.

'Bonjour madam,' the receptionist said, raising her head and smiling. Natalie felt their eyes engage for what seemed an eternity.

'Mademoiselle,' Natalie replied, throwing a flirtatious smirk. She thought it was cute that the receptionist went coy with embarrassment. Natalie composed herself again, passed the receptionist her British passport and signed the paperwork.

She used her deep-cover guise as a political advisor researching the economic and sociocultural issues of the UK and EU to check in. There was no need to change any of her cover, which existed naturally.

Natalie's bags were taken to her room and she made her way to the bar, making mental notes on the hotel's layout. She sat alone at the long bar for a while – only half a dozen guests were present in the large open-plan lounge, most of them watching TV. She decided that she needed to be regularly seen typing on her laptop in either the small lobby or the bar area. On other occasions she decided she would sit on the terrace overlooking the extensive gardens and lawns with views to the coast. She knew Sean would surface at some point in the evening or morning. And if Melissa did too, it would be a real bonus.

Two of Gregory's team covered the front entrance and the exit point for the road, and monitored it from a public right of way some forty metres away in the woods. They worked in shifts so that they could cover the area twenty-four hours a day.

Natalie felt compelled to succeed with honours on this task. She would not let anyone, or anything to stand in the way of demonstrating to Moscow her total and ruthless competence. She excelled in her intelligence tradecraft as well as in her more natural spy talent of nurturing senior political and Whitehall figures, and listening to them reveal their secrets. She was an accomplished lone operator, but for now, she had to rely on a team of seasoned Russian SVR agents to undertake the surveillance operation to find Melissa, and ultimately, Alfie and his files.

Natalie closed her laptop and walked outside the hotel, pausing at the double glass doors at the entrance to have a cigarette. It was a still and clear night. Checking who was around, she wrapped her shearling scarf around her neck, and turned a dark corner. A lone figure was sitting in the driver's seat of a blue Citroën vehicle, hidden behind a line of trees and in a lay-by off the main road.

'Anything?' Natalie asked, closing the car door.

'Nothing at all so far.'

'OK. Keep your men sharp tonight. The redhead was a tough bitch to crack,' Natalie said to Gregory. 'But now she's got us here I want you to gather as much information as possible on what they're doing.'

Natalie's SVR team had conducted a mock execution on Jane, administered electric-shock torture and subjected her to waterboarding. It was the chemical that had made her talk though. Jane had held out for a long time and didn't reveal anything about where Alfie was or what Sean was doing. She didn't know. But she did reveal the French location. Natalie had felt an almost orgasmic pleasure in seeing a female adversary suffer so badly, during which time Jane had revealed where she had been in France. The SVR team had taken Jane's laptops and phones and then trashed the safe house in Southwold. Jane's body was disposed of by the SVR agents as they sought to hamper the ensuing investigation by MI5. It was a good piece of work, Natalie thought. A good start. But what exactly was the British agent up to? And where were the files?

'Tomorrow will be our day,' Natalie said, passing Gregory a plan of the hotel. 'I want tracking devices on their vehicles, get the cyber team to trace their phone data and follow them if they're up and out of here early in the morning. I want to know what they're fucking well doing in this shithole.'

She watched Gregory nod, mindful that she had been assured by her masters that Gregory was a solid operator, although she harboured concerns about his abilities on the ground. His real name was Mikhail Trovich. He was the Second Secretary in the Political Section at the Russian Embassy in London and was operating under standard diplomatic cover. Gregory had four officers available to conduct mobile and foot surveillance once they had identified who Sean was. Not enough people, she found herself saying, not enough at all.

'What about getting into the rooms,' Gregory asked. 'I've got the kit in the boot. Listening devices and cameras.'

'Leave all that to me. Just make sure you get the surveillance done properly and find a suitable place to stay tomorrow away from the town. I'll get on with the real business of getting the information I need.'

Natalie stepped out of the car and grabbed the bag of tricks from the boot before making her way back to her hotel room. She kicked off her high heels and laid the devices out on the desk to the side of the long mirror: batteries, pinhole cameras, tiny bugs and a small box containing SP17. She felt exhilarated, despite the late hour.

An hour later she had tested all the equipment and took a moment to undress and slump onto the sofa, wearing only her purple underwear. She reached over for the wine she had poured. This will be my crowning glory, she mused, as she thought about her life as a sleeper agent. This was the one that would make her a star. If people did as they were told. And gave her what she wanted.

Natalie Merritt had been born Anna Katchalyna in the cosmopolitan city of Rostov-on-Don in September 1981. Her father, Andrey, was of Cossack heritage and had reared five well-to-do children. Natalie was his sixth and was the only child of his destined to become subsumed into the illegal programme, his enduring legacy to the Fatherland. To the West, he was a relatively unknown KGB general and he had sent Natalie at the age of nine to study in the Czech Republic, where she was fostered by a family with Canadian and Russian roots who were embarking on their own illegal careers. The family had emigrated to Canada under the Russian illegals programme in 1991, where they had built a backstory as a typical North American family and awaited instructions from superiors. Natalie was provided with the name of a deceased Canadian child and the beginnings of her 'legend' started to develop. She studied intensely in Ottawa and was eventually released from the care of her foster parents to attend St Andrew's University in Scotland, where she began her immersion in British life. Her father maintained a close eye on her progress via his brother, who worked within Directorate 'S'.

Natalie thrived on the chase and the crush, as she referred to them. That was her type of spycraft. The chase to befriend those right on the edge of executive government back home in London, and the crush to seal their utter infatuation with her, so that they continued to reveal their innermost secrets. She found that massage and touch were the best ways to relax her foes to get them to talk.

The sex was simply a means of getting them to keep returning. Her two pleasures in life were to extract national secrets for her masters at Directorate 'S', in return for which she was able to maintain a luxurious lifestyle, and to inflict pain and watch people in pain. On one occasion, she had nearly killed a British scientific officer from the Ministry of Defence through a series of sadomasochistic sexual acts that were nearly catastrophic for the man's sexuality. It had crushed him so much that his mental health was never the same again. He loved extreme bondage. She delivered pain. And she took it to its absolute limit because he had failed to supply material of any use to her. She secured the scientist with bondage ties, attached electrodes to his nipples and genitals and wired them up to their sex battery, as he had called it. She increased the current until he fell unconscious. She then discarded him with disdain.

Natalie caught herself standing in front of the long mirror in the hotel room with her third glass of wine, admiring her persona. She had put her heels back on. The bra had gone.

As she admired her pathological superiority, she picked up a syringe, pulled gently on the lugs and watched a jet of liquid shoot into the air.

She took the small bottle of unopened water, injected the SP17 serum into its base and plugged the hole with a dot of glue.

Everything was ready, for when the time was right.

Chapter 25

Côte Vermeille

Sean was up early, eager to talk to Jugsy who had finally agreed to travel to France and to meet him at the hotel for breakfast. He headed straight down to the pool at 7am and decided on a short twenty-minute swim before breakfast.

The pool was empty except for one woman who was doing gentle breaststroke, taking care not to get her hair wet. Sean became aware that this woman was looking at him as he walked around the side of the pool. He was conscious of his battle-scarred body, which annoyingly drew the eyes of people when he was bare-chested. Sean stepped into the pool as Natalie drew close to her last strokes. Sean smiled and very quietly said 'Good morning'. Natalie smiled back and emerged from the pool, walked up the shallow steps and headed over to the jacuzzi. Sean couldn't help admiring her shapely figure clad in a red bikini.

He finished his swim and quickly changed for breakfast. He made his way down to the terrace, where it was a morning worthy of sitting outside in the warm weather. He read *Le Monde* and looked up occasionally at the splendid views of the garden's lawns, whilst thinking carefully about the next stages of the plan. He had arranged to meet Liz later that morning at the gîte where the dogs were resting and enjoying plenty of playful fun with Billy Phish.

Jugsy arrived at 8.30am and Sean looked up to see him come bounding across the terrace with a cry of 'Mucker!' Sean grimaced at the less than discreet entrance Jugsy had made, as was his norm. Sean had known Jugsy for about eighteen years. Hawkeye, as he was also known, was a leading expert in imagery analysis, and covert terrorist surveillance from helicopters and drones.

Sean folded his paper, placing it on the table, and stood up to shake Jugsy's hand. 'Great to see you mate. Now settle down for Christ's sake and try to be a little inconspicuous eh?'

'No worries mucker, you know I can't help myself,' he chuckled.

'You're worse than Billy Phish's dogs when excited.'

'And just as bloody good if you don't mind. Now where's the coffee? Oh and, erm, my fee,' Jugsy joked. Sean smirked, shook his head and smiled broadly before sitting down, indicating for Jugsy to do the same.

Jugsy was in his late forties with swathes of grey hair, a thinning but noticeably radiant red face and a prominent nose. His lean, strong figure gave some indication of a fit man who had formerly achieved Special Forces glory with the Special Boat Service – but his active social life was beginning to take its toll.

They sat on the terrace and reminisced about the last few years and what they had both been up to since they had last met.

'Jugsy, this is a tricky op mate. I'll need your thoughts on reference points, so we can narrow the search down. And you can't mention this job to anyone. It's not officially sanctioned.' Jugsy took a sip of coffee as the sun rose above the hotel's treeline.

'It's official enough mate,' Jugsy said. 'I got a job number and a release note direct from MI5, so as far as my bosses know, it's official. They always know these jobs are heavily compartmentalised, so they will never hear the detail of the job.' Jugsy held his arms out wide, palms turned upwards. 'Use me as you want.'

Sean smiled with approval and quietly talked Jugsy through his plan, using cryptic speech to guard his words against prying ears on the terrace.

'I've brought my new boy's toy too. A nice, shiny, unmanned air vehicle. It's a fixed-wing, military-grade UAV fitted with imagery sensors that'll knock the socks off you mate. Slovenian technology and proper top drawer,' Jugsy said, grinning heavily.

'Well, we'll have a couple of hours up at the farm to discuss the search plan and how we can use your Gucci plane to hunt down what we are after. Once you've seen the full job you might baulk at it and say, no thanks, I'm off home.'

Jugsy's role and profession ensured he pretty much lived out of helicopters or was flying high-grade drones and UAVs. He was a typical old-school former Royal Marine: loud, gregarious and exceptionally non-politically correct. He used colourful, lucid language and had extreme views on all aspects of life. But he was also a bubbly, effervescent character who lit up the dullest of rooms. He was a well-known and well-loved icon in the intelligence community and had legendary status for getting the job done.

'What about Billy Phish's dogs then? What did they find?' Jugsy asked.

'They had a big hit in the cottage that Alfie had been using.'

'What, you mean a dead body?'

'Yep, and Foz hit on the blood too. Liz has confirmed this morning that it matches Alfie's blood group, and the DNA matches too. We think he was killed in the cottage and his body moved shortly after that.'

'Any idea who did it?'

'Not a clue at this stage. They tried to clean it all up but couldn't remove all the forensic traces. All we know is that they left in a car, with the body probably in the boot, and made their way up into the hills.'

'OK. So that's where I come in I guess?'

'Yep. We've only traced the car so far into the hills, but it gives us a starting point for the hunt.'

'Have you looked at possible burial sites?'

'Not in detail yet. We'll do that this afternoon and look at possible car-parking spots and work on the basis they wouldn't have carried the body too far. I want you to take a look from the air and see what ground markers might lead us into a smaller search area.'

Jugsy nodded. 'OK, let's get on with it then. Just like the old days eh?'

They relaxed and finished their breakfast. Sean made a few notes in his pad and scanned the terrace, which was now full of guests.

Natalie caught Sean's eye fleetingly and smiled, before returning to her laptop.

Five minutes later, Melissa joined Sean and Jugsy at the table.

Chapter 26

Languedoc-Roussillon

Sean, Melissa and Jugsy drove to Billy Phish's farmhouse. Sean had decided to take Melissa with him and noticed it had lessened her edginess by feeding her hunger to get involved. When they arrived, they were greeted by Billy Phish and Liz, who were sitting around the large wooden table in the kitchen which had by now become their office, covered with laptops and notebooks.

'Great to have you lot together again,' Sean announced. 'Normal fees apply and I've put fifty percent up-front, with final payments into your accounts when the job is done. And I know it doesn't need saying, but enhanced operational security applies right the way through this job, whether here or back in England.'

'Or Barbados for the posh buggers,' Jugsy chipped in, pointing at Billy Phish. His comments alleviated the nervous tension.

'OK, listen up. You all know each other and we all know how we operate. Let me introduce you to Melissa, who will be helping us on this job from here on in. She's an investigator too.'

Melissa looked nervous but smiled and said 'Hello'.

'And a big thanks to Liz who has cut her holiday short from across the pond.'

Sean rolled the maps out on the table and asked everyone to grab some tea and sit round them. 'Just a quick reminder too. This is a sensitive task, and I'm certain that other agencies are looking for Alfie. You all know the score – let's keep it tight and make sure we're thinking OPSEC on all elements of this job from this point onward.'

These were professional intelligence and forensic operators and he felt comforted by the knowledge that they knew the seriousness of it all, with OPSEC being paramount. Sean noticed that Melissa looked slightly bewildered by it all.

'OK everyone, settle down. I'm going to start the briefing with Liz's assessment first.'

Liz looked pensively at Sean as he stood up while everyone else sat, and then she began. 'Well, I've spent a long time at the cottage conducting a full forensic analysis with my portable equipment. I managed to find different types of soil on the carpet in Alfie's cottage, some fibres and even some pollen residue. The most revealing items though, seem to be the hairs.'

The team were leaning forward over the maps, listening intently to Liz's melodic Scottish accent. 'I hope you don't mind but I had to ask Larry the Italian to do some analysis too, and he's eager to find out what's happening.'

Liz paused, and the rest of the team simultaneously glanced at Sean to gauge his reaction. Sean scratched his stubble vigorously and threw a wry smile. 'You'll all be sad to hear Larry won't be coming out on this job but he's sending me his chemical analysis kit to use if we need it. Glad he's helped out on the analysis too Liz. That's fine.'

'Well he's the one who has helped on the hair analysis really. His supercomputers are able to data-mine the reference material so quickly nowadays, and he had the results to me within four hours.'

'OK Liz, what did you find?'

'Well, we've confirmed from DNA and blood that the body that was in the cottage was Alfie's. I've also managed to eliminate contamination from hairs that were left at the scene by Sean and Billy Phish. But I did find hairs that didn't belong to Alfie either. Curiously he didn't seem to have many visitors, and I'm making a bold call here, because the hairs we did find and analyse are more than likely those of his killers.' Liz paused and looked across to Sean.

'OK, good. But do go on. I can't reveal the location of where one of the killers may have travelled from, but the forensics are clear. You'd better explain Liz.'

Liz nodded. 'The chemical analysis of the hairs has shown us where the killers had recently been in the world. And they haven't travelled anywhere in the world apart from one location in the last year. Except here.'

Sean had spoken with Liz that morning to let her know what information he wanted the team to know, and which information he didn't want to release yet. The human hair analysis had identified someone who had been in the Missouri region of America in the last year. The use of Larry's chemical forensic database had shown exactly where this person had been during that time and was based upon what he had been eating and drinking. Modern-day chemical forensics could identify from a person's hair where they had been in the world based on the food they had eaten. Larry's chemical analysis was so good it even showed that the individual had drunk beer from a specific town in Missouri. There were no traces of food that had been eaten anywhere else in the world.

Liz then explained that some traces of soil, just tiny particles, had been left at the scene. She had also checked Alfie's shoes to see if any of his footwear matched the soil. It didn't. It had to have come from his killers.

'So, you see, it may be useful for us if we assume one of the killers wore the same shoes when he undertook his reconnaissance on the moors to find a suitable location to hide the body. That soil ended up in Alfie's hallway. Unbelievably, but luckily for us, the soil samples could only have come from a certain part of the Pyrenees. The map trace is here and shows the area the soil could have come from.'

Liz pushed the A3 piece of paper across the table. It showed a balloon-shaped shaded area right in the centre of the Languedoc hills.

'I then looked at some pollen particles. It was slightly more difficult to pinpoint where they were from, mainly because some of the traces could be from many areas of Southern France and Languedoc.' She paused to cough and clear her throat. 'Some of the peat particles I looked at came from a certain part of the Pyrenees, and a particularly precise location of about four to six square kilometres or so.'

The team could immediately see on her map the small area of the Pyrenees she was referring to. Sean enjoyed watching the team's reactions to this revelation. He knew that Liz's high-tech equipment and her databases on soils, pollens and grains could provide very precise geographic forensics based on decades of global research on the subject.

'None of this is perfect,' Sean said. 'And you can see some of the issues we have with confirming the analysis. But it gives us a great steer to begin searching these areas in earnest. It means I can use imagery analysis next before we target certain areas for Mike to have a go at. I'll use Larry's chemical equipment when we get a little closer, but for now, we'll all stay here and let Jugsy do his stuff.'

Sean had drawn a map showing the various overlays of the dogs' scent trail. This showed some large shaded bubbles of the soil and peat analyses and some circles he had previously drawn on the map indicating potential drop-off sites for vehicle access.

The map now showed they had closed in on a specific area of the Languedoc Pyrenees. It was still huge, but they were narrowing the search down using geo-forensic methods. They had gone from hundreds of square miles down to a few square miles and had identified specific areas of interest they could exploit further.

Liz returned to the UK that morning and Jugsy set off to launch his UAV with Billy Phish at a predetermined site high on the hills. That left Sean and Melissa alone at the farm. He decided a walk with Mike and Foz would help Melissa to adjust and relax before they sat down to chat again to try to recall the many conversations she had had with Alfie.

Jugsy returned with Billy Phish just after 3pm having collected the overhead imagery of the zones they had decided to check. Sean stood in the kitchen watching Jugsy set to work on four separate seventeen-inch laptops. Jugsy zoomed in on an area of his image and started to look at small tufts of peat and major geographical features. He labelled large granite rocks, horse tracks and the occasional small paths, as well as zooming in on potential burial sites. It was Jugsy's trained eye that would identify the crucial intelligence that Sean required. He started to look for any change in the terrain and for signs of shallow graves.

Sean left Jugsy alone for a couple of hours and returned to see the images that Jugsy had cropped and annotated with black letters to show the key marker points.

He showed Sean two major features that he had named. Target 1 was a small waterfall and was around ninety-five metres from the road. 'Looks like a great area that sits in a hollow, so they could easily dig without anyone seeing them,' Jugsy said. 'It would concern me though that the car would stick out and could be seen for miles around so I'm not sure I'd want that. It's quite easy to track your way back to the area after completing your initial recce to see where you'd bury the body though.'

'They must have recced where they were going to bury him first,' Sean said. 'These guys were experts. Have they got the right type of cover and reference points do you think?'

'The main reference points are the waterfall and this huge granite rock, Target 2. They could easily relocate themselves back to this location. I think when we get on the ground we could look for another marker from these points. You know, another distant object that's reasonably obvious so they can move from one point to the other.'

Sean nodded. He then pointed to another area further beyond the waterfall.

'What about these areas Jugsy?'

Jugsy looked at Billy Phish, with an expression suggesting they had both discussed this area. Billy Phish took his pencil from behind his ear before pointing accurately to what looked like small runnels, each running perpendicular to each other and up to the plateau. 'This is a remote area, especially the waterfall area. The runnels are about three metres high and quite narrow, so you could stand up in them and no one would see you at all if they were looking from a distance away. It could take less than twenty minutes to dig a body in there.'

Jugsy jumped back into the conversation. 'I have a lot of work to do tonight to see if we can find any obvious changes to the terrain or any ground that has sunk, possibly showing a shallow grave. I'll look for signs of digging and potential shallow graves by checking the old imagery against the new. I reckon it will take me a good six hours to try and find anything obvious. I'll get on the phone to our man Larry the geologist too. Just to ask his thoughts about the geology and body deposition indicators.'

Jugsy looked for Sean's approval of his thoughts and plan.

Sean tapped him on the shoulder, and stood. 'Great work. Get to it mate.' He picked up his map and lifted it in front of him. 'You know, we still have a vast area to search here. Each of these areas are huge. I think Mike will cover the ground fast to home us in. We'll get up there tomorrow at daybreak, while Jugsy continues his analysis here. It's time to let Mike loose.'

Billy Phish, Sean and Melissa would head to the Pyrenees as soon as the sun was up.

Chapter 27

The Pyrenees

It was drizzling, and the Pyrenean moor looked bleak, cold and mysterious. The mist was lying low, with sporadic pockets rising from the ground as the dreary first light began to break. Sean could smell the peat bog and he caught the lingering aroma of recent rain in every breath. He sensed this would be a long tiring day, and that it would be wet underfoot.

He and Melissa were up and out of the hotel by 5am. They joined Billy Phish and left the farm in his pickup truck with Mike and Foz at 5.25am. Sean only saw one other vehicle on the road at that time in the morning on their way to Target 1, high on the hills. The team were kitted out with small rucksacks, Thermos flasks and wet weather gear. They arrived at Target 1 at 5.50am.

Sean knew that the team's map analysis could only count for so much. There was no substitute for getting down and dirty on the ground. This was where he could really tune in his thoughts by getting into the minds of the killers. He would see the obvious reference points, the obvious terrain they would want to use to conceal a body and the best drop-off point to remain discreet whilst they conducted their burial. This was when he would get a feel for the case. When he was in the remote parts of the hills. Could he out-think the killers? Or were they smart enough to have concealed the body in a way that would defeat his techniques? He wouldn't know until he had spent some time on the moors and he was itching to start.

There were no fences to cross before getting onto the hills, just small undefined tracks leading off and down into the two shallow valleys. Billy Phish let Mike off the lead and shepherded him around the drop-off site, in case he picked up any scent immediately. Sean then looked at the natural fold of the terrain into the lower hills, where a stream branched off into two valleys. Mentally, a person would be drawn into taking this route he thought. Mike was revelling in this unexpected exercise. He ran crazily everywhere, most of the time thirty or forty metres away from Billy Phish. He darted into small peat recesses, smelt the ground vigorously, then looked up for 'dad' again, before scurrying off, head in the air, smelling the wafts of swirling wind to try and find what he had been trained to hunt down: a dead body. Sean marvelled at the grace and tenacity of this amazing canine in action as he searched for the scent of death.

Billy Phish steered Mike to where he wanted him to search but at times the dog was out of sight, hidden amongst the many varied high peat hillocks. Mike would always pop up though – all the time making sure dad was still there. He was like a small vulnerable child, happily playing away in the distance but wanting to have the comfort of a parent close by.

Sean could now see the waterfall and he meandered around the area looking for any natural features that might act as another location marker. He spotted a series of large rocks and a very distinctive runnel. He looked in the runnel and pulled at the peat recess to see how easy it would be to excavate and dig. The grassy tufts pulled away easily and he used his hands to dig a small hole. The peat was deep black and seeping with water. He then replaced the peat and tufts, which moulded themselves back into position, leaving no trace of their disturbance. This was a massive area to search and everywhere was too easy to dig and hide a body.

Mike ran and jumped around in the stream below the waterfall, enjoying a splash. There was no sign of any alerts or indications from him, he was just like a kid having fun, tail wagging wildly. Billy Phish moved him along the plateaux and up to the long runnels that Jugsy had indicated on the imagery about another sixty metres further on from the waterfall.

'These runnels are ideal,' Billy Phish mentioned to Sean. 'Especially as I can stand up in them and not be seen digging a body in from anywhere around here.'

Sean had hoped for a quick win from Mike, especially as this drop-off point would have been the best for the killers. A gloomy thought of failure came across his mind, but he kept his anxiety tucked away so that the others wouldn't sense it. He trusted his instinct and felt sure that one of the first four target areas he had marked would be the right one. He had twelve such areas to search and hoped it wouldn't take more than two or three of those.

The team were soaking wet with the incessant drizzle and covered in black wet peat from underfoot. They returned to the pickup for a break and for the tea and pastries that Billy Phish had picked up at the local bakery the day before. They chatted and relaxed, each of them enjoying the solitude of the wild Pyrenean hills. The sun began to peep through.

Sean's phone vibrated in his pocket. He glanced at the text sent on 'telegram', noticing it was from TABASCO – the codename for Samantha. The one she had chosen herself. He always smiled at that. He opened the page up and walked a few paces away from the vehicle.

'*Update/one eye on you/love you/call me.*' was the first line. 'Typical Sam,' Sean muttered. He opened his GCHQ app for voice calls and tapped the secure call button. The secure call was connected within seconds.

'Hello my lover,' Samantha said. 'Some good news and some not so good news.'

'I haven't got much time Sam, I'm out on the ground right now,' Sean answered. 'Go on. Send.'

'Well, One-Eyed Damon has been busy. I'll make this brief,' she said. 'The good news is he's tracked Big Bang Frazer down, put a tracking device on his vehicle and paid a few people off to provide the dirt on him.'

'Excellent. Keep going.'

'He's also going to set a few things up that you can use as collateral, and in the meantime, I'm in the process of doing a cyber phish on him.'

'Just what I want,' Sean said. 'You're ahead of me already.'

'I'm always, erm, on top of things as you know,' she said sassily. She mentioned how she would bait Frazer with an email that would trick him into clicking on a link in it – a cyber phish – which would then download a malicious software node direct into his computer.

Sean listened to her plan, which matched his. 'In which case, you'll know I want you to hack into all his emails and contacts, all his business dealings and every aspect of his financial transactions. We are going to nail this bloke hard to the mast for what he did to me.'

'Indeed,' Sam replied. 'Now, listen to this. One-Eyed Damon has left a 'marker' with him as you asked. Are you ready for this?'

'Go on,' Sean said pensively.

'Well, One-Eyed Damon rigged his house up in Surrey. He only went and rigged it up with army grenades and booby traps.'

'Fucking hell,' Sean said with a gasp.

'Yep. They were all dummy grenades and explosives, lined up in his windows for all to see, just to get an effect and put the shits up him. He'll know it was military and you're on to him. One-Eyed, erm, went a tad further too.'

'Go on.'

'He rigged the back garden metal gate to an electric transformer with 100 volts running through it. That's his normal route into the house apparently. Knocked the bloke clean up and back ten yards by all accounts, blowing the fuck out of him.'

'Jesus Christ,' Sean said. 'One-Eyed certainly took the marker to weapons-grade eh?'

'He did. Best bit is that the bloke was fully unconscious, taken off to hospital and the police took over eight hours to clear the bloody building!'

'A proper job then. Fair play. One-Eyed is OK right?'

'Oh yes, he's had a ball. Videoed the fucking lot, then walked down the street with his white stick past the coppers manning the cordon.'

'Top class,' Sean said. 'Give him the payment and get back to me when you've done the data mapping.'

'Love you,' she said in a whisper. 'Stay away from any tarts.'

Sean finished the call and saw a small black Citroën approaching the lay-by. He saw a waving hand appear out of the window, quickly followed by a cigarette being thrown to the ground. It was Jugsy.

Jugsy had worked through the night on his analysis and finished at 4am to grab a few hours sleep. He had then set off in his car and arrived at Target 2 just as the team were taking a break. He parked up and urged Sean to come and have a look at what he had found. Sean could see he was excited. Jugsy pulled his imagery out of a small brown briefcase to show Sean what he had analysed during the night.

'Looks to me like a sunken piece of ground. Could be a grave,' Jugsy said keenly. 'I found a similar one at Target 3 and also an area where there was significant change in the ground near here,' He was pointing to Target 3 again, which was an open plateau above a small copse.

'Well, let's go and have a look,' Sean said, glancing up to see Mike scuttling around the target area sniffing away, hunting for his treat. Mike was soaking wet but loving his extended time in the outdoors. The area was full of small valleys, and a high-topped plateau dominated the area some fifty metres away that had not been visible from the track. It was here that they looked at Jugsy's sunken grass. It was probably too open to dig a body in the peat there – and Sean wasn't convinced it would reveal anything. It was a curious feature nonetheless. Billy Phish used his metal rod to probe some vapour holes into the sunken area and about two feet down. It did look like a shallow grave. Mike then had a sniff. Nothing. Not a thing. Jugsy used his bare hands to prise open the turf and used a small trowel to probe further. Nothing. It was a very curious shape but just a sunken piece of ground.

The weather had improved but large clouds were moving briskly across the sky, allowing sudden bursts of the sun followed by the occasional shower as the wind swirled high above them. Mike continued searching across the wide expanse of the Pyrenean moors and Jugsy investigated other markers they had identified from his photography. It was 5.25pm and Sean could see the whole team were exhausted. They began the long walk back to the trucks, Melissa occasionally slipping on the grassy hillocks. Sean felt gloomy, but occasionally smiled at the escapades of One-Eyed Damon.

'How confident are you that we can find Alfie then?' Melissa asked, as they trudged across the dank moor.

'I don't quite know at the moment. All I know is, if this team can't find him, no one ever will.'

'And what do we do then?' she asked.

'Well it'll be game over for me I can assure you. I'll be shafted again but hopefully you'll get back to some sort of normality.'

'I don't think normality will ever come back my way again after this,' Melissa calmly said. 'But why don't I use my police contact? She might be able to help in some way.'

'How?' Sean asked, head down into the breeze, tramping faster now as the vehicles came into sight.

'Well, she blew the whistle on the Met Police some years ago. She has some great contacts and we could use her to drip-feed some of the more juicy and corrupt stories Alfie discovered, without revealing ourselves as the source.'

'Great idea. But my job isn't about that,' Sean said dourly, not being keen to have such discussions until he had found the files.

Melissa retorted. 'The way I see it Sean is that I owe Alfie. And I want to help him get some recognition now his life has been taken from him. Surely you can understand that?'

'I know. It's not quite that simple though. When we have something tangible to look at, I'll decide what we do next, so you'll need to trust me on that for the moment. My bosses have only one aim and that's to stop something getting out. But I don't know yet exactly what that is. They don't really care about you and me, but I do care about making sure we do the right bloody thing for both us and Alfie.'

'Thanks. I can see you know what you're doing but do please remember I'm good at what I do too.'

Sean glanced across at her face, hidden now below her hood, which was dripping with rainwater. She was appealing to him and she was genuine. He looked at the peat bog stretching ahead of them and thought a little about how indeed Melissa could help.

'So, what will you do when this is all over Sean? Will you stay in the service?'

Sean stopped, adjusted his rucksack and took a drink of water from his CamelBak drinking system. He turned to look at Melissa, noticing her dishevelled hair and pale face without make-up. She was breathing hard but her eyes were mesmerising. Sean smiled, knowing full well she was tugging his emotions again.

'I'm out of the service now Melissa and there's no going back. But they've given me a lifeline here and I'm going to bloody well take it. I'll probably move overseas and set up a small art business somewhere – or just disappear.'

'Good,' she replied. 'Let's get this done properly and get the bad apples shafted at the same time.'

'If I don't get to these files it's me who'll be shafted hard. So, you need to trust me when I say we don't talk to anyone.'

'Bit bolshie today aren't you?' Melissa teased with a smile.

Sean sighed. 'Bolshie works with you, suggestion doesn't.' He looked for her reaction.

She smiled cockily. 'As you wish, but when you need some proper investigative skills let me know.'

Sean walked by her side in silence as they headed for the car, and then he stopped for a while. He pulled out his Thermos and poured coffee.

'Actually, you could do a bit of work for me Melissa, with your copper friend in the Met Police.'

'Go on. What?'

'There's one other bastard I need to see to before I retire and get back to painting pictures. He's the man who caused me to be here now and nearly had me killed.'

'At last. Something meaty I can get working on.'

'I've got a couple of people working on it for me, but your police contact, is she open to doing the right thing? Or is she a yes-woman?'

'Nope. She's dynamite, a real maverick in the Force. She forced through the exposure of child abuse rings when many were trying to cover it up. She's got balls. And, what's more, she's still a mole for the Investigative Bureau on the inner goings-on within the Force. She'll give me access to archives I would need to check.'

'Good. I'll get you some secure comms to connect to her. Can you find out everything we have on this man, his connections within the establishment and government circles? He was a copper for a short while then turned into an international crook and murderer. Somehow he managed to get loads of government contracts in Iraq and Afghanistan and I can't fathom out why. He must be doing something shifty with people high up.'

'OK. I'll get onto it. What exactly did he do to you then?'

'Killed me. For a short while at least.' Sometimes Sean knew he had to give a little and open up. This was one such occasion.

'Sean, I just wanted to say something to you.'

'Go on.'

Melissa looked down slightly and grabbed her plastic mug. 'I'm really grateful for you looking after me, you know that right?'

'Yes of course. You just show it differently. I can see that.' Sean handed her a chocolate bar and stood up.

'Thanks. I do. But I feel really safe with you. I know now how dangerous this is, and you've been very kind to me. I like that.'

Sean looked at her. She was drenched. Her eyes looked up at his and she seemed tearful. The tough exterior was seeping an emotion, revealing Melissa's softer side.

Just as Sean was about to speak, Billy Phish appeared over the small crest. He took off his rucksack and sat on its edge. Sean poured him a coffee, throwing in six sugar lumps.

'Not looking too good is it?' Sean said. 'I was convinced this was the best site for the killers to get to.'

'Fear not, it's early days right now. You're in a good position mate, so don't give up on us just yet. I still reckon we'll find the body. Your boss needs to trust you on this and he has no choice but to sit tight and wait until you get the answers. Unless of course he's running another concurrent operation – an official one.'

Sean wondered about this. 'I'm not sure but I do know they'll cover up Alfie's disappearance and keep it low profile and say nothing more than him being AWOL. But I suspect someone else is also at play here. Everything points to an American agent having killed Alfie. The analysis Liz gave me showed that one of his killers had been in the United States for a long time before coming over to France.'

Billy Phish looked thoughtful and retreated into humour.

'You see, I was right mate. I knew the Yanks were involved somewhere along the line.'

Sean took a last swig of his coffee, put his Thermos flask away and pulled his rucksack over one shoulder. 'It doesn't quite make sense to me though Billy. Why would they need to kill him? It was the files they were after and they probably haven't found them yet unless they are hacking into all sorts of accounts, fishing for where he left them. Maybe Alfie talked and now they have them anyway? Or Alfie was bribing someone, and they've just had him killed for the hell of it? Sean turned to start walking. 'Plenty to find out yet mate.'

Billy Phish followed, right on his shoulder, with Melissa listening to the exchange eagerly.

Billy Fish raised his voice, so Sean could hear him in the wind. 'On the other hand, I'd have thought governments would be getting pretty pissed off with all the embarrassment of these whistle-blowers popping up every ten minutes and exposing new state secrets.'

'Go on.'

'So, what I find odd is that Alfie was a careful and competent hand. It makes you wonder what sticky hands, our lot in MI5 and MI6, have been up to here. And what exactly did Alfie uncover? It could be pretty potent stuff.'

Sean's pace increased, his thoughts murmuring at him, as he walked doggedly in the grim conditions with Billy Phish's voice over his shoulder. Something didn't seem right.

Sean continued to the third site and headed straight for the rocky outcrop that Jugsy had indicated on the imagery. This was an obvious location marker and they looked for others such as smaller rocks, distinctive bushes or distinctive natural features such as hollows or even tiny ground scarps. Sean knew that the killers would have tested how easy it was to dig the ground where they had planned to bury Alfie. They would then have tested that they could return to that site, having timed how long it would have taken to dig the hole.

'There's one other consideration we need to be sharp about,' Sean said to Billy Phish.

'I know exactly what you're gonna say.'

'Go on, what?'

'There's every chance the Yanks will return to the body once they get an inkling they have missed something.'

'Exactly right. We need to stay sharp. Keep your eyes out whilst we're on the hills and don't mention this to anyone.'

Sean moved on towards the vehicles, very conscious that there were probably a few nations in play in this deadly game, and he was in the cross hairs. He continued to think through his options as he watched little Mike running around ahead of him. Mike seemed reinvigorated from his little reward and ran around the hills, stopping occasionally, moving his head and with his tail wagging like crazy. But yet again, he did not hit. The team had covered considerable ground during the day but it was now approaching 7pm.

It had been a long day and Sean felt calloused and weary. They had covered dozens of kilometres but found nothing.

Chapter 28

Port-Vendres

Sean had a fitful night. He had been ruminating in his semi-conscious state and awoke with a curious thought still burning. He wondered why the hell Alfie had written his own obituary. It suddenly dawned on him that finding the hidden Photobucket account hadn't been a difficult part of the job, but what was difficult was finding a clue as to where he had hidden the secret files.

He had managed to extract a significant piece of information from the hidden depths of Melissa's memory, but needed to find the body and clothing to verify that. Had he missed a more obvious clue in what he had seen in the Photobucket account? Was Alfie so egocentric and arrogant that he wanted his own obituary published after he had exposed to the world all the secrets he wanted to disclose? Or was there a clue in the obituary? Was there a coded message contained within it? He kicked himself for so easily forgetting about the obituary and decided he needed a cryptologist from GCHQ to have a look at it. He contacted Samantha to arrange the detail before heading for the moors to continue the search.

Sean, Billy Phish, Melissa and Jugsy arrived at Target 4, which was closer to where the scent dogs had lost the trail. Mike worked his way around the saddle and outcrops, but although loving the exercise, he did not hit.

They sat on a small knoll and Sean reached for his map. He looked carefully at all the circles he had drawn on it and wondered if any of his assessments were wrong. 'But the scent dogs and the soil analysis led me to this area,' he reminded himself. His doubt transformed into positive faith in his instincts. Courage in his own conviction was needed. He finished his sandwich and coffee and led the team to Target 6, which was closer than Target 5.

This site had a vehicle lay-by on a narrow road and, surprisingly, gave Sean a mobile-phone signal. Sitting in the pickup truck alone, he decided to speak to Jack, who answered after a lengthy delay.

'Jack, I've found something on the hills. It's only a tiny cache of stuff but I need some documentation analysed by a cryptography expert from The Doughnut in Cheltenham. I've asked Samantha to get onto it.'

'That's fine,' Jack confirmed. 'You think he's been using steganography as part of the trail then?'

'Almost certainly. He probably had a number of methods in play.'

Sean explained to Jack that it was a breakthrough, enough to keep Dominic happy, and that Alfie may have hidden more caches, which might lead to something. Sean was careful to ensure he had enough information to keep Dominic satisfied that progress was being made, but also that he could subtly change that information if required in order to buy himself time.

'I need to task him directly Jack, as this could be important and link in with what I've found so far and what I'm now looking for.'

'OK Sean. I'm happy to go with that and I'll work on getting a formal tasking note out to them today. We need a result quickly though so don't hold back or elongate this where it's not needed. Also, don't forget I've got Jane back here on standby to escort Melissa home whenever you need.'

Sean managed to keep Jack and Dominic onside whilst keeping the information he had found very close to his chest. He didn't trust anyone and wanted to solve this puzzle himself before deciding which bits of information to give to his masters. He wiped the condensation from the nearside window, peered out at the high Pyrenean mountains, which twinkled with ice through the clouds, and continued to explain his thoughts to Jack. 'It might be that Alfie has left a purposeful cryptic trail to follow. It seems that way to me at the moment, so I'll keep following the clues.'

'No problem,' Jack said. 'Just be aware that there are some nervous people back here in the centre of this storm, so we need to know as soon as anyone else comes on the radar trying to follow any clues. It must be us that wins this prize Sean. For you, and I.'

That was a curious thing to say, Sean thought. Jack sounded calm but tenacious, reminding him in veiled speech of the need for success and how his future life may depend on it. Sean knew that Jack wouldn't be completely fooled by his charade, but for now it seemed he was content to keep allowing Sean to progress unimpeded.

Sean followed Jugsy down a steep bank and over a small ditch into a secluded valley. The ground was covered with bracken and large clumps of peat, making it awkward to walk without twisting an ankle. Jugsy steered the team to a valley that traversed leftwards and continued curving below a concave hill. Sean remembered this area from the aerial imagery. It was the one that Jugsy had explained to him had five good peat runnels and some interesting features on the hillside worthy of a good inspection. An area that was ideal for the killers to dig without being seen.

Sean watched Mike scarper up the concave hill, with Billy Phish busting a gut to stay with him. Sean wandered slowly to the top of the hill, looked up at the peak bog stretching ahead of him and was shocked to see Mike going absolutely crazy.

He was running around sniffing at four or five places within a ten-metre area and was barking wildly at his dad. He got his dad's attention and then moved to the next place and barked uncontrollably again, each time turning and barking furiously at Billy Phish.

'Fucking hell,' Jugsy shouted. Everyone looked at each other, bedazzled.

'He's only gone and done it mate,' Jugsy shouted ecstatically. He was pointing to where Mike was going crazy. Melissa stood still, stunned, and not knowing what would come next. Billy Phish was his calm gruff self and went straight into a series of double-checks with Mike before he would reward him.

'Sensational,' Sean said, rushing up to Billy Phish, relieved at last to get a result. Sean was panting heavily now, caked in ankle-high bog and spiked with a surge of adrenalin as he sensed a breakthrough. He watched Billy Phish move Mike around the peat to try and home in on the specific site of the scent. But Mike kept indicating at all four areas situated closely together.

'Looks like he's found a scent which is travelling around in the air passages,' Billy Phish explained as he rewarded Mike.

Sean gave Mike a few pats on the head and stroked his back. 'What an amazing dog you are.' He looked at the ground where Mike had hit. The scent spot was in a shallow dip on the crest of the hill but, worryingly, was an area that could be observed from quite some distance away. Nonetheless, this was a major breakthrough. A major find. Sean had confidence that a body was buried here – somewhere.

Billy Phish probed the ground with his extendable metal rod to release more vapour trails and Mike did his stuff all over again. They didn't have spades but Jugsy used a small trowel to start digging. It was pure peat underneath the grass and there was no real sign of any ground disturbance to concern Sean. There were also quite a few gaping holes in the peat suggesting small tunnels like a series of rabbit warrens.

After thirty minutes checking the potential burial site, Sean decided it needed a proper dig. He would return with spades later in the day. But, before that, he insisted on finishing the pre-planned route to check the entire area. Mike was bouncing around on the terrain like a jack in the box, happy and playful after his success. Billy Phish steered him over the back end of the hill and then turned right into the valley. Sean was worried though. 'Why has he hit, but found no body?' he murmured. The adrenalin seeped deep into his veins as he laboured those thoughts. He felt the gooseflesh on his neck.

Sean noticed Jugsy and Billy Phish were wearing the biggest of smiles, chirping away to each other as they finally, after so long, had something tangible to work on. When they entered the low valley, Mike went crazy again. He hit again. He started barking incessantly and stood rigid next to a small flow of water coming off the hill and into the tiny stream. The peace and solitude of the area were broken as Mike barked relentlessly.

'What the hell?' exclaimed Jugsy. 'What's going on now? This is bizarre. Has he found another body or what?' Sean was speechless. Mike was going crazy and Billy Phish moved him around again to try and determine the primary area of the scent, all the time filming the activity with his chest-mounted video camera. Mike remained in the same area, barking furiously. Sean could see it was the far side of a tiny stream by a pocket of peat next to some small rocks housed in the cascade of water coming off the shallow hill. Sean listened to the gentle torrent of water rupturing as it broke over the rocks, and only Mike, barking wildly, dimmed the sound of its fall.

'I think there are pockets of air moving through the aerations in the peat,' Billy Phish said to Sean. He lit his pipe as he always did when he was nervous. 'This isn't going to be as easy as we thought. I think the air is moving from the top of the hill to the bottom and vice versa. We have some digging to do my boy.'

'Bloody typical,' Sean said. 'Well, at least we've narrowed it down quite a bit. This is one hell of a result Billy. Well done.'

Sean called the team together in a huddle. 'Right, let's work the entire area and see if Mike hits again. This is going to be a long day guys,' he said fervently. He was exhilarated knowing they had homed in on Alfie's burial site, or at least the rough area. It was still a huge area to search in detail, but Sean had planned for that.

Billy Phish moved them all further into the valley, with Mike leading about twenty metres ahead. The shallow stream curved gently to the right where the peat runnels cut into the hillside. The drizzle had stopped but it was still a grey, bleak morning.

Mike hit again as he went halfway up the second runnel. He was barking wildly and stood stock-still as he picked up the scent inside one of the folds of the runnel banks. Billy Phish looked at Sean, and Sean looked at Billy Phish. Neither spoke.

Sean eventually broke the silence. 'It's almost as if Mike has triangulated a large area with all these hits. It's quite strange to see him hitting everywhere.'

'Totally,' Billy Phish answered quietly, composing his mind before explaining his thoughts. 'And I'll tell you this for nothing, this could turn into a right mess. It could be very tricky to solve –

and very time-consuming.' Billy Phish grumbled in his typically dour Yorkshire way, but Sean could tell that, under his impassive face, Billy Phish was chuffed to bits with Mike.

Sean watched Billy Phish put his spectacles on to look at the map. He was puffing heavily on his pipe, which had now gone out. 'I'll look at the markers and see what kind of route the bastards may have had in their mind to follow back to this burial site. This is a great site and my money is on the runnel.'

Sean nodded. 'We can start digging after we've completed this last recce,' he said. 'Let's get it marked up on the map. I'll need to use the chemical kit now to see if that helps.' He now had three potential body deposition sites. But he knew he could have an even larger site to search if each area didn't give him a quick result. It was confusing but stimulating at the same time.

They returned to the vehicle and had a twenty-minute lunch break before returning to the sites with spades, ready to dig. It seemed to be the ideal site, with good markers to lead the killers back to an area they may have tested for digging, and it provided them with great cover whilst they dug.

Jugsy started the dig and Melissa and Sean helped place the cut peat neatly to one side. It was easy digging, but very wet as Jugsy dug deeper into the bank. The peat then became soggy and crumbled at his feet the more he dug.

The sun broke through the clouds and Sean spotted a couple of walkers high up on another hill adjacent to where they were operating. He was perched above the bank, satisfied that no one would be able to see into the runnel and spot Billy Phish digging. The fractured black peat now smelt like rotten eggs. Mike indicated and barked again at the area central to the entire hole and Sean walked down the incline to inspect the dig. He could see the pockets of air in the peat, almost like an Aero chocolate bar, and deduced that such air gaps probably went deep into the hillside. There was no body. The dig had revealed nothing. He looked at the team, seeing the disappointment etched on their faces.

It was late in the afternoon and Sean wanted to set up another piece of forensic work. There was no other way than to try and zoom into the exact burial site using different forensic techniques.

He asked Jugsy to return to the vehicle and collect the chemical equipment, which he could use to try to identify the exact area of the hillside where Alfie was buried. Jugsy obliged.

Sean and Melissa spent forty minutes placing the small plastic vials in the ground, pushing them deep under the wet grass and peat. Sean placed them strategically at points that he knew would easily collect the water he wanted from the many surfaces of the hills and valleys.

'What are these for then?' Melissa asked, watching as he placed one directly under a crevice on the eastern bank of the hill. Sean looked round from his kneeling position and beckoned her to look at how he had placed it.

'The idea is that we can collect some of the water running off the hillside to analyse the chemicals. The water will make its way down overnight and seep into these sunken crevices, dripping small drops into the vials. I can then analyse whether anything that is dead is making its way into the fabric of the hillside. It might help us work out which side of the hill he is on and which slope.'

'Fascinating stuff,' Melissa said coyly. 'I love how you do this work.' Sean stood and felt Melissa grab his shoulders as she tiptoed to kiss him on the lips. He sensed the moment of her first real affection for him but turned swiftly to avoid it, knowing full well she would be affronted. Like most of his emotions, he placed that one in a drawer in his mind and closed it shut for the time being. He was intensely focused on the job in hand.

By the time Sean and Melissa returned to the farm that night, the rest of the team had eaten and were merrily chatting away with the open fire roaring as the chilly spring night wore on. They left their equipment and bade farewell to the team, returning to the hotel late.

Sean accompanied Melissa to her room, where he caught a final sad glance from her. He then made his way to his room further down the corridor. He slipped the swipe card into the door, expecting the light to turn green, but it didn't. He tried twice more and cursed under his breath. He then made his way down to reception to explain that his card wasn't working.

The receptionist issued Sean with a new key card and he went back upstairs. He knew straight away that someone had been in his room. He checked the fibres he had left covering the set of drawers next to the bed – sure enough they had moved. Someone was onto him. He started searching for any secreted bugs or covert cameras using a small hand-held detector. He found a covert camera and two bugs carefully concealed in the room, including one in the fabric of the high headboard.

Finally, he took the shower he wanted and then sat with his thoughts on the double bed. He grabbed the small bottle of water from the side table.

Chapter 29

Port-Vendres

Natalie's frustrations and impatience had now become insidious, but she had a new plan. Her powerful and influential resolve meant she knew she had Gregory where she wanted him and that he would do whatever she wanted.

'I don't care what your normal procedures are on these tasks Gregory – it's a fucking shambles and won't work.'

She knew he wouldn't disagree, and it was now time to get him to bend his operational rules.

'You lot haven't been able to maintain surveillance on the farm, you don't know what's happening there, who has been coming and going and you can't follow more than one vehicle at a time – so we're blind to what the fuck they are doing.'

Natalie stood and looked out of the window into the moonlit gardens. She clutched her black hair and put it in a ponytail, adjusting it using the reflection. She was incensed. She was right and always right, and no one would stand in her way of doing things the way she wanted them to be done – even if she didn't have experience of hard-core surveillance operations. She poured herself a glass of vodka and took her Arcus 94C high-power pistol from her bag. She loved the feel of the Bulgarian weapon in her hand and it eased her tensions when she gripped the walnut handle firmly.

'We don't have the resources I need,' Gregory said.

'Bullshit. You're responsible for this and, in the words of the British, you need to get a fucking grip of it.'

'I need better men to get this done properly.'

'Properly? I'll give you fucking properly,' she said, raising the weapon. Solid and beautiful, she stroked the smooth stainless-steel barrel, feeling an urge to fire the first of its thirteen-shot capacity right into Gregory's head. Natalie turned and walked towards Gregory, releasing the safety catch. 'I'm dealing with a bunch of fuckwits and you need to get sharp quickly.'

'We are sharp, and I'm not convinced we can do anything more than what we are doing. We're all well trained in this you know.'

Natalie began to fume. 'You idiots haven't given me anything so far, I've had to do it all myself. I really ought to pump a bullet into you right now and get someone in who can do a better job of this for me.'

'We haven't had anything to go on though.'

Natalie took one stride and smashed the weapon into Gregory's head with a sharp backhand swipe. Her ring cut his cheek with a sharp slice. Blood began to pour down his face.

'Don't make me fucking angry ever again,' she growled.

Gregory held his hand against his cheek, lurching forward for the tissues on the table.

'It's only a matter of time before Sean finds out that his red-haired woman in Southwold went missing,' she said, turning away. 'I can't keep up the charade of pretending I'm her on the phone. Someone will find out and then we'll be fucked. He'll simply pull out and get away,' she said with increasing rage.

Natalie had been answering Jack's texts to Jane – stringing him along and deceiving him into thinking Jane was still alive. She also had Jane's passwords for her laptops, the codes to her phones, and had sent messages and emails as if it was actually Jane sending them.

'We have to be bold now – if we aren't bold and daring, we'll lose everything,' Natalie stressed, standing above Gregory. 'You will now do everything I say – no fucking questions.'

Gregory nodded.

Natalie knew her next moves were vital to give her the upper hand on Sean. And she would force Gregory to comply.

Chapter 30

Port-Vendres

Sean was up early and decided to forgo the swim that he had promised himself. Instead, he stretched to warm his muscles and then banged out forty-five press-ups without interruption. He followed this with a series of sit-ups, showered, went straight to the breakfast room and sat in the far corner waiting for the others.

He noticed a brunette woman dressed in a white blouse, blue tailored skirt and blue high heels wander over to his table. She smiled at him. Sean recognised her as the woman he had seen in the swimming pool. Natalie asked if she could sit down, at the same time not waiting for an answer. She crossed her legs, Sean noticing the slash of her thigh.

'Hi, I'm Natalie,' she said piercingly. 'I've seen you around here over the last couple of days. I thought I'd come and introduce myself.' She smiled, and Sean sensed an air of supremacy as well as her hugely attractive disposition. He was curious at such an approach and wondered what was coming next. He gazed at her face.

'Meet me in my room in thirty minutes,' Natalie instructed. 'It's number 247 on the second floor. I have something that might interest you.' She stood up and, as she began to leave, placed a small piece of paper on the table with a photo on it. It was a photo of Melissa with Gregory – and a morning paper with the date clearly shown. They had taken Melissa and she looked as if she'd been drugged. She looked close to unconsciousness.

'Fuck, fuck, fuck,' Sean thought. He crumpled the paper and clenched his fists under the table, searing with inner rage.

At that moment he felt as though he'd botched every decision in the previous few years, and he was not overly confident that he could put this one right. His mind went into overdrive and he felt sick in his stomach. He was devastated. 'What a fucking mess,' he mumbled, continuing his inner rage. He wondered what Melissa's fate would be.

He composed his mind quickly, went into the garden and walked down to the flower beds. He felt numb. His trauma was fierce. His hands were shaking. How had he let himself turn his back and fail to secure her?

He texted Jugsy and told him to leave for the farm without him. He would catch them up.

Chapter 31

Pall Mall, London

Jack sat next to Dominic for lunch with an elderly gentleman in the Carlton Club in St James's. They occupied a quiet corner of the exquisite Wellington dining room, very content with the discreet manner of the waiters, who were impeccable in their service.

The gentleman was a hugely popular Member of Parliament and a very powerful figure in the Cabinet.

Dominic chose claret for lunch, with a dessert wine for later. Jack knew Dominic expected high standards of service and the waiters' distant vigilance meant that they were ready to give him dedicated service. Jack had primed the waiters about this highly important lunch, letting them know that Dominic expected people to serve him and serve him well.

Jack sat quietly, observing how Dominic would handle this delicate gathering.

'Things are moving along nicely sir,' Dominic began. 'I expect we can put this unhelpful issue to bed quite soon.'

'Splendid. I knew you would understand the commotion Dominic. Which of course is a damned unwelcome distraction. Do please tell me more.'

'Jack, why don't you explain to the Minister what we have so far?'

'Well sir, the entire operation is under control at this stage,' Jack said looking at the Minister. 'The police investigation has been shaped as we want it to be, and the media are conforming nicely. We have traced where the intelligence officer has been and I'm very confident we will find the files quite soon.'

'Very good. I'm grateful for your excellent efforts. What about government circles?' the Minister asked.

'Dominic has covered the internal avenues I believe,' Jack answered glancing over to Dominic.

Jack knew that Dominic was the gatekeeper for government circles on everything to do with national security. So he fed him occasional disinformation knowing Dominic would push it out to wider circles. Dominic had his finger on everything that was briefed to the Cabinet Office, Number 10 and the Home Office. Jack revelled in the fact that he was mastering each strand of critical intelligence brought to Dominic and his ministers, and relished the fact that each sought Dominic's judgement first before trusting their civil service mandarins or intelligence chiefs. Intelligence chiefs were not to be trusted after the debacle of the Iraq dossier some years previous. But Jack was also savvy enough to know that Dominic also needed his own powerful allies too – especially if he was ever to achieve his life's ambition of becoming Chief of the Secret Intelligence Service.

Dominic smiled at Jack before assuring the Minister. 'Everything's currently fine internally and you have my word that I'll tidy this all up in a timely fashion.'

'Good. This is very, very messy for me Dominic,' the elderly gentleman said. 'It needs fixing, or I lose a lifetime's reputation. I'll personally make sure you are both rewarded for this. And Dominic, I'll make sure you're lined up for Chief of Service if this awful thing is made to go away.'

Jack knew that the elderly gentleman was hugely popular with the public, and was seen as a man of the people, and someone with great character and humour. He had the ear of many equally powerful figures in the government and had spent his lifetime generating a first-class reputation as being a shrewd politician, adept at the bluffs and deceptions of his world, and a master of political tactics that could sway prime ministers and lobbyists alike. His influence meant that he was seen as the alternative powerhouse to Number 10 and his chums followed his lead with utter loyalty. He carried huge sway in the murky workings of politics and was masterful at smear campaigns against his detractors. He also had a closely entwined team who magnified his appeal to the public using a very carefully devised publicity campaign.

'It really was a long time ago you know, and no one would ever understand, Dominic. I was a young man then...,' the Minister said.

Dominic used his napkin to wipe his mouth. 'So far as I can tell, this wayward intelligence officer has left a very difficult trail to follow,' Dominic suggested. 'The police are nowhere near finding him, but Jack here has uncovered a full set of clues. I don't think any other agencies are onto what we are doing but do let me know if you hear any whispers emanating from your people in the services.'

The minister approved. 'It's only one file you need to find gentlemen. One file that will create utter mayhem in mine, and other people's worlds. Just find the file that incriminates me – and all will be well for you Dominic.'

Jack saw the anxiety on the Minister's face, knowing him to be a Russian spy. He could see that fear was rooted in every vein of his body.

Chapter 32

Port-Vendres

Sean had no idea who had kidnapped Melissa, nor which agency was on his trail. His mind was thrown into a maelstrom as he fought to make sense of it all. Melissa's life was in critical danger, and he was devastated by that. And who was this woman with the posh British accent?

'Get probing amongst your sources in MI5 and 6,' Sean demanded on his call to Jack. 'Any idea who's onto me?'

'None at all Sean. I've tasked Swartz and an SAS team to fly out this afternoon to try and find her. I've also scrambled all our signals intelligence teams and I'll bring to bear all the power we need through Dominic. Don't worry, we're primed and will chase this down quickly.'

Jack reminded Sean that finding the files, and that one in particular, was vital. He didn't need to encourage Sean to spin a tale to buy him time with the kidnappers – that was obvious to both of them. They had played this game long enough to know the dark world of cross and double-cross. Jack explained he would get Swartz on the case immediately to find Melissa, but that Sean must concentrate on getting the file.

They both agreed the only rational reason for taking Melissa was to carry out an extortion operation on Sean. They wanted something, and Sean had it. Or so they thought. Melissa would doubtless be interrogated but she was the collateral to make Sean hand over what they wanted, which was most probably the elusive and incriminating mole file.

Sean knocked on room 247. He calmed himself for the encounter. He buried his disdain and hatred. Tamped them down, hid them somewhere inside, in a drawer he could close. Regulating and surviving came as second nature to him.

Natalie opened the door. 'Come on in Sean,' she said. 'We have plenty to discuss.'

Sean noticed that Natalie had changed and was now wearing a red dress cut above the knee, black high heels and her hair up in a bun. She ushered him to a round table next to the window and offered him some bottled water, which he declined. Natalie sat down opposite Sean and began.

'We both know there is an easy way out and a hard way out,' she said. 'And you know I need to get the files that Alfie has hidden somewhere. I'm sure we can come to some sort of arrangement you know.'

Sean was still fuming inside. His face was tense, but he controlled his anger with professional calm.

'I'm not exactly sure who you're working for,' Sean began. 'But Melissa is hardly the key to all this you know. You'll be very aware that I don't need her to do my job, but I'll happily listen to your proposal.' Sean kept his resolve, determined more than ever to manage this conundrum in a number of ways.

'That may be so Sean, but it's so obvious to me you have feelings for Melissa. You can have her back totally unharmed if you help me get what I need. I'm sure there is a way it can work for both of us.'

'OK, and what might that be then?'

'We both have our own motivations here – so we just need to find a common way. We probably just need to talk it through and I'm sure you know it makes sense at this stage to work with me rather than against.'

Sean felt Natalie's flirtatiousness and the sly grin on her face hardly cloaked her ruthlessness. He sensed her narcissistic ways immediately, but also wondered how much she knew. And he wanted to extract that from her. 'OK, let's talk. What do you know so far?' Sean said. 'And what do you want?'

Natalie sat back in the dining chair and crossed her legs. 'Well I know that you are not flavour of the month in the corridors of Whitehall. Nor indeed anywhere else in your beloved ministry, never mind box or 6,' Natalie teased. 'I suspect you've been deceived by them a little, and so your motivation here is to find an exit strategy. I can help you with that.'

'You seem to know me rather well.'

'I think so, yes. You don't really care any more about protecting these morally corrupt bastards, and I don't care for them either. I simply want the information Alfie held and was going to disclose to the world. I'm sure you understand my resolve here Sean – and of course, a woman's needs.'

Natalie smiled, looking Sean in the eye. He held her gaze and it was only the sun shining through the window that caused her to concede. Sean glanced at her legs, and watched her gaze down at his.

'So, you see, if we really think about it, we both have something we desire,' Natalie said. 'I shall ensure you are well reimbursed and that Melissa goes free. I can see you both living rather happily together,' she smirked sarcastically. Sean was conscious that Natalie was pulling on all his strings. Very skilfully. She knew of Sean's inner disdain of the establishment and what it had done to him. Once a hugely loyal Crown servant, he had been betrayed by the powers that be. Hung out to dry. Why should he do this job for anything other than his own needs? He had puzzled over his options for some time and of what to do once he had found Alfie. Natalie's proposal was not all that unattractive anyway and she knew that.

'So, what's in this for you Natalie? What are your needs? Why is this so damned important and why should I trust you?'

'Oh, you know my needs Sean. Very well I'd imagine. I'm young and ambitious as you can see.'

'Indeed, that comes across rather shamelessly.'

'I'm sure you recall being just as cut-throat and clinical. My bosses will reward me with the success I want. My woman's need is of course for prestige and recognition – as well as some power, you understand?'

'Perfectly clear and obvious.'

'And I have nothing against you or Melissa, indeed I find her rather attractive too in all honesty. Why would I need to do anything to both of you if you hand over the special goods? Neither of you present me with any danger to my future you see.'

Natalie's confidence grew. Her tone charming and thoroughly influential. Her female persuasion, coupled with persistent conceit shone through. 'You both want to go your own ways having an easy life not being pestered and I know you're not arrogant enough to want to pursue any other motive Sean. Your time has come, hasn't it?'

Natalie's argument was compelling. She poured some water and continued. Sean caught a whiff of her perfume as she walked behind him.

'I'll set you up to move forward Sean. I'll set you up with a good sum of money and whatever you need, anywhere in the world. I'm sure you can tell a simple story to stop your side probing about what's happening here.'

Sean smiled just very slightly. A contrite smile. The thought of just disappearing with a good sum of money was very attractive to him. 'That all sounds very tempting, but there's one small delicate problem I'm afraid.'

'And what's that Sean?'

'Quite simply, I don't have the special goods to give you. I don't actually have anything to give you. I have found nothing so far. And I can't guarantee I'll find what you want.'

'Well, I know you better than that. You haven't been brought here to fail and I'm sure you're very close to finding what we both need. No need to delay me Sean. Neither of us are fools. I know every delaying tactic in the book.'

'OK, so let's view this as some sort of purchase then,' Sean intimated. 'You pay me for the goods if I find them and I shall ensure you get what you need. It actually seems quite a simple way to finish all this off.'

'I'm glad you agree. And be under no illusion. Of the files he has, I only need one. It contains some specific information that my chef de mission needs protecting.'

'I see. Well here's the story,' Sean began. 'I think Alfie left a trail of clues but it's proving difficult to follow them. This won't be finished quickly, and it could take some days you know. And I know you need the list of Russian moles that he had. That's all quite obvious.'

Sean kept all of his options open. He could take the money and run but needed some assurance that Natalie would deliver. Or he could hope Swartz found Melissa first and then he could deliver the file to Jack as agreed. He still had another financial arrangement in the bag with Dominic if he delivered. He had plenty of options, so that he could swing whichever way he felt was right.

'I need to see some genuine goodwill here and a large deposit, so I know I can trust you,' Sean said, leaning over for a pencil and paper. He wrote down the details of two bank accounts and asked for deposits to be made to each of them. He wanted €1 million in each account first, to act as a retainer.

'I'll arrange for €100,000, but no more at this stage,' Natalie said. And my goodwill will extend a little further too.' She leant forward, providing Sean with a glimpse of her cleavage.

'So, if you didn't kill Alfie who did?' Sean asked. Natalie smiled and sat back.

'We would have killed him if we'd got to him first. He knew too much, and the price was too big not to have him sidelined. Just find the files and hand them over Sean, and then walk away. It's a simple and clean option.'

Sean looked over to the window, stood up and walked across to the curtains to pull them shut.

'OK, I'll do it. Just don't harm Melissa. I've interrogated her, and she knows fuck all. There's no need to hurt her and my motivation will change if you fuck her around. No need to get me to turn and come after you, is there now Natalie?'

Natalie walked a few paces and stood right in front of Sean. She was immaculately dressed, wore expensive jewellery and red lipstick and smelt divine – she was a woman who was clearly very adept at getting what she wanted from a man.

Natalie turned and suggested they should spend some time dealing with the details. Sean agreed, watching her undress.

Chapter 33

London and Cheltenham

Jack continued to monitor the operation from Thames House and instructed Samantha to begin pulling the rescue operation together. He wanted a full team of GCHQ cyber analysts on the case, and brought in Swartz with a full team of SAS troopers. Jack ran the operation from his side office, in which Samantha was now fully ensconced.

'Get Sean on regular communications please Samantha,' Jack asked. 'And get a message to him that we're tasking all of our assets to come and play for this.'

'I'm on it,' she said, juggling with a couple of phones and looking at a bank of screens she had established as the basis of a mini ops room in Jack's side office.

Samantha started her communications log and contacted Sean by encrypted text.

'Why haven't you asked me to come onto the ground yet – are you with a tart?'

It took Sean less than ten minutes to reply.

'Too busy. Big job, as you know. Need immediate help.'

'What?'

'Standby. I'll send full details in the next hour.'

'I'm always on bloody standby for you.'

'I know. I'm sorry. This is important. Lives at stake.'

'OK. I'm standing my teams up and Swartz is en route. With two armed surveillance teams. You have full capability now – go well.'

She tasked a high-readiness cyber team at GCHQ in Cheltenham to monitor all outgoing phone calls from the hotel that afternoon and evening. They looked at every single social media transmission, every mobile phone call and text and every landline phone making calls out of the building. They were tenacious in looking at every single transmission, following up every destination for calls or texts and converting their analysis into triangulated locations from telecoms masts around the country.

They monitored specific mobile phones and sent a telecoms message to each mobile phone which placed an unknown app right in the heart of each phone. The app, once initiated, allowed the communications experts to download and analyse every single text and phone message and internal documents, including all social media messages. They had infiltrated thirty-seven mobile phones within the hotel and worked through the night to establish which was Natalie's phone, where and who she had called, who her contacts were and who she had sent texts to. Jack retrieved the various locations and forwarded them to Swartz, who now had a team of eight SAS soldiers on their way to a bolthole in the wilds of south-east France to chase down Melissa's location.

Jack was able to set the operation up very quickly using predetermined high-readiness teams thanks to Dominic's stealth strategy, which enabled tasking without the direct oversight of ministers. It was underhand stuff, and a frenzied and intense operation. Jack had the authority to permit the covert activity, knowing full well Dominic backed him to the hilt.

GCHQ had a few leads that were being verified and data-mined. The teams would close in fast.

Chapter 34

The Pyrenees

Sean returned to the search site late in the afternoon to see the team hard at work examining in detail each of the potential burial sites they had identified. As he walked closer to the team, he saw Billy Phish was using ground-penetrating radar to provide alerts of anomalies under the ground at the likely burial sites. His LED screen showed a series of blue, yellow and red streaming bands which would indicate whether anything of large enough volume was buried beneath.

Sean watched Billy Phish mark the sites with metal pegs and blue tape before Jugsy dug through the peat to a depth of about one and a half metres. Sean kept his own counsel and let the team continue without alerting them to the fact that Melissa had gone. He simply explained that Jane had returned to take Melissa for safe keeping.

Sean was eventually alerted to Jane's death by Jack and learnt that the safe house had been trashed. He now knew that Jane had never actually replied in person to Jack's texts and this added to his despair. He had got so close but now had a dead operator to answer for and had seen his charge kidnapped. He knew he had to fight back and be dogged in his next moves and also that he had to conjure up a master plan if he was to regain any semblance of self-respect.

Sean pondered the options. Could it be Russians, or a team from MI6? Or were the Americans in play, as Billy Phish had said all along? Who the hell was Natalie working for?

He began to see it didn't really matter at this stage. And he realised in his quiet moments on the moor that Jack held all the cards to shape the entire operation and was no mug where classic extortion ops were concerned. Any rescue op that was mounted would again be deniable, with no links to the service, Jack or Dominic.

Sean thought about Melissa on and off during the day on the hills. Gentle sleet began to spiral across the moors and his turmoil increased as he thought about the connection he had with Melissa. Her absence felt like torture, and he finally opened up his drawer of emotions. He heard her nagging and teasing him, and in his mind's eye, saw her being sad with him. He wished now that he hadn't retreated from the clumsy embrace she had thrown at him. He felt the chemistry and knew they had a curious, but unique, bond.

He stayed quiet out on the hill, but inside him, a steely edge of retaliation was beginning to return. His internal anger sharpened his mind as he plotted his options and he felt an edge coming back to him. The best way out was to take the money, nail the reprisal, get the hell away from the country and run as fast and deep as possible. Why should he stay loyal to the agencies he served now? He pondered Natalie's offer again.

Billy Phish came over to Sean on the windswept hill. The sun was occasionally popping out from behind the clouds and the sleet was subsiding. 'I've got another five sites that have shown something big under the peat. The trouble is the radar is picking up all the voids in the peat too. Probably because the water table is high.'

'Mate, we're now at the point where we need to dig and dig fast. That's where we are now. Time has run out.'

'OK. We're not far off but it'll be bloody hard graft mate.' Billy Phish put an arm around Sean's shoulder. 'It's gonna work out mate. I know about these things, so keep your chin up. We're all here for you, you know that.'

Billy Phish wasn't normally one for emotion, but it gave Sean a lift. 'You're looking bloody gaunt right now. Do you need anything?'

'I'll be fine Billy. How do you think the scent trail might have dispersed around here then? I don't understand how Mike could hit near the cascade of water but not here?'

'Could be that they buried the body not in a shallow grave, but a deep one, and the scent is making its way through the aerated ground to that spot. My money is on him being buried near those rocks over there.' Sean turned to face Billy Phish and looked him straight in the eye.

'Mate. You're damn right. It's easy to dig so they may well have dug very deep. Right, let's get on with it. Let's get to the rocks, probe the ground and get Mike to go over the area again.'

Billy Phish and Jugsy used long, black, metal probing rods to burrow deep into the peat. Mike came over from where he had been basking in the sun out of the wind and went wild when he walked over the area they had just probed. He barked incessantly, as crazy as ever, and Sean knew instinctively they had found Alfie.

It was a good area and easy to dig as well as being out of sight of any walkers. But Sean couldn't see any ground signs, not even a dip in the ground, that could be a possible sign of a shallow grave. Jugsy put his magnetometer and radar over the area. Nothing on either instrument. After a brief discussion and a long chat about why Mike had hit, with different views about why other equipment hadn't picked anything up, Sean stood and thought hard.

'Right boys, let's dig and let's dig deep here. I know this is it.'

It was Jugsy who dug the hardest – he loved the grunt of physical work. It wasn't long before he had burrowed down a full metre and Sean stepped in to take over. Sean probed the peat again and again, then felt a twinge of excitement as the rod hit something and stopped.

'I've hit something boys,' Sean shouted. 'The rod has stopped. I think we bloody well have something here.' He moved the rod and thrust it into the peat again, this time giving it a short sharp tap with a mallet as he stood on the tips of his toes. The same thing. The rod was stuck and had hit something below.

'It could be bedrock,' Billy Phish said out loud.

'No, this is a body.'

'Wow,' Billy Phish said, looking for his pipe.

'Right, no excitement here boys. I need composure because there's every chance we are being watched. If we find Alfie we need to stay calm and not give anything away with our body language. I need you to trust me on this. If we find him, we leave him here, re-turf the trench and move on to the next site. OK? I can't afford for anyone to know we have found him.'

He looked at them sternly, feeling the sweat dripping from his forehead. They both gave a whispered agreement and Sean asked Billy Phish to carry on with the magnetometer at another area they had previously marked out.

Sean and Jugsy would finish this one off. They dug down another half a metre until Sean moved some peat and saw what appeared to be blackened white cloth. He used his hands to peel away the remaining layers, which were compacted. He then uncovered Alfie's torso – dressed in a peat-stained white shirt.

'Fucking hell Sean, we've only gone and done it,' whispered Jugsy. 'What's your thinking now?'

Sean used his hands to try and uncover Alfie's head and shoulders by pushing the peat clumps to the side of his body.

'I'm not sure yet,' Sean said. 'All I know is we can't give away the fact that we have found him. Those fuckers are watching us, and I need to buy some time.'

Alfie's corpse was rigid, ingrained with peat, and his eyes were closed. The body appeared to be miraculously preserved because it had been buried so deep in the peat. Sean noticed the bullet wound in Alfie's temple and then used his phone to discreetly take a few pictures. He then removed more peat and soil to uncover his legs.

Alfie was still fully dressed, except his shoes were missing. Sean pulled out a small scalpel blade, cut the shirt and carefully made an incision under Alfie's left armpit. He felt around for a tiny data transmitter, then made another incision to cut it out. Using a pair of tweezers, he removed the tiny electronic device, which was only a few thousand microns thick and used Bluetooth technology. He tucked it into his breast pocket, then stood up, with only his chest and head visible above the trench.

'OK Jugsy, can you start replacing the peat? Replace it all carefully. I'll explain later.'

Jugsy nodded and just got on with the job. 'Poor bastard,' he muttered.

PART THREE

REPRISAL

Chapter 35

The Pyrenees

Sean called it a day on the dig at 6pm and made his way back to the hotel – alone. He was gripped by the case. And astonished at finding the body after all the false positives. He had trusted in his resolve and it had paid off. He felt sure he now had the clues to find the files.

It had taken a series of attentive questions from Sean using neuro-linguistic programming techniques to tease out what appeared to be an innocuous piece of information from Melissa. She didn't really recognise it as being important during her recollection of her conversations with Alfie. It had been buried deep in her subconscious mind. The clue she had uttered related to Alfie putting his hand under his armpit regularly. And grimacing as if in pain. She always thought it was a foible, but each time Sean asked where Alfie had put his hands, she recalled this curious habit of keeping his hand under his armpit. It had taken Sean many hours of interrogation to reveal these innocuous clues, but they came out eventually and he immediately recognised them as being the keys to Pandora's box.

The anticipation of opening the files from an ultra-slim electronic implant was thrilling for Sean. Before he left the hills, Sean briefed the team on the moor to keep searching the other areas. This deception would provide the cover and time he needed with Natalie, and with Jack. The safest plan right now was to carry on with the search as if nothing had been found.

Sean arrived back at the hotel at 7pm. He took his laptop out of his rucksack, plugged it in and waited for it to boot up.

Meanwhile, he took Alfie's data transmitter, cleaned it up and laid it on the desk next to the laptop.

Sean configured the Bluetooth technology on his laptop and let it search for any local devices. It seemed to take an age to him but eventually the laptop identified the tiny transmitter, which Alfie had given the name 'CHIME'. Sean's excitement peaked as the devices paired, and the transmitter requested a password. Sean scrabbled around for the papers he had found at the Baker Street flat. The passwords were a mixture of letters and numbers, tight enough security to stop a password generator cracking the code. The second one on the list gave him access to the data. He was in.

Alfie had somehow managed to find a bioengineer, a so-called flesh engineer, to insert the biomedical implant into his skin. It had probably been done in Germany, Sean thought. This novel electronic device had a Bluetooth connector and a computer chip and could connect wirelessly to any device. Alfie would simply have pointed his arm at any device, let them pair and then the data he had inside his body could have been accessed.

Sean wondered in how many places Alfie may have stored the files in the cloud. He still hadn't heard from the cryptographer about the obituary and suspected that the transmitter also held a code for entry into another account. He assumed that Alfie would not stick all his Crown jewels in one basket.

Sean clicked the data link and watched a screen pop up with large red file icons, each of them given a name. A second password was needed to enter these, which he again found on the list from the Baker Street flat. Sean began to scan each folder. There were literally thousands of files, most of which appeared to have different classifications, but in the main the top and bottom of the pages were marked 'SECRET'. Many were marked 'TOP SECRET'. Some of the documents used different caveats for release and disclosure, such as 'SECRET UK EYES ONLY' or 'SECRET US/UK EYES ONLY'. He flicked through a few files and scan-read some of the information, just to get a feel for the story in each file. He felt tired but knew he would need to research the files through the night. It would be an exhausting trawl. He made his first coffee and stripped down to just a T-shirt and shorts.

Sean took a break and then looked inside a file that provided all the cloud locations in which Alfie had stored his caches. The implant could only hold so much data. Sean then went to the main cloud site to delve deeper into Alfie's secret hoard.

What he read astonished him. Alfie had been meticulous in keeping notes on his detailed research and he gave specific locations of where he had found the data – all of it obtained by Alfie trawling and searching online intelligence systems, which he clearly had full access to. Sean began to see that Alfie had conducted brute-force hacking to get directly into digital compartments he didn't have access to. The more files Sean uncovered, the more he could see they were part of a compartmentalised operation, where each person only knew a small part of the entire intelligence collection operation. It was high-grade intelligence on multiple British and American operations that Alfie had uncovered – and he had then hacked into other areas of intelligence to retrieve follow-up information. He had put together a huge jigsaw puzzle.

Sean felt a chill and a shiver went down his spine as he recognised the scale and scope of what Alfie had wanted to do. It was phenomenal.

There were a few files that stood out for Sean because of the capital letters that Alfie had used in his file-naming convention. One was called 'MPS and LAWYER corruption' and related to the Metropolitan Police and legal firms. It contained hacked emails as likely evidence of endemic corruption that was rife amongst many senior officers who had ingratiated themselves with lawyers. A quick glance showed Sean that Alfie had hacked into key senior officers' voicemails, emails and personal files, some of which related to the Iraqi inquiries and paedophile rings.

He made a mental note to contact Samantha to find out how she and One-Eyed Damon were getting on with investigating his own quarry, Frazer, the bent ex-copper who had framed him and who haunted him at night.

There was one particular file marked 'Wilshaw' that provided Alfie's own intelligence and investigations into the death of the scientist Professor Margaret Wilshaw before the Iraq war, transcripts of which the government would certainly not want released. They all related to the dodgy dossier, the precursor intelligence record that had eventually led to the war in Iraq. This began to get personal for Sean.

What Sean read worried him. He read about his own intelligence gathered back in 2002 surrounding the Iranian missions in Central Asia to find and collect radiological sources, the focus of his very own undercover operation in Uzbekistan. This began to make him feel queasy as he recalled his memories of tracking and tracing the passage of isotopes across the borders of Kazakhstan and Uzbekistan and finally into Iran. The folly of it all was that Sean's own mission had been to verify that it was the Iraqis who were actually buying the material – in order for the US and UK governments to justify on intelligence grounds that Saddam Hussein was in the forefront of developing terrorist-related weapons of mass destruction. Sean knew otherwise: it was actually the Iranians, and this had disturbed him for many years. But it had all been kept under wraps.

Sean then read how Alfie had undertaken a lengthy investigation to uncover the depths of deceit regarding Iraqi intelligence and the more sordid details surrounding the death of Wilshaw. Alfie had explained in his investigative files how he had been able to hack and crack personal accounts of those involved in the affair, in order to expose the killing of Wilshaw by the Americans. This was staggering stuff, and the evidence Alfie had revealed was platinum-grade.

Alfie had uncovered evidence that indicated that Wilshaw may have been murdered, instead of taking her own life. Alfie had surmised in his notes that this was because she was regarded as a traitor by someone in the MoD or British Intelligence, or because the Americans feared she would disclose the Pentagon's fabrications intended to influence British government's opinion over the war in Iraq.

Alfie had written about this. '*The bottom line is that Margaret Wilshaw was probably killed because she somehow cocked up the secret avenues of communications between American military intelligence and the British government whereby lies, not just those involving Iraq, were fed to the British government to influence British actions along lines that helped the Pentagon.*'

Sean moved on to another file highlighted in yellow. He read through it for a while before lurching back into his chair. This was gripping stuff. It took Sean back to his forays into Central Asia over twelve years ago. He was reading how Alfie had hacked into the personal files of a foreign spy.

Sean read Alfie's written transcripts of the affair. '...the extent of emails and personal files shown on his computer, often in hidden areas, provides total and unambiguous proof that he was leaking classified intelligence documents to the enemy via a third party. From the evidence I have uncovered, he had been doing this for many years, leaking data to the host country and other Asian and middle eastern states by dead letter drops using Bluetooth technology to transmitters & receivers hidden across the city. He kept photo shots of the information he was passing on from London-generated intelligence through the Foreign Office. The leaked documents can be seen here.' Alfie had embedded a link in the Word document.

It was information linking the British Ambassador to Russia in the early 2000s. He was a spy, right in the heart of the highest echelons of the British establishment. He had leaked information direct to the Russian government, and possibly to others.

Sean sighed and made a face. He mumbled expletives to himself, agog at what he was reading. Sean knew that this was likely to be the person who had nearly got him killed all those years ago. But how did the Ambassador know of his pursuits and mission? Sean clicked the link and searched. Sure enough, Alfie had settled it. He had discovered who had leaked his, and other missions to the Iranians. It was the Ambassador. Sean reflected on how the Russians had had a very close relationship with the Iranians in state-sponsored pursuits, and it certainly fitted with the Iranians' pursuit of harnessing fissile material. It all seemed to tie together. He made a mental note to find out more. 'Bastard,' he said, as he smacked the desk.

Were the Iranians now in this game? It would be no surprise if they were, he thought. Or was this a piece of intelligence unrelated to the needs of Dominic Atwood and Natalie? He took a break from reading, leant back and thought carefully. What had he missed? Think. Analyse. Read.

There was another key file on the list – and Sean left this to last. It was a file called 'QUERY'. This seemed a curious name as Alfie had diligently named everything else with a title that related to its contents. Sean became engrossed in this file and its contents. Was this the tinder-box information that Natalie wanted? And was it the file that Dominic needed?

Sean had hit another jackpot. 'At last,' he mused as he scanned and read the detail. He could now piece it all together and get the unadulterated truth about why he had been brought in from the cold – and why these files were so desperately important to people.

Sean began to piece together the different types of intelligence contained in this file – it was complicated, and it confused him as he tried to think through the permutations. There were so many memos, intelligence reports, archived data and historical evidence. It seemed to involve a lot of people. He decided to use i2 intelligence software to begin connecting the individuals to see who was connected to who, who knew what and who may have hidden information from who.

The crux was that the QUERY documents contained a list of names alleged to be high-grade Russian moles within the British establishment.

He started with the individual who had been given the information and list of names from someone in Moscow – Sean gave him the code-name 'FITZROY'.

The information handed over in Moscow was a list of names pertaining to Russian moles in the UK intelligence services and the sources they had recruited to provide ongoing high-grade intelligence to the Russians. Sean wasn't quite sure who was who at this stage.

But who else had known about this list? One document suggested that the initial primary source, 'WYNTHROP', had concealed this list and hidden it before it was finally given to FITZROY, and from the account Sean read, it had taken many years for this information to fall into the hands of FITZROY. It had remained deeply hidden for a long time: 37 years in fact. It must have been like gold dust, he thought to himself, when

FITZROY opened it and saw this devastating list of names within the British establishment. He wondered if he had read the names or whether he had been under strict instructions to pass it on to his intelligence masters. But who had FITZROY given the list to? And why?

This was Alfie's very own mole hunter investigation which he had planned to expose to the world. This was a classic anti-mole intelligence investigation, enhanced by the additional skill set that Alfie had of brute-force hacking into digital systems. The old anti-mole teams in MI6 had long since gone, but this list gave Alfie a nudge back in time to the hinterland of cold war spying.

'So, this was what drove Alfie on,' Sean said out loud. 'Bloody good stuff too,' he thought. Sean relaxed back in his chair, feet up on the small desk, looking intently at the list of names in front of him. He didn't recognise any of the names – except one.

The name came with two initial letters attached to it. And whilst the surname stuck out, was it the person he was thinking of? Or was it just a coincidence? It was the name of a very well-known British political personality in the current Cabinet. He stretched and arched his back, and knew he had to push on with the i2 map to see who was linked to whom.

He wrote down WYNTHROP on the paper. This was the name or codename that Alfie had uncovered as being the person who had initially written the list of moles in 1979. He then wrote FITZROY below WYNTHROP and connected them with a dotted line. FITZROY was the person who had received the list of moles in a small rusty tin in Moscow in 2005. FITZROY would have given the list to someone back in the UK. Sean assumed FITZROY would be MI5 or 6. He then had to make a few assumptions in the absence of any evidence and began to write the interconnections on an A3 sheet of paper. He wrote FITZROY in the middle with the date and place – 2005. MOSCOW. He then drew a circle below FITZROY and named this individual 'CHIEF', for the Chief of MI6. London 2005. He then drew a circle on the right-hand side of the page with the name next to it, QUERY, to represent the high-profile British personality – in other words, the Russian mole.

He scribbled some of his own conjectures below these circles and then tried to fill in the blank circles with questions – such as, who had killed Alfie? Who had informed the foreign or home agency that had killed Alfie? How did they know about Alfie? And who was Natalie working for? Who was Dominic connected to? And was there a direct link with the intelligence services or a specific individual?

It was 4.20am when he began to see what was happening. He was totally exhausted but alive to the fact that time was of the essence here, with Natalie on the prowl for the information and the QUERY list.

Sean was now carrying on where Alfie had left off. Alfie had had no idea who had been on his tail – nor had he known that other dark forces knew of his plan to whistle-blow these devastating secrets. All Alfie had known at the time was that he held highly precious information that would probably destroy certain men on the Russian and British sides – and probably cause earthquakes within the intelligence services and government.

Sean recognised that whoever got the list first would ultimately determine which men would be thrown to the wolves and which would survive.

He saw that Alfie had had a fantasy side to him and that his egocentric nature had lulled him into the sense of being immortal if he became the greatest whistle-blower of them all. And, to add the icing on the cake, he would have exposed the highest-profile British mole in history. That was what Alfie wanted. To be famous forever.

Sean reflected on how this staggering piece of research had revealed a long-lost secret that had re-emerged from the cold war days to expose a Russian sleeper agent of the highest magnitude. His final actions that night were to copy and paste hundreds of files into a separate cloud-based account so that all the information was easily accessible to him and could be accessed and used as he desired. A few surreptitious thoughts crossed his mind about what he could do with it all.

He felt himself gently drifting off to sleep, realising that he now had an exit plan. He could play both cards and provide the list to both Natalie and Dominic. Either way, the mole would be exposed, and others would fall too – something that he knew deep in his soul he had to do.

He knew he didn't have much time on his side with Natalie, but he judged he had just enough to make his plan work. He could then depart safe in the knowledge he had done his job and could quietly exit this dark world of deceit.

But he wanted Melissa too.

Chapter 36

Languedoc-Roussillon

Swartz was poised and ready for action. He had prepared his team in short order and watched his SAS operators prepare their equipment as dusk began to fall. The bolthole was a hive of activity as he watched his men go through the well-versed ritual of sorting out equipment, rehearsing assault drills, checking communications kit, memorising maps, taking tea and toast and reading before sleeping.

Swartz had brought with him a bomb disposal officer, Phil Calhoun, to conduct the specialist target-site reconnaissance using a variety of special equipment. Happy that the SAS troopers were settled in with their kit, he asked Phil 'The Nose' to have a chat with him on the terrace.

Swartz sat down on the upper terrace of the split-level building which offered a glorious view across a secluded valley to the limestone hills. A daylight moon shone across the vast expanse of rolling meadow that lay below them, with the gentle trickle of river water providing the only sound. A perfect place for rehearsing the assault, Swartz thought.

'What I've got so far is that the GCHQ analysts have tracked and traced the Russian team to a wooded farmstead near Corsavy and the Gorges de la Fou. I think they've created all sorts of defences to protect the place, which is where you come in Phil.'

'No problem, I've got plenty of tech kit and a good bit of bang too. We're good to go. What's been happening there?'

'Not sure yet. I've got a surveillance team sitting in the undergrowth watching every aspect of life inside and outside the two-storey cottage. I need to find out quickly if Melissa is inside and what we're up against to rescue her.'

Phil the nose stood up and leant over the wooden rail to take in the view before turning. 'This is a marvellous place you know. Total solitude. My kind of place for a stealth operation and a bloody big bang,' Phil the nose said, with a glint in his eye. 'OK, let's get on the ground tonight and we'll have a quiet peek inside the place and throw a bit of kit around to see what defences they've put in place.'

Swartz had ultimate faith in Phil the nose to cover the technical side of the operation, which was needed to give the vital intelligence to his shooters before any assault took place. Phil the nose was an explosives legend. He was only five foot eight inches tall but well-built with a very distinguishable boxer's nose, wide shoulders and a trademark number 1 haircut. He was the font of all knowledge on bomb disposal and technical surveillance and had received many bravery awards during his distinguished career in the army.

'Good. I'll go and grab some plans of the place and we can look at how we can get up to the building,' Swartz said. 'GCHQ will keep feeding us signals intelligence from the targets and I'm expecting to get an order to strike within forty-eight hours, depending on what we see is happening inside.'

Swartz's team had set up their small bolthole some five kilometres away from the target cottage and were briefed every six hours on the Russians' movements by the surveillance team leader. Swartz had been instructed that no further operations on the target were to take place without Jack's authority and without Sean's approval of the plan.

Swartz had been receiving Sean's instructions via messages he had placed in the drafts folder of a Yahoo email account. OPSEC was vital now. They would communicate remotely using the method of leaving instructions in the drafts folder, which would mean that no information was ever transmitted. They both checked in regularly to see what messages and instructions had been left for each other in the folder.

Swartz grabbed some maps and returned to see Phil the nose preparing his explosives on the terrace deck. He had a range of equipment, including detonator cord, wiring, remote initiation devices and a couple of ammunition tins full of PE4 explosive.

Phil the nose would be handling the explosive means of entry into the target and would use high-tech passive and intrusive surveillance equipment that would be needed for the rescue attempt.

This job was no different to all the other stronghold takedowns Swartz and his team had completed over the years except that, this time, they were getting paid a bit extra but with no protection against prosecution on foreign soil. Swartz was acutely aware of the risks of this mission going wrong. He recognised that Sean could only bide his time and trust in his men to provide the information he needed before he, and only he, would decide to spring the operation.

Chapter 37

Languedoc-Roussillon

Swartz and Phil the nose led the search team along a narrow, muddy ditch adjacent to a line of trees that eventually gave access to the house. It was pitch-black and they wore night-vision goggles with ultra-sensitive optics to carefully observe the extremities of the building and the best approach routes to the target.

Swartz crawled the last twenty metres in the ditch before popping up in a small gulley. He was flawless in checking how the Russians may have deployed their defences to provide them with early-warning systems of any approaching intruders in the gardens. He checked for any signs of ground radar or infrared lighting before making his approach to the skin of the building. He was aware that local wildlife could easily set off any radar but he suspected the Russians had only placed active or passive infrared alarm systems on the building itself, backed up with night surveillance optics if a sensor was set off. These were highly professional foreign agents and he had no qualms about being ultra-cautious.

Swartz followed Phil the nose as he moved around a small copse and then approached the cottage along a ten-metre hedge line. This provided them with superb observation and cover from view as they scanned the approaches to the cottage with their night-vision goggles. Swartz noticed the rear garden consisted of a large expanse of oval-shaped lawn with a few shrubbery plantations, rose bushes on the perimeter and a small terrace by the dining room. Swathes of ivy hogged each side of the cottage and the remoteness of the area meant that there was very little light pollution.

Swartz had identified which areas of the grounds might be covered by movement sensors and was confident he could pick them up using the team's detection equipment. He was also confident that he would be able to guess the exact locations the foreigners had used to alarm the ingress and exit routes to the building. The only problem, he mused, was that these adversaries were far more skilled and capable than the average terrorist cell, so he had to ensure he thought of every little trap they may have set.

Swartz watched Jim and Chris, the two searchers, check their small hand-held sensors, which would detect any other active defences if they were being used. With their equipment, they moved cautiously to their start point. Swartz then ushered them to begin their journey around the entire cottage to detect any electronic defensive or detection alarm systems. This was slow, laborious work, but vital to identify and avoid any high-tech detection systems the Russians might have put in place. They moved with supreme stealth and skilfully used the cover of night and the environment.

Jim and Chris returned an hour later and met Swartz behind the main hedge, where they briefed him and Phil the nose on the situation.

'The house is only protected by six external infrared sensors,' the lead searcher, Jim, whispered.

'OK. Anything else in place?' Phil the nose asked.

'Nothing. But if they're triggered, they'll probably illuminate the areas of the patio, the front door and the kitchen door. That's about all we could see.'

'But we don't know if they'll trigger an alarm in the house?'

'That's very possible but for now we can avoid them. Other than that, the external faces of the building are clear. We couldn't see any CCTV cameras either, but there could be covert cameras in place to trigger a black screen and an alarm inside the house. I can't be sure.'

Phil the nose reached inside his pocket for his plan of the farmstead. 'OK, let's mark this up before the next run,' he said.

He marked the drawing of the house with the four faces of the building. Their approach to the face in front of them, which was the back garden, was marked as the purple face, the front was amber and the other two sides were grey and blue. Swartz watched Phil the nose crouch to brief Jim and followed suit.

'Jim, I want you and Swartz to start on the corner of the purple and grey faces, and I'll take the corner of the amber and blue faces. Let's move clockwise and return here once we've done the recce of the brickwork of the building.'

'If I see an opportunity, can I exploit it to look inside the building?'

'Yes, but only if you're happy there are no sensors inside the room you choose. I want to know what's happening in each room downstairs and upstairs, through the windows and through any apertures you find that give us a look into the place. Let's map out the rooms and see what the hell is going on inside.'

'No problem. Just be aware that the swathe of the external infra-red detectors' is about thirty degrees with a distance of about twelve metres in front of them.'

'Fine. Any space to squeeze below them?'

'Yep. The downward angle is about five degrees, giving us about a one-metre gap to crawl past without triggering them. Tight but should be OK.'

There was a slight wind rustling through the high oak trees that provided a useful background noise as they started their next runs. Each of them wore night-vision goggles strapped to their heads on top of their black balaclavas. They carried a Glock pistol in thigh holsters with endoscope equipment strapped to their waists on black webbing belts. Their small drills and toolsets were attached to the rear of their belts.

Swartz and Jim crawled the last few metres from the rose bushes to the corner of the building and then stood up slowly to stand against the side of the walls. Their first target was the narrow room facing the back garden, which was the kitchen. The kitchen lights were on. Swartz watched Jim kneel, place his endoscope through a tiny gap under the door and look at his two-inch chest-mounted screen, which was shrouded with a black veil to hide the light and disguise his presence. He stretched to push the three-millimetre endoscope camera under the draught flap. He twisted the camera head using the toggles on his chest controller to look around the room. He let Swartz view the inside. The kitchen was empty. There was no one inside. He looked up to the right, making a mental note of the layout and furniture. He then looked to see if there were any PIR sensors in the corners of the ceiling, and then checked upwards to see if he could see a lock system on the back of the door or a key inside that lock. There was an old iron key with nothing else attached to it and quite a substantial bolt lock on the top and bottom of the door. He then carefully turned the door handle to see if it was locked. It was.

Swartz indicated silently to Jim with a thumb that they were done with the kitchen. He then moved slowly in a crouched position to the next room, which had a protruding extension with bay windows on both sides and ivy leaves on the extremities of the walls. He started to stand up against the wall when suddenly a fox in the garden made an almighty screech.

'Shit, stand still,' Swartz whispered. He quickly looked through his night goggles to the area of sound and saw two foxes copulating under the far hedge line, next to an old tree stump. The noise was piercing as the vixen screamed in pain and tried to release herself from the clutches of the male, whose coital tie had trapped her. Swartz and Jim froze as the screams continued for what seemed an age. They didn't see any lights come on but remained alert to anyone coming out of the cottage to check on the noise. They willed the male fox to get it all over with and release his grip on the vixen.

Once the noise had subsided, they gave themselves some soak time – and did nothing for five minutes after the screaming had stopped.

Jim identified a small area in the bottom left-hand corner of the wooden window frame and used a tiny hand drill to make a small hole. He chose an area that might allow them to slip the long endoscope inside the frame, which could then be adjusted using the toggles to make it look below the curtain. The endoscope head could then be swivelled to look up and beyond into the room. Swartz pushed the endoscope in gently and kept feeding it in, turning the head until eventually he could see the wooden floors. He then turned the camera head to view directly into the room. This was risky stuff if the probe was seen from inside.

'Damn,' Swartz muttered under his breath. 'There's a chair right in front, can't see a fucking thing.' Jim tapped on his shoulder and directed him to move to the furthest extremity of the window and try again. Swartz nodded. 'I can see now,' he whispered. 'Only two chairs and a sofa in here – it's the lounge. Nothing seen.'

It was slow and tedious work as both teams mapped out the inside of the building. Their plans showed that there were three rooms on the lower floor: a kitchen, lounge and dining room. There were two bedrooms on the second floor and no cellar. The chill in the air began to bite as Jim started to drill the next hole, taking less than three minutes to get through the wood. This time, when Jim popped the endoscope in, he immediately saw movement in the dining room. What he saw was quite shocking.

'Fuck, this is not good mate.'

Chapter 38

Languedoc-Roussillon

'I want the entire cottage rigged with booby traps,' Natalie said firmly to Gregory. 'I want Melissa to be well protected but killed if it all goes wrong.'

'Exactly what I'm trained to do,' Gregory said confidently. 'This is right up my street now.'

'Good – because there's no room for error anymore and nothing must be attributable to me at the end of all this. I'll deal with Sean. You make sure Melissa goes up in smoke if I don't get what I need. On my call.'

Natalie had instructed Gregory to protect her quarry using all necessary means to ensure any rescue attempt failed. Natalie wanted no one left alive if it all went pear-shaped, and especially if Sean decided to renege on his deal with her. The whole operation had to be carefully planned to ensure that the Russians were not implicated in this if it went wrong. It was vital that she walked away scot-free.

Gregory had enormous experience in explosives and weaponry from his background in the Russian Special Forces and he was determined to ensure that, if a rescue took place, then the whole cottage would be burnt down and Melissa killed at the same time. They had recruited three Russian thugs from Marseille to watch over the cottage and Melissa.

Gregory rigged the cottage with a number of explosive booby traps and CCTV systems that would allow him to monitor the place remotely. He placed a series of explosive incendiary charges around the cottage that he could detonate remotely in the event of the operation being curtailed or abandoned or if it failed in any way. Natalie was wary of MI5's extensive capability to find Melissa, and also wary of any rescue attempts or assaults on the place. She was even more determined that, if everything failed, Sean and Melissa needed to be killed, and rigging the house with explosives gave exactly that opportunity. Her deep cover in Parliament was a high priority and she wanted no one left alive after this operation.

'I want every angle covered here,' Natalie explained to Gregory in an over-anxious manner. 'I won't allow this charade to go on forever and if Sean tries anything smart, we take him out and kill Melissa. Simple as that.' Natalie was increasingly nervous about failure and wanted a simple get-out clause if it all went awry.

'I'll give him forty-eight hours and no more,' she shouted at Gregory. 'Make this a fucking good job and make it work well.' She gave firm instructions on how the Russian minders were to manage Melissa, and that they had to follow her instructions precisely in order to earn their handsome cash reward and keep their lives too.

Gregory and his agents had installed a series of security systems in the farmstead cottage, including covert cameras and electronic intruder systems, all of which could be viewed remotely on his laptop. The alarms would be diverted to his smartphone if any activity took place in specific areas of the cottage that needed his intervention. He had also installed a series of high-tech booby traps. This gave him the full capability to remotely trigger the detonators to devastate the building, burn it to the ground and kill any occupants.

Natalie had prepared a plan to ensure Gregory pressed the trigger once she had received the files and codes from Sean – and after she had killed him.

Chapter 39

The 'bolthole', Languedoc-Roussillon

Sean sat opposite Swartz at the SAS bolthole as the distinctive odours of sweat and dampness spread throughout the room. He could see Swartz's eyes were red and he wore an ugly face after a gruelling eight hours of reconnaissance.

'It's like nothing I've ever seen mate. It's a well-defended target with Melissa thoroughly trapped,' Swartz said. Sean made a face and listened in to the debriefing.

'To be fair, I'm damned worried about what we may have missed,' Jim, the lead searcher, said, looking at Phil the nose. 'We can't just take this on blind. He's got wiring, booby traps and movement sensors everywhere. Those incendiaries alone will easily blow and destroy the room if we make one wrong move and we'd never get her out in time.'

Sean watched Phil the nose wipe his brow as he added to the debate. 'Well, my assessment tells me he's set this up either as a victim-operated device to blow the lot up in the event of an assault, or he may even have set it up to blow it remotely at a time of his choosing. It looks to me as if you wouldn't go to all that trouble without planning to blow it all up at some stage anyway. It's pretty fruity and we'll need to kill some of those sensors to have any chance at all.'

Sean watched inquisitively as Phil the nose pointed his pencil at the sketch map he had drawn. 'Looks like we have an approach route but it's right here that we need to penetrate and take out the sensors. If I was him, I'd also have some sort of covert camera inside covering our main entry points, so he can see when people are in the room and then just blow it.' Phil the nose stretched a little as he paused. 'How many Bravos have we got then Chris?'

Chris put his aluminium mug down before replying. 'Three. We have three to deal with. Ugly twats too from what I saw. Will be a pleasure to take the fuckers out. The ground team haven't seen anyone come or go for over eight hours and we have pictures of the three Bravos inside. They only seem to congregate in the kitchen and large hallway, which gives them access to the stairs. They're all carrying pistols but no long-barrelled weapons in sight.'

The atmosphere around the table was tense and the information Chris relayed concentrated Sean's mind on the seriousness of what they were facing. This was a high-tech adversary.

Chris carried on describing the Russian thugs in detail, the team listening intently. 'They seem pretty gruesome but not the sharpest of characters from what I observed and listened to. They broke into Russian and French, but looked more like local hoods to me. Definitely not military.'

Jim then spoke about what he had seen in the living room and the large dining room. The boys were absorbed. 'It seemed bizarre when I first saw it. But, given his modus operandi of wanting to destroy the place anyway, his techniques and procedures seem to fit with what you're saying Phil.'

'What's the main obstacle then?'

'Booby traps, and plenty of them mate.'

'Go on.'

'It seems to me that the three goons can only walk in certain parts of the building, as the rest appears to be booby-trapped. That fits the assessment if he wanted to defend the main access points an assault team would use. So, he seems to have thought about how we might get to Melissa and has protected all those areas.'

'And it's all rigged together to be blown remotely?'

'Yes. He's rigged it so he can detonate it all from wherever he is in the world. He's using the internet to transmit any alarms we set off across the net to his laptop and he's able to watch the imagery from his cameras on a smartphone or computer.'

Sean watched Phil the nose nod and scribble some writing in his notebook before Jim continued.

'His Crown jewel is Melissa, and he's protected her well. I can't believe how he's done it. The only access door to her in the dining room is through the lounge, and from what I saw, the Russians could only walk in a small part of the room. It's almost as if the remaining part of the room is cut off to them, and protected with some sort of booby trap along the windows and in the bulk of the room. He's probably done the same with the dining-room window.'

'What about Melissa?' Phil the nose asked.

'Well, she has an explosive necklace on her. Only about a quarter of a kilogramme – but enough around her neck in plastic tubing to take off her head. I couldn't see the wiring, but it looked to me as if it was a hard-wired detonator to a trigger somewhere else in the room. Hard to tell. She's also surrounded by infrared light beams, probably just below ceiling height, and about four feet either side of her. Walk through those invisible beams and bang, off she goes. The whole cottage would go up and her head would go through the roof with it.'

Jim didn't exaggerate the gravity of what would happen if they triggered any of the sensors. Sean was astonished that the Russians had set up a virtual fence around Melissa in the room – an ingenious way of stopping anyone getting to her, and also stopping Melissa just getting up and walking out. Break the light beams and the explosives would detonate.

The boys looked eager to crack the conundrum as Sean watched Phil the nose pass some pre-prepared plans of the cottage to them all. 'OK guys. Take the time to get these drawings accurate. I want everything you saw tonight drawn in full detail and to scale. I'll then brief Sean later this morning and see what we can do. Have we got the kit to do this?' he asked uneasily.

'Yes, we have,' Barky, the kit man, replied. 'But we might need to improvise and move quickly to get away with it. It's also a crazy ask to get out of this with no damage to somebody.'

Barky's assessment left a sober mood amongst the men but Sean knew he was right. There were no guarantees about who would remain alive if they took this on.

Chapter 40

London

Jack was not at all happy with Sean's assessment and his ideas for releasing Melissa. This was now becoming too high risk and there could be huge repercussions in London if such an unauthorised mission failed. There would be lots of questions and intense probing, not to mention the high risk of the deaths of Melissa and the assaulters.

Jack asked Sean if it was feasible to find out who had the trigger, rather than risking a full-scale assault on the farmstead cottage.

'Virtually impossible,' Sean replied, leaving Jack with a hell of a dilemma. He didn't have a clue how long it would take to find Alfie, and now he had a marauding bunch of Russian agents trying to grandstand the entire operation. Jack was angry but controlled his thoughts.

He knew that Natalie would not remain patient for very much longer and Sean could not carry on buying time. Sean had provided very precise timings for the assault and the aim was to kill Natalie and the Russians, while rescuing Melissa alive. But to do that they needed to get to Melissa first. It was too high risk in Jack's eyes, and he didn't want his career toppled through a maverick at play on the ground.

Jack pontificated quietly in his office in London and mulled the options over before agreeing – in part – to Sean's plan. Jack remained calm, hoping to avoid any catastrophes in France and London if it all failed. There was a huge amount at stake and Dominic had been continually on his back urging a breakthrough.

He wondered if Sean was straying. Was he concocting his own deception plan? Had Natalie got the better of him? What was

Sean's motivation? What would happen if Jack made the wrong call now?

He felt he knew Sean well. If Sean wanted to go through with the assault, then that meant he probably hadn't turned and given in to Natalie's extortion. He knew Sean would be vulnerable to taking an easy way out if Natalie had been convincing enough. But what if Sean was trying a double bluff here? Setting it up to look like an assault with a view to releasing Melissa and then providing the data to Natalie and giving him a false set? Surely Sean could now see it was fruitless to even consider such an option?

It wasn't beyond the realms of possibility, Jack thought, for Sean to set up a deception knowing full well that only he could give the order from London to mount the rescue. It was difficult to gauge from a distance exactly what Natalie had planned and how close she and Sean had come to striking a deal.

Jack concluded that it looked as if the Russians had no other intention than blowing the place up at some point and that the extortion attempt on Sean was heading only one way: total destruction of the house, Melissa killed and Sean executed at some point when the time was right after the information had been passed to Natalie.

Time was running out if Jack was to salvage the entire operation, which was now in danger of getting way out of control. He chewed over the dilemma and realised how far this operation had come, knowing he needed to wrestle back some sort of control. This was his head on the line. He needed to look Sean in the eye. There was only one way and Jack knew Sean held all the cards.

He made a couple of phone calls around London and headed for France on his own.

Chapter 41

Languedoc-Roussillon

Sean worked all through the night on his plan while Swartz's team conducted further reconnaissance on the target cottage.

He also spent some more time looking at Alfie's files. He went back to the one Alfie had marked QUERY. He decided to look at some of the other documents he hadn't previously had a chance to and felt a surge of adrenalin shoot through him when he opened a file relating to the handover of the rusty tin to FITZROY in Moscow in 2005.

This written intelligence report, classified as 'SECRET UK EYES ONLY', reverberated strongly with Sean, who was now engulfed with a sense of déjà vu. He sat shocked at what he had just read. And about what had happened when he was last in Moscow in 2005. It was him – he was there – and he remembered the mission well. He spent a moment or two reflecting back to that night in Moscow, standing on the bank of the Moskva river, with the city lights shining brightly in the distance. Sean had been the team commander that night.

He remembered his team throwing the sacks into the river after he had completed the month-long undercover mission when he had handed the goods over to FITZROY. The list of moles.

He looked at the findings of Alfie's obituary. The cryptographer had found nothing he could see to decrypt so far but would try with other steganography software systems.

Sean then made sure he had enough files and information to hand to Natalie on a USB stick and also via a web-based cloud account. This was his final twenty-four hours on this operation and he had to get everything absolutely right. Nothing could be left to chance. He drafted a long operation order for Swartz to conduct, and contacted Jack with the same plan and timings. Jack, he sensed, would not be very happy but hopefully he had given him enough to convince him to agree – and to give the vital order and authority to conduct the assault. He had explained to Jack in his message that he had some files, but not all of them.

Sean made a set of duplicate files to be given to Jack and Natalie, allowing him to keep his options open and to retain the data on QUERY. His master plan involved carrying out the high risk rescue of Melissa. His second plan was to negotiate with either Natalie or Jack to get the best deal he could in return for the QUERY files. He still didn't know who was batting for which side and who was protecting whom. He developed his own insurance policies for both options, allowing him and Melissa to walk away from the mess that Dominic had orchestrated.

He thought long and hard that night about what he was about to do, but in the end, he did it anyway. It was an act driven by his deep regret for Yuri's death, the Iraq war duplicity and his disdain for those establishment figures who had pushed him over the edge.

He released around six-hundred files in links to five Twitter accounts, connected to botnets that would push the tweets to two investigative journalists used by whistle-blowers. He used Alfie's name in the tweets, and configured his botnets to wake up and send the information twenty-four hours from now to the direct mail of the journalists and then, twenty-four hours later, to send a reduced number to the public at large.

'My turn to run the show – and Alfie will have his day,' he muttered as he pressed send.

Sean had just released the entire case files of the Margaret Wilshaw murder and the tantalising evidence of Iran's nuclear smuggling in Central Asia. It was enough to see many ministers implicated and probably put on trial for falsifying intelligence. He also added the damning police corruption files that Alfie had found, which would probably see many serving and former senior police officers in the dock.

He smiled as he imagined the nuclear fallout of such revelations in the public arena.

His last act was to prepare two time-delayed emails. His own act of reprisal, which would be sent four weeks after he pressed the send button, just in case he was killed. The emails contained damaging evidence against the former Ambassador, Jonathan Hirst, the list of names provided by WYNTHROP in the QUERY files and the information about the high-profile serving Cabinet minister, plus the full list of Russian moles within the British establishment. Sean felt a sense of retribution and finality about this act – one that he knew would help him to move on in his life.

The recipients of the leaks were the Global Investigative Journalist Network. A whistle-blowing receptacle for global intelligence exposés.

For finality, he added his own whistle-blowing nugget – the one that would see Dominic Atwood crushed.

Chapter 42

The 'bolthole', Languedoc-Roussillon

Sean sat down with Swartz and Phil the nose to look at the many options for releasing Melissa. They sat in front of some poor-quality imagery and photographs taken from the endoscopes of the inside of the house, together with a series of room plans with the exact details of what had been seen inside.

'I'm not sure I can fit with the timings that you've given me Sean. It could all go horribly wrong if we fuck up the first phase of the operation and then any timings from there go straight down the pan.'

'I agree,' Sean said. 'That's why we get the first phase bang on. The timings are crucial, and speed and surprise will give us the win.'

'Well, let's go through this in detail and get the timings worked out to the second,' Swartz piped up.

Swartz looked at the plan in detail to try and get the optimum timings, and to work out how long each phase of the rescue would take. He mulled over each phase and kept coming back to the same concern. 'If we missed anything on the recce the bloke on the end of the trigger could blow the lot up before we can get to her.' He scrunched his face at the prospect.

'But we might get lucky too,' Phil the nose chipped in. 'If he's off the ball for just a few seconds we will win.' Phil the nose pointed out all the known defences the Russians had put in place. 'We've seen these incendiaries in each room. Simple initiation mechanisms using accelerant fuel and a small charge on the top of the containers. Some are well hidden, but others are obvious. They're all connected to fuses with electric initiation and all the connections seem to go back into a small area, probably underneath the sofa in the lounge. We can see the fuse and wire trails but not the trigger and power unit to set them off. I'm guessing it's initiated by mobile phone but can't be sure. If he's any good, he's probably put two or three mobile phones there to ensure wrong numbers don't set the cottage ablaze. Chances are he's set up an automated dial-and-trigger system on his laptop that will zoom in over the 4G network. But he may also have a backup – we don't know.'

Sean watched Swartz put his hands behind his head and stretch, releasing a lengthy sigh. 'You know what Sean, there are too many fucking "known unknowns" here for my liking.' Sean smirked at his Donald Rumsfeld moment.

Quiet pauses. Private thoughts. Each of them absorbed by the bizarre nature of it all. Sean realised that their trump cards were speed, guile and instinct.

'The best way is to act dynamically,' Phil the nose said chirpily. 'We'll look at taking the fastest way to release Melissa from the explosives. My gut feeling says he hasn't put anything complicated like a collapsing circuit on the explosives around her neck, which will make it easier for us.'

'OK, what about the hired hands inside though,' Sean asked.

'It's tight,' Phil the nose explained. 'It seems the guards simply come into the room by following a marked route and then slip her food and drink under the active beams, making sure not to break them. She has an area of about eight square metres to sit in and sleep, but effectively she's a prisoner within an invisible fence.'

Phil the nose then described in detail the trigger mechanisms surrounding Melissa, referring to the active infrared beams and the power systems that made them operate. 'I expect the neck explosives are on a remote-trigger system, possibly even a Bluetooth system from beneath the sofa. That's the command centre of all his explosives and incendiaries. I expect she is paralysed with fear, pretty much expecting that her time is up, but not knowing at what minute of the day it will come.'

Sean pondered the sheer terror that she must be feeling with a bomb around her neck and asked Phil the nose what would happen if the primary system failed to detonate or was tampered with.

'Well, if I'd put this together, I'd have a time-delay device that would be triggered but I'd set it up as an anti-tamper switch too, with a fallback if the power failed.'

Phil the nose drew a small diagram to explain to Sean how a timer device could be triggered if he cut a wire or removed a detonator, or indeed if the circuit's power failed. 'It would immediately transfer to the secondary initiation switch,' he explained. 'Which would be the timer and could be set for one second upwards. This is high-end capability mate, and it will be a hell of a task to keep Melissa alive in the short time we have to raid the house and then to extract her without the explosive traps blowing her up.'

Sean watched as Swartz and Phil the nose led the rehearsals with the team to get the timings right, and to get the technological interceptions right. The soldiers were kitted out with their MP5 assault weapons, Glock pistols, ammunition and flash bang grenades. They were dressed in dark jeans, boots and lightweight black jackets.

They practised on the safe house they were occupying, setting up white tape in the garden and in the rooms to signify the exact routes they would need to take, and the exact distances. It wasn't perfect, Sean thought, but they had scaled their own bolthole to suit the target-site layout, adapting and building makeshift walls and doors using a variety of carpentry skills and odd bits of junk hanging around.

Sean knew they would have to carry a lot of technical kit on the assault and he knew each phase was dependent on the equipment they had to guide and steer the assault team to success. Swartz was making sure they tested the kit and then tested it again, and that they had a contingency plan if the equipment failed. He instilled into each and every man that this was ultra-high-risk and beyond the scope of any previous operation they had conducted. But it was doable.

Sean sensed that the feeling amongst the team was electric, and that it helped numb their fear. No allowance was being made for incompetence or failure to be precise on this job. There were explosives and electronic booby traps everywhere.

Chapter 43

Languedoc-Roussillon

Early morning rain. A day for a kill. Sean was deep in thought as he watched Jack walk soullessly across the dank moor, gradually getting closer to the rendezvous. The black storm clouds were gathering and a few scudded overhead, providing an ominous setting for such a vital meeting.

'We all look like grave diggers,' Sean said, looking at Jugsy, who was covered from head to toe in black peat on an horrifically wet day. Sean sniggered as Jugsy looked himself up and down and tried to clean himself up a bit. 'It's not a ministerial visit you know Jugsy,' Sean said, chuckling.

'Piss off,' Jugsy said, giving him the finger. 'I'll shove this shovel right up this bloke's arse if he doesn't play ball mate.'

'Fear not Jugsy, it's all in hand,' Sean said, noticing Jack was right on top of them now. He took off his glove and shook Jack's hand. 'Welcome to hell on mud Jack.'

The intensity of the rain matched that of the rendezvous. Sean pointed to a small tent where they could talk without the Russians watching them. At that moment the clouds broke – opening with a riotous volley of hail, followed by a torrent of rain that engulfed them.

They crouched together inside the sodden tent.

'Well, have you found him yet then Sean? Or is all this a smokescreen?' Jack asked.

Sean smiled and looked Jack in the eye as he handed him a mug of coffee and a chocolate bar. 'I've found him alright Jack. He's lying in a grave about four metres away from us, still fully clothed, and not decayed. It wasn't a small cache that I was looking for, it was his corpse I needed all along.'

Jack, unsurprised, took a sip of his coffee and looked at Sean, waiting to hear the whole story. Sean knew the time had come to reveal all, or at least most of it, to Jack, and vice versa. Cards on the table.

'You see Jack, I knew I had to have some sort of insurance policy here. I still have no idea why you got me out of that godawful jail to do this job when you could just have easily got another agent with similar undercover experience to do it. I've been wondering why Dominic needed Alfie's files and what the hell was so big that he had to put such a large cover-up in place.'

Jack nodded, and Sean offered him a small stool to sit on, just as the rain splattered the tent with what sounded like loud bullets.

'It's inconceivable to me that you don't know the full picture,' Sean said fiercely. 'But I still haven't got it all. I've been piecing it together and I've set up a few things to let me finish this off for good and move on. You can either run with my plan or not Jack.'

Sean was careful to make Jack witness the steely nature of his own position – he was focused, sharp and ready for action. For Sean it was now fight or flight. This was his big moment. Their exchange felt honest and straightforward. The raindrops on the canvas got lighter. The tent poles creaked in the howling wind.

'Well Sean, I think you should give me your plan and we'll see what I think from there. I'm guessing that you have access to the files or know where they are. Am I right?'

'Yes, I've got them all,' Sean said. 'I know exactly where they are. But I've taken the liberty of placing the most sensitive secret files in other areas of the public domain, to ensure I'm not shafted. And I've put in place some instructions to enable others to expose them all, based upon what happens to me in the next twenty-four hours.'

Sean had saddled Jack with the conundrum of highly sensitive information falling into the wrong hands. 'So, you see, I think I've figured out who Dominic is protecting,' Sean revealed, 'And the information he doesn't want exposed in the press and public arena. But it will find its way there unless I have my exit firmly mapped out with you Jack, sanctioned by Dominic and whoever else has their fingers in this damned muddy pie.'

'What have you seen in the files then?' Jack chipped in.

'Bad stuff. It's gold dust if you want to see heads roll. Alfie might not be alive but by fuck this stuff can still be released in his name. And it would send some people into orbit with the furore that would result from his whistle-blowing. I think it's time we came clean and sorted this out. Otherwise, Alfie will get the opportunity to release those files, because I'll make sure he gets what he wanted. I'll make sure his obituary is published and show how the government had him killed.' He held back on which government, to see if the statement triggered Jack.

Sean looked at Jack's thin face. His eyes told him the stakes were high. His look had a fatalistic air. His manner, as always, was fastidiously calm. Doubtless he was aroused by the intellectual aspect of it all, yet he remained unprovoked. Sean had raised the tempo, had poked him, and he was now ready to listen.

'Let me have your plan and your wish list,' Jack said. 'Let's get that dealt with now.'

Sean unzipped the inner pocket of his black Gore-Tex jacket and pulled out a plastic zipped wallet with some documents inside. The first brown A4 envelope, which had mucky folds across its centre, concealed an operation order for the release of Melissa. It was meticulously typed and written with precise military orders outlining the mission, scheme of manoeuvre, phases of operation and timings.

'We have less than four hours now to get the boys over the start line. I need you to authorise this.'

Sean didn't try to bribe or coerce Jack any further – he just let Jack read it and left the tent to get some fresh air.

Jack spent fifteen minutes digesting the detail of what was proposed and looked at the last phase, which involved Natalie. He wasn't too happy about what Sean had recommended which was too high risk. Jack felt a twinge of relief though that his thoughts about Sean were spot on. He knew Sean still had some loyalty – and his own mantra of doing the right thing. His plan was risky, but the fact that he had presented this as his first option encouraged Jack that Sean's loyalty to the Crown had still not fully deserted him, angry though he may be at having been disgraced and pushed out into the cold.

Jack checked his thoughts, put himself in Sean's shoes and wondered if he had presented a similar plan to Natalie.

Sean sat on a rock, gazing over towards the small waterfall, mindful that he would present a similar plan to Natalie that evening – but the detail depended on Jack's responses now. Sean was well aware that Natalie's ruthless edge would involve having himself and Melissa slain, but he had a simple plan for that. And it involved a kill. Jack could have first bite at the cherry though to deliver Sean's exit plan into a new world.

Sean was still trying to piece the puzzle together, and had continued late into the night mapping out who he felt was working for who, who was connected to who and who was covering who. He took his 'mind map' out of his pocket. It was now covered with dotted lines linking individuals to other people, and contained an array of short sentences written in pencil, some of which had been rubbed out a few times, to try and piece together each individual's motive and who was linked to the moles and the conspirators. It was *Spycatcher* stuff – the pieces of the puzzle were slotting together but a few gaping holes remained for Sean to decide which way he would jump when the time came. Sean knew the end was coming and he was confident he could make the moves to win.

Sean returned and sat opposite Jack. 'If you agree to this Jack, you get the second envelope tonight.'

'I presume that the second envelope will have the access codes to the files I need?'

Sean nodded.

'OK, I'll give the order. It's bloody high risk and if people are killed, I'll have some serious explaining to do,' he said. 'But you have to agree to give me the codes and files whatever happens, or else I can't sanction this. I need the files, not Melissa. I can let the Russians go, it doesn't matter to us.'

'In which case you can have the files now. Just give me what I need. The money and a cover story to leave the country. I've done my bit for you.'

Sean handed him the second brown envelope. Jack held it in his hand.

'It's already set up for you Sean, just as we agreed when you set out on this journey.'

The atmosphere was unruffled, both men focused on the night operation. A feeling of full trust had occurred for the first time.

'It's damned risky,' Jack said. 'You know she may not make it out alive?'

Sean didn't answer but instead pulled out his i2 relationship mind map of his ideas on what this was all about. 'This is what I think Dominic is up to,' Sean said. 'Alfie called the files QUERY. An agent I've called FITZROY was handed a list of Russian moles in Moscow in 2005. That list had never surfaced in over forty-odd years. On that list is a current Cabinet minister – a Russian spy at the very centre of the British establishment for over four decades, who no doubt gave the very best of our secrets to the Russians all the way through. It was me who was actually tasked to find that hidden list and I handed it over to FITZROY in the rusty tin. But I didn't know what the fuck it was all about at the time.'

Jack looked shocked at the revelation. Sean noticed his reaction and then continued. 'I handed a cache of stuff to a British bloke on the banks of the river Moskva, never knowing quite what the hell it was. I was tasked by the FCO to take a team to search for a whole raft of stuff before handing this special list over to the guy I named FITZROY.'

'But who's this man WYNTHROP on the drawing? Who was he?' Jack asked, pointing to the name on the paper.

'I've no idea but what I do know is that Dominic Atwood is providing cover for the mole. What kind of British loyalty is that? He's nothing but a devious bastard hell-bent on his own egotistical aims, and a traitor to boot. Alfie managed to hack into his accounts to reveal how he had set up the rendition programmes for the CIA in Uzbekistan. That's exactly when I met him for the first time all those years ago in Central Asia. I knew he was a dangerous man the moment I met him. What is he to you Jack? Why are you so loyal to him?'

The rain was now pelting down, and the strong wind was rustling the small tent like a mainsail in the sirocco. Jack took a large gulp of his coffee. Sean sensed more was to come.

'I can tell you now Sean that I didn't know the details on this list until you just showed it to me. But Dominic needs that list of moles and it's my job to get it to him. If this name gets out, the government will fall but, worse than that, it will create the conditions for a new subversive government to take over. None of that is in anyone's interests but I'll make sure the endgame is played out properly. And for the benefit of the public too.'

Jack, as ever, kept his council but showed that he too was not happy with all that was happening around him.

'There is one other thing you probably want to know Sean. It was my idea all along to find a job for you and get you out of that jail. Dominic gave me this mission and I needed to make it happen. It was me who wanted to see you redeemed and brought back in from the cold. No one else.'

Sean looked up into the eyes of Jack, totally surprised at what he was hearing.

Chapter 44

Port-Vendre

S ean arrived at Natalie's room at exactly 7.25pm.
'Time to get down to business I think Natalie,' Sean said cheerily as he walked through the door, acting chirpily.

'Why? What's happened?' she inquired, holding the door open.

'Well, it's all good. I have the files for you. It's time for you to transfer that money into my account if you don't mind. The files are all on a cloud site that Alfie uploaded them to. I also want to discuss the conditions under which Melissa is released.'

Natalie closed the door, simultaneously responding with a large smile. 'Great, let's have a celebratory drink and get down to business then.'

Natalie, looking elegant in a red dress and black heels, walked behind Sean as he strode purposefully to the round table next to the balcony.

He sat adjacent to her laptop, the smell of Natalie's perfume permeating the air. He placed his phone next to the laptop and gently aimed his covert live-feed camera, hidden in his jacket button, towards the keyboard.

The live feed went directly to one of Samantha's operators sitting at his desk in London. Sean visualised the activity of Samantha and her operators back in MI5, who were watching as Natalie typed in her login name and password on the keyboard. Sean's phone, issued by GCHQ, had a very powerful Wi-Fi encryption scanner inside it, and it began to lock onto the ports within Natalie's laptop. The technology had been designed by GCHQ and started to retrieve data via vulnerabilities to break through the firewalls of the laptop's Wi-Fi system creating a data tunnel. It then retrieved a series of files and operating system codes which were immediately uploaded across an encrypted point to point link allowing an operator in Cheltenham to grab the files. The operator would soon be able to mimic the Wi-Fi and 4G connections that Natalie would link to, and then breach the established data security software to retrieve all elements of the operating system held on her laptop. He would effectively have full command and control. Once he had confirmed he had control, Samantha authorised him to embed a small application – and he began retrieving the files he wanted.

Sean asked Natalie to transfer the funds, so he could then hand over the files. Natalie opened up an HSBC online account, one of many she used, and Sean captured the keystrokes she made on the keyboard via the covert camera. Samantha was immediately able to penetrate the account using the apps that had been placed on the computer as well as the typing her operator had picked up from Sean's still photographs. Natalie then transferred fifty percent of the funds to two of his accounts. Sean sat back and passed the logins to Natalie for the cloud account holding the data. He passed the envelope to her, and before long, she had gained access to the site and files.

Natalie was in. Sean could see her elation and sensed her thoughts. She was joyous that she had succeeded and was thinking about the effect it would have on her Moscow overlords. She looked over her shoulder and smiled at Sean. She then began trawling through all the files. Sean felt pleased.

'Look at the one called QUERY,' Sean said wryly. 'Quite a revelation if you ask me.' He then stood up and made his way to the drinks bar.

Chapter 45

Languedoc-Roussillon

Swartz and the eight SAS soldiers remained pensive as they waited to move out of their bolthole. Few people talked, most just sat checking their kit, some had the odd discussion and each of them visualised their mission-specific tasks for the night ahead. There was no gung-ho behaviour, no high fives, no pre-match banging of heads. They were just waiting for a concise and highly charged set of orders to be given to them by Swartz.

The guys knew they'd be in for yet another of Swartz's stirring speeches for this set of orders. They all knew him well and responded to him. They would follow him anywhere. He looked around each of the faces as they sat close together in a semicircle in the room.

He gave each person one short nod and a curious smile before he began speaking. The smile meant, 'Follow me boys, you'll be fine.' Swartz had a real knack of being personable and genuine when it came to delivering such a crunch briefing, which he relished. His brief focused the hearts and minds of every single soul in the room.

Swartz did not make the briefing too long. To have effect, he knew it had to be short, sharp and to the point. But he did know he had to raise the tempo and give a morale-boosting uplift to the assembled team, which he did with aplomb.

The atmosphere was tense as he finished going through the timings. With professional control, the small team were now at the apogee of their instincts – primed like elite athletes, high on adrenalin, immersed in courage.

They moved quietly to mount their vehicles and headed to the drop-off points. The first phase would see Phil the nose taking control of how they entered the building: he would provide the 'eyes on' the three Russians that they would take out and kill. Phil the nose assigned Jim and Chris to take control of the sensors and central initiation switch, as well as searching for any covert cameras that might be in play.

The first four men made their way to their pre-identified positions around the building, hard up against its skin, whilst avoiding the external PIRs. It was now 7.45pm and reasonably dark. Swartz would lead the shooters who would execute the kill. Radios would not be allowed to transmit until Phil the nose had done his job by means of an explosive entry through the windows on the ground floor.

Chris set up his endoscope and immediately had eyes on the room that Melissa was booby-trapped in. The other team had eyes on the kitchen and hall. It was quiet, with only the slight noise of distant traffic in the air.

Meanwhile, Jim was poised to take out the initiation switches, which he assumed were under the sofa in the lounge.

They sat silently and waited.

Swartz watched Phil the nose assemble a small line of explosives on the two windows and door to be used for entry. It took him a while to carefully lay out the detonation cord and detonators, and then make his way around the house to each entry point he would soon blow open. His fingerless black gloves allowed him to calmly twist the initiation wires and accurately prime the detonators deep within the line of blue plastic explosive. He pre-prepared his detonation cord connections and used small metal clips to make sure it lay in a structured manner. Then he rolled the small coil of black wire back to his start point.

Swartz helped him with the coil, feeling the sweat emerge on his brow and hearing the sound of distant thunder as he watched Phil the nose configure the remote detonating device. Phil the nose used his teeth to expose two wires through the plastic, twisted them and then finally pressed them into a spring-loaded capsule which he held between his knees.

Phil the nose was good to go. He took a long breath and checked the time on his army-issue watch. Swartz heard Phil the nose curiously hum the Welsh national anthem, 'Land of my Fathers', as he always did, keeping his fingers crossed and hoping that the foreigners were not watching the CCTV. Swartz then watched Phil the nose mimic his next moves: mind and movement rehearsals for his actions in the room – something he had watched Phil the nose do all day during the quiet periods. It was vital Phil the nose moved with great speed to the bomb if he was to keep his life – and save Melissa's.

It was all set. They didn't know exactly where the Russians were, but they knew where they could and couldn't go, with the myriad of booby traps inside the house.

Melissa was lying on her bed, curled up in the foetal position with the bomb around her neck. Swartz switched the MP5 safety catch and checked that Phil the nose and the other operators were primed to spring into action. The explosive means of entry was set.

Swartz heard the distant thunder, knowing it would get closer, as a deep blackness drew in. He waited.

Chapter 46

Languedoc-Roussillon

As Sean leant over to lift his cup in Natalie's hotel room, all hell broke loose. He heard the boom of a thunderous explosion as the door was smashed open and saw the black outlines of two very large men, who pounced on him, smashing him to the ground.

He heard the crack and thump of a double tap gunshot as he watched Natalie stand and fire two shots into the second attacker, who kept coming straight for her despite bullets hitting his chest. The body armour repelled the nine-millimetre shots. Natalie was pounced on by a huge man, who punched her straight in the face before turning her onto her chest and thrusting her head into the carpet. Sean was bundled to the ground, his arms and shoulders pinned down, and a set of plastic tie-wrap handcuffs violently strapped around his wrists. He felt the pain of his nose breaking as he was brutalised into submission.

'What the fuck?' Sean screamed, before being kicked firmly in the ribs. They pulled him to his feet as the shock of capture registered once again with him.

'Right. Get these two out of here, do a check for weapons and make sure you search them thoroughly before you get them into the wagons,' the commander shouted. He gestured to his team to get a move on.

Sean was frogmarched outside the hotel. All he saw was blue and white police tape and flashing blue lights everywhere. The hotel had been quietly evacuated and he caught the eyes of a crowd of people watching from a distance behind a cordon manned by the gendarmerie.

Chapter 47

Languedoc-Roussillon

It was 9.55pm. Cold dark shadows. A gloved hand firmly placed on the shoulder.

'Fucking hell Sean, you're cutting it fine,' Swartz said, shocked by the silent approach.

'Late but primed mate. The bloody French overdid it a bit.'

'Shit, I can see that. You look like Phil the nose now. Your conk is bent to fuck.'

'It breathes. All set to go?'

'Yep. Let's do this.'

At 10.05pm Sean moved round the corner, tapped Phil the nose on the back and gave the order. He watched Phil the nose stand, then glide his thumbs across the small detonating equipment until he felt them reach the recessed buttons. Sean heard the whispered words 'Three, two, one, firing now.'

Phil the nose pressed the two buttons simultaneously, sending the electric current down the wire and into the detonation cord.

'BOOM.' The air around the cottage vacuumed and the over-pressure of the explosion rocked every timber of the building. The noise was deafening and each of the three men inside were semi-frozen with shock. The blast wave forced the two windows out and the doors blew off their hinges – all with simultaneous precision. Phil the nose had given two firm presses on his radio switch to signal to the rest of the team, followed by another two presses which signified five seconds until explosion. Each of the men heard the short crackles of the button being pressed, tensed up poised to strike and shot into action as soon as the doors and windows were blown off.

Sean threw a stun grenade into the kitchen and waited for the six rapid flashes and explosions. He counted the fifth bang and entered the kitchen on the sixth. The flash bangs were over in less than three seconds as Sean stepped around the corner into the room, with Swartz slightly behind him on his left shoulder. Sean saw a Russian at the end of the room, frozen with shock, and aimed the red laser at the middle of his forehead. He fired two shots to the head and another two shots at his torso. The Russian slumped to the ground and within a second, Sean had sprinted past him and turned right into the hall, moving quickly but breathing hard.

Jim leapt into the lounge seconds after the windows had exploded and was at the sofa within four quick strides. 'Fuck!' he shouted, as he saw an incendiary device to his right explode, making a loud crack and a shallow pop before it burst into flames. The flashback engulfed him, before the flames swamped the wall and curtains at the end of the room.

'Must have set off a bloody sensor,' he muttered, as he looked at the flashing motion detector located high above him to the left. The fireball reduced in intensity and he cracked on at speed, pushing the sofa backwards as quickly as he could. The heat in the room was increasing. He was faced with two square plywood boxes and black wires connected to two mobile phones strapped to the side: the command box for all the booby traps in the house. He shuddered, knowing that at any time someone could detonate the devices from a remote location many miles away. He was staring into the abyss – and he froze. One of the phones was ringing. He knew he had seconds to live.

But the seconds continued. 'For fuck's sake,' he ranted. 'This is crazy.'

Nothing happened.

The phone continued to ring. He knew he had seconds before the next one would ring, and he instinctively grabbed the phone, ripping the wires from its connection. The fire inside the room was raging and he knew he was in trouble.

'The bomber fucked it up and something failed,' he mused instinctively. He had been staring at a complex multi-initiation bomb and watched the phone screen light up in green as it rang. He knew the first phone had to ring followed by the second, before full initiation would take place.

He had done it. He had stopped the entire house from being blown up. He lay there for a few seconds, gripped by the sheer luck of a failing circuit. The fire was searing, and the flames were now whipping out of the windows and shooting up to the second floor. The heat was intense.

Sean and Swartz had moved through the hall at pace and were starting to climb the stairs when they heard the explosion above them. It was a deep pounding blast that reverberated around them, rocking the staircase violently. Sean saw Swartz blown backwards and was showered from the debris falling from above. Sean recovered from the shock and saw a gaping hole in the roof where the landing had collapsed, with one of the Russians falling through it. He pumped four shots straight into him before moving back down the stairs to the hall as a huge fireball swamped the second floor of the cottage. The building was now in meltdown and Sean assumed that no one would have survived the explosion on the second level. He rushed into the dining room where Melissa was coiled up shaking with fear on the bed and screaming.

He watched Phil the nose leap through the window into the dining room and heard the crack and thump of the explosion next door where Jim would either win or lose the day.

Phil the nose ran a wire onto the first active infrared beam, pressed a switch on his equipment, watched the power lights drain down and gave the thumbs up to Sean. The beams of the virtual fence were de-armed.

'Stay perfectly still Melissa. Lie on your back for me,' Sean instructed as Phil the nose de-armed the other active infrared beams. 'We'll sort you out now, just stay quiet and lie perfectly still. I need to sort this bomb out on your neck, then we'll have you out in a jiffy.'

Melissa was shaking incessantly and crying with intense fear. Her feet were trembling from the panic and Swartz held her legs down as Phil the nose crouched to deal with the bomb attached to her neck. He ripped her gilet open to reveal a black harness with a tiny aerial, a 12-volt power pack and a tiny electronic LED timer.

'What the hell?' Sean mumbled as he saw the secondary initiation system in front of Phil the nose's face. It was an electronic timer that would initiate if the Wi-Fi signal failed at any time.

'Shit,' Phil the nose said. 'Sean – move that bloody Wi-Fi router to the window. If we take her out of the room and the Wi-Fi goes down, the timer will kick in. I don't know the countdown, but it will trigger if we take her outside the Wi-Fi area.'

Sean responded instantaneously, and then moved straight back to watch as Phil the nose checked how the bomber had set up the circuitry. Sean knew immediately that the bomber had put together a damn good system. If these were collapsing circuits then Phil the nose wouldn't be able to cut any wires, and if he did, the explosives around Melissa's neck would detonate, taking her head and torso off and killing him and Phil the nose instantly too. Sean held Melissa still whilst Phil the nose entered his world of instinct. Phil the nose pressed a button on his waistband and, to Sean's astonishment, he heard the canned music of 'The Triumphal March' from *Aida* – Phil the nose's favourite tune to accompany his hands and mind working in rapid synchronisation to defeat the bomb.

Despite Sean nursing her, Melissa shook continuously like she was having a fit – he noticed her breathing was shallow before she fell unconscious.

Gregory was lying on his hotel bed when his laptop alarmed loudly. Foolishly, he didn't have the CCTV screens open on his laptop and had to scramble quickly to get the software booted up. He then reconfigured the six screens, so he could quickly see what was happening in the cottage. Using the mouse, he dragged the screen to show the view of the dining room and enlarged it.

He saw Melissa curled up on the bed with two dark figures just beyond the active-beam stanchions that had been placed around her. In a panic, he brought the wrong screen up to make the phone calls to the three detonating units he had set up in the house. He had placed two under the sofa in the lounge and one upstairs in a small cupboard on the landing. He hit the 'Call' button on the first unit downstairs to initiate the phones. Nothing. He then pulled up the second screen using his mouse and cursor and retyped the password. He cursed as he had failed to keep the screens open and was losing vital time. He looked at the CCTV screen again and saw Phil the nose moving towards Melissa. He clicked on the call button with his cursor. Again nothing. Phil the nose had managed to rip out the wires. Gregory's irritation grew as he repeated the same routine for the last unit upstairs. It took him another thirty-five seconds before the explosion finally occurred on the second floor.

Gregory smashed the desk with his fist, raging as he watched the CCTV pictures disappear from his screen.

The panic and delay had allowed the assaulters just enough time to disarm the downstairs phones that would have initiated all the explosives. The speed of the assault had defeated Gregory and his high-tech booby traps. Only the bomb around Melissa's neck remained.

Phil the nose decided he could not take the risk of moving Melissa and looked frantically for the power unit that would allow the time-delay initiation switch to work. He couldn't find it.

'Hurry up Phil, this place is falling down,' Sean shouted anxiously.

'I'm on it, give me a break,' Phil the nose snapped back without looking up. 'Where's the fucking detonator?' he mumbled frustratingly as Sean watched him feel around the back of Melissa's shoulders before turning her over to finally reveal a small pack on her back that held the power switch and wires. They were connected to the plastic explosive ring around her neck, all of which was held together with black masking tape. The lights went out in the room as the blaze caught hold. Smoke was billowing into the room and began rising high into the dining room.

'The fucking timer's flashing mate,' Sean shouted to Phil the nose, shining the torch on Melissa's chest while Phil the nose was looking at the power unit on her back. The explosions in the house had caused the electricity to fail along with the Wi-Fi router and the timer had now been initiated and was blinking rapidly.

Phil the nose held his breath and quickly cut a number of wires. Sean heard him exhale loudly when nothing happened. His threat assessment was right – it wasn't a collapsing circuit. 'Safe!' Phil the nose shouted.

'Everyone out!' Sean ordered as Swartz burst into the room with Jim. They picked up Melissa's lifeless body and passed her out of the window to Chris and Barky. The cottage was now fully ablaze. Sean coughed and spluttered as he scuttled out of the window before sprinting across the lawn to where Melissa was now lying. He took a quick look at the timer, now set to zero, and fell to the floor on his back, breathing heavily. He then heard the mellifluous sounds of the 'Chorus of the Hebrew Slaves' from *Nabucco* fill the smoky air as he turned to see Phil the nose working through his motivational tunes.

Sean finally caught his breath and crawled to Melissa. He stroked her hair before picking up her limp body and walked across the lawn to the gravel driveway to place her in the unmarked ambulance – Jack held the door open.

Chapter 48

Perpignan

Sean had been quickly taken out of the hands of the French Special Forces team by Jack immediately after the arrest of Natalie. Both of them had been whisked off in a fast security car straight to the target site, whilst Natalie had been flown back to London and then to a safe house for interrogation by MI5. In a very short time, Samantha and her GCHQ operator had been able to incriminate Natalie with holding thousands of the nation's secrets on her laptop, which would be analysed forensically and used as evidence for criminal charges or horse-trading with the Russians.

Sean had figured that she was a deep hidden sleeper of the Russian SVR and that her capture would allow Jack's team to oil the wheels of international spy diplomacy for a suitable trade-off with Moscow.

Melissa was taken in a traumatic condition to a private hospital near Perpignan, where she slowly began to recover. Jack arranged early next morning to have her transferred by plane to a secure hospital in Marylebone. Sean flew back with her and Jack having bidden farewell by phone to Billy Phish and Jugsy, who were still none the wiser as to the covert events of the last couple of days. He made a mental note to go and visit them both and let them know the final outcomes once the dust had settled. He wanted them both for the next job he had planned in his head – a big one. A reprisal.

On the plane, Sean looked at Melissa strapped into a bed. He was content that his precision tactics had worked despite the horrific pain suffered by Melissa and the carnage that had ensued the night before. Sean admired how Jack had everything in hand

and everyone on call to tidy up the mess, so that the aftermath could be dealt with quietly by MI5 and the French General Directorate for Internal Security without any fuss.

Sean took Melissa's hand and gently stroked her forehead. 'It was a damn close thing you know, but you'll be fine now,' he whispered.

Melissa smiled, still groggy but conscious of Sean's presence. 'I've no idea what happened but I bloody well hope you've sorted this out once and for all,' she said tenaciously, before holding his hand and beckoning to him to kiss her. He didn't resist this time.

'Anyway, what on earth happened to your nose?'

'Had a slight hiccup whilst playing Russian roulette,' he said sarcastically.

Chapter 49

Knightsbridge, London

Sean emerged from the Tube station into a glorious London evening. He felt revitalised and cheerful as he wandered past the grand old Georgian terraces of Knightsbridge. It was a time of calm contemplation that would bring finality to this case before he would slip away from the service, quietly knowing he had kept to his values. His hair had grown back, and he'd blissfully asked the hairdresser to apply a light wax after he'd had it tidied up. He chose to wear a light grey suit, white shirt and club tie for his meeting with Jack, which he sensed would reveal the gaps in the operation.

'Who is still alive on the list of moles, he wondered? Who bloody well killed Alfie? And what cover-ups would the establishment put in place now?' His mind was full of these thoughts as he took a gentle stroll to the club.

Jack had suggested to Sean that they should meet that evening at the Special Forces Club, which was discreetly located amongst the Knightsbridge mews and was a place where they both knew they could talk in confidence.

Sean stopped for a moment on the street to send a message to Samantha. He needed to tee up the final job with the team and punched out the text quickly.

'*Thanks for all your help – can you drop those drugs running files onto Frazer's company computers please? With the child abuse photos. Can you also get Jugsy to have his drone ready to go in the next few days. Stand up Swartz, Phil, and One-Eyed Damon too please. I'll send dates and timings and RV shortly. Critical job. Will grab a coffee with you to say Hi when I get back.*'

He watched the screen indicate that she was online and responding. '*Consider it my pleasure – You're a lovable, avoiding bastard,*' she replied seconds later.

Sean walked up to the door of the club and pressed the buzzer. The door opened and Sean walked into the club, a place of mystery and intrigue where his old commanding officer, friend and mentor had often met him for lunch.

The Special Forces Club had been founded at the end of the Second World War by the surviving members of the Special Operations Executive and it had remained a meeting place for those who had served in the SOE and for members of the Special Forces and the intelligence and security communities, along with others, such as experts from bomb disposal and counterterrorist units.

It felt strange for Sean to step back into the club having spent so much time outside of the fold. He sensed that Jack wanted to bring him to a place that was evocative of the Special Operations family, but totally secure and discreet. He wondered what the meeting would reveal.

He walked up the long winding steps from the hall to the bar, taking his time to look at the portraits on the wall of Special Forces legends who had accomplished deeds of derring-do. Sean caught a glimpse on the way up the stairs of a watercolour showing 'Gentleman Jim' Almonds in the North African desert standing next to his boss David Stirling, both of whom were founding members of the SAS. He finally walked into the bar and saw Jack in the far corner. It was a quiet evening and there were only two unassuming elderly ladies sitting near the entrance. Two younger men, clad in jackets and ties, arrived and stood at the bar drinking ale.

'Great to see you Sean. Take a seat and I'll get you a drink. Red wine?' Jack inquired. Sean agreed and stood for a while, looking at a small oil painting in memory of the massacre of a number of long-forgotten SAS heroes in France during World War Two. Thirty SAS soldiers had been captured and executed by the Germans during Op Loyton in October 1944 – a mission behind enemy lines to create havoc in the Vosges region. It was one of the greatest-ever losses of SAS soldiers and Sean was touched to see a small brass inscription from the family of Wallace Hall, one of the young troopers who was believed to have been tortured and killed in a German camp near the village of Moussey in the Vosges.

'I expect you're wondering what happens next then, after all the furore?' Jack asked. Sean smiled and sat back in the corner of the soft bench seat below a large painting of a wartime SOE parachute drop in France.

'Well, I thought we'd chat about how all this came about and about the history behind the operation Sean. It's rather complex I'm afraid but a worthwhile story to tell in here, of all places.' Sean smiled, allowing Jack to continue.

'You remember the job you did in 2005 in Moscow which led to all this? You know, the one where you handed over the small cache?'

'Yes, of course,' Sean said knowingly. 'It was a great job, but it had some unusual historic complexities as I remember.'

'Exactly,' Jack said. 'Well, this operation we have just unravelled was linked to that cache, the rusty tin's contents and the list of moles that you handed over to the spook in the van. It's just sheer coincidence that it was you who undertook that job in Moscow. The tin contained, amongst other documents, a list of names of British sleeper agents who were being groomed by the Russians at UK universities at the time. The agent who buried that tin and knew of the list and its contents was a chap you have called WYNTHROP. The names on the list were from the '70s and those who are still alive are quite old now. The list was never seen again after WYNTHROP buried it, and not known about until you uncovered it in 2005.'

Sean cast his mind back to the small civil servant, Edward, who had handed him the file to read in the FCO basement before Sean had undertaken the job in Moscow. Edward had occasionally been in touch with Sean over the years.

Jack continued. 'Well, the backdrop to all this is the deeply strained relations between America and Russia during the cold war crisis of 1980. Under President Carter, America deployed hundreds of Pershing nuclear missiles in Western Europe, causing a toxic stand-off between the two countries. Relations just plummeted and both nations pretty much had their fingers permanently on the nuclear trigger. You'll recall this was a highly charged game of deception, with the Russian army fully mobilised for months. The stand-off between the Americans and Russians took the world to the brink of nuclear war, as you know. In March 1980, as it all flared up virulently, the staff at the British Embassy in Moscow made plans to evacuate the Embassy. This included plans to destroy tech systems, cassettes, video tapes and files.'

Sean remembered the red file marked 'Top Secret' and how Edward, the mild-mannered civil servant, had recounted the story, all fully documented in the file, of how the Embassy staff had decided in angst to bury and secrete a considerable quantity of tapes, files, secrets and weapons in numerous holes that they had dug in the basement of the Embassy.

Sean revelled in the story as Jack filled in the gaps. 'The man in charge of burying all the stuff was a double agent that you have now called WYNTHROP. He was an old-school, Eton-educated MI6 officer. WYNTHROP was gay and the Russians had recruited him in 1971 to provide secret information to his Russian handlers. WYNTHROP buried the cache you handed over – next to all the other stuff. And he drew a map of its location once he had concreted it over. WYNTHROP defected to the Russians shortly after that, comforted that the list was safe and that Russian interests had been safeguarded. But he made a mistake.'

Jack took a sip of his wine and showed Sean an old letter. 'Before he defected, he told a close friend of his in MI6 that the list existed – and this is the letter he wrote. His close friend eventually became 'C', the Chief of Service for MI6, in the '90s. C decided not to pursue the list of moles, when it eventually surfaced, but passed the knowledge onto his successors. It was known as The QUERY.'

Sean looked at the letter, which was now very stained and its handwritten ink hard to fully decipher.

'So, this was why Alfie had used the word to title his files,' he mentioned quizzically.

'The story is something of an MI6 legend, especially regarding the frantic activity of evacuating the Embassy with lives at risk in

1980. They had to quickly destroy vital top-secret documents, prepare to destroy their key communication equipment, pack up their belongings, seal the British territory and put plans in place to evacuate the children, wives and support staff.'

Sean listened intently, before explaining to Jack his memories of the Moscow job in 2005. 'I remember Edward saying the caches they had buried had been left untouched for decades. I remember the precise drawings Edward gave me of the locations of the caches in the basement. Where did they come from?'

Jack leant forward. 'Well, no one except for one man actually knew that the secret list of British graduates being groomed existed. So, no one sought to dig them up. Until, that is, the map and letter were posted to C shortly after WYNTHROP died. Maybe it was his final act of loyalty to the Crown? And that is why C called it The QUERY.'

'Fascinating,' Sean said gleefully. 'WYNTHROP clearly had a conscience. I do remember the map, finding and digging the stuff up and throwing all the bags of kit into the river before we handed the rusting tin over to a bloke in a van.'

Jack listened to Sean's story and they enjoyed talking about the clandestine activities of cold war Russia that had now spilled over into both of their lives in 2016.

'So, who arranged for me to dig them up Jack? Who actually tasked that job?'

'All I can say Sean is that FITZROY was sitting in the car when you were throwing stuff in the river and that he was operating for C in 2005. He was an MI6 agent.'

Jack paused. And Sean sensed he was carefully crafting his words.

'FITZROY left MI6 in 2012 but during that time he became the guardian of the QUERY list. Now that C had the list, the query was solved – and he was able to feed disinformation to the Russians. He ran those deception ops for many years until he passed it on to the next C. It was only later on that the Chief of MI6 found out that our man Alfie had somehow hacked into C's account and found the list during his research. We needed to ensure it didn't get into the wrong hands. The Russians clearly didn't want that list to be exposed as it would have implicated them in grooming on a massive scale and given away the names of some of their most distinguished establishment sources in Britain. What's more, if Alfie had released the list of names, it would have destroyed the careers of the people at the very top of the tree and stopped C's ability to deceive the Russians with high-grade counter-intelligence. We wanted to make sure only the bad apples on the list were destroyed and not the ones who were of use to us. We achieved that. The current C obviously knows I'm running this operation – and he's looking forward to seeing Dominic suffer, if you get my meaning.'

'Wow, that's some piece of deception.'

'The current C also managed to convert three of the four people still alive into double agents, and he continues to run a highly secret disinformation operation by passing worthless information back to the Russians. So you can see we couldn't have run this as a fully sanctioned operation as word would have got out across the agencies. The QUERY, as we now call the list, is exactly that. It is for C's eyes only and, of course, for those of his most trusted of aides who exist within a special operations group. C is now ready to oust the Cabinet minister. He never converted him, but we monitored him closely. We bided our time until he became useful to us in exposing him as a spy – and that time will come very soon. We'll start to leak a few snippets to the press to line it all up for when the time is right.'

Jack paused and then leant forward. 'The Minister and Dominic have no idea we are about to shaft them both. We have now managed to locate the rottenest of apples in our establishment – and the most disloyal – and Dominic is at the top of that list.'

'Because Dominic is trying to protect the Cabinet minister?' Sean asked. 'The last of the Russian moles you mean?'

'Exactly Sean. Dominic had taken the bait, no doubt having been handsomely paid by the Minister so that he would protect him, and C managed to stitch this all together as a ruse, knowing full well Dominic was corrupt in many ways and had been for some considerable time. This also stops Dominic becoming the next C.'

'So is Hannlan the mole?'

'Yes. Sir Joe is indeed the Russian mole.'

'Fucking hell – Sir Joe Hannlan,' Sean exclaimed. 'I knew it when I saw that name on the list in the QUERY file of Alfie's. Strewth, the shit will hit the fan there.'

'Yes, it's Sir Joe Hannlan, the current Foreign Office Minister in the Cabinet who oversees aspects of national security. Sir Joe was groomed at a late stage of his university career by the Russians to act as a direct source of political information to the KGB. Recruitment in British universities was not only the preserve of MI5 and MI6.'

Sean sat back, let out a long sigh and thought deeply. He sipped his wine as both men paused to gauge the other's thoughts. Jack carried on.

'He's a very close friend of the Foreign Secretary Sean, and therefore carries great influence. You can see why we have had to act carefully on this, can't you? We can't expose Sir Joe just yet until we've got all our ducks in a row and decided how to progress things – one shot at a time, so to speak. Many of the other names have long since died, but Sir Joe is quite crucial as he would be the highest-level politician ever to be exposed as a Russian spy.'

'So, Dominic will of course be held in great favour if he protects Sir Joe from being exposed,' Sean remarked.

Jack nodded as Sean's thoughts crystallised. Sean then continued. 'I see. I'm beginning to think that Dominic would want Sir Joe to carry huge weight and to favour him in return for keeping his affiliations with the Russians under wraps. In other words, Sir Joe could easily get the Foreign Secretary to make sure that Dominic became Chief of MI6, in return for stopping his name being exposed. Well I never.'

'Indeed Sean. But what Dominic doesn't know is that C had teed up this operation all along. It was a genuine counter-espionage operation, only it was run by a small cabal called The 'Court'. A double deception. Allowing Sir Joe to know that the list was about to be leaked would create a swathe of underground activity. All C needed to do was to see who Sir Joe turned to for help. And who would come crawling out.'

Sean smirked and held his wine glass up to gesture 'Cheers'. Jack obliged. 'Listen Sean, there are other angles to this too. The government could easily topple over all this, and the Prime Minister could be culled. There are some big discussions going on right now to decide which chess piece is moved next. I suggest we meet up in a week or so and see what the likely outcome is.'

'Sounds fine to me. But tell me Jack, what have you found out about the Ambassador and what will you do about him after all those leaks? The bastard nearly got me killed.'

'Oh, we have plenty up our sleeve on that one. The man is a traitor of the highest order who was put out to roost long ago. But we'll decide who to expose first, and when, and then we'll deal with the others at a point where we can get some return and value. A bird in the hand, so to speak...'

Sean sensed that there was a lot more mileage in this case and he had a slight niggle in his mind about the establishment politics of it all. 'Treacherous bastards,' he mused. It could all just be covered up and forgotten about, it depended on how the current C planned to expose Sir Joe and Jonathan Hirst. Either way, Sean knew he was just a small cog in a bigger political wheel and he wondered how long it would be before that wheel turned and Dominic was finally sacked from government service.

'And by the way Sean, to avoid any doubt, you are now a free man.'

'Free? Not quite. I'm nearly free Jack.'

'I understand. Do you need anything from me?'

Sean smiled. 'No thanks. I just need you to turn the other way for a short time Jack. Nothing more.'

'Mucky business all round,' Sean thought as he left the Special Forces Club that night. He reflected on the fact he was now unshackled, had one last act to perform to neutralise his ghosts and could then pursue a new life. He started to imagine the shape, colour and style of the painting he wanted to create of his i2 map – Moscow and WYNTHROP would be dead centre he thought. He did wonder though whether Jack was again testing his loyalty and whether or not there were more skeletons hiding in more cupboards.

Sean's phone vibrated. It was TABASCO. '*All sorted. All on standby for the next episode of mayhem. Talking of fun – stay away from any tarts. Your fun is here.*'

Chapter 50

London

'Can you rig up an initiation device with passive infrared telemetry?' Sean said quietly. 'One with dual sensors that can be kept forensically clean?'

Phil the nose looked around the nicely adorned Soho pub, glanced at the Victorian-themed stained glass panels and nodded. There were two senior citizens drinking half pints of Fuller's London Pride in the corner, and a group of builders standing at the bar. The music from the retro jukebox muted enough of the conversation to allow Phil the nose to expand further. 'All very doable, but where will we get the bang from? And what type of bang?'

'Shaped charges,' Sean said.

'For fuck's sake,' Swartz spluttered, spilling his pint of Rebellion real ale. 'That's my fucking pension gone again.'

The three of them sat awaiting the arrival of One-Eyed Damon, who had promised Sean he could get the bang.

'One last soirée for the team then?' Phil the nose inquired.

'You could say that,' Sean said.

'Another fucking ruse,' Swartz added, slurping his beer loudly.

Phil the nose, forever the optimist, shrugged his huge boxer's shoulders and asked Sean what the plan was.

'It's a final nail,' Sean said. 'Something that needs to be done to take an evil bastard off this earth before we all move on to a normal life, and await the next adventure.'

'A life, I hope, with my pension intact,' Swartz said. 'Between you, Jack and the rest of the crew, I've seen my twenty-six years disappear down the pan on three occasions now. I love a rumble, but can we make this the very last one please? I've only got days to go.' They all laughed.

One-Eyed Damon walked into the pub and they all looked at him. Sean watched him meander calmly to the bar, ask for a pint of Guinness and fold his white stick up – almost indicating he was ready for a session.

'I'll get that,' the tall cockney builder said, undoing his high-visibility vest. 'You're an army veteran mate and it's my honour to get you a beer.'

'Ta very much, you're a real gentleman,' One-Eyed Damon said. 'But you better get that lot over there a beer too. They're hard-core veterans too mate, and they can sink a few.' Sean winced at the attention being drawn to his crew. One-Eyed Damon winked at him. Sean sensed the boys were up for some mischief. One-Eyed Damon shook the builder's hand, grinned and brought a tray full of beer over to the lads. 'A fine gesture,' he said.

'Damon, before we get on it, we have some pretty key business to sort out,' Sean said keenly.

'Never a problem. Beer helps us all to focus mate, as well as giving us a good laugh. Bless the great British public for buying us ales, eh? Don't you just love 'em to bits?'

'Tell the guys what you picked up on with Frazer.'

'Well, all I can say is you're dealing with one nasty bastard,' One-Eyed said. 'It was my pleasure to put the shits up him, as he's an evil twat. He's running a full-on organised crime syndicate with the Albanians. Pop-up brothels across London and the South East, running drugs mules via Turkey and across the EU and shipping in women from the Balkans like there's no tomorrow.'

'Our target then,' Swartz chirped.

'I think that's the plan,' One-Eyed continued. 'We've figured out his pattern of life and he always has two Albanian minders with him wherever he goes. But he has the same routine on a weekend, a religious routine.'

'Rugby religion?' Phil the nose asked teasingly.

'Fuck no. The bloke's a real wimp. But he does like to throw his weight around with women. He busted the arms of two prostitutes he felt weren't performing. I've arranged for them to be extracted and looked after properly. He's a real nasty bastard and vicious in every way. Fuck knows how you got involved with him Sean.'

'Bad judgement whilst in a deep mire,' Sean replied. 'Just so we all know, Damon has done a great job on this. He has followed the guy for weeks, seen his movements, tracked the stashes of drugs coming from Afghanistan and worked with Samantha to nail the fucker by finding evidence of all of his ruthless operations across Europe. The time has come to take the bastard out.'

'Not least because he fucked you over,' Swartz added. 'Pension or no pension, we're a team and I'm with you. This needs to be done.'

Phil the nose and One-Eyed Damon raised their glasses and they toasted Swartz's endorsement. Sean was touched. He composed himself. 'OK guys, love the sentiments. In fact, I love the lot of you, but we need to sharpen up for this one. It's a complex plan and kill. But one we must get absolutely right to stay out of jail.'

One-Eyed Damon picked up his pint and downed it in one. 'Right guys, follow me. We have a meeting to make with a few scrotes.'

Sean and Damon led the way to a gentleman's club a few minutes' walk from the pub. They were expected and escorted down a narrow set of steps deep into the bowels of a club owned and run by a high-grade Bulgarian syndicate. It fronted up as a British business, with Damon's former army mate, a Brit, acting as the company boss. The Bulgarians were all close friends of Damon with whom he had operated in the Balkans. They were Damon's go-to team for weapons, explosives and strong-arm men when dirty business was called for.

The club had a centrepiece stage surrounded by white-leather sofas and armchairs. On the flanks were two small pole-dancing stages, on which stood topless women entertaining clients who chose to meander around the club. The centre stage was dominated by a teenage blonde from Moldova and she winked at Damon as he led the team to the bar before going to the back office. The pert dancer kept her gaze on the four men as she wrapped her legs skilfully around the pole, before sliding down to adopt a spreadeagled position, much to the joy of those in the front row. Along the bar and across the floor spaces were plenty of women dressed in bikinis who were eager and ready to take money from the clientele.

'Like it,' Phil the nose piped up, taking the beer from Damon as the bartender ensured the men were all served first.

'Don't get too comfy,' Sean said. 'It's you who will be negotiating for me in a few minutes.' Phil the nose nodded, shook his beer at Sean and tapped his boxer's nose.

A few moments later, Damon returned with his Bulgarian friend Naz. He was a small beast of a man built like a beer barrel with a thin face and two gold front teeth. One-Eyed Damon introduced Naz to the team and led the way to a private room.

'So, gentlemen, how can I help you today?' Naz said, smiling. He waved to a very pretty girl clad in a yellow bikini and white high heels who was standing by the salubrious bar. She came over and poured Sean a large beer, and a second woman placed small pots of olives and chilli bread on the table.

Sean took an olive and leant forward towards Naz, who was sitting directly opposite him. 'I need some shaped charges,' Sean said. 'Small copper ones, but if you have tantalum and the price is right, I'll think about those too.'

'Well, I think we'll drink to that gentlemen,' Naz said, raising his glass. 'It means you're on your way to a bit of action, and as we're all military men, who can deny us such deeds?' Naz was a former Bulgarian Spetsnaz soldier who, according to One-Eyed Damon, had the market share of all military-grade weaponry being smuggled through the EU from the Balkans.

'Never seen tantalum ones. They're really special I think. I do have some copper ones in stock, stolen from an Iranian gang I think, but let me check where.' Naz beckoned to his second-in-command behind him. Sean noticed he was wearing a chest holster as he leant over to listen to Naz whisper in his ear.

'I need them very urgently,' Sean said, 'like yesterday and I'll pay well for quick delivery.'

'How much explosive do you want in them, and what about firing mechanisms?'

'Enough for four or five inches of copper to be projected. Don't worry about the initiation, we have that in hand.' Sean looked across to Phil the nose, who nodded.

'OK. Where do you want it delivered?'

Sean passed him a small business card showing the address of a lock-up in Battersea. 'Tomorrow morning at 6.30am would be ideal.'

Swartz looked at Sean quizzically as Naz stood up and left to make a phone call. 'What the fuck?' he said. 'Are we doing this tomorrow?'

'We are mate, and we don't have much time to prep for it. Jugsy is on the team and will launch his C-Astral unmanned air vehicle at 9am, ready to track Frazer as he heads to his villa on the coast. He'll be in the first of two armour-plated Range Rovers, with his protection team following. He never had protection before until One-Eyed decided to leave a marker that scared the shit out of the bloke, and now he's gone for high-end security.' One-Eyed Damon laughed, the glint in his false eye showing a Yorkshire rose.

'So, we're gonna launch a full-on hit job using shaped charges? For fuck's sake Sean, great idea but this isn't Afghanistan you know. Why don't you use an under-vehicle device?'

'I checked on that option,' One-Eyed chipped in. 'I found out he has his vehicle fleet fitted with Precipio under-vehicle detectors. They pick up tracking devices and bombs mate.'

'Good skills,' Swartz said. 'I guess a full-on ambush Afghan-style is as good as anything else.'

'Don't worry. Your pension will be fine Swartz. I promise you,' Sean said. 'We have a big party planned that involves a top-drawer ruse.'

Phil the nose chuckled, and patted Swartz on the back. 'You know it makes sense,' he said, waving the pretty girl over. 'One for the road anyone?'

Naz returned with a big smile on his face and gave Sean a note. 'This is the courier's number. I've told him I'll kill him if he fails to deliver exactly at 6.30. He's doing a recce now and will take them off the shelf. I have three if you want to go for a third?'

'Perfect. How much?'

'These are very special stores my good man. All in, it's eleven grand with a third, and I'll slip in a couple of Glocks too.'

Sean nodded to Phil the nose and a small rucksack was lifted from below the table and handed to Naz's right-hand man.

Sean looked at his Samsung tablet to study the live images of two Range Rovers slowing down at a roundabout before turning into the countryside on a B-road. Jugsy was operating the two-metre fixed-wing UAV from his Sussex farmstead. He had launched it at exactly 9am using a catapult system. The UAV had a four-hour loiter time and could zoom right into the occupants of a vehicle from a height of two thousand feet, where it whirred silently. The imagery was sharp and clear, and Jugsy relayed data to Sean using the chat system of the air-imagery software.

Sean sat with Swartz behind a four-foot-high hedge monitoring the screen. They were located halfway down a narrow country lane that gave access to Frazer's villa and provided a perfect escape route on their Enduro motorbikes through woodland which provided excellent cover. Sean had sat in the bushes with Swartz from daybreak and had walked the road to precisely determine the points to place their three copper explosive projectiles. The projectiles would penetrate the armour and wreak havoc inside the vehicle, creating a searing fireball.

'Are you in place and ready Tango two?' Sean said over his radio to Phil the nose and One-Eyed Damon. His earpiece was under his black woollen hat, and his tablet was attached to his chest rig.

'Roger,' came the reply.

'Good. They're currently at red five, moving to red six. Astral has checked the road and we're all good to go. Watch and shoot.'

Swartz stood up, patted Sean on the shoulder and began to make his way to his position further along the hedgerow. 'It's the right thing to do mate, and you know we have your back mate. We're family.'

Sean was humbled that his mates had given him the nod that the past was the past, and that what had been had been. This was a new era but he knew he had one last demon to expunge. And his mates agreed. He looked back at the screen. Jugsy had now zoomed into the front car, just as Sean had asked him to from the map position red six onwards.

'Locked in,' Sean heard over the radio. 'Trigger and set.'

Sean put his gloved right hand inside his jacket and pulled out his firing device. With both thumbs he simultaneously pressed the two arming buttons. 'Game on,' he whispered. At exactly that time, Phil the nose and One-Eyed Damon staged a car crash at the main junction providing access to the narrow road, blocking it entirely.

The two vehicles drove round the right-hand bend, known as green two, and were now in the ambush zone. The rear vehicle was thirty metres behind the lead vehicle, exactly as One-Eyed had said from his previous surveillance of their pattern of life. They were now heading slightly downhill, with one blind bend left before the hit zone. Frazer was sitting in the passenger seat of the front vehicle.

'At green three,' Sean heard in his headset, as he crawled beneath the hedgerow. He stood and walked right into the middle of the road, raising his Glock pistol to head height. He stood still, feet slightly apart, shoulders tensed, knees bent and his left eye closed. He peered through the sights.

The lead vehicle came around the bend slowly, right into Sean's sights. He paused, took two deep breaths and let off a volley of shots straight into the windscreen. The windscreen shattered and the car sped up, driving directly at Sean as it screeched in second gear. He saw Frazer lunging forward to clear the screen and then bam!

Whoosh! Zing! The passive infrared sensor hidden in the hedge had initiated the explosive projectile which was five metres further forward and precisely three feet off the ground on an aiming stand. The copper inverted itself, and with a loud crack, formed a high-speed jet of metal that seared through the passenger door at thousands of metres per second directly into the occupant of the car, killing him instantly.

The car slewed to a halt, and Sean heard the second projectile flash and boom as the rear vehicle went straight into its escape drill of a handbrake turn, to turn back on itself. Swartz had armed the PIR sensor after it had gone past, knowing full well their drill would make them turn to escape, straight into the ambush.

The front vehicle had halted abruptly, and Sean watched intently as it was engulfed in flames. The rear door opened, and Sean took a few paces forward, raising his weapon with two hands to chest height. A dark figure fell to the ground in the foetal position, looking up to see Sean raise the Glock to eye level. He double tapped the weapon twice. Only the sounds of the gushing flames and an aircraft high above broke the deadly silence. Sean walked to the vehicle and made one last check before jumping the fence into the meadow.

'That's called a re-gain,' he muttered as he fired the Yamaha Enduro up.

Chapter 51

London

Jack caught his normal morning train from the home counties and felt fully vindicated by his judgement and work on the case. He was a happy man and smiled incessantly as he strode purposefully on his way to meet his boss for a debrief on the case. He decided to walk along the river Thames from Westminster, wanting to have a long early morning walk.

He strode along the river past Victoria Gardens and onwards to Millbank, taking in the chilly but clear spring day. He stayed on the river side of Millbank and then crossed towards his office in Thames House. He wondered how this meeting would pan out, what decisions had been made about Sir Joe and what would constitute finality for this case.

He entered the historic building and made his way immediately to see 'D', the Director General of MI5. The Director was expecting Jack, and his secretary ushered him into the large office.

'A splendid result all round I would say Jack. It has really helped a lot, so thank you for all your magnificent efforts.'

D invited Jack to take a seat on the comfortable Chesterfield sofa. 'I wanted to see if you agreed with the next steps I've put in place this week, and also wanted to check we haven't missed anything.'

Jack relaxed, gave a slight smile and replied. 'Of course, I was delighted to help, and yes, I think in the end it worked out perfectly, albeit with some small collateral damage last week. All in all, it was a good result given the complexity of the case.'

D then explained his thinking to Jack. 'I certainly didn't think we would weed out a Russian sleeper agent in all this, but she has given us some extra value with the Russians. It could work rather well as a bargaining chip when we need one, and will help with a new government in place, if you get my meaning? In the meantime, we'll let her, the Russians and some ministers stew whilst she awaits trial. We can expose her at our will, and it's unearthed a lot of other stuff, some of which will be helpful to start disrupting their active-measures cyber campaigns. We found some good data on her devices and it seems we have plenty to go on from her house search too.'

Jack could see that D was delighted at having unearthed a deep sleeper agent and he knew he had a number of interrogators probing Natalie and her secret life. D settled into his brown-leather seat, straightened his dark red tie and unbuttoned his grey suit jacket.

'Anyway Jack, some first-class revelations have come to light and it's given us some bargaining power. It's a bloody good job we knew about that devious ambassador bastard some years ago passing stuff to the Russians and others. It's never a great thing to have an ambassador exposed but the damage is done, and I have a thought about him for later. His head will be Sean's prize.'

Jack listened intently as D leant forward to pour some coffee for them both. He added some milk and lifted his Walpole bone china cup to his mouth. Jack watched him savour the taste.

'I'm rather delighted about how you handled this Jack. A great deception. Anyway, I plan to do the Home Secretary a favour that might just elevate her into the spot we'd all like. I see her as Prime Minister soon and it would be a great improvement for us here if that was to happen. We have a rather special plan for that already underway for next month, the month when Britain will no doubt vote to exit the European Union.'

Jack looked up at D somewhat bemused.

'You see Jack, the world of operating in the shadows is changing and we need to adapt to the way the Russians have operated by focusing on cyberspace, hacking, generating disinformation campaigns and using the media as a vehicle to help us. Operating in the dark web, hacking to steal secrets and running better deception operations is what we need to get better at. They are bloody good at it, as we have seen, and you can bet your bottom dollar the Russians already have a hand deep in the US Presidential elections. It's a new world of hybrid warfare Jack. They taught the Stasi the dark secrets of manipulating the populace, using active measures and influencing agents by growing Department X in 1962 and implementing its doctrine – *Auftrag Irreführung*, or Mission deception.'

D paused and stood. He walked with his coffee to peer out of the large window overlooking the Thames. He studied the London skyline and continued. 'Brexit, Jack, will be our catalyst for change. Make no mistake about that. It will be a year of disinformation and propaganda the likes of which we have never seen before in this country – and it will surely divide us all. But we have planned for that landscape of disinformation and we will use it to our own ends to get the team we need into Downing Street.'

D turned from the window and smiled at Jack knowingly.

The intelligence services had long been sidelined since the Iraq war as being untrustworthy and D saw the time was ripe to change all that. Now was the time to harness the trust of any frontrunner to take over from the current Prime Minister and D saw Sandra Wolstenholme, the current Home Secretary, as exactly the person the intelligence services needed to bring them back into the fold with the government. Intelligence chiefs had been derided for too long.

'Enough of the future… Let me tell you about now,' D said as he sat back down.

D explained to Jack that it was time to drop Dominic in it and put him out of the game. And the time was right to expose Sir Joe as being the spy he was. The Home Secretary would then see the value of D and his operations for retaining the integrity of HM Government, whilst opening the door again for MI5 to the inner workings of the Home Office, instead of Dominic Atwood acting as the gatekeeper, as he had for so long.

D had always been incensed by Dominic Atwood's devious methods within the Home Office and his incessant win at all cost nature, together with his ambition of becoming the Chief of SIS. It was now high time to declare him persona non grata. 'Enough is enough, we will out him,' he said.

'My only regret in all this Jack is that I suspect C may have told the Americans about the plan young Alfie had to expose all these secrets. They clearly had him killed, probably by non-agency people. I suspect because it was too much for the Americans to bear with all these whistle-blowers running amok and spilling all the US secrets, just as elections were looming. If that's the case, it was a foolish error by C.'

Jack smiled and concurred with everything his boss was saying before D continued. 'And so, to the business of the day. Let's get Sean brought back into the fold. You were right to identify him for this. And the next episode. He has all the right skills and attributes for our small team. It was foolish to have such a talent wasted and you've looked after him well Jack. Well done. Let's mould him and bring him into the team. These Russians are about to play a nasty game in the coming years, and we need to be on top form for all this.'

D sat down, placing his cup on the small glass table. 'You know what Jack... Churchill once called Russia "a riddle wrapped in a mystery inside an enigma". He may well have been talking about you and your splendid operation too.'

Jack smiled. 'Right you are sir, I'll get Sean on board. And thank you.'

Jack stood up to leave. 'Sean came very close to turning you know. And who could blame him? But his nerve and loyalty came through in the end.'

'A good test of mettle Jack.'

'Indeed sir. It verifies his resilience for us. He still thinks it's all an MI6 set-up, so I'll need to read him in properly to 'The Court' and our small team. I'll also need to let him know that Natalie is the daughter of an ex-KGB general – and that there is a price on his head now.'

D nodded and politely shepherded Jack to the office door. He gave him a pat on the back. 'I'm very pleased that the secret of C remains very much in our safe hands Jack. And not in C's. Get the file closed down in good order.'

Chapter 52

Tuscany

'No one in the secret services can keep a secret,' Sean proffered to Melissa. 'They are all treacherous bastards you know.'

'Incredibly devious too. You were right not to trust anyone Sean. That's for sure. You've been proven right all along.'

Jack had debriefed Sean on Friday, and that evening, Sean and Melissa had flown from London to Pisa for a few days rest and recuperation in Tuscany. Sean had managed to finish drawing his i2 intelligence map after Jack's discussion and finally all the pieces had fallen into position.

Sean marvelled at his piece of artwork, which now had all the scribbles, lines and faces of all the key players in this game. It included 'C', 'D', Sir Joe, Jack, Natalie, Alfie, the Russians and the Americans who had killed Alfie. WYNTHROP and FITZROY remained central to his drawing. He made all the connections of who had passed information to who, and who was running who. The picture came alive and Sean smiled at it all. He would turn it into a painting one day.

Sean and Melissa were free – for now. Free to explore their own journey whilst the grand and murky politics of the British establishment whirred away in England before the news bombshells would fall. Sean smirked at his vision of the media headlines and the field day they would have each and every day for the coming weeks. What would happen would rock the establishment like never before he thought. And he wondered if D had judged it right and that Sandra Wolstenholme might now be propelled towards being the next Prime Minister. Only time would tell – but he felt D was a master of all the dark forces that were operating.

Sean and Melissa hired a car in Pisa and drove to a small villa overlooking San Gimignano. The countryside was spectacular in mid-May and the weather a pleasant twenty-three degrees with wide blue skies. The villa was magnificent – it was situated in the hills, with superb views looking across to the old medieval town. It had lush vineyards and quiet walking trails in the hills, and its swimming pool was located next to the old Tuscan cottage. Orange and lemon trees grew in the gardens and it was an ideal place to linger and relax, with one eye to the future.

They spent their time relaxing by the pool and visiting the splendid old cities and towns of Tuscany. They explored the hills and walked amongst the vineyards, smiling at the quirk of fate that had inadvertently brought them together. Melissa had entered the agency underworld, unaware of its deadly traps and deceptive nature, and Alfie had paid a vicious price for straying from the fold. Sean felt he owed Melissa some explanations about the intricacy of the circumstances that she and Alfie had found themselves caught up in – and the subsequent aftermath. He took his time over the days to explain the story.

Melissa sat in a purple bikini at the poolside, where they had the small pool and sun loungers to themselves.

'So, you mean to tell me that this was all about protecting one Minister? And that Alfie had uncovered something so sensitive that it led to his own death?' Melissa asked.

'That's pretty much the case, but what Alfie was also going to expose would have pissed off the Americans massively,' Sean answered. 'He was giving away some of the biggest secrets about their Iraq cover-ups. He was going to directly implicate them in the killing of Wilshaw, and the impact on certain American officials would have seen many of them jailed. This was huge. I admire how he investigated the secret list of moles though. It must have taken him months to do it properly.'

'Bastards. But where did Alfie get it wrong then?'

'Well, his fatal mistake was to inform the editor of the Bureau that he had this list of spies among many of the other devastating secrets he had found through hacking.'

'Yes, but he did all that to give credence and strength to his plan to expose the secrets, very much with the intention of showing the editor the veracity of what he had.'

'I know. But unfortunately, the editor then contacted D directly to explain what Alfie had – and what he wanted to expose. The editor was a long-running source from the media into MI5 and had been close friends with D for many years.'

'Bugger,' Melissa exclaimed.

'D then informed the current C that Alfie was about to expose thousands of secret files, and C in turn probably informed the Americans. He didn't know about the list of spies. MI5 monitored Alfie for some considerable time, but the Americans chose to take the easy line and kill him just before MI5 could get to him. Not sure we'll ever find out who killed him, which is a big shame. But it seems he's probably an agent living in Missouri from Liz's forensics.'

'This is so sad though Sean – there was no real reason to kill Alfie and why did the security service not do anything once he left his post?'

Sean touched Melissa's arm and smiled at her, whilst trying to think how best to answer that.

'Well, you know, even I was amazed at how all this came about. There are some smart, very smart, people in the intelligence services, but the smartest guy I have met in a long time is Jack.' Sean collected himself to explain the intricacies of the operation.

'The whole episode was devised by Jack in MI5 – on behalf of D. He is the genius in all this. It was Jack who spotted how he could influence an irregular side operation to trap Dominic, put the microscope of suspicion on him, and at the same time, find Alfie and his files.'

'I'm confused now though. How did Jack do that?'

'Well, it wasn't a side operation at all – it was an MI5 counter-espionage operation all along. Authorised by D and only known about by a small team subservient only to D known as The Court – a special compartment group within MI5.'

'Fascinating. So Jack led this team?'

'Pretty much so. Jack spoofed me and Dominic into thinking it was a side operation. Jack set the bait, hooked him, played him for a while and then smashed him. And we bagged a Russian red under the bed for good measure.'

Sean continued to explain the foggy complications. 'It was all very risky stuff for the Director of MI5,' he said. 'If it all went wrong he needed a scapegoat, to avoid him and Jack carrying the can for any fallout. Their careers and the reputation of the service were at stake. He decided that the only way to operate was to have a high-level fall guy that the Home Secretary could blame and cull if it went wrong.'

'This is brilliant,' Melissa said, 'if it weren't for the suffering everyone's gone through. They certainly had balls going through with this.'

Sean glanced across to the vineyards, watching the gentle spin of the sprinklers spraying the hard soil. He noticed a Tuscan hare dart into the bushes.

'Jack would see Dominic on a daily basis and the two of them had built a very close working relationship. Jack knew the WYNTHROP case would need a side operation to avoid the inevitable chit-chat across intelligence circles. It was a calculated gamble. Jack's shrewd judgements were proved right. Dominic had an inner anger given that MI6 had moved him out of the service and into the backwaters of the Home Office. This operation, carefully proposed to him, would give him an opportunity to get back in as the Chief. Power and control were Dominic's addictions.'

'An arrogant bastard, eh? How did the Russians find out though?'

Sean had thought about this for a while through the fog of war on this job.

'Sir Joe told his closest friend that his name was on the list of moles. His friend is a cross-party peer in the House of Lords, knew for many years of Sir Joe's connections with the Russians and had protected him all along. It was their secret that they would take to their graves. That is until Natalie found out – and she then warned Moscow.'

'Bloody hell – you mean honey-trap stuff then?'

'Indeed. Sir Joe's friend had been having sex with Natalie for many years on and off, and was inadvertently giving away a number of secrets and sensitive matters to Natalie. It seemed innocuous at first to Natalie, but on one occasion, he told her about Sir Joe being horrified that he may be exposed as a Russian spy. Natalie just listened and plied him with more red wine.'

Sean grabbed a beer and explained to Melissa one of the biggest secrets he had unleashed. 'One of the journalists I leaked to, plans to run a series of articles on how an inner sanctum of dodgy lawyers and ex-police officers manipulated evidence for the Iraqi Historical Allegations Team.'

'Juicy stuff then.'

'Yes, and the paper will reveal hidden files, taped meetings and testimonies of ex-policemen and lawyers which will show how a small, Mafia-style cabal ran amok with racketeering on IHAT and other private contracts.' Sean smirked as he knew the entire exposé in the press would see an outcry from the public, who hated seeing British soldiers being hounded. It would create thunder throughout the entire political establishment.

'But how the hell have you gotten away with all that?' Melissa said. 'I'm pleased you did it though – because that was going to be my next case. You just beat me to it you swine.'

Sean laughed and lay back on his sun lounger.

'It played out well for D really. He's been quite happy for me to leak all of this.'

'Why though? This is now officially sanctioned whistle-blowing from MI5,' Melissa exclaimed.

'All rather simple my darling. Deception tactics, manipulation and active measures to achieve an aim. D wants Sandra Wolstenholme to become PM – and exposing these kinds of secrets will provide the launch pad he needs to show her being competent, powerful and anti-corruption.'

'Next stop PM then.'

'That does appear to be D's plan.' They both grimaced at the immensity of the plot – and at the murky world beyond it.

Sean relaxed in his sun lounger, looking across the vineyards to the distant town of San Gimignano. Melissa came across to him, sat on the lounger and kissed him, before holding his hand.

He imagined the sea of change across the political spectrum that would result from the huge amount of whistle-blowing. Politicians would fall. The gravitas of such leaks would force wholesale change – this was shock and awe on an extraordinary scale and the political fallout could be cataclysmic.

The Tuscan sun gently fell as Sean and Melissa revelled in each other's company. 'Well, thanks to you and your policewoman friend, we managed to nail Frazer and his establishment chums too,' Sean said, checking his phone. 'He had paid off a lot of people to win those contracts and it should make a good splash in the papers too on corrupt links to organised crime.'

'Seems we're knocking off quite a few bastards now – I assume he's been put away now?'

'Permanently it would seem, yes.'

Sean smiled at that and he smiled too because he had been offered a new job – of sorts – to return to.

Chapter 53

London

It was a bleak Thursday afternoon when the government decided to spring the news of a high-level Cabinet minister who had been exposed as a Russian spy. Sean sat in his favourite Fitzrovia bar alone. He watched the entire commentary unravel on Sky News. Half a dozen local punters gathered round the TV suspended from the ceiling, the cockney landlord leading the cheers as the exposés were announced. Politicians were being culled. Phrases such as 'Sleeping with the enemy', 'Iraq corruption' and 'A traitorous mole' were mentioned.

Sean listened intently to the news reporter. A silent hush filled the room.

'The Metropolitan Police have this morning released a statement to the effect that an individual has been arrested because of breaches of the Official Secrets Act, and the Prime Minister has decided it was in the public interest to identify who that high-profile minister was. We are expecting an announcement from the Prime Minister within the hour.'

Specific well-timed leaks to the press provided the snippets needed to show that this was the highest-ranking person in British history to be exposed as a Russian spy. Sean checked his Twitter account. There were lots of rumours of a Cabinet minister being a Russian spy. The hashtag 'Whistleblower' was trending.

Sean sat on the bar stool, a glass of cold beer in his hand. Should he have another? An array of newspapers lay on the bar. He began to sketch the people in the lounge and the gesticulations they were making at the TV. It was an image to be captured.

Kay Burley was the news anchor. *'A second statement from the Metropolitan Police this morning reveals that a number of high-profile arrests were made in dawn raids this morning. We understand they all related to the Iraq intelligence dossier from over fourteen years ago. Let's go to our correspondent now outside New Scotland Yard – Frances Dawn.'*

'Hello Kay.'

'Frances: what's been happening then?'

'Well Kay, it's all been moving very quickly here, but my understanding is that the arrests include a number of MPs and a spin doctor and I'm hearing news right now of a former ambassador too...'

Sean sighed. The locals were going spare at the revelations. It seemed as if it would never stop. The day saw a frenzy of media activity, with Sandra Wolstenholme and the Prime Minister personally orchestrating the approach to both the media scramble and the political fallout of such media exposés. Sandra Wolstenholme benefited hugely from the media spotlight as it was her department that had the responsibility for the intelligence operations on home soil and the subsequent high-level 'catches'. The Prime Minister knew he was done for. It was a bombshell right out of left field.

'Think I'll have one of those big beers too,' Jack said, pulling up a stool. 'A small celebration I think.'

'Jeez, don't sneak up on me like that. Lesser men have been floored for that,' Sean quipped.

'Oh well, I live to tell you another tale. Just thought I'd update you personally and no better place than a London pub to do so.'

'Go on, I'm intrigued. Ale or lager?'

'Pale ale please,' Jack said, pointing to one of the hand pumps. 'Well, this morning I accompanied the Cabinet Secretary when he visited Dominic Atwood. We'd kept it under tight wraps for a while and it was all over pretty quickly actually. He was simply told it was now time to go.'

'Wow, what did his face look like?'

'He pretty much went white and stiff as a board.'

'Brilliant. Quietly escorted from the premises, through the back door and into a cab I'm guessing?'

'It was along those lines, yes. Mission accomplished with some aplomb I suppose. The Cabinet Secretary explained how the

Home Secretary was aware of him concealing information about a Russian spy but was content to allow him to retire early in a quiet, no fuss manner.'

Sean passed a beer to Jack and they clinked glasses. 'Tremendous news. Really wish I'd been a fly on the wall for that.' Sean thought of how the chief spook would have known all too well that he had been set up and would have been resigned to all his accomplishments being destroyed, and his lifetime's ambition lying in tatters. The smell of the fresh kill had already begun to permeate through the establishment and the gossip and rumours from the intelligence services had started to amass.

Sean glanced at the TV, where the news cameras were now capturing the views of people on the street as Sir Joe was outed. National disdain seemed rife. A whiff of revulsion and disbelief spread across the country as the scandal of the biggest spy catch since the Burgess and Maclean episode steamrollered across every club, community and establishment in the country. The country was stunned.

Sean turned towards the bar and scanned inside *The Times*. There was a full-page article on organised drug crime in London. He was delighted to see the piece refer to a major car explosion in the quiet backwaters of Hampshire and the story of the death of an international drug runner, who was linked apparently to ultra-violent Albanian gangs.

Buried deep in a Ministry of Defence magazine was a short obituary for Alfie. His body was repatriated from France and the story broke of his death, which was still under investigation. To Sean, it looked clear that it would become an unsolved case and that the American murderers would never be brought to justice.

Sean and Melissa attended Alfie's funeral in Hastings, along with a large contingent of military officers. Sean was pleased Alfie would have his day in the media at some point in the near future, as the most notorious UK whistle-blower ever.

'So, what exactly was his failsafe?' Melissa asked as they meandered through the cobbled streets of Rye that evening.

'He always wanted to have the codes on him in case he was kidnapped,' Sean said. 'In case he was incarcerated for a lengthy period and could use it as collateral to obtain his release, or even get to a computer or phone. He also used steganography to encode pictures with hidden text. Like his obituary.'

'You mean he sent pictures on to someone for decoding?'

'Yep, and I've no doubt you'll be receiving a set of pictures and a software key to decrypt them in the coming weeks,' Sean said, looking for her reaction.

'Bloody hell!' Melissa exclaimed.

'I read it in his files. He had a plan to send delayed emails with a series of pictures and then, some days later, a decryption key. He had all sides well and truly nailed.'

Sean now had his mind set on that rugby match he had been promised and a few pints with the team to celebrate Swartz successfully reaching retirement age. These were fine, gregarious men, he mused. Gregarious men, living life on the edge, avoiding their destiny of one day making the journey to their own special Valhalla where they would all gather no doubt. For now though, they were all living their dreams.

Sean smirked when he thought about the embarrassment of the parliamentarians who had all been exposed as sleeping with the enemy. Natalie's legacy would leave a long, deep and malodorous seal on the immoral lives of many MPs and Lords alike.

Jack had warned Sean in the pub that there was now a new and formidable danger for him. It had caused him to have quite a few more beers. He wasn't overly pleased that this job meant a lifetime of being on the run from the Russian SVR, who had happily put out a contract on his life after he had exposed and nearly killed their finest Russian spy, who had operated for years within the British parliamentary system. The beer had helped him to formulate a plan to deal with that and Jack would help him make those clandestine moves.

Melissa and Sean smiled a lot as they walked arm in arm through the cobbled streets towards the harbour. They were just another couple with their very own story and their own secrets to be told at some point down the line.

'Remember I told you about that job in Moscow where we threw a load of sacks into the river?' Sean asked playfully.

'Yes, I do. What of it?' Melissa asked, turning to face him.

'And when I handed that old rusty tin to a spook in the van?'

'With the list of Russian moles? Yes, go on.'

'Well, the one piece of the story I recently found out about over a beer, is that the spook who I called FITZROY in my drawings, was actually Jack. I handed the rusty old tin to Jack.'

They looked at each movingly, puzzled by the extraordinary life of this genius spook and how, together, they had pulled off the coup of a lifetime.

Epilogue

Westminster

Edward remained in the MI5 basement in Thames House, still working the same civil servant job he had done for over forty-five years. He was ageing now, his grey hair had been lost to baldness, and his sight was getting worse. He had given all his life to serving the Crown. He was a modest civil servant who made his daily commute and minded his own business. He had seen many comings and goings whilst in office and had seen and heard many tales of derring-do and of clandestine secret missions across the world. He held many a secret in his head but just continued to enjoy gardening, the occasional bet on the horses and a beer with his local chums in a small pub in Hertfordshire. He would retire in the coming year. He had served his country well.

Edward started his search for the file, which was hidden deep in the archives amongst row upon row of grey-metal sliding cabinets. He turned a very large wheel on the side of the cabinets and the tall rows moved slowly to the right, opening a gaping corridor into the depths of the files. He walked with his gentle limp and went straight to the battered and tatty red-coloured file tightly bound with grey ribbon.

He brought the file to a small desk outside the cabinets and looked at the cover. '*Placed in suspended animation*' it read.

He smiled knowingly, remembering how some years ago he had placed that sticky label on the front. He untied the file. He then placed a single sheet of typed paper inside the file and signed the inside cover to provide evidence of his amendment. He dated it 15 July 2016, meaning that it was over eleven years since he had last touched it.

He remembered the face of Sean all those years ago and made a mental note to invite him to his retirement party. He continued smiling, a proud man. He was overjoyed to hear the news of a new Prime Minister. He then put a large sticky label on the front cover which read:

TOP SECRET
Closed in Perpetuity – July 2016
'For D Eyes Only'
TOP SECRET

Edward closed the red file and retied the grey ribbon, knowing he would never touch the file again. He gave a mental salute to Sean and Jack and walked back to his desk.

***

Acknowledgements

I dreamed for many years during my military and intelligence career of writing a thriller, mainly because the fascinating men and women I served with had left an indelible mark on me. My friends and colleagues were hugely charismatic, robust, and resilient in every way, and immersed in honour and commitment. I wanted to bring some of the traits of those colourful characters to life in a thriller that drew upon my experiences in a range of disciplines. The characters are entirely imaginary of course, as is the story. And I also wanted to celebrate the wonderful life of Eddie, who was probably the world's most successful cadaver dog. He is now dead but was a fine friend, as is his master. A big thanks to my wife for her encouragement, which helped make this novel happen – it sat in draft form for many a year. Thanks also to Richard, a friend from my local pub, who provided crucial feedback on the early drafts. It's very hard to move from being an intelligence officer to an author – so huge thanks for the encouragement of my editors, Craig Taylor and Derek Collett, and to Unbound for making this happen. Also, to Liane Hard and Emma Mitchell, who gave me some great advice during their beta read and edit, and to David Thorpe for his superb coaching during the early drafts. Finally, a big thank you to my remarkable supporters. I have always said that, in life, teamwork makes incredible, unimaginable things happen. And my team of supporters who contributed to this publication are all legends in my mind. Thanks to you all for your generosity and support.

Michael Jenkins MBE
London
May 2018

Did you enjoy this book? If so, I'd be delighted if you would take the time to submit a review on Amazon and Goodreads, which really helps make a difference to authors. Honest reviews are our lifeblood and are so helpful for readers and authors alike. I'm very grateful to every one of my readers and supporters, who inspire me to write more.

Other novels by Michael Jenkins:

The Kompromat Kill
The Moscow Whisper

You can follow me or join my readers club at:
www.michaeljenkins.org

Featured author on www.londoncrime.co.uk

Glossary

Active measures: Political warfare activities conducted by the Russian security services to influence the course of world events

Badged: A term used to describe a fully trained member of the Special Air Service who is qualified to wear the SAS badge

Bolthole: A safe place from which to plan and conduct military operations

Box: Nickname for MI5, after its official World War Two address of PO Box 500

Bravos: Enemy terrorists

Close-hold: A term describing secret information that should not be disclosed

Crack and thump: Sounds generally heard during an explosion. The crack is the primary detonation and the thump is the main explosion

Directorate 'S': The department in the Russian foreign intelligence services responsible for the gathering, studying and dissemination of illegally obtained intelligence

Double tap: Two bullets fired in very quick succession

Doughnut: The nickname given to the Government Communications Headquarters (GCHQ), a British cryptography and intelligence agency based in Cheltenham

Drive-by: Conducting surveillance on a target by driving past it in a vehicle

Eyes on: Having a direct line of sight to a target

Flash bang: A stun grenade used to incapacitate an enemy within a building by way of a powerful flash and loud bangs

Great Game: A political and diplomatic confrontation that existed for most of the nineteenth century between the British and Russian Empires over Afghanistan and neighbouring territories in Central and Southern Asia

Illegals Programme: A term describing Russian 'sleeper' agents operating under non-official cover in Western countries

Marker: A geophysical reference such as a tree or boulder, used to help relocate buried items

OPSEC: Operational security measures designed to reduce risk on military operations

PIRs: Passive infrared detectors that detect motion and then trigger an alarm

Shooters: Soldiers assigned to kill terrorists or other enemies in a stronghold situation

Side op: An intelligence operation that is not officially sanctioned or known about, i.e. a 'hidden' secret operation

Skin: The brickwork or external walls of a building

Soak time: A period of waiting to judge a threat or to see if any danger materialises

Stronghold: A building or structure housing armed terrorists or other enemies

Track and trace: The skill of tracking where a person or object has been and tracing its whereabouts

Two eyes: UK intelligence only to be seen by UK- and US-vetted Nationals

Virtual fence: A fence that cannot be seen and can be configured using infrared light beams to trigger an alarm when it is breached

Dear readers,

This second edition of the book you are holding is entirely published by The Failsafe Thrillers, whereas the first edition came about in a rather different way to most others. It was funded directly by readers through a new publisher, Unbound. I am indebted to the following people who provided fantastic support to help me start my author journey:

With special thanks to the following supporters who went a long way to make this novel come to fruition:

Special Acknowledgements

Rebecca Jenkins, Ian Trayling, Martin Foster, Mark Weatherley, Russell Vincett, Matthew Brodrick, John Malcolm, Mark Verard, Justin Lewis, Dean Davison, Nick Atkinson.

Super Patrons

John A, Geoff Adams, Nick Atkinson, Matthew Avery, Mic Badger, Jason Ballinger, Katie Barber, Brian Barkworth, Stuart Batey, John Bebbington, Alissa Bell, Jim Blackburn, Lance Bradwell, Matthew Brodrick, Andrew Brooker, Joseph Burne, Ali Burns, Dave Campey, Trev Canner, Dean Carrick, Andrew Clarke, Lucas Cohen, Rebecca Cole, Chris Conneally, Simon Cosh, Jason Creswell, Dale Creswell, Malcolm Davies, Dean Davison, Shane Deakin, Christian Donelan, Neil Drew, Steve Duff-Godfrey, Mariana Dumitrascu, Stuart Fairnington, Mark Foskett, Martin Foster, Joan Frazer, Simon Gately, Alisa Gill, Peter Goodwin, Alice Gould, Shane Greene, James Gregory, Jo Hall, Glyn Hannah, Ben Hawkins, Chris Hawthorne, Greg Henson, David Hirst, Jim Holl, Guy Horne, Tom Hughes, David Humphrey, Mark Jackson, Sarah Jane Duff-Godfrey, P.I. Jenkins, Luke Jenkins, Ramina Jenkins, Matthew Jenkins, Rebecca Jenkins, Dan Kieran, Vincent King, Joe King, Richard Knowles, Chris Lambert, Jon Leighton, Justin Lewis, John Malcolm, Mark Simpson, Peter Markham, Guy Marshlain, Gary Merritt, Bryan

Miller, Jason Miller, John Mitchinson, Mark Molyneaux, Nicholas Mould, Carlo Navato, Mark O'Neill, Gary O'Shea, Bryan Osborne, Sean Owen, Phil Paul, Justin Pollard, Paul Potter, Ray Powell, Dave Robson, Steve Shores, Toni Smerdon, Bruce Springett, Nina Stutler, Phil Sullivan, Mark Swindells, Graham Symes, Martin Thomson, Gary Toombs, Spike Townsend, Ian Trayling, Will Turner, Terry Vass, Mark Vent, Mark Verard, Russell Vincett, Paul Wakefield, Mark Weatherley, Matt Williams, Andy Wood, Jeremy Wray, Darren Young,

Patrons

Alan Beeton, Lance Buttress, Penny Carr, Ian Clarkson, Robin Courtney Bennett, Jimmy Coyle, Clare Darbyshire, Amanda Elliott, Brian Lunn, Richard Mallinson, Neil Manchester, Stuart McKears, Diego Montoyer, Tim Pass, Matt Pilborough, Darius Smith, Kevin Strauther, Jon Washington, Derek Wilson

Printed in Great Britain
by Amazon